THE
MACHINIST

JD KLOOSTERMAN

MONTAG

First Montag Press E-Book and Paperback Original Edition July 2022

Montag Press ISBN: 978-1-957010-12-0
Design © 2022 Amit Dey

Montag Press Team:

Editor: John Rak
Cover Illustrator: Eris Mandrake
Managing Director: Charlie Franco

A Montag Press Book
www.montagpress.com
Montag Press
777 Morton Street, Unit B
San Francisco CA 94129 USA

Printed & Digitally Originated in the United States of America
10 9 8 7 6 5 4 3 2 1

DEDICATIONS

Dedicated to Dr. Christian Dickinson, who told me to bite the bullet and just write a novel instead of constantly talking about it.

To Sir Terry Pratchett, whose Discworld series introduced me to the wide world of steampunk and the potential of centering a story around a postal department.

And as with all my stories, this writing is also dedicated to the Lord God, from whom every good thing comes.

TABLE OF CONTENTS

ACKNOWLEDGMENT

I'd like to thank my older brother Steve, who talked me into signing the contract, and my younger brother Neil (who's not in the dedications because I've dedicated too many books to him already), who was one of the first people I talked to about this story back in high school and whose response when he saw the first draft was: "It's so exciting to see this *finally* on paper." I should also thank my high school teachers for being (mostly) tolerant of the sketches and notes I would write on my assignments on this as well as other stories.

CHAPTER 1

4::139400::2405

Find and kill interlopers. Waycar system has been locked down; they will be on foot within the Detroit area. Send a complete report once all items have been recovered.

0::000000::0000

The door to the shop banged open in a way it really wasn't supposed to, nearly jangling the bell off its hook. Iosif had just registered the gun in the man's hand, and was groping for the shotgun under the counter, when the man tossed something onto the counter in front of him.

"Woodpecker," he gasped. "Take care of this for me." And whirling on his heel, in a hurried manner that made his overcoat swirl dramatically, the man was gone again out the door.

Iosif blinked as the door slammed shut. The entire exchange had lasted less than thirty seconds. Slowly, he let go of the shotgun, and stepped up to the counter to see what the man had tossed onto it.

To his surprise, he did not recognize the item at all. There were very few things that he was unable to repair (the natural exception being federal appliances, for legal reasons), having had frequent cause to dabble outside the various watches that were the (stated) purpose of the shop. 'We fix anything' had been tacked beneath 'Whisterhorn's Watches' for nearly two years now, and Iosif had never failed to fix, let alone recognize, a single device.

Yet this was most peculiar. It was not quite a cylinder, as he had thought at first—the shape was broken into six distinct sides—and it was certainly not a 'woodpecker,' whatever the customer might think. There was no real joint or obvious opening—even a magnifying glass under a gaslight revealed nothing more than beautiful scrolling patterns etched in the metalwork. The only clear thing he could recognize was the hexagonal button set mid-way up the cylinder (which was jammed—that must be the problem.)

Perhaps Master Whisterhorn would know more about it. He should send him a message.

The mail machine had a few stuck buttons of its own, but Iosif was used to them. He typed out:

4::534322:8943

Customer has left 'woodpecker' here. No name given. What are the details of the job?

4::2345233::2324

He pressed *"Send"* and watched as the machine ripped off the paper and folded it into the envelope. Valves hissed as heat clamps sealed the letter shut—the left clamp got stuck again, but Iosif freed it with an impatient movement—there was a *clickclickclick* noise of pins punching the destination sequence along the top-left corner, then a hook cleanly poked through the top of the letter, carrying it along the track and up into the mail chute.

Iosif shook his head to clear it and turned back toward the shop. "Is crazy," he muttered to himself. "Is so crazy." He could have fixed that side clamp ages ago, but it wasn't worth the jail time. Without so much as a machinist license, much less a Federal Engineering degree, Iosif was barely allowed to touch the machine. That left clamp would doubtless stick for five years more, and maybe longer, until the maintenance request finally came through.

For a moment he looked over the shop, his eyes flitting across the wide array of machinery he'd added to it. He was reluctant to use a power saw or a steam drill on the strange device until he knew more, but perhaps the vacuum seal... Iosif pulled the machine out from under the table and lifted it onto the workshop. Clambering onto the barstool (one of the less-fancy but more-necessary additions Iosif had made), he connected the vacuum to the steam line on the wall, opening up the valve to set the machine to purring and humming.

He'd barely started examining the strange item when the mail machine chattered again, and he looked over to see an envelope arriving on the track.

Hurrying over, he ripped the letter off the hook and slit the envelope open with a nail.

4::2345233::2324

No such item scheduled, but sounds like a toy. Put it aside until you finish the Vernweiler watch.

4::534322:8943

Iosif rolled his eyes. Mrs. Vernweiler was not only very rich, but very exacting, and it was important the job be finished correctly.

The workroom only had space for the one workbench, but all the watch tools were kept in closed drawers, where they could be kept relatively clear from dust. Iosif dragged the barstool over to the set of drawers, climbed on top of it again, and opened up the corresponding drawers, finding the watch after a few moments' search and setting to work with a pair of tweezers.

Iosif's eyesight was not much better than his boss' in some ways, and he found himself forced to use the jeweler's eyepiece in order to properly look over the watch. It was very fine, and very intricate, showing the movements of the stars and moon in small windows in its face. One of the gears had been misaligned—possibly by Mr. Whisterhorn.

The troublesome gear was badly jammed in there, and Iosif had barely managed to work it loose when the bell over the door clanged again. He exhaled loudly through his nose, but there was little choice. Setting down the watch (and the eyepiece), he hopped off the barstool and exited the workroom. "I help, hold on," he said, grabbing a rag to wipe his hands.

The gaunt-faced gentleman at the counter didn't actually recoil when he caught sight of him, but his eyes definitely widened and there was a sharp intake of breath. Iosif barely noticed-- he knew what his face looked like and after having it for so long he'd grown used to the reactions. He just smiled as he came up behind the register, his head and shoulders just barely above the counter. "I help." He repeated. "What is problem?"

The gaunt-faced gentleman blinked at him. "Is your father in?" he asked.

Iosif sighed internally. "I sixteen," he assured the man. "Apprentice. Whisterhorn not here today. What is problem?"

Usually the very next question was about his accent, but instead the man seemed to shrug it off. "I'm here for a piece of merchandise," he said. "It would have just been dropped off a few minutes ago... frightful accident, my friend meant to drop it off at a shop down the alley. It was long and thin..." The gaunt man gave a smile. "I'm afraid I don't know what it was for, but my friend's anxious to get it back."

Iosif frowned and tapped the sign on the register. *Items left for repair must be collected by original customer.* Too many shifty-eyed customers came in claiming to 'own' the expensive timepieces sitting in the glass case.

The man looked at the sign, then back at him. "Surely you can make an exception—my friend caught a tramcar moments ago, he'll be half on his way to Toledo by now. It's all perfectly simple; I only need to move it to the watch shop down the street."

Iosif was not in the habit of breaking contracts, but even if he was, there was another problem. "No other watch shop on this street," he said quietly, watching the man.

The man's gaunt face froze, his deep-sunken eyes flickering over Iosif. "Well, aren't you a clever boy."

5

"I sixte--" Iosif stopped as a revolver whipped out of the man's coat, lining up squarely with the middle of his forehead.

"Now listen here, mongoloid." The man's thin lips twisted in a snarl. "You and I are going to walk into that back worksh—"

BOOM!

The buckshot tore out through the thin plywood of the counter, slamming into the man's chest and turning a significant portion of his face into hamburger. The blast knocked the man to the floor, but he was already starting to get back up when Iosif clambered onto the counter and leveled the second barrel at his face.

BOOM!

Iosif winced at the way the man's head spread across the floor. Glancing around, he dug the spare shells out of the cash register, reloading the shotgun in case the thief had friends. He let out a long, shaky breath. Gangsters were getting bolder, no doubt about that. But this needed to be cleaned up. He laid the shotgun on the counter and hopped off onto the floor of the shop.

The bell over the door gave a cheery tinkle.

"My stars!" Mrs. Vernweiler nearly screamed, recoiling at the sight of the headless body on the ground. "What in heaven's name…?"

Oh dear. "Was attempted robbery, miss," Iosif said, spreading his hands. "No danger now. All is good, yes?"

"Robbery!?" Mrs. Vernweiler's eyes latched on to him. "Not my watch, I hope!"

"No, no. Nothing stolen."

"Oh, thank goodness." Mrs. Vernweiler fanned herself. "Are you all right, dear? Not hurt?"

"I fine," Iosif said, managing a smile. "Is Detroit life, eh?"

"Oh... oh my." Mrs. Vernweiler swallowed and looked away from the corpse. "Well, have you mailed the police?"

"Not yet," Iosif said. "Soon." For all the good it would do.

Mrs. Vernweiler seemed satisfied with this. "And is my watch ready?"

Iosif sighed. "Not yet," he said, picking up the man's body. "Soon."

∽ం∾

"Good day at work today?" his mother asked him, later that night, as he shook off the mud on his boots.

"Yes," Iosif said, unwinding his scarf. No sense in telling her about the robber, it would just worry her. "Busy day." A detective had, oddly enough, showed up to take his statement, so between that and cleaning up the blood he'd barely had a chance to look at the strange object, which was currently in his coat pocket.

"Did you have fun?" His mother pressed.

"... had interesting job." Iosif was already turning for the stairs.

"Dinner will be ready in thirty minutes," his mother called after him, as he went up the stairs to his room.

"Is good." Iosif closed the door to his room. It was small, but so was Iosif, and the space that would ordinarily be filled by a large bed had instead been devoted to a small table, where Iosif kept a few modest tools of his own, to work on 'rush' orders.

Taking the cylinder out of his pocket, he laid it on the table, and then laid the jeweler's eyepiece next to it. It'd been an idea he'd had while mopping up the blood. Settling behind the small table with a sigh, he put the eyepiece in place, adjusted the setting, and grinned. Properly focused, the eyepiece revealed several joints, cunningly hidden in the geometric designs of the knot-like scrollwork. More than that, they revealed that several tiny dots, seemingly part of the design, were in fact infinitesimal screw heads, scored with a triangular indentation.

Iosif made a small clucking noise. Such delicate craftsmanship! Such fine detail! Iosif couldn't begin to think why such detail would be needed, but simply the accomplishment...!

Reaching into a small box of odds and ends, Iosif pulled out a length of wire. He laid the end of the wire next to the screw head and frowned in concentration. The head was a tiny little hexagon shape, while the wire was perfectly circular. This would take some finesse.

∞o∞

After dinner, Iosif went straight back upstairs. "Don't stay up too late, dear," his mother called after him. "You're no good to your job dead on your feet. And don't forget to leave out some crumbs for the boggart."

"Yes, yes." Iosif waved his hand. Father Piotr would not approve of his mother's devotion to the "little people," but there was no sense in arguing the point.

Seated again at his desk, Iosif took the wire, which he had nearly finished sanding to a proper shape. It was tiny, exacting work—just the sort of thing that he excelled at. A few more strokes with the sandpaper, and the wire fit neatly into the hole. Iosif grinned with satisfaction.

There were ten screws. One by one, Iosif delicately teased them out, dropping them in a bottle cap to make sure he did not lose them. The metal casing was stubborn, and rusted in places, but with some firm pressure it lifted away.

Iosif was an unemotional soul, generally, but even so he could not withhold a small gasp.

A loom of tiny metal wires, like the inside of a piano, lay exposed to his eyepiece. Gleaming strands of some unidentifiable metal ran back and forth and along the length of the cylinder, and crisscrossed over its length in a glittering tapestry of metal.

And in the center was lodged a bullet.

Iosif's mother came to the door. "This letter just came for you in the mail, Iosif," she said, holding up a standardized envelope.

Startled, Iosif glanced out the window. It was pitch black outside, who could be sending mail at this hour? He took the letter and opened the seal.

4::555343::2344

Dear sir,

I apologize for my abrupt greeting today; I mistook you for someone else. I believe I left a personal item of some personal value with you. Due to other matters, I cannot collect it before next week, but if you would mind it until then, I would very much appreciate it.

"Woodpecker"

P.S. Please keep this affair discrete.

2::131412::4309

There was no signature.

"Who is it from?" asked Mother, clearly as curious about the letter as he was.

"I not know," Iosif replied, honestly. "Customer from shop." He glanced down uncertainly at the cylinder on the workbench, with the bullet lodged in the center, and tried not to think of the gaunt man's head spread across the shop floor. "Customer," He repeated.

∽∘∾

The day Mr. Whisterhorn came back, Iosif told him about the gaunt man. Mr. Whisterhorn chewed his lip. "S'possible he was from the Families The customer, I mean."

Iosif hadn't considered that. "Is… is Mafioso job?" he said, looking at the cylinder.

"Maybe." Whisterhorn shook his head. "Best to be on th'safe side. You focus n'that. I'll mind th'shop. Do it right."

Iosif resisted the urge to roll his eyes. He would have 'done it right' regardless of what was going on with the customer, almost out of sheer curiosity. But he appreciated the chance to work completely uninterrupted.

Prising out the bullet was fairly simple, but Iosif was in frightful distress over the wires. They were of an unusually strong material, and far thinner than he could possibly hope to match. The closest he could come, steel wire, was much thicker and clumsier than the original, making it impossible for him to tie it to the end anchors. Copper wire, in the end, had to be used instead, but Iosif knew it would not be as sturdy as the usual. Bolts were no good, so in the end he heated an iron red-hot and melted the thin cord onto the anchors.

Overall, it was uglier and probably weaker than the original, but it fit within the bronze-gold casing. And more importantly, it worked. Now, when you pressed the button, the flat tip of the cylinder would elongate and unseen plates would shift to narrow to a point—one with a very specific shape. A triangle. One very similar to the insets on the tiny screws he'd removed.

Iosif had, in fact, found a screwdriver.

The discovery amazed him, mostly because of its implications. Simply that such a tool was *necessary* implied a vast array of finely-worked devices just as delicate and intricate as this. Not only that, but Iosif found that if one rotated the button and pressed it again, a wholly different point would form. A star. A hex. Even a surprisingly normal Philip's Head point would form when the right button was pressed. There was, apparently, a wide variety among such marvelous devices.

The man returned, as he had promised, nearly a week to the day from when he had left, and oddly enough again on a day when Mr. Whisterhorn was too sick to be there. Iosif was standing anxiously behind the counter, waiting, as the man entered the shop, scanning the room as he did so. "You have my item?" he asked.

Now that the man was talking—and moving—at a normal pace, Iosif could tell that he had grey hair that was thinning at the top, and a lined, serious face. There was a smoldering cigar in his mouth, and he was wearing, as before, a voluminous raincoat.

The raincoat did not quite hide the revolver in the man's shoulder holster.

"Yes…" Iosif said, bringing out the screwdriver. He licked his lips. This would be tricky. "But… very sorry. Not able to fix.

It work, you see…" he said, pressing the button and allowing the plates to twist into the appropriate shape. "…but… is no perfect."

Iosif's gaze was fixed on the screwdriver, or else he might have seen his customer's eyes get very round.

Iosif retracted the point and lifted off the top panel—which he'd left unscrewed--so the man could see the inner workings. "You see… bullet… lodge here. Wires, no more. I make my own… patch up hole." He indicated the panel he had taken off, with the bit of tin patched over it. "But not right supplies. Steel—not as tough as these others." He tapped the other wires for emphasis. "Break, you use too much."

He finally looked up, straight into the stranger's wide eyes. They looked skeptical to Iosif, and he wondered if the man had seen through his ruse already.

"I melt wire onto anchors." He indicated the ends within the screwdriver. "Only way to fix, but… if you want to change now… expensive. Maybe break." Again he licked his lips, knowing that was a giveaway but unable to stop himself. "Apologies. Offer refund… value of item…." He looked up. The man did not seem to understand. "I… buy… this…" he said, tapping the screwdriver on the desk, "…from you. Because… I… break… it."

The man shook his head, slowly. "I don't want a refund, son," he said, in a deep, gravelly baritone.

Iosif's hopes plummeted. "New offer…" he plunged on desperately. "Value of item, plus any watch in case… all watches in case!" Technically he did not own those, but he could always work it off.

"Forget it, kid," said the man. "It ain't for sale." He gestured. "Now, screw the top back on, please."

Iosif did so with a heavy heart. It'd been a lost cause, but he'd had to try. Now he couldn't even charge the man anything, since he'd admitted the repair hadn't really worked. He handed the screwdriver over. "Wire cost money," he said, without much hope. "Value of materials…"

A sheaf of hundred-dollar bills thudded down onto the desk. Iosif's eyes widened. He looked at the clip of bills, then back to the customer.

The man had his entire focus on the screwdriver. He clicked the button on and off, watching the tip narrow and retract. "How long did you work on this?"

Iosif did some rough calculations. "3… 4 days, maybe?" It was hard to say, a good chunk of his time "working" on it had just been marveling at the overwhelming beauty and complexity of the marvelous device.

The man nodded. "Do you know what it does?" he asked.

Now Iosif was even more confused. Was this a test? "It is screwdriver," he said. But that was not accurate; he struggled to think of a better term. "…adaptable… screwdriver."

"Is it? Hm." The man hefted the device in his hand. "Never actually seen it work before."

Iosif gaped.

The man caught his expression and offered a dry smile. "Never been able to get any of them to work." He turned the device over in his hands. "Artifacts like this… yeah, they look fancy, but we've maybe managed to get one out of twenty of them to work."

Iosif literally could not think of what to say.

"But you can," the man said, studying Iosif again. "You managed to figure out in one week what my best engineers have been spending the better part of several years on."

"…oh…?" Iosif managed.

"I could use a man like you," the man said. He tapped the "artifact" against his knuckles. "Would you like a job?"

Iosif noticed, for the first time, that the man's knuckles were bandaged, with crusted red showing through the rough cloth. He caught the glimpse of the massive revolver he'd seen before, underneath the man's coat. He thought, again, of the shotgun underneath the counter.

He thought of the marvelous, glittering device in the man's hands.

"…where?" he asked.

✼

"The… Post Office?" Mother said.

"He said is called Au-to-ma-ted Postal Department," Iosif said. "Enforcement Division."

Mother mulled over this for moment. "They run the mail machines?" she said, glancing doubtfully over at the box in the corner.

"Yes," Iosif said. He hadn't asked about 'Enforcement Division.'

"And you said yes?"

"Yes." Iosif was turning the screwdriver over lovingly in his hands. The man had said he could keep it until he came to work. A "signing bonus," he had called it.

"Why?"

Iosif's finger caught against a button on the screwdriver he had not noticed before. Again the plates shifted, but this time, instead of a rod, one of the plates themselves slid out, smooth, unadorned metal exposing itself to the naked eye.

"...not sure," Iosif said, staring at the plate.

Etched into the plate with hasty, desperate strokes were the words: *HELP US.*

CHAPTER 2

4::555343::2344

IOSIF RUSVAL

Welcome! This letter is to inform you that you have been offered a MAINTENANCE position as the MACHINIST of the UNITED STATES AUTOMATED POSTAL SERVICES ENFORCEMENT DIVISION in PITTSBURGH. We are excited to see the talents you will bring to the team.

The UNITED STATES AUTOMATED POSTAL SERVICES ENFORCEMENT DIVISION is an elite team of focused individuals who provide critical civil services to our citizens, and no position more than its MACHINIST. To be awarded this position out of all the applicants is a great honor, and we look forward to working with you. It carries with it a monthly salary of 2000 dollars, along with on-site housing and cafeteria services. To accept this position, simply fill out the enclosed form and return it to the destination address printed on the bottom.

And again, welcome!

2::235225::2341

Iosif wasn't even out of Detroit before his waycar was hijacked. His mother had said he should never have gone, that no one could possibly pay 2000 dollars for such a position. Beyond belief, she'd protested, even as she picked out new clothes and forced them into the brand-new steamer trunk. Ridiculous, she insisted, as she pressed her ash-wood prayer necklace with the silver engravings into his hand. Some sort of elaborate prank.

But the ticket that'd come with the letter was clearly no prank, as the terminal on the waycar platform accepted it without protest, and, after the customary clicks and clacks, spat out a receipt marked with "AUTOMATED POSTAL CENTRE-PITTSBURGH" marked on it. So when a waycar rattled up to the terminal and opened its doors invitingly, Iosif picked up his brand-new steamer trunk and stepped inside.

Iosif had not had much cause to ride the railways, but he found them endlessly fascinating. Sitting on the threadbare seat, he listened to the clatter as the car left the terminal to join the line on Mavon Street. From Mavon Street, he knew, it would take a sidetrack over to Surrey line, and join the Grand Column to Pittsburgh.

Iosif nearly shivered. *The Grand Column.* He had not ridden it in ages—not since he and mother had taken that trip west to Chicago. It was childish to feel glee about something so mundane, and yet Iosif could not help bouncing on his seat a little and craning around his neck to look at the line ahead.

Not that he could see much. The windows in the car, stained with rust and salt, were so grimy as to be nearly translucent in places. The faux-wooden paneling in this car had long been stripped away, and the metal lay bare in many places. There was a metal box just to the left of the seat, marked with a bright red tag: WARNING: TAMPERING WITH THIS FEDERAL APPLIANCE IS STRICTLY PROHIBITED BY FEDERAL LAW AND MAY BE SUBJECT TO A PENALTY OF UP TO FIVE YEARS IN PRISON.

Reaching out a hand, Iosif splayed his fingers out over the box, and closed his eyes.

Iosif's fingers, unlike the rest of his rough, calloused body, were, smooth and soft to the touch, and were surprisingly sensitive. Not to temperature—he could pick up hot plates like anyone else—but to vibration. "He could hold a watch and feel it tick," Mr. Whisterhorn had bragged on occasion to customers. Not even Mr. Whisterhorn, perhaps, knew how true that was.

Now, as he held his fingers against the WARNING tag, he felt the light vibrations of the machinery underneath as they shivered through the thin metal. *Click. Click CLACK.* The way car turned left suddenly onto Surrey Line. *Click. Click. Click. Click. CLACK.* The car jerked toward the right, continuing down the road. *Click. CLACK.* It jerked left. Changing lanes, steering around something. *Click. Click. Click…*

THUD.

Something slammed into the side of the car, sending Iosif sprawling over the seat. Snapping his eyes open, he saw an enormous man clinging to the outside of the waycar, grinning broadly at him through the glass. A leather duster whipped around the man's muscular frame, and his face was smooth— slightly puffy, giving him almost a boyish look.

Before Iosif's startled eyes, the man brought out an oddly-shaped tool (like a crowbar, Iosif noted, though the angle was different), and wedged it into the crack between the door and the car. With an enormous heave, the man dragged the protesting door open. "Heya, kiddo!" He smiled at the terrified Iosif.

As the man swung himself into the narrow car, the gleaming barrel of a Tommy gun peaked momentarily out from the folds of his coat, clanging briefly on the sides of the door. The man did not seem to notice (or care), and he dropped onto the seat opposite Iosif with a loud exhale. "Ah…" he said, as the doors screeched shut again. "Didn't know if I was going to make it. That was quite a jump." He glanced at Iosif and laughed. "Whassa matter, kid?"

Iosif had never been good at speaking with strangers, even ones that had not just broken Federal law while carrying automatic weaponry. His hand, frozen against the metal box, registered the workings of the machinery. *Click. Click. CLACKE TYCLACKETYCLACKETYCLACKETY…*

The way car slid into place on the Grand Column with a *thump*, locking into place snugly behind another waycar. Through the window just over his car-companion's shoulder, Iosif could just see the olive-green hats and uniforms in the next compartment. Soldiers. Perhaps on their way to New York. Perhaps armed...

The big man's eyes followed his to the soldiers, and his demeanor changed swiftly, silently. "Oh, don'tcha worry about them, sonny." He chuckled. "They've got their own business to attend to. So long as no one causes a ruckus, we should get on just fine, eh?"

His coat shifted ever so slightly, and the barrel of the Tommy gun gleamed.

Iosif swallowed and leaned back against the seat. He'd been in cars that were Jumped before, but never in one that was actually Jacked. Technically, forcing the door counted as 'interfering with Federal Appliances'—even here, Iosif could see the indents in the metal of the door frame—and carried the same penalties as any such 'interference.' This tended to make Jackers more... unpredictable, by all reports. And this 'Jacker' was well over twice his size, much closer to the emergency lever, and also carrying a gun.

So Iosif sat back and tried to relax.

The man seemed to sense his decision, for he also relaxed. "There ya are." He laughed again. "Ya seem like a sensible kid."

"Sixteen," Iosif said. There was a *thud* behind his head as another waycar joined the Grand Column.

The man cocked his head. "Sorry?"

"I sixteen," Iosif repeated. The response was nearly automatic by this point, customers were always calling him "kiddo," "sonny," or "little monster." Iosif knew it was barely worth correcting them, but he'd just passed the milestone rather recently and it was something of a sore point with him. The big man still looked puzzled, so he tried again. "I, sixteen," he said, jabbing a thumb at himself.

The man looked at him, then shrugged. "Good to meetcha, Sixteen," he said, grasping Iosif's unresisting hand. "I'm Snorky."

Iosif felt his hand being shaken. "Yes?"

"It means Sharp Dresser," Snorky said, sprawling all over the back seat, his Tommy gun cocking at an odd angle. He gestured to the coat and tie he was wearing. "Issa nickname, kid. Like yours, amiright? Unless your folks actually called you Sixteen, in which case, jeez." He reached into his pocket and dug out some cigarettes. "What's it mean?" he commented, eyeing Iosif critically. "Ya kill sixteen boys in a fight or somethin?" He shook his head. "No, sorry. Old habits. Probably something more like sixteen at jacks, right? Or sixteen warts? Sixteen… smallpox infections? Seriously, kid, what happened to your face?"

"Er…"

"Actually, forget it. Doesn't matter." The man stuck a cigarette in his mouth and dug around in his coat for some matches. "Ya headed to Pittsburgh, right?" He pronounced it *Pitts-baugh.*

Iosif nodded.

"Ah! Great place." Snorky grinned, lighting his match on the stripped metal. "Ever been?"

Iosif shook his head.

Snorky blew smoke at the ceiling. "I," he said, with great confidence, "know all the best stories about Pittsburgh. I can tell ya all the sights to see, all the holes in the wall. Ya couldn't ask for a better guide than me, kid."

Iosif would have asked for one without a Tommy gun, but he nodded anyway.

"Whereabouts in Pittsburgh…" *Pitts-baugh* "… are ya goin' to?"

Iosif hesitated. Part of this was his normal shyness, part of this was born of the stranger's Tommy gun, but most had to do with the letter—the smaller, hand-written letter dropped in the envelope of his employment contract.

> *Tell no one about this. Don't reply to this letter, don't send a query to the main offices, SEND NOTHING THROUGH THE MAIL. If you want the job, just show up. But TELL NO ONE.*

Technically Iosif had already violated that three times over. Mother had had to be told, of course, and she had insisted he tell Father Pyotr for his blessing, and Mr. Whisterhorn needed to be given notice so he had enough time to find a new apprentice (a tarnished gold watch, a going-away present from the old man, was currently stretching the leather of Iosif's overcoat's breast pocket). But telling a random stranger on the waycar was something else entirely.

The big man did not seem terribly interested anyway. "Well, wherever you're going, the first thing you ought to see is the old Carnegie tower. Mostly abandoned, now, but the observation deck's still in good shape—you can see for miles from up there. The Five Quarters boys, they used to meet up there." He grinned and leaned in close. "This one time—I used to work for Johnny, Johnny Torrio, ya know? And he wanted us to send them a message. So we took this insider of theirs, that we'd caught, and we took him up on the deck, and…" He gestured. "You get me?"

Iosif did not, but the man was looking at him expectantly. "Ah," he said, nodding. His mind was more fixated on the name "Johnny Torrio," it sounded vaguely familiar.

The man seemed disappointed with his reaction. "Jeez, you are a hard one, aren't ya? It was a whole thing, we needed to find a way off the top quick after we bumped the guy off, so we had these ziplines set up…"

Iosif's mind suddenly clicked, and he felt a cold pit of unease settle in his gut. Visions of newspapers flashed in his eyes, lurid photos of murdered bodies and robbed banks plastered across them. Five Quarters Boys. Johnny Torrio. *Bumped off.* Iosif's mind rendered the unfortunate visuals and he winced.

His storyteller noticed and grinned. "Yeah, it was a tight squeeze, but we got on the Column before the Feds thought to close it down. That's what kicked off the Five Quarters war, you know." He tapped his chest meaningfully. "Read about that in the papers, didn'tcha? That was us. Johnny didn't let nobody mess with his business. He got his start back with the old Carnegie 'strikebreaker' boys. He told us once about this job *they* pulled..."

Iosif pressed back against the seat, keeping his face absolutely still as his companion launched into another story. People might not *talk* much about Johnny Torrio now that he'd been put away, but his hold on Detroit had not weakened, and his ruthless method of "business" was the stuff of bar room gossip. Iosif felt the weight of the artifact in his coat pocket and thought again of the gaunt man from the store.

"Oh man! This other time, in Pittsburgh, we'd hooked up with this rail wizard—these guys who can hack the way cars, you know? And we were doing this bank job..."

Did this man mean to kill him? Even if he were, Iosif realized, there was nothing that could be done. The man had a gun, the column was moving at nearly 60 miles an hour, and prying the doors open would be a federal crime. He was this man's cell-mate for the next ten hours or so.

Iosif couldn't help but wonder how often most hitmen talked about their crimes. And what happened to the people they talked to about them.

∽o∾

"...and we had this idea, to use the Environmental Monitoring Station as a smugglers den, since they're supposed to be all automated and no one else would mess with a federal facility. You ever seen one of those, kid?"

Iosif shook his head without looking up. He'd ended up slumped against the side of the car, arms folded and head bent at a strange angle that was probably going to give him a crick in his neck. He was studying the man's Tommy gun, now openly laid out on the seat. The way the wire stock folded up struck him as particularly clever.

"Don't they have them in Detroit? They're supposed to be in all major cities—port cities anyway. They're *supposed* to monitor the water quality, they say. You'd think they'd make for great smuggler's dens, but it turns out the feds just *pepper* the water around 'em with mines. Crazy, right? Who guards a water monitoring station with—oh hey!" his head lifted suddenly. "Kid, get up, you're going to want to see this!"

Iosif sat up obediently, and then stared.

Ahead of them, just across the grey of a massive river, tall buildings loomed against the sky, large and dark and formidable. Smoke stacks belched forth black fumes to the skies, their smaller factories nearly lost amidst the great ash-white cloud that fogged the city. Along the shores of the inlet, Iosif could see waycar tracks rising in double levels—triple levels, in some places—with cars busily whirring back and forth on them. His gaze traveled to the docks, but it swiftly turned from searching for ferries to marveling at the many-tiered cranes and steam lifts servicing the barges.

Snorky laughed at his wide-eyed staring. "Damn, kiddo, it really IS ya first time heah, ain't it?

Iosif withdrew a little from the window, abashed.

"Ah, heck, stare all you like, it's quite a sight, even if it ain't Chicago." The man pointed. "Lookit! That's one of those Environmental Stations I was telling you about. See? That thing like a black beetle, out on the water? Perfect for a smugglers' den, right? Issa close enough to shippin' lanes, but so far out no one'd bother ya. But just try and even land on one." He pointed again. "We ended up putting the den over by that dock, with the crane arm hanging all crooked like a spider's web. Locals said it was haunted. Spirit of old Mrs. Flibberjabber, who drowned in a giant—hey!"

Iosif had the Tommy gun in his hands, and was examining how the ammo magazine connected to the main weapon. He barely heard whatever it was Snorky was shouting. The catch for the magazine looked sound in principle, but the metal must get awfully hot. That was probably what'd caused the deformation he'd spotted—the small ripple in the socket for the magazine. He pressed the button and popped out the magazine, still barely attending to Snorky's yells. Yes, that was a ripple… could be dangerous. Luckily the metal seemed fairly pliable… he applied some pressure with his thumbs and smiled as the metal flattened out.

"There," he said, snapping the magazine back in place and handing it to his companion. "Less chance of jam now." He smiled at the other man, who seemed to have taken out a knife at some point. "Sorry. Please continue with story. Very interesting."

The man looked at him. He looked at the Tommy gun he'd just been handed. He looked at the bowie knife in his hand.

"Kid…" he said.

There was a rushing roar as the Grand Column entered the city, a great *click- CLACKETYCLACKETYCLACKETYCLAKETY*

CLUNK CLICKclickclick as the waycar disconnected, and suddenly the two of them were rattling down the streets of Pittsburgh.

To Iosif's surprise, the under-streets were not all one foggy mass, as he had supposed from a distance. It seemed the constant bustle of the way cars swept the mist away, creating a vacuum of sorts where the lower streets could be seen, if through a slight haze. High elegant fronts with Doric Columns and grotesque statuary flashed by the window. It was all much too fast. Iosif felt his breath fogging up the glass.

"This is Main Street, yes?" he said, turning back to the other.

Snorky seemed to have momentarily lost his poise. "Huh? Yeah … yeah, this is Main Street. Oughta take us to Polk Ave, and from there … Yeah." He put away his knife and shouldered his Tommy gun. "Notta cop in sight … yeah, good."

Iosif blinked. Right. This man was a criminal. This man was dangerous. This man had given him detailed confessions of several extremely criminal acts. Handing him back his gun had probably not been the wisest thing to do.

Iosif sat back down, somewhat hard. He had nothing to bribe the man with—his whole life was in the steamer trunk at the man's feet, and the only remotely valuable thing in there was the costume-jewelry praying necklace his mother had pressed him to take. It wouldn't buy anything. Iosif felt very nervous again suddenly.

Snorky, on the other hand, seemed to have regained his good-humor. "Yeah, this'll be good," he noted. "Oughta take us straight to the heart of downtown. Ya can see the clock tower from there. Ya wouldn't think ya could, cause of all the great buildings they got down there, but right at the station, if ya stand by this pillar, ya can just see it due west. I've won sooooo many bets with that trick…"

Iosif eyed the door. The man had needed a crowbar to pry open it open, but Iosif thought he *might* be able to force it open barehanded. He was pretty strong, for his size. It would be a felony, but it wouldn't be death, though jumping on a four-lane tramway would be risky, especially when the man still had the gun. If the car jerked suddenly… say, if the control box received a shock…

As Iosif's hand inched over the DO NOT TAMPER WITH sign, his palm picked up again the tremors from the machinery. *Click… click… click CLACK clickclickclickclickclickclick CLACK clickclickclickclick…*

Iosif frowned. That felt… odd.

"Damnit, is we… is we slowing down?" Snorky glanced around, and his face collapsed in annoyance. "Ya gotta be kidding me." he muttered. "How did they know?"

The waycar jerked off to the right, sending Snorky and Iosif lurching against the side. Again it jerked sideways, off the main road entirely, slowing as it pulled under a concrete archway. The doors shot open, and Iosif was confronted with the grey uniform and whiskered face of a police officer.

"Papers please," the officer announced, in a very officious tone.

There was a moment's pregnant pause while Iosif realized that the officer meant him. "Oh!" he said, feeling through his coat pockets. "Yes, of course…" In his fluster, he checked the same pocket three times, fully aware of the stares of both the officer and his raincoat-clad fellow passenger. "Here it is!" he said, producing the identification papers triumphantly.

The officer took them with a nod. "Please wait here," he said. "You too, Snorky."

The big man just waved. "Yeah, yeah."

Iosif did not have long to gape. The officer was soon back. "Everything checks out," he said, handing back the papers. "Have a good day, sir. Good seeing you, Snorky."

"And the same ta you, Jefferson." Snorky gave an easy nod.

Iosif was speechless as the doors slid shut.

Snorky, though, had plenty to say. "How do theys keep doin' that?" he snarled, the easy smile evaporating as he glared back at the police station. "They ain't got no reason ta flag ya car, why would they... Inspection my ass..." He slumped against the seat, muttering. "Every dang time... no matta what we do..."

He fell silent, and the compartment was filled with the clicks and rumbles of the waycar. For the first time on the trip the car was silent, and Iosif wondered if he should say something. But he had no idea what to say, what to do, or even what to think; whether he should still be plotting his escape or if that was a moot point. Did the mob have enormously strong police connections? Did that mean the man wasn't afraid of what he might tell them? Had the officer just given some sort of secret approval for his execution? Was...

At last the waycar began to slow again, and this time, Iosif realized with a thrill, it was approaching a platform. His platform. The sequence address was clearly stamped above it in gold lettering. This was it, the end of the line.

The waycar ground to a halt and its doors slid open, presenting both passengers with a completely empty, fog-choked terminal platform.

For a moment Snorky and Iosif watched each other from across the car, waiting for the other one to make a move. Then Snorky jerked his head with a grunt. "C'mon kid. It's ya stop, ain't it?"

Iosif made a desperate grab for his suitcase and nearly fell over himself stumbling out onto the platform. He darted into the fog, pulling his trunk along behind him, moving as quickly as he could, just in case the big man changed his mind The wisping steam was too thick to see through, but he could make out a row of granite steps at the back, beyond the brickwork pillars.

As he climbed the steps, a sudden gust of wind blew back the steam, and he looked up and gasped.

The building directly before him had a certain faded grandeur about it, visible in the remnants of chipped plaster still clinging to the old brickwork of the seven-story building with its long, narrow, salt-stained windows. *United States Automated Postal Department Central Office*, read the sign just to the left of the entrance, in green-bronzed letters.

But it was the shadow of the complex beyond that had made Iosif gasp. Cleared of the steam, a massive complex loomed clearly above, its multitudinous boilers gleaming dully amidst the labyrinthine network of pipes, valves, and chutes which surrounded the massive, barn-like structure of steel and aluminum in the center. For a moment, the sun gleamed between the four massive smokestacks that capped the assembly, shining on the hundreds of thousands of sprawling mail-chutes, collecting and collating countless messages from all quarters of the city to be digested in the Sorting Machine before being again sent out to their proper destination.

For a moment, Iosif caught a glimpse of all this, and was dazzled by the beauty and complexity of it all.

Then the wind died, and the steam rose again, and all he could see was a foggy outline of the doors and their bronzed letters, with the old man standing next to them, smoking his cigar.

Even without the raincoat, it was easy to recognize the man's balding temples and steely gaze. His shirt-sleeved arms were crossed in a manner strongly suggestive of impatience, and his dark brow was knitted in what looked like displeasure. Iosif approached his new boss with a slight feeling of trepidation.

The old man regarded him for a moment, then took the cigar out of his mouth. "Well?" he asked.

"No dice, boss." Iosif jumped at the voice behind him. He turned around to see Snorky behind him, Tommy gun easily held in the crook of his arm. "They found it out somehow. They called the car and checked his papers. He's in the system now."

The older man's mouth twisted. "Well, damnit." He sighed, knocking the ash off his cigar. "Worth a try." He gestured to Iosif. "C'mon. Let's get you settled in."

CHAPTER 3

4::555343::2344

IOSIF RUSVAL,

Thank you for giving us the chance to review your application. Unfortunately, we find that your records do not suit the requirements of the Carnegie Federal Engineering Institute Early Entrance Program.

The backbone of not only our nation's security, but also its economy and culture, depends on the fine men who produce and maintain the Federal Applications that keep our great nation running. The Grand Columns, the Automated Postal Service, the great Steam Drives, and the wondrous Babbage Analytical Engines rely upon the integrity of the Federal Corps of Engineers. Because of this, the Carnegie Federal Engineering Institute only allows the best of the best within its doors, and even the Early Entry program must select its applicants carefully.

Do not take this rejection as a judgment upon your character. Simply getting to this stage is a major achievement which reflects well on your abilities. The review board remains confident that you will find your own role to fill in the Great American Economic Engine.

Otis Ostermausen

Dean of Admissions

Carnegie Federal Engineering Institute Early Entry Program.

P.S. A review of our records shows that this is the third time you have applied to the program. In accordance with Regulation 12b.4, we must inform you that we can no longer consider any further applications. Any correspondence from this sequence address will be discarded unopened.

4::118741::9520

"**H**e's an alien."

Iosif was not sure how to respond to the woman. "I Iosif," he decided to say, tapping his chest. "I new machinist. I sixteen."

"Oh, *that's* what ya meant." Snorky, currently taking his gun apart on one of the many desks scattered in the near-empty office, looked up. "Thought that wassa weird nickname."

"He's an alien, Alphonse," the woman said, not turning around. "Some sort of Martian."

"Martians don' look like that," Snorky objected. "They's all tentacly and stuff."

"If you rely on dime-store speculative novels, then yes, I would agree." The woman was not particularly pretty. Her thick eyebrows and coarse dark hair just intensified the glare on her roughened tan face. She *looked* slim, but Iosif suspected that might have more to do with her height than her build—though it was hard to tell, with the enormous grey trenchcoat she was wearing.

"Eh, what would you know?" Snorky waved, turning back to his work. "Aliens ain't even our department. He don't look nothin' like that thing in the vault."

The woman put both hands on her hips. "Well, he's clearly not *human*."

"So ya agree he's not an alien." It seemed this sort of argument was fairly common; Snorky was carrying on with his work as he talked with the woman. "Whatcha falling back on now, them Wendigos?"

The woman rolled her eyes. "Wendigos were fables devised to enhance taboos against cannibalism and the like. Much like the story of Ut'lunta, who could take any form until she used her hooked finger to pierce men in the eye and eat them out from the inside."

"Great stories, Edi. Ya oughta be a governess or somethin', rock babies to sleep at night, feed 'em all your psy-whatever and your monster stories"

"If I were going to choose a monster, I would call him a skin-walker. *They* were at least shapeshifters."

"So ya gonna stab him with an ash arrow or whatever it was?"

"No, because he is not a skinwalker, because they do not exist. " She turned back to Iosif. "He is an alien."

"Aw, for the luvva…" Snorky groaned. "What's with ya today? Something happen at the tax office? Somebody stick a knife in the wrong place?"

"Quite the opposite. A great many bullets found their proper homes in other people. My point holds that he is an alien."

"Look, don't an alien wanna avoid attention? Why he gonna choose a face like that, then, eh? Sorry, kid," he added.

Iosif shrugged, though he couldn't help the stab of pain. He'd never been pretty, but he didn't really like being reminded about it.

Snorky turned back to the woman. "He's a good kid. Cut him a break, will ya?"

"I sixteen."

"Just because he can tolerate your endless stories without telling you to shut up does not make him a 'good kid,' Alphonse," the woman said.

"You two still at that?" The conversation was broken by the old man, as he came walking in the door, a large file in his hand. "Look, let's just settle this now. Son." He stopped and bent down, looking Iosif dead in the eye. "You an alien?"

Iosif found this all very confusing. "…no?"

There was a beat of silence as the old man stared solemnly into his eyes. "Well." He clapped his hands and stood. "That settles that, then."

The woman gave an annoyed huff. "Mr. Hougan, I really don't think that that is a sufficiently comprehensive answer, and it explains so little about…"

"Not an alien, Kilroy," Hougan gave her a look. "That's the end of it. Now get the paperwork on the Berhousen job together, and see the doc about that eye before it starts to swell. Snorky, see what you can find out about the name 'Pryor.' Found a reference to him in the stuff from the tax office. Check with your old pals and see if anyone recognizes the name. Grey's working the federal angle."

"Sure thing, boss." Snorky pushed off the desk, firing a mock salute.

"...Yes. Sir," the woman responded with gritted teeth. She made no move to go anywhere.

"You," Hougan said, pointing at Iosif. "My office. Grey wants to take a quick look at you."

The woman's glittering dark eyes followed Iosif as he followed Hougan into the director's office.

೦೦೦

"Iosif Rusval." The slight man in the three-piece suit regarded him narrowly over his spectacles.

Iosif, unsure of what to say, gave a little nod.

"Hm." The man made a note on the papers before him. "4'2', 140 pounds, German descent. Yes?"

Iosif hadn't weighed—or measured—himself in some time, but he nodded.

"Known medical conditions." Again the man consulted his notes, and again he frowned. "Asthma, Rosacea, and Foreign Accent Syndrome. From birth?"

Iosif blinked. The man talked too quickly. "Sorry?"

"The way you talk. Has that always been the case?" The man looked at him over his spectacles.

"Er... yes," Iosif said. "My mother, she say is always how I speak."

"But she doesn't speak that way."

"No." Iosif shook his head.

"Probably some sort of birth trauma." The man looked over to Hougan. "The few cases of FAS we have in administrative were tied to head injuries they suffered in the line of duty. Haven't heard of a case from birth before; I can talk to the doctor about it…"

"Don't bother." Hougan waved. "We won't be paying him to talk. What's that other thing you mentioned, the one after athsma?"

"Rosacea," Grey noted, consulting his notepad. "It's a skin condition, not uncommon in people of Eastern European descent; causes red skin and rash-like swellings on the nose or face."

"Mm." Hougan grunted.

Iosif cocked his head. Rosacea. It was interesting to learn that there was a *name* for a face like his—that his swollen collection of warts, moles, and rashes were some sort of recognized symptom. He liked it; it made it seem like his ugliness were something outside that had infected him, not something that he just *was*.

"Also generally associated with eyesight problems." Grey turned his gaze back onto Iosif. "Do you ever wear eyeglasses?"

Iosif simply nodded. He already knew the name for that—astigmatism. This whole procedure seemed largely unnecessary. He hadn't realized there would be all this… whatever this was. He'd sort of assumed he'd show up and be ushered into a room full of magical wondrous artifacts to repair.

Yet there was something terrifying about this man in the three-piece suit with the eyeglasses. Something about the way he moved—smooth, like silk—that seemed… dangerous.

"Will it impact his duties at all?" Hougan asked.

"Not so long as we get him some decent spectacles." Grey made a last few notes. "I'll file the paperwork and get him on the payroll. Reserve him an office in administrative…"

Office? Iosif felt a strange stab of panic. Was this an office job? He wasn't much for reading, writing, or even talking. He couldn't man the front desk at Whisterhorns without driving away customers. He was good enough with figures, but he hadn't thought…

"Ah…" Iosif half-raised his hand. The men looked at him and he quailed. "…is nothing." He gave a quick smile. It couldn't be too hard, he'd pick it up.

Grey gave a satisfied nod, then continued speaking. "I think we have a place up on the fifth floor that should…"

That Iosif did need to object to. "Is there… anything… lower?" He'd been to a customer's house on the fifth floor once, and he wouldn't care to repeat the experience.

Grey looked at Hougan. "Rodrigo's old room should still be open…"

"Give him that one, then," Hougan said.

"Very good, sir." Grey gathered up his papers. He pointed at Iosif's steamer trunk. "Those are your belongings?"

Iosif looked down, then looked up and nodded.

"I'll have those sent to your office, then." Grey bent, dropped the papers atop the trunk, and lifted it easily.

Iosif was too confused to protest. "Yes… ah…" Mustering his courage, he turned to Hougan. "…office?"

Hougan glanced over. "Sorry, kid, should have explained. 'Administrative' is the dormitory here, the 'offices' are basically apartments. It's this whole…" He waved his hand vaguely. "Anyway. Grey's just going to take your stuff to your room."

"Oh." Iosif thought that was very odd, but he was more interested in another question. "So... I not desk worker?"

"What?" Hougan looked at him. "No. Machinist. Got a workshop for you downstairs."

Iosif felt a surge of relief.

"Suppose I should show you that," Hougan said, knocking the ash off his cigar. "Come along, then."

∽∘∾

"This is the central shipping warehouse," Hougan said, over the clatter of machinery. "Handles larger packages that can't fit in the mail chutes. Everything for Pittsburgh comes here straight off the Grand Column. We ship it out to different mailing centers across the city."

Iosif craned his neck around with interest. The warehouse was filled with endless shelves that stretched nearly two stories high, packed with random assortments of boxes marked with tags. Between the looming shelves, hardened men in coveralls piloted hissing carts with motorized claws, rattling back and forth on tiny rails bolted to the floor. On his left, Iosif could see cargo doors leading to the outside; on his right, he could just barely make out the steam pressure valves for the carts. And against the far wall opposite him, he could see the Grand Column itself running through the warehouse, cargo modules detaching and re-attaching like clockwork as packages came in from out of town.

There seemed to be just one thing missing. "Where... letters?" Iosif asked. Hougan looked at him and he clarified. "Where you handle letters?"

Hougan gave a humorless grin. "That's all handled by the machinery in the back." He gestured vaguely. "*Automated* Postal Department, after all. The whole back of the compound is for the Sorting Engine that all the letters run through. *We're* not even allowed near it; there's this great fat door keeps everyone but the eggheads out." He growled. "Assholes."

Iosif's brow furrowed. "Is ... is that my job?"

"Hm? No, no. Federal Engineers only back there. Public Works Department runs them. You're a Machinist, and you work for me." Hougan clapped a hand on his shoulder and steered him away from the warehouse floor. "Officially, your job is to provide maintenance on the warehouse luggage carts and keep them working properly."

"Ah." Iosif looked over his shoulder at the luggage carts. He could not say they looked extremely interesting.

"You're also Chief Renovations Director, naturally." Hougan continued.

Iosif frowned. "What?"

"This place is old, kid." Hougan took the cigar out of his mouth. "Government took control of it in 1894 or so, but Carnegie actually built the place back in the early 1870's. It's pretty much never been properly refitted. We don't even know what half the stuff in here was supposed to do when it WAS working. So we need someone to fix up and upgrade all the old machinery." They came to a large metal garage door set in the near wall of the warehouse, and Hougan paused. "And, of course, fix up those *other* artifacts I hired you for."

Hougan pressed the button on the side of the door and the metal curtain began to rise up. Slowly, Iosif's fascinated eyes took in a large storage space, stacked high on each side with shelves full of bizarre paraphernalia, cast haphazardly every which way like an insane sort of dust heap.

"Sorry the place is such a mess." Hougan grinned ruefully. "My ex-wife'd die of shame if she saw this. Apparently, this is where they used to have the workshop, but we've just been sort of throwing whatever in here. Will it work for you?"

Iosif did not answer. He was studying the wide desk against the back wall and the cubby holes above it, taking in the steam lines running directly across the ceiling and the valves for the gas lamps linked along the wall - the solid concrete floor under the rubbish heaps and the luggage cart track running straight toward the back. He was seeing brand new glistening tools all set in a row next to cans of grease and oil and ball-bearing fluid.

"I'll take that as a yes, then," Hougan said, with a look of faint amusement. "Anything you need, just talk to Grey. He'll be down in a sec to take you up to your quarters. Any questions?"

"Ah… yes." There was indeed one question, one vital question that Iosif had nearly entirely forgotten. "Please… what is… 'Enforcement Division'? What we do?"

His new boss took a long drag on his cigar. "We beat up people and break into secret bases," he said, no variation in his tone. "Sometimes even foreign ones." He stubbed the cigar out on the wall. "And we make sure that the mail gets to where it's supposed to go." Turning, he walked out of the workshop. "Welcome to the Post Office, kid."

CHAPTER 4

4::555343::2344

Dear mother

All continues well here in Pittsburgh. The quarters they have settled me in are neat and comfortable, and my neighbors are friendly. My boss says I am not to speak much about work to you in letters, so I will just say that it is good work that keeps me busy and is interesting. It also pays well—did you get the money I sent last week?

Glad to hear of Mr. Whisterhorn's new apprentice and that things are going well for you. As you suggested, I went to St. Olaf's church last Sunday and met Father Boris. He seems friendly, and I will go there as often as I can, work permitting. I forgot to ask Father Boris about making offerings to the household dvergrs, but I will next week.

They say I am to have a 'review' at work today—someone from the paperwork department is coming in to check in on me. I am not sure what to expect, but I am eager to please.

Hope everything is going well at home,

Love,

Iosif

2::324523::4234

Iosif put the letter in the auto-mail receptacle and grabbed his bag as he heard it rattle away. He was more curious than ever how the auto-mail system worked, now that he was, in theory, only a few hundred feet or so away from a live, working example. But he'd seen the vault door—and the guards—and had no ambition to test either.

He was nearly out the door when he remembered the last part of his letter. He quickly dug through the kitchen cabinets, found a stale slice of bread and some old grapes, and dropped them on a plate in the corner. He doubted they would attract anything besides mice, but his mother was bound to ask if he'd "fed the gnomes," and Iosif hated lying to her.

He walked out the front door, and cast a look up. Twenty stories of plaster-painted concrete stretched up above him on all sides of the bare courtyard. The morning air was crisp and cool, but even so Iosif could see some forms moving about on the upper balconies—old grey-haired men and fresh-faced women in white coats. Dark wooden doors dotted the balconies at exact intervals of forty feet, each one marked with a bronzed plaque. Iosif turned momentarily to study the sign on his own room. "Chief Executive Renovations Director of Central Office," and below that, in smaller letters, "Machinist." The letters gleamed dully in the morning light.

The doors next to his read: "Assistant Director of Internal Accounting" (an 80-year old man who thought Iosif was his daughter), and "Executive Archivist of Human Resources" (a 76-year old woman with a wooden arm). Iosif hadn't meant to meet them, but it seemed everyone here was keenly interested in him—there had been at least thirty curious faces peering out of windows when he returned to his apartment, and five casseroles on his doorstep the next day. The visit from his neighbors had been inevitable.

Iosif grimaced and turned quickly to the path, trotting across the courtyard toward the building's exit at the far end. One pleasant thing, the housing was nearly adjoining the Enforcement Headquarters Building; so he barely had to walk five minutes to work. It was through a door and up a staircase once you left 'Administrative.'

"Hey! Junior!" Snorky called as he entered the front office. "Just the man I was looking for! Think ya can fix the stock on this Tommy gun?" Snorky grabbed the weapon off the desk in one massive hand and tossed it easily to Iosif.

Iosif tried to catch the gun, but merely batted it to the floor with a wince-inducing clatter. "Perhaps," he said, picking it up. Snorky had understated the damage as usual; not only was the wire stock hopelessly mangled, but the framing and most of the back end of the gun were all bent out of shape. "How this happen?" he asked, not looking up from his examination.

"Jammed door. Tried to smash it open with my gun," Snorky said.

"Why you ever thought that would work in the *first* place…" Ms. Kilroy spoke under her breath but loud enough for the entire office to hear. She was working at a typewriter with one hand, picking out the keys with her fingers. Her other arm was in a sling.

"Better than the alternative, sweetheart." Snorky gestured. His hand was all bandaged up, with several fingers splinted together. "Anyway, depends on the door. This one time, me and a couple boys was taking out a rival operation based in an old Carnegie Distribution Centre. The side door was locked, see, but we...."

"Is Rusval back there?" Hougan's voice floated. "Tell him I want to see him!"

Iosif still couldn't tell what his boss's angry voice sounded like—or at least, how it differed from his normal voice. Neither Snorky nor Ms. Kilroy *seemed* very concerned, but then again, they weren't the ones getting called into the office.

Hougan was behind his desk, still in shirtsleeves and smoking a cigar. There were several bits of sticking plaster on his face, and he was picking at the bandages around his knuckles. On the desk was a gleaming suitcase—aluminum, Iosif noted with surprise—with a handcuff fastened to the handle.

The cuff was splattered with what looked like blood.

"You know anything about locks?" Hougan asked, nodding at it. "Grey could probably pick it open, but he's attending to other business right now."

Iosif did indeed know a few things about locks. Unlocking things had been a big part of the miscellaneous sort of jobs they pulled at Whisterhorn's when watches were slow (or rather, when the business was slow. Watches being slow actually made business go fast). Walking up to the desk, he picked up the suitcase to study it. The lock itself, though, was perfectly simple, a three point combination. Quickly he spun the dials. 3-5-4 9-1-5.

The suitcase sprung open, to reveal a pile of papers and folders.

"That was fast," Hougan muttered, standing and turning the suitcase around so he could see its contents.

"Is default factory setting." Iosif pointed to the suitcase. "All Vosterhofen suitcases start with that combination."

Hougan chuckled. "Well, for such a secret message, that messenger wasn't thinking too securely."

"It's a shame," Grey said, as he entered the room. "The sort of people they let in the Black Chamber these days.... The quality of training has really gone down."

Hougan grunted. "The analysis on those codes ready yet, Grey?"

"No, sir." Grey's mouth had an unusual twist. "The ... senator is here, sir."

The air in the room chilled suddenly.

"Shit." Hougan slammed the suitcase shut and slid it into a desk drawer. "How long?"

"About five minutes, I should think ..."

"Perry!" The door boomed open and a man, not quite as tall as Snorky but undeniably *bigger*, entered the room. He was clad in an immense, black three-piece suit with a golden watch dangling from the breast-coat pocket. "Perry, Perry, Perry, how are you!

Hougan noticeably grimaced, but he still extended his hand. "Senator Blackthorne," he said, extending his hand. "I didn't know you'd be dropping by."

"It'd been too long!" Senator Blackthorne chuckled. "I needed to come down and see how my old chum Perry is doing! See how the business is going, you know? They don't just appoint anyone to be Director of Public Works, after all; I need to take seriously how things are run."

"Commendable." Hougan nodded. "If you'd care to follow me, I can take you…"

"Sir," a spider-haired underling behind Blackthorne whispered. "There is, ah, the matter of the new employee…"

"Ah!" Blackthorne turned around. "Perry, I've heard you've taken a new man on! What's all that about, eh?"

Hougan grimaced again, more pronouncedly. "The review of new postal employees falls under my…"

"Oh, Perry, Perry." The senator's chuckle was deep and thick. The chain on his watch shook as he laughed. "I'm not trying to step on your toes! But you know the budget, Perry, there's always the budget! The Postal Department has one of the largest budgets in America already; do they really need to keep adding to it? And new employees can be so expensive, Perry! And then too…" He shook a finger at Hougan, "I need to make sure you're following regulations. You don't always follow regulations, Perry, now you know you don't."

Behind the senator, Iosif saw the door open and Ms. Kilroy slip in. She leant against the back wall, arms crossed, watching.

"*I* follow regulations to the letter, Mr. Blackthorne," Hougan said. "My problem is with those other subordinates of yours who *don't.*"

Blackthorne coughed and gave another smile. "Well, in any case, I'd like to meet this young man, say hello! He *is* a man, eh Perry?" He nudged Hougan in a way the older man clearly did not appreciate. "Not another little typist of yours, eh?"

Ms. Kilroy's lips thinned, but she remained silent.

"Sir." The spider-haired attendant again. "I, ah, think this young... man..." He gestured toward Iosif.

"Is this him?" Senator Blackthorne turned fully on Iosif.

"Iosif Rusval is my new employee, yes." Hougan inclined his head.

Iosif had the uncomfortable sensation that all eyes were on him. "He-Hello." He gave an awkward wave.

"Perry, Perry, Perry!" The senator's smile had vanished, and he shook his head, making a tt-tt-ing noise. "This is beneath you! We don't hire children, Perry! You know that!"

"I sixteen." Iosif sighed.

"I have Mr. Rusval's paperwork all prepared here." Mr. Grey handed the senator a folder. "I submitted it all to your office a few weeks ago. Mr. Rusval's birth record demonstrates that he is, as he says, 16."

The senator immediately passed off the file to the spider-haired attendant, who did not even bother to open it. "Sir, if you, ah, recall, we discussed this earlier," he said, with just a hint of reproof.

"Er... yes." Senator Blackthorne looked lost for a moment before rallying himself. "Ah, but Hougan, I didn't see any interview transcript. Surely you must have interviewed him?"

"There was no reason to," Hougan said. "Mr. Rusval's expertise spoke for itself."

"Nonsense! The Federal Automated Postal Department is one of the most crucial services in America, Perry! One can never be too careful." Senator Blackthorne turned on him, and Iosif felt himself confronted with the entire mass of man. "You, young man. What are your qualifications, eh? Where were you trained?"

"Er..." Iosif felt a growing sense of panic. *Trained.* He saw marble columns, gleaming floors. *Sorry, Mr. Rusval, but the early entrance program only accepts the finest...* He felt paper crinkle in his hands, saw the red marks stare back at him accusingly.

"Hmm!" Senator Blackthorne looked keenly at Hougan. "Tell me, young man," he said turning again. "How would you fix a diluted pressure valve on a 53-X Federal Babbage engine?"

"Sir." The spider-haired attendant. "Mis-ter, ah, Rusval is listed as a Machinist, he would not be required to perform maintenance on a Babbage engine..."

"Hm." The senator looked irritated. "Or, ah, shall we say... a broken drive shaft on a Lindvarne Steam Lift Luggage Cart?"

"Er..." Iosif felt relatively certain of what the man was talking about—those carts in the warehouse, but how to explain... "I remove... I remove casing... not shaft casing, but outer casing, that covers shaft... oh, before that I unscrew screws. Yes, I unscrew screws, I remove outer casing, yes. Then I disassemble shaft—oh, after shutting steam off, of course, after shutting everything off, probably even before removing casing— removing screws. Then, I disassemble assembly, and grease… or perhaps…" His voice trailed off. He felt this was not going well.

"Hm." Senator Blackthorne's brows knit together, he looked grimly pleased. "Well," he said, bending over to stare at Iosif, "Your skills do not seem so evident to me, young man."

Iosif stared at the senator's golden watch, its chain dangling before him. A sudden idea seized him. "A moment," he said. He dug into his pockets and brought out the antique watch Mr. Whisterhorn had given him out of one, and his oil-cloth-wrapped tool kit out of the other. "Sir…" he said, looking up at the senator. "I borrow watch, please?"

The senator looked askance at him. "Whatever for?"

Iosif did not have the courage to explain. Instead he turned to Hougan. "I borrow watch, please?"

Hougan looked puzzled. "I don't have…"

"Here." Iosif turned at Grey's voice, just in time to see the man throw a silver watch at him. He tried to catch it, but instead batted it away, sending it thudding against the floor. Mr. Grey winced. "Do be careful, Mr. Rusval," he said, as Iosif bent to pick it up. "It is not quite the clockwork nightingale the mountain gnomes made for the emperor, but it is very dear to me."

"A bit fond of fairy tales, your man." The senator laughed, staring at Grey. "Unusual in such a professional line of work." He caught sight of Ms. Kilroy and smiled. "Caught some habits from this one, maybe?"

Ms. Kilroy's lips twitched in a smile. "The *nirumbee* in our stories live underground, but they made no nightingales," she said "The shared legends are possibly reflective of a universal fear of darkness and the unknown."

"My ex-wife used to say; nothing more terrifying than a dark empty room," Hougan said, watching with interest as Iosif cleared out a space on his desk.

He laid out first his watch, then Mr. Grey's watch, then his tool kit, all spread out.

Tick   Tock   Tick   Tock   Tick

TOK   TIK   TOK   TIK   TOK

The two watches ticked, arrythmically, Whisterhorn's considerably off Grey's more precise timing.

Mr. Grey came to stand beside him, cocking his head to look down. Iosif felt the considerable bulk of the senator loom behind him on the other side, with his attendants in tow. "What's he doing?" the senator asked.

Iosif closed his eyes.

Under his fingers he felt the table, the rough grain of the wood. By memory, he raised his hands and brought them down on the watches. He flipped them both over, then reached for his screwdrivers.

"Mr. Rusval...!"

"Quiet! Let him..."

Sounds faded as time slowed to only the two watches. First Whisterhorn's. Back casing, gears, small wheels, cogs, coiled spring—considerably uncoiled, by this point, he should really have cleaned out this watch earlier. Quickly, smoothly, systematically, he disassembled the watch down to its core parts, laying each piece out in a carefully selected spot on the desk.

Next. Mr. Grey's. Back casing, gears, small wheels, cogs, coiled spring… wire? There was some sort of wire wound around the casing on a spool. Curious. He uncoiled it and set it aside. Everything was now all spread out on the desk. His eyes were still closed, but in his mind, every part was perfectly distinct.

He started back. The spring in Grey's. The spring in Whisterhorn's. Two wheels in Grey's. One in Whisterhorn's. One coiled wire. Four cogs. Watch movements. Face. Glass. Outer casing. Iosif flipped over the watches and reached for the keys to wind them up. One, two, three turns… Whisterhorn's took an extra turn before the spring was tight. He laid aside the key, picked up both watches, held them up, and opened his eyes.

Tick   Tock   Tick   Tock   Tick   Tock
TIK   TOK   TIK   TOK   TIK   TOK

The watches, ticked alongside each other, in perfect harmony. Iosif didn't even bother to check the time. He knew it was right.

Hougan had a quiet smirk on his face. Mr. Grey looked slightly pale, but he too was nodding. Even the attendants behind the Senator were whispering.

The senator seemed unsure of how exactly to proceed. "Well…" he coughed. "A nice trick."

Iosif shrugged. "Thank you." He'd done similar tricks every so often at Whisterhorn's, to impress customers.

"... but obviously planned." The senator coughed again, with growing confidence. "Yes, a regular flying circus. How many times did you have to practice that, eh?"

Iosif shrugged again. "I can try again," he said, reaching with a grimy hand for the senator's gold pocketwatch.

"No!" The Senator withdrew a few paces. "No, er... that will be fine, Mr. Rusval." He turned on Hougan and Mr. Grey, as if daring them to laugh. "But this does not really answer as to whether he can repair steam lifts, eh?"

"Mr. Rusval has been steadily maintaining the steam lifts in the warehouse for the past few weeks," Mr. Grey said, producing another folder. "He has restored 30 percent of our decommissioned lifts to active duty, and increased the efficiency of 40" of the working models currently in operation." He handed this folder also to the senator, who again immediately passed it off to his spider-haired attendant. Mr. Grey gave a small smile. "The overall estimate in savings is well in the thousands of dollars."

The bookkeeper was reading through the folder at an alarming rate, his eyes magnified impossibly large behind giant spectacles. "These, ah, figures seem quite accurate, sir." He looked up and peered directly at Iosif, his overlarge eyes blinking. "It seems Mr. Rusval is, ah, quite talented."

"Hm." The Senator studied Iosif for a moment, and then broke into a huge grin. "Well, then, welcome to government service, Mr. Rusval!" He smiled broadly, reached forward as if to shake Iosif's hand, seemed to remember that that hand was covered in grease, and swiftly withdrew his hand. "We, ah, we hope you enjoy your time. Hougan, you have a good man here!"

"Thank you sir." Hougan collected Grey's watch off the desk and tossed a fast overhand back to his lieutenant, who caught it left-handed. "Now, you mentioned you wanted to see how the rest of the facility was doing…?"

"Er… sir?" The spider-haired attendant, who had wandered close to the desk, poked open a drawer that had come just ajar.

The shiny aluminum suitcase lay exposed to view.

The senator's eyebrows rose. "My, my, Hougan, what is that?"

"A messenger suitcase." Hougan answered, lifting the item out onto the now-greasy desk. "Similar to the sort carried by federal Black Chamber agents."

"And… where did you get it?"

Hougan looked at the senator. "We chopped it off the arm of a man we shot," he said.

There was a quiet gasp.

"You… what?" The senator gaped.

"We were investigating possible tampering with the mail," Hougan said. "In the process of our investigation, we met a man carrying this suitcase. He refused to offer any identification or respond to any of the normal call signs, and instead attacked my men and me. Thus, we shot him. And, I regret to say, killed him. My associate Mr. Grey severed the man's hand…" Here Hougan indicated the bloody cuff, "… so that we could bring the suitcase back to the forensics department for further investigation. Mr. Rusval here just opened it for us."

Iosif felt he'd really rather have been left out of that speech.

"Director Hougan." The Senator's grin was entirely gone. "Are you telling me that you killed a federal agent and chopped off his hand to steal secret missives?"

Hougan simply stared back. "I don't know, sir. I don't know the man, or his missives. You tell me. Was this man …" He picked an identification card out of the suitcase, "… Howard Trollope …" He looked up at the Senator, "… part of the Black Chamber? And if so, were these your secret missives?" He swiveled the suitcase around to the Senator. "Because if so, sir, then both you and the Black Chamber are guilty of tampering with the Automated Postal Service, which as you know, is a capital offense under Federal law. So." He gestured to the suitcase. "Is this yours? Because if so, by all means, take it, sir."

Beads of sweat were standing out on the Senator's forehead. "Hougan." He growled. "You have been *ordered* to give up this silly investigation …"

"I must stop you there, sir." Hougan crossed his arms. "Tampering with the Automated Postal Service rests under the jurisdiction of the Postal Enforcement Division and the Enforcement Division alone, and as such, is only answerable to the Director of the Automated Postal Service." His eyebrows leveled. "Me."

The Senator's lip curled, but he remained silent.

"So." Hougan continued to stare at the man. "I ask you again: Are these your messages?"

There was a pregnant pause. Iosif, who was trying to move out of the way without actually moving, could practically feel tension crackling in the air. The senator's attendants had grown utterly quiet. Two very large ones at the back were stepping forward. At some point, Ms. Kilroy seemed to have pushed herself off the wall and was now standing poised, alert. On the other side of the room, Mr. Grey slipped a hand into his waistcoat.

"No." said the senator. He turned away. "Now show me around the damned department already, Hougan. And you'd better hope you've got a clean bill around here."

"Of course, sir." Hougan closed the suitcase and picked it up, walking around the desk toward the door. On his way past Grey, he handed him the suitcase. "If you'll just follow me, we first have the administrative department to overview, then the engineering..."

"Skip the cripples. The eggheads too, we've wasted enough time already. Show me your damn warehouse."

Hougan and the Senator filed out, followed by the senator's many attendants and bodyguards. Iosif was left alone with Mr. Grey and Ms. Kilroy.

Both of the agents exhaled loudly. "One day..." Kilroy said.

Grey pinched the bridge of his nose. "It works. You can't deny that it works."

"I can't deny it, I just don't know *how*," Kilroy said. "Was he like this back in the service?"

"Yes. It drove our superiors in the Black Chamber crazy." Grey shook his head and looked at Kilroy. "Any observations?"

"Early onset dementia possibly, almost certainly some form of compensation for past trauma, possibly related to his..."

"About the senator." Grey closed his eyes.

"He's nervous. Didn't know about the suitcase, so it must be the op in Detroit that's got him rattled," Kilroy said. "He's looking to isolate the Director, rob him of manpower, that's the only explanation for why he would be so fixated on a new employee. He's never done this before. Why visit expressly just to meet Iosif here?" She looked at him. "Can you think why?"

"Er…" Iosif was surprised at being asked for an opinion. "The… one man… reminded him. The secretary. With the hair and glasses." He realized that was not a very distinctive description.

"Really? Didn't see that." Kilroy frowned. "Then maybe you weren't the main point after all. Maybe it was just to intimidate us." She looked at Grey. "His mannerisms are getting more desperate, though. The director's pushing him. It's only a matter of time before…"

"The Director," Grey said with finality, "knows his job. We just need to make sure we know ours." He looked to Iosif. "Can you crack a safe?"

CHAPTER 5

1::159188::2864

Senator Blackthorne,

In regards to your request, I must refer you to the Veterans Bill of 1918. It is functionally impossible to remove any Federal Employee from work in the Postal Department. It is, perhaps, possible to restrict their movements limited to the Administrative grounds, but that requires permission from the Central Postal Director, who I understand to be the person under consideration in this circumstance.

Declaring a Director 'restricted to office duties,' as the form reads, you would need the signature of all three of the immediate members of APD board—the Central Assistant Postal Director, the Postmaster General, and the Marshall-At-Arms of the Postal Enforcement Division. All would need to come to an agreement that the Director was no longer fit to serve.

Of course, if the Central Director and his subordinates were found guilty of crimes, that would be a separate question. Yet it seems the limits of the Central Postal Director's power are very broadly defined. The circumstances of the APD's formation were so unusual; Congress seems to have given them a wide latitude of powers in order to allow them to expedite the widespread installation of auto-mail machines,and, of course, to give them the latitude to fight back against Carnegie's mob connections. (There are even exceptions for Tampering with Federal Appliances, since naturally the auto-mail machines constitute Federal Appliances. Only the Sorting Engines themselves fall outside the Director's purview.) Thus, it seems that actually arguing that the Central Director had gone outside the law would be a very difficult proposition which any lawyer would hesitate to make without the strongest evidence.

On a wholly unofficial note, I must thank you for this request. It is a fascinating legal question that never seems to have been fully tested. No one has attempted to remove a postal director since 1902, and no one has issued any serious legislation against the department since 1911. It was a delight to look into the legal question, and I can only express regret that I could not give you a more satisfactory answer.

Frederick Laroche

Deputy Attorney General

0::231778::1278

"**P**urely speculative, of course," Mr. Grey assured him, as they walked down the hallway. "But, should the occasion arise, in the course of your duties as Chief Renovator, that a safe might somehow get lost in the mail…"

"A safe?" Iosif frowned in puzzlement.

"As I said, speculative." Grey waved. "In any case, if one did, unlocking the safe would be your responsibility." He glanced back at Iosif. "You say you have no training?"

Iosif was still frowning. "I unlock Ms. McGuillicutty's safe one time—but she keep combination on a tag on the side."

"Hm." Grey gave a sharp nod. "Perhaps we should speak with someone in Administrative who may be able to help you."

∽o∾

Iosif had never been around the Administrative Centre in the daytime, and he was surprised to see that it wasn't busier. A few elderly people were sitting in the garden, a few others were walking about on the balconies above. A great many of them seemed to be young women—secretaries, Iosif presumed. But where was everyone else?

He glanced after Mr. Grey to ask, only to realize with dismay that Mr. Grey was making for the *stairs*. "Coming?" the man called after him. Iosif had no choice but to comply.

"We had a lift installed, but the staff doesn't trust it," Grey said, when they had gone up about two or three flights. "For good reason, I would add. It's useful for large-scale deliveries but too risky to rely upon fully. Though I do pity Pikwing, having to walk up these stairs every day."

Iosif didn't answer. He was too busy trying not to calculate the load-bearing capabilities of the concrete at that particular angle. He was trying not to calculate the odds of several missing nuts in the stairway railing. He was trying not to think of what might happen if those iron spanners folded in half and sent them all smashing to bits on the ground.

He was failing. He was also, with each step, feeling the tightness in his chest growing. He paused on the step to dig out his inhaler, but Grey was fast climbing the stairs ahead of him.

"Here we are," Grey said, after what seemed like an eternity to Iosif. He stepped out onto the narrow balcony running around the interior of the apartment complex. "Come on, lad, don't loiter. This way. Briskly! What's the matter with…" He stopped. "Oh, ah."

Iosif stood on the top step, bracing himself against the door frame, taking quick draughts from his inhaler.

"My apologies. I had forgotten." Grey had the grace to look abashed. "Please, take your time."

Shaking his head, Iosif held up a hand. "I fine," he said, pocketing his inhaler. "Ready." A quick grin.

"…very well." Grey turned back to the balcony and began to walk.

Iosif looked at the balcony and its all-too-thin railing, and realized another problem. But there was nothing for it. Taking a deep breath that had nothing to do with asthma; he followed Grey, trying not to look out the wrought-iron railing at the six-story drop below. Instead, he tried to focus on the other people walking about on the balcony. A few old people with walkers. A young man missing an arm. And there were the young women, again—clearly visible in red-and-white uniforms. One of them was wheeling the young man around, talking to him. Some others were pushing around carts of towels. Two had what looked like a stretcher.

Not secretaries, Iosif realized with something like embarrassment. *Nurses.* And then he realized that that was even stranger.

Grey stopped outside of 618A (The plate underneath read: *Deputy Director of Waste Removal Allocation, District 14*) and rapped on the door. "Mr. Pikwing!" he called. "It's Grey!"

There was some muttering behind the door and at length, some bolts slid back and a wrinkly face peered out. "Grey," it said noncommittedly. "What can I do for you?"

"Not for me." Grey shrugged off the question. "For Hougan." He jerked a thumb at Iosif. "This is his new can-opener. I need him to learn how to open safes."

"Really." Pikwing glanced over at Iosif, looking him up and down. He shrugged. "Well, that's his choice. Come into my office, kid, and we'll see what we can do." The man drew back from the door, and for the first time Iosif realized the man was in a wheelchair.

To Iosif's surprise, Grey did not accompany him into the man's "office," but remained outside and shut the door behind Iosif. The room inside was dim and musty, piled high with loose memorabilia. "Here." Pikwing said, digging through a pile of junk on the desk (Iosif momentarily saw a pistol disappear into a desk drawer). He tossed a padlock in Iosif's general direction. "See what you can do with that."

Iosif tried to catch the lock, batted it instead, batted it with his other hand, juggled it around for a while, and finally lost it on its way to the floor.

Pikwing watched without interest. "No combat training, then." He wheeled over to him. The man had no legs at all, Iosif saw now; only a pair of stumps that ended at the knee. "Well, never mind. You don't need to be a rugby player, just see what you can do with it."

Iosif gave the lock a quick once-over. He'd seen this sort before, though this looked to be a much older model—the gears moved a bit more clumsily. All the same, he tried the factory default—33 left, 41 right, 59 left. Nothing. He looked at Pikwing, but the man's expression did not change in the slightest.

Iosif licked his lips. The factory defaults were his only real trick. Maybe he could feel it out? More slowly, this time, Iosif rotated the dial first one way, then another. There seemed to be a small resistance at 5... Iosif called that his first number and moved on. The second one he lost for a moment, but after some experimenting he found somewhere around the 45 area. That just left the last one—Iosif spun the dial wildly and pulled back on the hook,

Nothing happened.

Shamefacedly, he handed it back. "I sorry."

"No need to be." Pikwing did, in fact, look a little impressed. "Good thought at the start, there, trying the factory setting. And you were picking out the numbers there, I could tell." Taking the lock, he spun the dial. 63-5-45. "Safes and combination locks work by lining the pins up to the proper gates—gaps in the interior lock," he said, popping open the lock. "That's the essence of the art, though there's obviously tricks and nuances the farther you get. Basically the safecracker needs to find the gates in order to limit his options. You seem more of a 'touch' safe-cracker sort. I do it more by sound—well, did, anyway." He indicated the wheelchair.

Iosif was a little embarrassed. How were you supposed to respond to something like that?

Fortunately it seemed Pikwing was not waiting for a response. "But the 'catch' you were feeling is when the pins line up with *one* of the gates," he said, wheeling back to the desk. "Any one of them—not necessarily the next one in the sequence. So you pick out the numbers first, and then try different combinations of the number. Usually the highest is first and the lowest is second, but that's entirely dependent on the person locking the safe. Of course, a safe's a lot trickier than a shed padlock." Picking another lock off the desk, he tossed it again at Iosif. "Here. Take that home, and come back once you've gotten it unlocked."

Iosif took that to mean he was dismissed, and he made for the door.

∽o∾

The next day, Hougan volunteered to accompany Iosif, much to the younger man's surprise. Again there was the grueling climb up the stairs, though this time Hougan paused on the landing a few times to give him a chance to catch his breath. "You sure you don't want to take the lift?" Hougan said, conversationally, smoking on his cigar as he watched Iosif struggle up the steps. "They're not really so dangerous as all that."

Iosif shook his head, wheezing. He'd had a look at the lift, and was heartily in agreement with the residents' appraisal.

"Suit yourself." Hougan stubbed out his cigar with a look of regret. "Y'know, they have a pharmacy on the fourth floor, if you want to pick up some more of those inhalers."

They arrived on the sixth floor and again walked along the balcony to the door. "Hey in there!" Hougan rapped lightly on the door. "Central Postal Director calling for the Deputy Director of District 14's Waste Removal Allocation!"

"Perry!" This time the door was opened immediately, and the wrinkled face was beaming. "What brings you here?" Pikwing caught sight of Iosif and his eyebrow jumped upward. "Already? Bloody hell, kid, that was fast."

"Devoted, if nothing else," Hougan said, with a look at Iosif's bandaged hand. "Kid tried to sand his fingerprints off to make them more sensitive."

"Oh. Yeah." Pikwing frowned. "That's a myth. Forgot to mention that."

"Yeah." Hougan looked to the man in the wheelchair. "I know. You always 'forget to mention that,' Latches."

Pikwing broke out in a wide grin. "Still remember you trying to sand your earlobes to improve your hearing. Never seen anyone try that before."

Hougan wagged his finger at the man. "I need this one well trained, Latches. No tricks, okay?"

"No tricks." 'Latches' raised his hands.

As it happened, Hougan came inside for a few moments and talked with Pikwing, while Iosif practiced on a safe cross-section, where he could see the gates lining up. They also had a short discussion on 'false gates,' which sometimes you could tell and sometimes you had to determine by trial and error.

"I should get going," Hougan said, standing to his feet. "Oh, Rusval." He dug through his pockets and brought out a small box, about the size of the sort used to hold cigars. "When you get a chance, see if you can figure out what this is for."

"You still at that, Perry?" Latches looked worried, but not surprised. "Where's this one from?"

"Navy Pier in Chicago," Hougan said. "They're doing something with the submarines."

"Damnit, that's a Shadow Site." Pikwing said. "They can shoot you just for being there!"

"They tried." Hougan turned toward the door. "Report to me when you know what it does, Rusval."

∽ₒ∾

When Iosif came to his workshop the next day, there was someone else there already.

"Can I help?" he said.

The scrawny man with the spidery hair turned around, with a somewhat startled expression. "Er… yes," He turned around from his study of the desk. "Mr. Rudkus, isn't it?"

"Rusval," Iosif said. "You?"

The man gave a little laugh. "Flistworth is my name," he said. "You may have, ah, seen me with Senator Blackthorne the other day… I am his, ah, secretary. Mailing secretary, you understand. I handle his paperwork." Extending his hand, he said: "Pleased to meet you, Mr, ah, Rusval."

"Yes," said Iosif, in utter disregard for everything his mother had taught him regarding manners. He was suddenly very conscious of the artifact box in his hands. Why had he brought it home last night? Why had he not hidden it in the desk with the others? Should he hide it behind his back? Would that look suspicious? Was it already suspicious? He stepped forward as casually as possible, up to his workbench, and shoved the box off to the side, almost as if it didn't matter.

It didn't seem to deter Flistworth. "Oh … what's that?" he said, following Iosif up to the desk. Flistworth wasn't a tall man, but he was still taller than Iosif by nearly a head.

"Family heirloom," Iosif lied, turning around to face the man. "Project I work on."

"Oh." Flistworth seemed to lose interest. "This is an, ah, interesting workshop you have here, Mr., ah, Rusval." He tugged at the lapels of his coat. "Do you not find it, ah, warm?"

Iosif shrugged. "Not really." He found it hard to focus on temperatures at the moment; he just wanted this man out of the warehouse. "You have reasons for visit, Mr. Flistworth?"

"I do, in fact." Flistworth clapped his hands together, as if in memory. "Thank you for reminding me. I'm conducting an audit of sorts, you see. A small, ah, irregularity to clear up." He fumbled with his briefcase and opened it, producing a few papers. "I, ah, looked over the figures your Phillip Grey provided … really quite, ah, remarkable … you've already saved the Automated Department quite a bit of funding. Really amazing work on those steam lifts, out there."

Iosif frowned. "You're … welcome?"

"Yesss… there is, ah, a slight problem, though." Flistworth winced. "You see, I inspected some of the steam lifts and noticed that several had been, ah, illegally modified."

Iosif froze. "Yes?"

"In-deed." Flistworth paused. "Several have, ah, received several new features, which do not appear in the original patents." He gave a thin smile. "I assume this is your doing?"

Iosif licked his lips. He wasn't really even good at talking, much less lying on short notice. There didn't seem to be any way he could deny this. He nodded.

Flistworth gave a pained grimace. "Of course, tampering with Federal appliances is, ah, prohibited."

"Of course," Iosif agreed.

"Well." Flistworth coughed. "As it happens, the steam lifts are *not* federal appliances. We subcontract them through a private firm—the developer decided to, ah, produce them himself. So tampering with them is not a serious, ah, offense. But they are still, ah, Federation *property*." Again fumbling with his suitcase, he brought out a thick sheaf of papers and laid them on the desk. "There are the, ah, records of the altered steam lifts. Please take them out of, ah, operation and return them to their approved state."

"Yes, sir." Iosif gave a broken nod.

"Do remember, Mr. Rusval." Flistworth smiled again. "You are here to, ah, *keep* things running. Not *change* how they run. Also." He opened up his suitcase. "This is the employee, ah, handbook." Flistworth produced a book that was thicker than the entire sheaf of papers and laid it next to it. "I shall return next week to administer the, ah, exam. *Do* read it carefully, Mr. Rusval…" He studied him critically. "Particularly, if I may say, the part about, ah, personnel regulations and how they are required to, ah, shave every day."

"I shave just in morning!" Iosif protested.

"Ah?" Flistworth looked strangely pleased. "Well… do continue, then. It is important all federal employees maintain a standard of, ah, appearance." He gave another thin smile. Iosif was growing nervous, the man was smiling so much. "Also, the department prepares a background check on all employees." He produced a clipboard from seemingly nowhere. "Might you provide us with the letter sequence for your, ah, mother?"

"…Certainly." Iosif answered, after a few moments of surprise. He stepped up to the clipboard and jotted the number down.

"Very good," said Flistworth, studying the signature. "And your, ah… father?"

"I… not have," Iosif said.

Again Flistworth seemed strangely pleased. "Well… that simplifies, ah, matters, then." Flistworth snapped his briefcase shut. He glanced around. "As a, ah, final point… is your workspace satisfactory? The lighting, the… heating?"

Iosif shrugged. "No. Is fine." He really wondered why the man kept harping on the heating problem.

"Hullo…" Something had caught Flistworth's eye—a cord, dangling in the darkness. "What is this, may I, ah, ask?" Without waiting for an answer, he pulled on the cord, and nearly fell over as a telescoping column extended down from the ceiling.

Iosif nearly swore (an extremity he had not yet been driven to, but had been often assured by his mother would send him straight to hell.) "Is... apparatus," he said.

That was really the only name he had for it, but it was perhaps his favorite part of the workspace, and it had taken him nearly two weeks to put together. He'd put a lot of work into refitting the workshop—cleaning it, for one, as it'd been mostly used as a loose storage room by the warehouse personnel. He liked the workbench he'd put in, and the tool shelves, and the (to his mind quite sufficient) lighting. And he'd fixed up some old machines, and ordered some more.

But he disliked having to constantly move things around. So, he'd requisitioned Snorky's help (with Hougan's blessing and the bodyguard's grumbling) and installed a pair of rolling tracks on the ceiling, one running sideways and the other one lengthways. To this he'd attached a spring-loaded telescoping column, which was counterweighted so that it could be easily pushed back up into the darkness when it wasn't necessary. On the end (and this was the part that he was REALLY proud of), he'd cobbled together a boltgun, alongside an industrial drill and a circular saw (all powered through a steam pipe that ran up the column into the block at the top). You had to fold up the appendages you weren't using, naturally, but it was still an amazing time-saver.

And now, apparently, it was about to be gutted by a government man.

"Ap-pa-ra-tus?" Flistworth cast an eye up at the device. "How, ah, fascinating. I cannot say I have ever seen one before. Is it, ah, standard equipment for a federal machinist?"

"No," answered Iosif, seconds before realizing he could have lied.

"Hm." Flistworth cocked his head. "Did you, ah, make it, then?"

"Yes." It was not a common emotion, but Iosif felt something break inside him. He had liked the little device, had pulled it down some times just to see how it looked and assure himself that it had been made well. He had been thinking of adding some...

"This is, ah, quite impressive." Flistworth clicked open his suitcase and pulled out another sheaf of papers. "You ought to fill out this, ah, Federal Application patent form. This is the sort of device that Senator Blackthorne is *most* interested in; it could be quite useful in, ah, other facilities across America."

Iosif didn't understand. "Federal application?"

Flistworth indicated the 'Apparatus.' "I would like to, ah, pass this on to the Public Works department as a new Federal Appliance." He smiled.

"This?" Iosif asked, cautiously. "As... a... As a..."

It had never occurred to him that all Federal Appliances must be invented by someone somewhere. If it had, he would have thought of a wise old man in a mountain industrial facility, staring at bubbling beakers and great clanging gears, shouting orders at obedient students. Someone great, and majestic, and brilliant; on another plane altogether.

It had never occurred to him that slapping a couple power tools on a pipe would have the same effect.

As if in a dream, he felt the papers being pushed into his hands. "Do fill these out in, ah, time, Mr. Rusval," a voice said. "I might mention that you will receive a, ah, stipend for your part in developing the application."

∽o∾

"Well, you could do that, certainly." Hougan grunted. "The stipend is more like a percentage—I believe they pay you a certain fee for so many uses of your product and so forth. Others opt for different job positions."

"What about the steam lifts?" Iosif asked.

"Yes, you'll have to take your little additions off." Hougan waved irritably. "Damn regulations. Wish you'd told me about what you were doing. Could have done the paperwork bit by bit, then."

Iosif hesitated. "My… my handwriting is…"

"Ask Grey if you need help." Hougan turned back to the desk. "You figured out what's going on with that artifact?"

"There's… nothing special about this one, sir." Iosif shrugged. "Is toolbox. Special lock—pressure activated. That all. Good handles on side. Small tray on top. That all."

"Fair enough." Hougan grunted.

"I could take another," Iosif suggested.

Hougan eyed him quizzically. "You've got over 20 forms to fill out, a bunch of modifications to work on, this new work order…" He tapped the paper on his desk, "…you just applied for, and you want more artifacts? How's the safe-cracking business going?"

Iosif considered how to answer this. "Is… good," he said, carefully. "Easy to unlock padlocks, now. Can usually feel out gates. Still not good on false gates…"

"Keep at it," Hougan said. "I've got the feeling we're going to need that skill pretty soon."

∽o∾

"Okay, let's take a field trip," said Latches.

Iosif had been working with the elderly cripple for about two weeks now, but even so he didn't enjoy venturing out onto the balcony. "We're going to the first-floor lobby." Latches expertly weaved his way around the nurses, "I need to take the lift, but no need for you to risk death."

"Is fine. I go with you." Iosif had been working on a side project this past couple weeks.

"Suit yourself." Latches glanced around as they squeezed into the closet-like lift. "Looks like they renovated it recently, anyway."

Iosif slid the wrought-iron grate shut behind them and compressed the lever to send them sliding toward the bottom floor. As they descended, Iosif took note of every shake and shudder, waiting anxiously for Latches to say something. But the old man was silent. "Be sure to be polite to Myrtle," he said, eventually. "She's been through a lot, but she's a decent girl."

They arrived at the bottom floor, and Iosif slid the grate open. They made their way quickly along the cement paths toward the lobby at the northern end of the Administration building. They passed Iosif's own room on the way there, but he saw no reason to point it out to the older man.

An elderly white-haired lady looked up as they entered the lobby. "Hello, may I ... oh, Latches!" She gave a sweet smile. "How can I help you today?"

"Hullo, Myrtle," Latches said, wheeling up to the desk. "We'd like to break into the lobby safe, please. Got to show this young man how it's done."

Myrtle rolled her eyes. "Oh, you. Very well, this way." She let them behind the desk and opened up the glass door just behind to let them into the office in the back. As they passed through, Iosif noticed the lettering: "Myrtle Whitehouser, Senior Manager of Operations, District 72."

To his surprise the room beyond resembled nothing so much as a living-room parlor. Cut-glass lamps and porcelain elf figures decorated elegant tables and nicely upholstered chairs, and tea was brewing on a low stove against the back wall. A small, but comfortable, bed was half-hidden behind a chiffon curtain.

"Here we are." Myrtle took a needlepoint of a barn with flowers off the wall to show the safe behind it. "Knock yourself out, Latches."

"Actually, it's the lad who'll be taking a crack at it." Latches nodded to Iosif.

"Oh ah? Well, while he's doing that, would you care for some tea? It's just brewing now."

The two chatted amiably as Iosif worked. He couldn't help but feel a bit resentful about this—it made it a little harder to concentrate. No matter. Closing his eyes, he turned the dial about one way and another, feeling for the parts where it 'caught', ever so briefly, and noting them down in his head. 12... 35....42...45...76...90...12... all right, so six. But a Grunwildsen safe like this generally had only five tumblers, so one of those gates was probably fake. 35, if he had to guess. Iosif took a breath and started.

12, 42, 45, 76, 90. Nothing

12, 42, 45, 90, 76. Nothing.

12, 42, 90, 76, 45. Nothing,

12, 90, 45, 76, 42 ...

∽○∾

It was nearly an hour later when Iosif wearily spun the dials to 90, 12, 42, 76, 35 and popped the safe door open.

Myrtle and Latches looked round at the sound. "My goodness," Myrtle said, putting down her cup. "He's ever so faster than the last boy you had in here."

"He's not bad," Latches grumbled. "Still going to get them killed if they have to take him on an op, though. Can't stand around for an hour when that happens." He waved Iosif over. "C'mon, take a break and have some tea. I'll give you some tips for making educated guesses later."

Iosif loathed tea, but he was too shy to mention it. Obediently he joined the two elders and accepted the porcelain cup with the steaming liquid. He glanced curiously at the fourth plate Myrtle had laid out.

The old woman caught his gaze. "For the elves." She chuckled. "Did you ever read that story as a child?"

"The story *I* read was about a miserly old shopkeeper who kept a gnome imprisoned in his closet to make clocks for him," Latches said.

"My goodness, what sort of books did you read?" Myrtle glanced over at the crippled man.

"The original ones," Latches said. "Those children's books of yours cleaned up the stories immensely. Surprised a modern woman like yourself still holds to superstitions like that, Myrtle."

"I... leave out food. For *dvergrs,*" Iosif said, feeling compelled to come to the old woman's defense. "Are... German elves. Dwarves." He corrected. "Perhaps like gnomes, yes?"

Latches snorted, but Myrtle looked pleased. "Well aren't you a fascinating young man?" She turned back around. "Tell me everything about yourself. I'm simply dying to know."

"Er..." Iosif glanced around for some sort of excuse. He did not particularly enjoy talking, and his own life was not an especially interesting subject. "Perhaps... is too long, yes? You have been away from desk so long..."

Myrtle gave a light, kindly laugh, which Latches joined in with a dry chuckle. "Oh, bless your heart, child, never worry about *that*. If someone wants me, they'll ring the bell. And if they do, they can very well wait."

Iosif still felt puzzled, and a trifle insulted. "But is busy job, yes?" He pointed at the "Senior Manager" tag she was wearing. "Is important job."

Myrtle's light laugh became a full-bodied guffaw. "Oh, you're too precious, child, you really are!" She patted him on the head. Iosif *definitely* felt insulted at that.

"No one here has an 'important' job," Latches said, coming to Iosif's relief. "No on here has a remotely *useful* job. Well, except the warehouse workers. And the Engineers, technically, though can't say I've ever seen them doing any maintenance work. All the rest is done by machines."

"There's no need for any 'administration' of an *Automated* Postal system," Myrtle said. "This place is really more of a… retirement home, for useless old agents like ourselves."

Latches smiled ruefully. "Top Black Chamber agent, I used to be, before a cargo crate landed on my lower half." He looked down at his stumps. "Not much use now."

"Nonsense!" Myrtle patted his hand. "You're training boys like this young man here, aren't you?"

"I sixteen," Iosif said, cautiously taking a sip. He winced at the taste and set it down again.

"Heh." Latches shook his head. "Myrtle here," he jabbed a finger at the hostess, "is one of the higher-functioning retirees. All she's got wrong is a small bout of schizophrenia several years back."

"I still feel terrible about what I did to that poor man." Myrtle frowned. She proffered a small jar. "Honey?"

"No," Iosif managed. "Is fine, is fine."

"My, the boy looks pale," Myrtle said, cocking her head. "Oh, don't worry, dear. I haven't had a relapse in *years*, and by this point I'm so old that Latches here could probably stop me if I went on a bender. Otherwise, I'd probably still be in the Isolation Wing with all the others."

Iosif looked to Latches, who nodded. "You don't see them much, obviously, but there's a good amount of crazies here too. Surprisingly common combination, insanity and government work." His gaze darkened a bit. "Though some…"

"Don't go on that again, dear," Myrtle said. "Director Hougan's done a *wonderful* job of finding out which inmates are actually insane, and which ones are simply being locked up for one reason or another. It's amazing how thorough he's been."

"Yeah," Latches said. "I suppose he would be."

Iosif accompanied Latches back, mostly to see, again, if he would say something about the lift, but also because something had occurred to him. "All employees here..." he paused, searching for the right word, "...broken?"

Latches glanced over at him. "Broken. Yeah, that's a good way of putting it." He grinned suddenly. "If you're still worried about the crazies, just figure that the ones with broken heads are the ones without broken bodies." His grin widened. "Ya like that? Pretty clever, huh?"

"Yes." Iosif had never seen the point of riddles, and right now he had a much more compelling mystery. "So... Mr. Grey, then. And Ms. Kilroy. And... Snorky."

Latches didn't answer right away. "They're the Enforcement Division," he said finally. "They're different. You're not crazy, are you?"

Iosif gulped, but he felt he had to know. "And... Director Hougan?" he said.

Another long silence. "Look, kid." Latches sighed. "If you want to know Perry's story, just ask him. But it's gotta be him, because I ain't tellin ya."

Iosif was about to ask what that meant when the lift suddenly lurched, with a horrible grinding noise.

Hougan actually came by the workshop the next day, but Iosif was not yet ready to ask him, and anyway Hougan gave him no time to ask. "You okay?"

"Yes." Iosif actually felt pretty pleased with how his redesigned lift had functioned. The cable had snapped, but the emergency catch system had performed flawlessly. The only real problem was that it had taken a while to signal one of the nurses—that was something to work on for the next model. Some sort of bell or escape hatch, maybe...

Hougan did not seem very interested in the mechanics. "Latches says you know how to crack a safe," he said.

"Er... that is so." He decided not to mention what Latches had said about getting the rest of the crew killed.

"Good." Hougan turned to walk back out. "Get any tools you need together, and be sure to be here by 5:15am tomorrow. We're headed out to DC."

CHAPTER 6

1::3412993::4824

INTERLOPERS EN ROUTE. DESTROY ALL BLACK CODED MATERIALS.

0::000000::0000

"Y ou don't know how to use a gun, do you?" Ms. Kilroy demanded.

"Is point and shoot," Iosif asked, squinting on the primitive eyesight. "Not hard, yes?"

Kilroy, sitting across from him on the waycar, glared at Iosif. "Oh, this is marvelous. Simply f—" She seemed to remember Iosif with a start and cut off whatever she had been about to say."... we're all going to die," she muttered, turning to stare out the window at the countryside.

"Eventually, yes." Mr. Grey had a wry twist to his mouth. "Take heart. Most people fire at chest height. They are bound to miss Mr. Rusval entirely, unless they are looking for him. Like one of your people's 'shadow men.'"

"That is not how the shadow men work. That is in fact the opposite of how they work," Ms. Kilroy said. "Looking *for* a shadow man is precisely what causes them to disappear. But thank you. I feel vastly comforted knowing that it is only we who will die. Mr. Rusval is likely to live to a ripe old age."

"Of several seconds longer than the rest of us, yes."

Kilroy snorted but seemed content to let the subject drop. Iosif was grateful. He was trying VERY hard not to look at the woman's legs—she was wearing pants, of all things—and it was more difficult if he had to talk with her. Or at least listen—he supposed he hadn't actually contributed anything to that last discussion.

The others were wearing long leather dusters and broad-brimmed hats. Not Iosif—the duster they'd gotten for him had been too big and the hat too small, so he'd gone back to his sheepskin jacket with his green wool scarf. He had seen Snorky (who was in the other car with Hougan) still carrying his new-and-improved Tommy gun, and Kilroy kept bringing out her Sten rifle out of her absolutely mammoth purse to check and clear different components on it. Grey did not seem to be carrying anything, but Iosif knew better than to trust that.

The weight of the Ruger pistol in his coat pocket felt like lead already. Iosif understood the mechanical principles of it well enough, he'd just... never actually shot one before. It probably wasn't all that different from the shotgun he'd used at Whisterhorn's.

He'd probably find out before the day was over; he doubted a mission like this would go totally according to plan. And even if it did—Iosif wasn't really clear on what the plan actually *was*. His part, as far as he could tell, was to follow the others, say nothing, and crack a safe if they told him it needed cracking.

A safe in a federal building. Presumably a federal safe. Locked by federal agents. Property of United States government.

Iosif still wasn't sure how he felt about that. Would cracking the safe be treason? Was going along with Hougan and the others treason already? Had he been party to treason his whole time in government service and not known it?

"How are we to get into Coastal Defense, anyway?" Kilroy was talking again.

"The Director's got that sorted out," Grey answered.

"I'm sure he does." Kilroy did not sound as confident. "One of these days, that trick of his is going to stop working."

"It's not a trick." Grey defended him. "And it's never failed him that I've seen."

"Then the failure is all the more overdue."

∾o∾

It was nearly 8 am by the time they got to Washington. Iosif had nodded off at some point, but he woke up—presumably Kilroy had nudged him, or perhaps simply moved—just as they were entering the city.

Unlike the smog-choked skyline of Pittsburgh, Washington DC's profile stood out clear and stark against the sky. Washington's Monument could be glimpsed above the marble and sandstone buildings, and there was a distant blur—Iosif put on his spectacles—yes, yes, that was the Capital dome, gleaming white in the sunlight.

Iosif heard a light chuckle, and glanced over to see Grey watching him with amusement. "America does not have Camelot, but we do have a City on a Hill."

"City in a swamp, you mean," Kilroy said.

They rattled onto the Warren G. Harding Bridge, tripping over the iron girders: *ka-thump, ka-thump, ka-thump.* Iosif noted with interest as they rattled over a small, hinged portion clearly meant to swing away and cut off the city if necessary. Directly outside the window, trains shot past on the Column out of the city, roaring as they went by, rattling the windows.

Then they were off the bridge and among the city, with tall, regal buildings stretching all around. Old masonwork buildings, Iosif was fascinated to see, with steam pipes and mail chutes bolted onto the exterior walls. Some were beige sandstone, some were granite grey and some were blinding white. And some, like the one their waycar rolled up to, were black marble.

"Well, time to go," said Kilroy, checking her Sten gun one last time and stowing it in her purse. She grabbed Iosif by the arm. "Good luck, Grey."

"I'm not the one who needs it," Grey said, watching as they stepped out of the waycar.

Hougan and Snorky stepped out of the car directly behind them. With scarcely a nod, they led the way up the marble steps, Ms. Kilroy following them briskly and Iosif more cautiously. He could not help but glance at the words etched high above on the stone arches.

UNITED STATES DEPARTMENT OF COASTAL DEFENSE.

"Identification, please." The guard at the front gate had an impressive mustache, Iosif felt. He had always wanted to grow a mustache, but Mother had been against it.

"Perry Hougan, Director of the Automated Postal Department." Hougan laid his card on the desk with a thud. "These are agents of the Postal Enforcement Division." Snorky and Kilroy produced their cards immediately; Iosif took a little longer before finding and raising his triumphantly. "We're here investigating a charge of tampering with the mail…"

"Yesss…" The guard looked uneasy. "They did say you might be coming, and they said not to let you in under any circumstances."

Iosif heard Snorky give a quiet hiss. Kilroy gave a not-so-quiet curse. Hougan just smiled. "And who are 'they', son?"

"I'm afraid I can't…"

"Of course you can't." Hougan grunted. "Nevermind. It doesn't really matter. Under the Postal Automation Act of 1889, Section D By-Law 14, the Enforcement Division has jurisdiction to enter and investigate any building they have reason to believe contains a non-functioning Automated Postal Apparatus."

"Is he makin' that up?" Iosif heard Snorky whisper.

"Does he ever?" Kilroy whispered back.

"That's a helluva jurisdiction."

"Accordingly, we're entering this building now, and you have no a priori cause to stop us." Hougan did a twirling signal in the air to the others. "Let's go." Grabbing his card, he made for the gate.

The guard was up. "Sir…!"

Snorky reached over the man's desk and pulled the lever. The gate sprung open, and Snorky and Kilroy strode purposefully directly after Hougan with no more than a backward look at the guard.

Iosif felt he ought to say something. "Sorry." He mumbled to the dazed guard, following the others.

The others did not pause or halt as they dashed up a set of stairs and through several sets of hallways. Iosif simply followed them; he got the impression that they were following a floor map they had all spent considerable time studying beforehand.

They came at last to a sturdy-looking metal door. Hougan tried the door. It was locked. "With me, Capone," Hougan grunted. The two men drew back a few steps.

Iosif understood their plan a second too late. "Wait, I can..."

The two men rushed the door and slammed into it, shoulders first.

"...unlock that..." Iosif finished.

The door itself buckled only slightly, but the frame buckled considerably more. It burst open, and as both men half-fell into the room, they reached into their coats and withdrew their weapons with a single, fluid motion. "Freeze!" Hougan shouted.

Iosif followed after Kilroy (whose Sten gun was already out and at the ready) into the room to behold a strange scene.

About ten to twelve men in rolled up sleeves with ties stood standing about in front of a row of filing cabinets. Four or five of them had frozen with great sheaves of paper stuck in their hands. One was half buried in a filing cabinet. Two were operating a great paper incinerator along the back wall.

There were also three uniformed guards with their revolvers out.

Iosif came to with a start, dug around in his coat for his gun, found it, dropped it, picked it up again, somehow forgot how to hold it, remembered, and then pointed it at the man half-buried in the filing cabinet.

"United States Postal Enforcement Division!" Hougan shouted, holding up his card. "Stand down immediately!"

The uniformed guards exchanged glances.

That was all the opening Snorky needed. He quickly swung his Tommy gun in a wide arc, clocking the first guard across the skull. Hougan grabbed the second's gun and knocked him up with a straight fist to the jaw. And Kilroy, who had been walking forward since she entered the room, elbowed the third in the solar plexus, making him double over so she could club him over the head. It didn't even slow her down; she reached the incinerator and shut it off. "Boss man said, 'immediately,'" she said, with a satisfied smirk.

Iosif decided he'd just keep his gun focused on the man in the filing cabinet.

"Right," Hougan said, holstering his pistol. "Where's the Head Archiver here? Gibbons, right?"

A scrawny man in a tie and glasses stepped forward defiantly. "You have NO jurisdiction..."

"That's an auto-mail dispenser, isn't it?" Hougan jabbed a finger at the device next to the door. "Then we have jurisdiction. Now, we're in the process of an investigation—help us along, and we'll all be out of your hair as quickly as possible."

"I officially protest."

"Protest noted." Hougan cast an eye toward the back wall. "Iosif. The archive vault should be against that back wall. Get it open."

Iosif's heart dropped into his boots. *A vault?* He'd barely mastered convenience safes, how was he supposed to manage a government vault? But he saluted and hurried toward the back wall. What he saw made him nearly collapse with relief. "Sir... is already empty." *And open.*

"Blast." Hougan sounded more tired than surprised. "All right. Capone, get the coastal records. Kilroy, see if you can find the maintenance reports. Gibbons, I've got some questions for you."

"What... I do now, sir?" Iosif asked.

Hougan looked at him with faint surprise, as if he'd forgotten about him. "...take a look around and see what you find," he said, after a moment's thought.

"Yes sir." Iosif answered, and turned immediately to the incinerator machine. He found it fascinating. There was a pipe coming out of the top, clearly meant for smoke, but nothing seemed to be coming out.

He examined it more carefully, ignoring the two attendants on either side, who were shooting him nervous glances. The central burning cavity was in the bottom, obviously. There was a gas line for the fire; that would create heat but little smoke. And there was a small box between the paper feed and the burning chamber, with a small door on the side. Iosif wondered what that was for.

Without further prompting he pulled the door open. Ah, saw blades! Fascinating! They must be meant to chew the paper up and make it easier to burn. Oh, but currently they were all jammed up with documents. He reached in to pull them out.

"Don't!" yelped one of the attendants.

The sudden outburst drew Hougan's attention. "What the…"

"Ah. Thank." Iosif smiled at the attendant. He shut off the drive to the blades. He could have lost a hand that way. Again he reached in and started pulling out the documents. Not terribly efficient, this design.

"Are those…" Ms. Kilroy was at his elbow. "How'd you know they'd be in there?"

"Hm?" Iosif glanced at the papers. They were not, as he had first thought, fully charred. Rather, they were printed on completely black paper, with only the words standing out in white. Iosif didn't think he'd ever seen a document like that before.

"No!" Someone tried to grab the papers from him. Iosif looked up in surprise at the attendant, moments before Kilroy clocked him across the face. There was a short scuffle in the main room, and Iosif turned around to see Hougan knocking the head archivist to the ground, while Snorky covered the rest with his Tommy gun.

"Stow the papers, Kilroy," Hougan said. He looked suddenly triumphant. "Where's our exit?"

"Back wall, behind that oak cabinet." Kilroy answered, stowing the papers in her rucksack. "Capone, would you be a dear…"

Snorky slammed his shoulder into the cabinet, sending it crashing to the floor, papers spilling everywhere. There, set into the wall, was a small, nondescript, metal door. It stood maybe four feet high.

Snorky looked at it and groaned. "Aw, ya gotta be kidding me."

"Chamber agents will be right outside the door any minute." Kilroy opened the door and ducked down. "Come on."

Snorky winced, but opened the door and crawled inside. His broad back brushed against the top of the door. Hougan motioned with his pistol. "After you, son."

The door—and the passageway beyond—were actually at nearly a comfortable height for Iosif. He had to bend his head over a little, but that was all. Hougan, behind him, apparently did not feel the same. "Goddamn arthritis," he muttered, pulling the door shut.

The passageway was plunged into darkness. "Damnit, boss, really?" Iosif heard Snorky groan. "Ain't like those archivers won't tell them where we went."

"Then may I suggest we hurry?" Kilroy's brisk comment came from the front. "These old maintenance tunnels only go so far."

Now that his eyes had had time to adjust, Iosif could more clearly see the inside of the hallway. It seemed to be made entirely of thick metal, with large rivets set near the floor and ceiling. "What is this?" he asked.

"Maintenance passage." Kilroy sounded a little out of breath. "Gap spaces between rooms, used in case they need to run an extra steam or gas line to a particular room. More modern buildings have them. They don't show up on blueprints—you need to find them by looking where things AREN'T."

Iosif frowned, tapping the metal of the passage. "Is very strong."

"How 'bout that," Snorky muttered. "Only place the feds don't skimp on issa stuff nobody uses."

"Oh, dear." That was Kilroy.

"What's the problem?" Hougan asked.

"There's... some sort of... intersection here, sir," Kilroy said. "Not really a problem, I just... wasn't expecting it. Hang on. I think we need to go left."

"You think?"

There was a clanging sound behind them.

"Go!" Hougan said.

Iosif would have gone faster, but Snorky was having a lot of trouble moving, it seemed. They came out to the vaguely spherical intersection Kilroy had described. There were six round doors, four for each point of the compass, one in the ceiling, and one in the floor. Snorky stopped to stretch, but Hougan shouted "Go!" again, and he quickly ducked into the left-hand door, which Kilroy had left open.

Iosif wished he didn't have to hurry. The gear work on the doors looked to be of fascinating intricacy, and there were some strange carvings along the edges.

Hougan very quietly shut the door behind him. "Absolute silence until we're out of here." He hissed.

"But..." Snorky started.

"Silence!" Hougan snapped.

Snorky shut up. For a moment there was no sounds from anyone except Snorky's heavy breathing, and Hougan's more labored wheeze. Even Kilroy's whispering pant could be heard occasionally.

Finally, Kilroy whispered: "Here's an outlet..." There was a small creak. "No... it just leads to this larger chamber..."

"Goddamn it, go in anyway!" Snorky hissed. "My knees are killing me!"

Iosif could see in the dark pretty well by this time, and he gazed around the larger room with interest as he stepped inside. It was the same sort of corrugated metal as the rest of the hallways, but nearly twice as high, and the floor underneath was concrete. They had come out one tunnel in the wall, through a tell-tale spherical door. But what was more compelling was that, directly next to that door, was another small door. And next to that another, and another, and another. Small, four-foot diameter circular doors of metal were set into the room's walls, floors, and ceiling. In some places there were two or three stacked on top of each other, with little metal ladders reaching to the higher ones. Queer little spiral ladders ran up to the ones in the ceiling.

Snorky ran into one of these. "Ow! Damnit all!" He groaned, rubbing his jaw. He looked back at Iosif and his eyes widened. "What the hell... who's that?"

Iosif frowned. "Is Iosif."

"The hell?"

"Oh, for the love of..." Kilroy looked back too, then froze. "Iosif?"

"Yes?" Iosif really did not see what they all found so remarkable.

"Your eyes are glowing."

"My eyes...?" Iosif held up a hand in front of his eyes. It didn't seem to be particularly illuminated.

"Ya look like a dog, kid." Snorky gave a nervous laugh. "Gives me the creeps."

"Ah." Iosif did not know quite what to make of that.

"That's interesting," Hougan said, coming alongside. "Iosif, can you see anything?"

Iosif did not see what all the fuss was about. "Of course."

"Bullshit." Snorky snorted. "How many fingers am I holding up?"

Iosif just blinked. "You ... not hold up any fingers."

Snorky's expression went blank.

"Where are we?" Hougan asked.

"Closed-up boiler room, is possible," Iosif guessed. That was the only explanation for all the maintenance shafts.

"Can you see a way out of here?" Hougan asked.

"Yes." Iosif nodded. The circular doors had locks on them, but a few were standing open.

"Perhaps you should lead." Ms. Kilroy said.

"Perhaps he should," Hougan said. "All right. Everyone grab hands and follow him."

Iosif felt a little silly, but with Ms. Kilroy gripping on to his right hand, he walked across the room, toward a promising-looking steel door,

About halfway across the room he paused. "There step here," he said, tapping the edge of the metal circle with his foot. It rang—very dully. The metal must be very thick. "Careful."

On the lip of the circle was what looked like a claw hammer, and Iosif knelt to pick it up as he stepped up onto it. He paused as he looked at the circle more closely. Something about it seemed odd—there were all sorts of valves and cogs set in the face. Some intricate scrollwork, too. Four circles, set within each other. The innermost was just wavy lines, but the one beyond that had strict geometrical designs, and he could practically make out human figures in the third, while the outermost had some scrolling patterns…

"Why are we's stopped?" Snorky growled.

"We're on something of a time-table here." Hougan reminded him. "Is there a problem?"

"No… no problem." Iosif assured him. He stood and continued across the room. Glancing at the small item he'd picked up, he saw again the scrollwork, and suddenly realized where else he'd seen them before.

They'd been etched into the surface of the screwdriver.

The maintenance tunnel terminated in another service ventilator, which was locked with a queer sort of latch that took Iosif a few moments to figure out. There were several hallways after they left the maintenance tunnel, and one nasty encounter with a querulous but stubborn old janitor, but when Snorky finally managed to wrench the burglar bars off a window, they found themselves exiting on a back alley. Kilroy jumped and landed in a crouch on the asphalt. Snorky half-fell after her. Iosif tried to climb out, lost his grip, and fell entirely onto a trashcan. Hougan jumped easily down beside him. "Kilroy?" he asked, wincing as they stood.

Kilroy was glancing around. "South side, sir. Harrison Ave ought to be… that direction." She took off running.

Hougan dashed off after her. Snorky urged him on. "C'mon, kid, I'm coverin' our asses here!" Already they could hear sirens warbling from within the building.

Iosif could not run. His legs were not made for it. The best he could do was to trot, desperately, after his companions. He could see them standing, at the mouth of the passageway. Suddenly Kilroy yelled and pointed to the right, then disappeared in that direction. Hougan ran after her.

Had they seen some guards?

Iosif would have turned back, but Snorky was pressing behind him. "We's gonna miss our train, kid, leg it!" They came out of the alley and nearly ran into the way line. The street in front of them was filled with waycars darting back and forth on the rails, weaving in and out of each other on their way to various stations. Just in front of them, waycars rattled from right to left with blistering speed.

Iosif glanced after his companions. Kilroy and Hougan were jogging along the margin, against the flow of traffic. They seemed to be looking for something.

Suddenly they stopped and began running in the opposite direction. Guards? But no, suddenly Kilroy leaped and grabbed onto a passing way car. Hougan jumped a second later and landed on the same car—it had a scarf flying from its window, Iosif observed, a bright blue scarf.

Snorky grasped him by the collar. "No time for gawking, short stuff!"

He hauled Iosif along the margin, running alongside the cars, and as the car with the scarf came alongside, threw him bodily at it. Iosif threw up his hands to protect himself and by sheer blind luck managed to grab hold of the ledge of the waycar.

The door slid open and a hand grasped him around the waist. "Get in here, Rusval!" Hougan roared.

They pulled him in and the door slammed shut. Through the window, Iosif could see Snorky disappear in the maze of traffic. "Wait!" he said, "We left…"

"Too late now. He'll be all right." Hougan grunted. "The man knows how to disappear. Kilroy, you still have those documents?"

"Here, sir." Kilroy held up her purse.

"Okay." Hougan seemed to think rapidly. "Nanninga's is over on Seventeenth. We should be coming up on it in a second. You and Rusval jump off there."

"Rusval?"

"Kid." Hougan looked at him. "You grabbed another artifact in the tunnels, didn't you?"

Iosif stared with wide eyes. "I… it was just sitting on the floor… I saw it and…"

"Forget it." Hougan waved his hand. "But we need to ditch it. It's evidence. Drop it off with Nanninga, he can hang onto it and send it along once the heat's died down." He checked his watch. "Okay, Seventeenth is coming up. Ready?"

"I…"

But the door was open and Hougan was picking him up and now he was flying out and oh there was the ground…

Iosif just managed to get his legs under him enough to run a few steps before fully faceplanting on the cobblestones.

Kilroy landed gracefully beside him. "Come on, Rusval!" she said.

"I… I coming." Iosif managed. His head was ringing, his knees throbbing and he knew he had skinned both his palms landing on the ground. His sheepskin coat, thankfully, had taken the rest of the damage.

They dashed up the alley. On the corner was a small shop—*Gnome's Workshop*, read the sign, next to a comical caricature of a wizened old dwarf in a red stocking cap—and Kilroy pushed open the door. "Woodpecker!" she shouted, darting up to the counter. "Woodpecker, Nanninga, we've got some documents for you to…"

She stopped. At the counter, a grey-headed old man was slumped over the cash register, like he was asleep. The dark iron below was stained a red hue, as if by rust.

"Shit!" Kilroy dove to the floor. Iosif nearly asked why, before a hail of bullets rattled over his head and smashed into the shelf of gaily-painted elven figurines just behind him. He dropped alongside Kilroy, who was already digging out her Sten. "Cover the door!" she shouted. "Don't let them in!"

Not quite understanding, Iosif half-ran in a crouch for the hardwood door as Kilroy fired a volley at the workshop door. He looked out the window and immediately understood. Outside were several large men in grey overcoats, hands inside their jackets.

Another hail of bullets cascaded through the shop. Several punched through the shop window, shattering it to bits, and the men in the grey coats seemed to come alive. Heavy revolvers appeared in their hands as they advanced on the shop.

Iosif fumbled for his revolver, only to realize it was gone. He must have dropped it when Snorky threw him onto the waycar. He watched the grey-coated men advance with a vague feeling of unreality. There had to be something he could use. Something!

He cast a nervous glance back at the shop, and saw Kilroy jumping over the counter, teeth bared in a fierce snarl as her boot smashed into the dark figure looming in the workshop door. A "Mad Aviator—Experience the Impossible!" kit came tumbling down from the shelf and smashed to pieces on the floor.

He remembered the 'Mad Aviator' line. He'd been obsessed with them as a kid, and even tried to make a life-size model, convinced it would work. He was going to get it up in the air with…

Inspiration. Surely this shop had some. Yes, there they were, over on the back wall. Brightly colored with sharp lettering, names like "Wizzpoppers" and "Devil Nuggets." Iosif dove for them, ignoring the pitched battle taking place behind the counter. He crashed into the back wall, sending dozens of the tiny balls crashing to the floor. He grabbed one in his hands, just barely absorbing the "Not for indoor use" label as he fumbled for his tinderbox.

A grey silhouette loomed in the window. Iosif's flame caught on the firework's fuse and he hurled it with all his might.

BANG!!

It was mostly light and sound, but it must have been terrible at such close range—you probably weren't supposed to throw them into people's faces. The man fell backward howling with pain. A second figure appeared and Iosif threw another—forgetting to light it in his excitement. The bomb didn't go off, but it struck the man somewhere below the chest and he doubled over, groaning. The third figure appeared. Iosif fumbled wildly for another bomb.

RATATATATATT!

Iosif looked round with wild eyes to see Kilroy, her Sten gun smoking. "Come on," she said, offering him a look. "There'll be more of them soon."

They darted out the front, but Kilroy quickly pulled him into a side alley. "There's a platform over at Robinson," she muttered, mostly to herself. "Nothing for it… need to risk it."

Iosif couldn't reply. His asthma was finally catching up, and he didn't know how much longer he could keep up this pace.

They ran right up to the platform and Kilroy punched in a destination. A waycar rattled up to the terminal and they climbed inside. Iosif collapsed on the floor, his head knocking against the control box. *Click. Click. CLACK.* The waycar slid out into the street.

"Okay…" Kilroy said, digging the papers out of her purse. "Let's see what we have… FMS Avalon… ten capsules of grubs to Fort Sumter… For crying out loud, Rusval, help me!" She shoved a sheaf of papers at him.

Iosif took them, unsure as to what he was supposed to be doing. He flipped through the papers. Diagrams, names, Dragon's Teeth project, I-X93 facility... He let the steady clicking of the control box soothe his thoughts as he tried to absorb the meaningless information.

Click. Click. CLACK. Click. Click. CLACK. CLACKclick. Click. CLICK. Clickclickclickclickclickclickclickclick…

Iosif cocked his head. Something was off about that.

The car jerked left, suddenly picking up speed. *Clickclickclickclicckclick…* Left again. It was slowing now. A shadow slid over the window, and Kilroy glanced up. "Damn it," she said, but there was no anger or surprise in her voice.

The door slid open. "Hello, miss." said the brown-suited police officer, smiling politely. Behind him, Iosif could see a squad of policemen, milling casually about in the station. "Sorry for the inconvenience, but we received orders to Call in this car for inspection." He peered at the purse in her hands. "Mind if I take a look at those papers, eh?"

Iosif looked at Kilroy. She looked more resigned than anything.

She handed over the papers.

CHAPTER 7

0::001022::1691

City Quarantine successful; see enclosed list of recovered documents. Involved officer was Private Frank O'Lunger. Postmaster General Kilroy and Chief Renovation Specialist Rusval have been released from custody, per Director Hougan's citation of "operating in the interests of perpetuating APD functions." He has issued the required statement to take "appropriate action" to ensure this sort of "cross-departmental conflict" does not happen again.

Archiver Gibbons has been relieved of his post.

0::000000::0000

"Well, can't be helped," Hougan sighed, collapsing behind his desk at the postal office. "Damnit, Nanninga was a good man."

"How did they get to him?" Kilroy asked.

"Probably worked it out from the last time we were in DC." Hougan shook his head. They were gathered in Hougan's office.

"Him, and McElroy last month." Snorky, who true to prediction had showed up a day behind them, was picking his teeth as he sat on the floor, slumped against the filing cabinet. "Ain't a good sign, boss."

Grey let the blinds fall back over the windows and turned back toward the group. "Maybe we should lay low for a while."

"We're just starting to make real progress on this," Hougan said. "Though it'd be easier if we could find some way to dodge the rail system, but no one's ever worked anything like that."

"There used ta be people who could do that for ya," Snorky said. "There was this bank job me and the boys did, back with Torino's gang—or maybe it was Rivaldi's—and we had this guy, the Wiz, he could…"

"Not now." Hougan waved his hand. "Rusval, you say you remember a reference one of the files made to an I-X93 facility."

"Yes sir." Iosif tried to recall. "Used for… 'Grubs.'" He shrugged helplessly. "Not much more I remember."

"Grubs?" Hougan frowned.

"Food, perhaps, or code for some sort of resource," Grey said, almost absentmindedly, digging through the papers. "I-X93 facility. I think that…" he glanced at the blue paper in his hands, "…should correspond to these blueprints we relieved the Chamber agent of."

"Hm." Hougan leaned over to see the files. "Looks right. What's this place for, did we ever work that out?" He took the blue paper, shifted it around on various angles, and as an afterthought, passed it off to Iosif. "Thoughts, Rusval?"

"Er…" Iosif's main thought at the moment was that the paper was very blue. And that the white markings looked vaguely like a large donut. There were other details—a donut broken up into segments, a small dollop of whipped cream in the very middle—but nothing along the lines of what Hougan was probably hoping for. He stared hopelessly at the mass of lines, and saw nothing but drizzled icing scattered haphazardly over a large, blue donut.

"I was very puzzled by the piping network and the corresponding valves." Grey noted, looking over at him. "There are more than seem practical."

"Perhaps some sort of chemical processing plant?" Kilroy suggested, looking over Iosif's shoulder.

"In that case, there should be significantly more." Grey tilted his head. Okay, not a donut. A building. Iosif was starting to get it. The donut on the page was disappearing. Some sort of tower-like building. Maybe an arena, made of many small boxes. With a lot of weird white lines running everywhere.

Hougan frowned. "The whole place is designed wrong—there's not even a foundation that I can see. All the stresses seem like they're calculated backwards, all the pipes run nowhere at all, all the valves seem to actually be operated elsewhere. It doesn't make sense."

There were small boxes with "x's" in them across the document, which really puzzled Iosif. They looked a lot like windows to him, but they were very oddly spaced.

"It looks like a structure within a structure, perhaps," Grey said. "There's an outside super-structure made of individual cubicles of some kind and then this circular construct in the middle. With the pipes running into the cubicles, and the valves controlled from the middle."

Why had no one mentioned the windows?

"Why do it that way, though? Thoughts, Rusval?" Hougan said again.

Iosif took a deep breath. "What happens if… valve gets blocked?" he said, stabbing with a finger at one of the mysterious little boxes.

There was a beat of silence.

"Hm. That's an interesting thought." Hougan reached over and took the blueprint from Iosif's hands. "Grey?" He passed the paper over, his finger on the box in question.

Grey took the paper and looked at it thoughtfully. "Well, if *that* valve got blocked… it would trip this system here… if we assume the pipes are for steam, it might… the pressure would stack up…" His fingers traced over the paper up and down and sideways, mouth moving in silent whispers. He looked up. "My word."

"What?"

"Well, if we assume the pipes and valves to be for some sort of steam drive system, generally there would be some sort of emergency vent. But here, if this valve were blocked, it would instead build up in this pressure tank…" He pointed at the corresponding room, "…and explode outward. Violently."

Kilroy stared. Snorky blinked. Hougan *hmmm*ed. "Is it supposed to?"

"Doubtful. In fact, I'd say probably the designers don't even know about this." Grey looked at Iosif. "How did you do that, Mr. Rusval?"

Iosif was too nervous to actually contradict the other man.

"Mr. Rusval has been astonishing us all with his tricks of late," Hougan said, taking the blueprint from Grey and rolling it up.

"In the meantime..." He tapped the paper roll contemplatively against his chin, "...I need to consider what our next move will be."

Next move. Iosif wondered which government building they were going to be breaking into this time, and if he'd be spending the night in a police station box again. He also wondered how he was ever going to explain this to his mother.

"Do you think this is related to Dragon's Teeth?" Kilroy asked.

"Possibly," Hougan said, twisting a rubber band around the roll. He handed her the roll. "Lock these back up in the vault. Take Rusval with you—you need some more artifacts to analyze, right Rusval?"

"Yes sir."

"Very good." Hougan turned away. "Capone—take a shower or something."

'What?" Snorky sounded insulted.

"No, he's right," Kilroy agreed, snagging the suitcase. "Come along then, Iosif."

Iosif followed the woman down through a half-hidden side door deep into the basement, down a rickety wooden staircase that seemed a long-forgotten renovation project. Iosif wondered where they were going, and what "the vault" was. So far he'd been brought the various 'artifacts' he'd been meant to examine (which apart from the toolbox, had turned out to be an adjustable wrench, a wiry little claw that could be used to reach into tight spaces, and an extremely ingenious device which now rested on Grey's desk, a miniaturized abacus). He'd often heard of "the vault" where these were stored, but never actually seen it himself.

To his surprise, it turned out to be a completely respectable vault, the sort of thing one might find in a bank. Better than that, even—the front was decorated, dials and all, with scrolling gold work, and the workings in the back were astonishingly intricate and involved.

"How was vault opened?" he asked, in disbelief, tracing the system of gates, false gates, and counter gates. 'Carnegie Innovations Incorporated' read the scrolling inscription on the side.

"Hougan said the last director had the combination written on a drawer in his desk," Kilroy said, putting the papers into one of the filing cabinets against the back wall.

Iosif looked around. The whole interior was far too large for what the department used it for, it seemed. There was a set of shelves against the back wall, which seemed to be filled at random with an assortment of "artifacts." Apart from that and the filing cabinets, there was a variety of strange boxes next to what looked like an old Stanley Steamer boiler, some dusty machines Iosif had never seen before, several piles of bagged mail, boxes everywhere, and something vaguely oval-shaped under a tarpaulin. And next to that...

Iosif's mouth went slack. His eyes grew wide. He stepped forward, cautiously, to the large steel cylinder resting on a wheeled platform. He had seen an iron lung once before, when he and his mother went to see Mr. VanMuellen in the hospital. The workings were fascinating enough, but Iosif found himself interested in the occupant.

He supposed it must be a girl, from the long blonde hair, but she looked like no girl he'd ever seen. Her skin was impossibly pale, and the closed eyes looked just slightly too wide. Her neck, too, seemed off-settlingly long, and looking through the lung's glass window, he could see the same was true of her arms and fingers. It wasn't quite grotesque, but it *was* unsettling. He could see an IV taped into her wrist just below her long white hand. Her chest rose and fell underneath the sheet, but otherwise she lay perfectly—deathly—still.

"Who... *she*?" he asked.

"Who... oh, Sleeping Beauty," Kilroy said, glancing back. "She came up in a military shipment that got 'misplaced' about... two years now, I guess."

"But... who she?" Iosif persisted.

"Alien," Kilroy said, turning back to lock up the filing cabinet.

Iosif blinked. "What?"

"Alien," Kilroy said again. "Extra-terrestrial. Being from another world. Martian, perhaps Venusian. Not of this earth."

"Alien."

Kilroy sighed. "I understand this comes as a shock," she said, walking over next to Iosif. "Believe me, neither I nor the director, thought aliens were anything more than dime-store novel speculation. Yet here she is." She gestured at the iron lung. "Lots of government agencies send their classified intel through the mail service. Hard to know where all of them come from or what the full story is behind them all."

A question occurred to Iosif. "Then... what makes sure she is *alien*?"

"Her spaceship." Ms. Kilroy kicked the tarpaulin next to the iron lung with a booted foot. It rang dully. "Hard to think of any other explanation what you would consider a creature being shipped alongside something like that." She gave a firm nod. "Alien."

Iosif was suddenly hit by a memory. "Like… you thought… was me?"

"Like I thought you were, yes," Kilroy said. She looked between him and the girl again. "I realize you don't look much alike, but then—you're a man, and she's rather obviously not. I can't be sure how alien genders work."

Iosif decided not to pursue the question. "Why she here?" he asked.

"No real reason… Boss ordered her stored down here the moment he saw her in the shipping container." Ms. Kilroy looked down at the girl. "We've never been able to find any link between her and our little 'mail tampering' investigation. Heaven knows what the government was doing with her. A number of agencies have come calling for her, but every time the Director asks them if they'd mind signing a receipt, they always back out. So for the moment, we hang onto her." She gave a little snort. "I don't think he'd hand her over even if they did. Old-fashioned chivalry, that's all he's got keeping her here." There was a surly sort of triumph in her face.

"She… asleep?"

"In a coma. Has been, the whole time we've had her. Oh, but that reminds me…." Bending down, she opened up the icebox next to the iron lung and pulled out another IV bottle. She replaced the current bottle almost nonchalantly, with an ease and boredom that spoke of long practice, then bent and replaced a different, opaque container beneath the lung.

"There," said Ms. Kilroy, wrinkling her nose. "That should hold her through for the rest of the week, I think. Come on, now." She clapped her hands. "We don't have all day. Pick something out and let's go."

Iosif was so distracted that he barely noticed it as he picked up a bland, utterly uninteresting-looking belt from the shelves. As they started to walk out he paused by the tarpaulin and started to lift it.

"No, you stay away from that," Kilroy said. "Director's forbidden anyone from messing with the spaceship. We don't even know how it's powered; could blow the whole place up if we're not careful. Now come on."

Iosif dropped the edge of the tarpaulin and followed her out. She swung the vault shut and spun the dials.

"How did you do that eye-glowing thing, anyway?" Kilroy asked, as they climbed the rickety wooden stairs back up.

"I don't know." Iosif shrugged. "Has never been mentioned before." Though it did maybe explain why Little Sally had run away screaming back in second grade. He supposed it must look a bit unsettling.

"Hm," Kilroy said. "Sure got us out of tight spot, anyway."

"Yes." Iosif's mind moved over to that track, and he realized there was a significant detail that needed clearing up. "Is... is government likely to kill us? Send... agents?" He didn't particularly like the idea, especially with all the new ideas that were flooding into his brain at the moment.

"Assassins, you mean? They haven't yet." Kilroy shrugged. "Grey says it would cause a great disruption if the Central

Director of any department were to be killed. Apparently, there's a mandatory investigation, and of course all the other Central Directors would be worried. Still. Wouldn't do the rest of us much good, hm?" Kilroy shook her head. "Grey says he's taken 'precautions,' whatever that means."

Iosif nodded, already forgetting about the possible peril to his life. He'd just noticed the insignia on the belt in his hands—four detailed circles set in a larger one. It wouldn't have held his attention, except it was the exact same insignia on the vault downstairs, and the same symbol he'd seen in the maintenance tunnels at the Coastal Defense building.

Iosif almost didn't hear the voices in his workshop before it was too late. He nearly walked inside, the stolen belt in his hands, before he recognized the senator's booming voice. Quickly, he stuffed it under his coat and entered the room.

Senator Blackthorne looked up. "Mr. Rusval!" he called, with his usual good humor. "I was just singing your praises to Perry here." Hougan, directly beside the senator, gave a short nod.

"Praises?" Iosif put his hands in his pockets and tried to look innocent.

"Well, of you and your remarkable invention here, naturally." Senator Blackthorne tugged on the cord dangling next to him, and Iosif's apparatus came sliding down through the dark, stopping with a jerk at about head-level. "Already we've deployed it in Federal Appliance stations across the country, and we're getting requests for more and more all the time!"

"Oh." Iosif decided having his hands in his pockets looked fishy, and folded them across his chest. "That... good."

"Sir." Flistworth, the spider-haired attendant, was back at the senator's elbow. He seemed the only staff present today; the workshop was empty except for them and the senator's guards. "There is his, ah, commission..." He handed the senator an envelope.

"Of course there's also this!" Senator Blackthorne handed the envelope over to Iosif. "There's a percentage rate for the number of facilities adopting your device—rather high, I must say—and also our usual flat rate of 500 dollars for new innovations."

"Sir..." Flistworth seemed to be speaking almost despite himself. "...innovations are, ah, new by definition, to call them 'new innovations' is repetitive..."

Blackthorne ignored his secretary. "Many thanks, Mr. Rusval!" he said. "I thought I'd come by and just let you know how much I appreciate what you've done! Haven't had a lot of innovations, lately, so yours was a real shot in the arm! Got to keep the voters happy!" Another laugh. "Do be sure to let us know of any further new innovations you have!"

Flistworth winced but said nothing.

"Is good." Iosif nodded, warming to the idea. He looked up. "Actually, several modifications planning to make to Apparatus...."

"Federal appliance..." Flistworth whispered.

"Ah, I must stop you there, Mr. Rusval." The senator's large head wagged back and forth, and he gave a sorrowful smile. "Still can't allow you to work on Federal Appliances, not even ones you invented. Rules are rules, you know." He tapped a fat finger against the apparatus, and the new "TAMPERING WITH THIS DEVICE IS A FELONY UNDER FEDERAL LAW" label.

"...oh." Iosif deflated. He hadn't seen that coming. It was a pity; that had literally been his next job. He'd thought of improving the steam drive before taking a harder look at the artifact belt... perhaps adding a mirror to the gas lamp...

"Quite the productive new member you have here, Perry!" Blackthorne turned to Hougan. "You did a good job, talking me into letting you keep him."

"I didn't." Hougan's arms were crossed over his chest. "He did that himself."

Blackthorne gave a dismissive wave. "You might learn a thing or two from him, Perry," he said. "Make some productive headway on something, eh? Stop messing around with these silly little field trips of yours. I heard one of your people was stopped in Washington the other day. Do you know what that was about, eh?"

Hougan looked at him. "They were stopped while carrying condemned Black-coded records that we'd confiscated from the Coastal Defense Archives," he said. "Someone ordered the police to confiscate them, and someone killed our contact in the city." He raised an eyebrow at the senator. "Do *you* know what *that* was about?"

Blackthorne seemed about to ask another question when Flistworth gave a small cough. "Sir," he said. "We have the... appointment with the, ah, general."

Blackthorne's smooth face wrinkled and he clapped a hand to his head. "Damnit, Perry! I just remembered, I've got some other business to attend to. But do think on that, eh? We'll talk it over more some other time."

"Of course." Perry shook the man's hand. The senator and his guards filed out, trailed by Flistworth.

"Business…" Hougan said. "With who, I wonder…"

"Secretary mentioned a… general," Iosif said.

"His secretary?" Hougan looked at him. "Grey." Iosif jumped as the man practically materialized out of the shadows. "See if you can find out which general they're talking about."

"Sir." Grey slid out the door after them.

Hougan gave a grunting sigh and knocked the ash off his cigar. "Of all the times for him to show up… Anyway, looks like your little project worked pretty well," he said, looking around at Iosif.

"Yes," Iosif said. He was examining his back desk; he thought he'd seen Flistworth lurking around his toolbox. To his relief nothing seemed to be missing.

There was a silence, which surprised Iosif, and he turned around to see his boss, leaning against the back wall and frowning at him, as if in deep thought. The cigar in his hand was swiftly fading away.

Apparently coming to a decision, the older man pushed himself off the wall. "Come on," he said. "There's something further I think you should see."

∽o∾

"Jeez, kid, calm down." Hougan looked at him. "You made this lift, you know how safe it is."

Iosif took a pause between breaths of his inhaler. "… yes…" he managed. He decided not to mention that he also knew how *unsafe* the lift could be, and that he was currently thinking of all the many different ways the machinery could break and send them hurtling down the ten-or-fifteen stories to the ground.

"You know, you could probably patent this thing too," Hougan said, glancing around. "Or the safety function anyway. That's a pretty major improvement. The whole lift's a lot smoother than it used to be."

Iosif thought about it. He did like the feel of that padded envelope in his coat pocket. He was already thinking about the new power drill he could purchase with it. "Would… senator come… again…?" he said. His breath was starting to come back.

"He can come as often as he likes, for all the good it does him." Hougan shrugged. "If he really bothers you, you could sell it to a private company, otherwise, though then you wouldn't get a commission. Or find a business partner of some sort."

Business partner. Mr. Whisterhorn had been a business partner, in a way. There'd been a time Iosif had made a little wind up *dvergr* clock, which Mr. Whisterhorn had sold to an old lady. That hadn't been a bad arrangement. More bothersome, though, than just filing paperwork.

A tremor shook the lift, and Iosif was brought forcefully back into the moment. "Who we visit up here?" he asked.

"Nobody," Hougan said. "We don't have enough people for these upper levels. We never even modernized most of the rooms up here." The lift slowed to a stop, and Hougan slid open the iron grate door. "Come on."

Iosif followed his boss out with considerable caution. They couldn't possibly be twenty floors up, he told himself. They must be only up four floors. That was it. That floor that he could see over the edge of the railing must nearly on top of the ground, because there was no *way* it could possibly be…

Iosif gulped and hugged the opposite wall.

His boss, who clearly had none of his paranoia, was walking around almost aimlessly. He wandered into an open doorway and motioned Iosif inside. Iosif gratefully darted inside and put his back against the wall, looking fixedly at the opposite wall and telling himself again that they were on the fourth floor.

The room itself was laid out in nearly exactly the same way that the ground floor lobby had been. Here, though, the paint had peeled away from the concrete walls, the tile underneath was broken, and the door leading into the back room was rusty metal, with gaping holes that showed the corrugated iron bunkbeds just beyond.

"These were the workers quarters," Hougan said, pulling up a wooden chair with a missing arm.

"…Quarters?" Iosif said, focusing on his boss's speech. He ought to find a seat himself. There was a stool—he pulled it over towards himself, picking up the daguerreotype off the seat. A large group of men in a cracked frame stared seriously back at him.

"In the old days." Hougan shrugged, lighting his cigar. "Back before Carnegie Incorporated got broken up by the courts and absorbed into the Public Works department. Carnegie had its own share of muscle, of course—they're still ferreting out all the mob connections the company had—but standardizing the mail? Putting mail machines everywhere?" Hougan shook his head. "That was a job and a half, and you needed more than engineers to make it happen and set the rules down." He looked around the room. "The Enforcement Division wasn't a joke, back then. They had a a helluva lot of freedom and jurisdiction. Heck, *I'd* be leery of them if they were still around. They were practically an army, and this place was their barracks."

Iosif thought about all the twenty floors of rooms. "Really?"

"Yeah," Hougan said. "Bizarre, I know. Doesn't make for getting people out super quick; that's why most barracks are built *out*, not *up*. They called them the workers' quarters for Carnegie's men... not that that makes much better sense. Carnegie wasn't great to his workers. When the Feds finally broke up the company and its hitmen a lot of folks came out to the papers with all sorts of stories—said he treated them like slaves." He glanced at the rusting door and grimaced. "Sort of see their point."

Iosif tried to see the room as it must have been. Metal doors, bunkbeds, hard concrete walls and cold tiles. Better than nothing, he supposed, but yes, he saw the point.

"There used to be a giant tower in the middle of this place." Hougan pointed out the door and Iosif tried not to think of the empty courtyard outside. "You can still see the foundations. Don't know what they had that for. They got rid of it... oh, ages ago." He scratched his head. "Probably sometime in the oughts? When the APD became more of a retirement home." He sighed. "When they started sending their cripples and crazies over here."

There was a silence. Iosif, who had been absently studying the picture in his hands (he was pretty sure that the whiskery man in the center towering over the small spiky-haired man with the large glasses was Carnegie), realized too late that he was supposed to say something. But by the time he realized it, the moment had already passed.

"Anyway." Hougan struck a match and lit his cigar. "No one ever bothered to change the laws on their jurisdiction." A cold smile filled his face. "Something Senator Blackthorne is bitterly regretting right now, I imagine."

Another silence, as Hougan sucked on his cigar. Iosif nodded instead of searching for something to say. It felt safer.

"Kid, I brought you up here, because you've probably figured out by now that we're about a bit more than delivering letters, here," Hougan said at last.

Iosif realized, quite suddenly, that he had left his pistol all the way down in the front office. He wondered if the director would mind if he got up quickly to go and get it.

"It's legal, what we're doing." Hougan took another long drag from his cigar. "Though whether it *should* be legal is a separate question. We're not breaking any laws, and we're serving our country. But you deserve to know that not everyone in the country, or even in the government, sees it that way." He sighed and let the smoke drift out of his mouth. "And you deserve to know that I'm officially insane."

Silence. Iosif nodded, slowly and carefully. The director was not particularly big, but he was still twice Iosif's size. And he had a very obvious pistol in a very obvious holster (a 'docker's clutch' Snorky had called it). And they were, after all, twenty floors up…

"'Officially', you understand." Hougan gestured with his cigar. "High-functioning, they said, 'no danger to anyone', they said—though again, I imagine the senator'd revise that diagnosis now." Again there was the cold smile. "But the point stands that they had a certified doctor certify my brain as certifiably insane." Hougan looked straight at Iosif, with calm eyes. "And you deserve to know that."

Iosif nodded, again, but it was clear Hougan was waiting for more. Iosif cast around, desperately, for something he could say. "Is… because… of truth?" Hougan frowned in puzzlement and Iosif hastily explained. "Because you. Telling truth, always saying… even when dangerous…"

Hougan's face cleared. "No," he said, a small grin twitching the side of his face. "No, that's not insanity, exactly, that's 'an eccentricity;' my ex-wife used to call it. I've always had it. Had it when I was a kid, had it when I was a teenager, had it when I worked in Black Chamber. Drove the bosses crazy, but, hell, I've always hated lying. Probably why I was so bad at it. So why bother?" He shook his head. "They let it go, though, because they knew they could trust me, and because I had—have— killer instincts for when someone's lying to *me*." He jabbed a thumb at his shirt. "Ask Grey sometime, if he's in a talkative mood."

Iosif nodded to show he was still paying attention. "Then… why?" he said.

"Why'd they call me crazy?" Hougan took another pull at his cigar. "Because a letter got lost in the mail."

Iosif stared.

"A letter," Hougan said, "containing photographs and critical evidence of a secret facility I had described in a report. When the report was called into question, they asked for proof. I said I'd sent them the photos; they said they never received them." Hougan shook his head. "I was given the chance to retract my report. I refused. The report was true, and the evidence had been sent. I insisted on both, but I didn't have proof for either." He shrugged. "So I was declared insane and appointed Director of the Postal Department." He considered. "Actually I guess I started somewhere as a Sub-Director of a branch division, but I worked my way up."

Iosif nodded again. He was frowning, he realized, and quickly wiped it off his face.

"Here's the thing, kid." Hougan jabbed his cigar in Iosif's general direction, "I told you I have killer instincts. I could tell they weren't lying when they said they hadn't received my letter. And my boss—he wasn't a bad man. He knew I wasn't a liar either. Otherwise I'd have had a court-martial instead of a psyche eval. So I knew something was wrong. As soon as I became director, I re-tooled the Enforcement Division to investigate that particular lost letter." He spread his hands. "And that's what we're working on now."

Iosif realized he was frowning again. Again, he made his face blank.

"Letter itself is probably long gone by now." Hougan waved his hand. "And I'd never get back my... job. Or any of the other things I lost." His face looked very old for a moment. "But that's not the point." He leaned forward. "Letters don't just get lost,

Rusval. Not in the APD. That's the whole selling point, that's what they always say. But if that's true, then ..." he sucked on his cigar thoughtfully, then let the smoke out. "...someone's been tampering with the mail."

Iosif shifted uncomfortably, and Hougan spread his hands. "Impossible, I know. It's all automated, right? And the machinery is locked up behind that huge vault door. It's the same way in every city." He shook his head. "But Rusval, I've been at this job for a while now. You start to see patterns. Lots of letters *do* go missing. The question is why."

Hougan leaned back in his chair and puffed on his cigar with grim confidence. "You think it's weird that my whole team is four people, and they're all in this building. I used to have a bigger network, more spread out. But when we tried to send each other messages, some would never arrive. Targets would already know our plans. Objectives would disappear before we even arrive on the scene. Agents would die." Hougan leant forward. "Someone in America---someone in the government, I believe—is tampering with the mail, on a wide and pervasive scale. And I don't know why, but it'd have to be something big."

There was a beat of silence. Iosif wasn't sure whether to nod or not. He was frowning again, but he felt too absorbed to correct it. Was what the Director proposing even possible?

"That's what we're doing." Hougan drew back, slouched in his chair, and took a long drag on his cigar. "We're finding out who's tampering with the mail, and how. There's links—those artifacts, for instance, keep popping up wherever we go. Public Works has something to do with it. And Black Chamber of course, though that could just be on an enforcement level… I told you, not everyone thinks we're serving our country this way."

Iosif felt the hard surface of the toolbelt under his coat.

"But I can't nail down any one person." Hougan frowned at the floor. "Or even any one group. Some of the pieces I've got, I don't even know how they fit together—that I-X93 facility, for instance. And this 'Dragon's Teeth' program that all these briefs keep talking about."

"Senator Blackthorne?" Iosif dared to ask. He didn't want to talk, but the question seemed so obvious.

"Possibly." Hougan nodded. "He's got the means. Public Works handles damn near everything these days. But he was only elected four years ago. This is older than that. Probably bigger."

Iosif just nodded.

"I should've told you all this, when I hired you." Hougan knocked the ashes off his cigar. "But I barely knew you then, and anyway I didn't know how much you'd be involved. Athsma aside, you're a kid."

"I sixteen." Iosif wondered why he bothered.

"And I'm sixty." Hougan grunted. "Or thereabouts. It's one thing for someone as old as me to go around dodging bullets You've got a lot of your life ahead of you." He bit his lip. "But you're just so damn useful, kid. If you stick around, chances are I'm going to be putting you in a lot more bullet-dodging situations."

Iosif frowned. He'd caught that. "*If* I… stick around?"

"Didn't tell you about the danger before," Hougan said. "Seems like a bad idea to force you into danger you never agreed to. If you want to leave…" Hougan shrugged, "…well, you can't actually, that's the other side of Postal Service. But..." He knocked the ashes off his cigar. "...I could probably find an unimportant role for you in the administrative building..."

"No, no..." Iosif hastened to assure him. "Is fine." He saw Hougan look at him strangely, clearly wanting more. "Is... is good job." He clarified.

Hougan looked skeptical. "Mr. Rusval, you just got back from assaulting a military facility, crawling through vents, jumping onto waycars, and being shot at, all of which, I should inform you, probably means that Black Chamber is doing a 'cost-benefit analysis' on the possibility of assassinating you."

"Is... interesting job," Iosif said.

Hougan studied him. "There's something more," he said. "What is it? I told you, I can tell when someone's lying."

Iosif swallowed. "Is... difficult to say..." It wasn't so much that he was *trying* to hide the truth, he just wasn't sure how to express it. "Old job... very boring. Fix watches, fix other things. Day in, day out. Nothing new. No challenge. This job... more interesting. Challenge." He shrugged. "Go places. See new things. See *secrets*. And *make* things, not just fix. Do projects." He hesitated. "New project... just thinking about starting now. Want to stay on. Finish."

There was a beat of silence.

"Hm," Hougan said. "And... the insanity thing? Attacking government buildings? You're all right with that?"

Iosif bit his lip, trying to decide how to put words to his thoughts. "I... not American," he said. Then he shook his head. "No. I born in America. I grow up in America, but..." again words failed him and he waved his hands. "Not speak America.

Not look America. Not friends. Not enemies either, just…" He shrugged. "…not." He felt he was doing a bad job of this, so he finally said: "Is no big deal."

He couldn't think how to explain it. There wasn't, he felt, a way to put into words something that didn't exist. He could maybe have explained it by talking about the small house he and his mother had lived in, describing the lives he had lived between the house, the shop, and the church, how Washington DC had barely been a concept in those spaces. He could maybe have even talked about how comfortable he felt working here, in a way he doubted he'd feel anywhere else.

But he didn't feel that really would have gotten at what his boss was asking.

Hougan didn't say anything for a while. "Well," he said at last, stubbing out his cigar. "That's fine."

"They say that when Carnegie was asked why he had modernized the entire city of Pittsburgh in one night, he said it was simply the challenge that excited him," Grey said, stepping through the door.

"Bit more recent than most of your stories, Grey." Hougan raised an eyebrow at his lieutenant.

Grey shrugged. "Not everything happened in ancient times, sir."

"You learn anything?" Hougan said, looking at his cigar.

"Senator Blackthorne's appointment must have been with General Winters, sir," Grey said. "The sequence they used on the waycar sent them to Charleston, where he's currently reviewing fortifications. Also the senator made a comment about his 'sea legs', so…"

"Fort Sumter." Hougan nodded. "Sounds probable. We'll do some sniffing around."

"Shall I take Mr. Rusval back to his apartment, sir?" Grey said, turning slightly to allow access to the door.

Hougan stood with a gruntwith a grunt. "Yes, do that."
"Rusval, before you go… do you realize your eyes have been glowing this entire time?"

Iosif blinked. "They have?"

"Yes." Hougan walked toward the door. "Might want to see somebody about that."

∽о∾

The lift ride back down was quiet, but not uncomfortably so. Iosif was too glad to have the ground under his feet to give much thought to awkward silences. It had grown dark, and as they stepped into the residential compound they could see the dark sky above the flare of the gaslights.

"I asked Director Hougan if I could walk you back so I could clarify something," Grey said, looking up at the stars. "Obviously a man is no judge of his own sanity. But I served beside the Director during his years at Black Chamber, and a more sane man I have never known. Nor a more honest one." He looked down, directly at Iosif. "I did not see the facility Director Hougan did, nor did I encounter the man he did. But I trust his account absolutely, and if you are to be part of our enterprise, it is critical that you do also. Not merely false trust, but abiding and absolute confidence in the fact of his honesty and sanity."

Iosif's brow furrowed. "Why?"

"Because there is no room for doubts in this enterprise." Grey said. "And because the director can also tell when people are lying about their trust in him. As he could with his ex-wife."

∽o∾

Around 12:05 am, all was quiet in the residential courtyard. The gas lamps hissed, and mice darted to and fro, and the cicadas were buzzing loudly. The roaring noises of the outside city floated in dimly.

The blinds over Iosif's window creaked open ever so slightly. Moments later, the door squeaked, and Iosif himself stepped out into the courtyard. He cast a nervous glance around—up five or six floors he could see some nurses making the rounds, but no one else could be seen. Just to be safe, he skirted along the underside of the balcony toward the exit.

The interior of the Enforcement Division Front Office was empty also. He could see the light on in Hougan's office, which didn't much surprise him. It didn't matter. He wasn't going there.

The stairwell was quiet. The basement was loud with silence. Iosif stole across the room, his feet padding lightly across the concrete toward the massive vault door at the back.

He'd seen the combination when Ms. Kilroy unlocked it, but even so it took him a few moments to get it open—the amount of pressure seemed to be important somehow. He swung the door open and paused a moment to look at the workings—they were really fascinating—but shook his head and kept on. He also gave a longing glance at the artifacts on the shelves, but those too were not his goal—he could get more any time. He looked, for a moment, at the iron lung and the alien inside, but then moved past her toward the tarpaulin.

He pushed back the tarpaulin. The alien ship stood before him, like nothing so much as a large raindrop wound inside grass-green spiderwebs fanning out on either side. He stared, for a moment, fascinated by its silvery finish, its flowing lines, its bubble-like glass extrusions.

Then he knelt next to it and began to take it apart.

CHAPTER 8

2::324523::4234

Mr. Rusval,

I was very surprised to receive your letter. Though I cannot imagine the APD's interest in my work, you have nonetheless flattered an old man's fancy, though I must warn you that to ask an academic to explain his work is akin to asking a farmer to show you his fields.

Air travel is of course theoretically possible---even practically, as zeppelins and hoppers can attest. Even longer-range, heavier-than-air flight is not beyond the realm of possibility. Few people, I think, are aware of the full developmental extent of "aviation," as the sport is called. At this point, the designs exist to carry man into the stratosphere—there are simply no reliable ways of ensuring his return.

The Marceloni 'Barrier' or 'Curse,' as it is commonly known, has no scientific basis, but the pattern is impossible to deny. Since the Marceloni Brother's disappearance in 1798, no less than 27 different aspiring inventors, or 'aviators', as we tend to refer to them, have vanished while in the midst of testing prototypes. While sub-strata air vehicles, or 'hoppers' have become common, no one has ever yet managed in breaking the Marceloni Barrier.

Experts differ on where the Marceloni arrier is actually located. The Marceloni brothers themselves were known to ascend to 500,000 foot heights, but in 1908 the Wright brothers disappeared at a mere 2000 feet above the ground. My own personal theory is that the barrier is not a particular layer of atmosphere, but more likely a toxic interaction with the clouds themselves, which cause them to disintegrate higher-altitude craft that wander into them.

I hope you do not object to the package I have sent along with this missive—as I said, asking an academic to explain his work is dangerous business, and I so rarely get people interested in what is, by this point, an obscure field of study. The history of aviation "science" is generally known only to a few hobbyists, and if your interest in the field is as great as you profess, I think you will not object to the sheer volume of etchings.

However, if you are thinking of entering into the field yourself, I must dissuade you in the strongest terms. Aviation is a fascinating curiosity, but as a field of innovation, it is fraught with dangers, and anyone associated with it has been killed by either the ground or the air. There is nothing wrong with professional curiosity, as I can well attest, but some things have been left to history for a reason.

Sincerely,

Dr. Alan H. Puudernikel, PhD
History Department
University of Pittsburgh

2::294013::3211::321

"That's the ZR-1 Shenandoah," Hougan said, pointing at the massive zeppelin floating over the harbor. "Old base commissioned during the war, used as a flying mobile command center."

"Is base?" Iosif questioned, eying it dubiously.

"Not anymore." Hougan shook his head. He and the others stood in a disused tenement building on the fringes of the shorefront. Iosif could see one of the beetle-like Environmental Monitoring Stations, half-hidden by the curve of the dock. "It was only ever commissioned as a propaganda piece to match the German's airships. Wasn't much use as a bomber or a command post, and by this point it's a rusting death trap. They don't even take field trips up there anymore. Supposedly it's there to commemorate Charleston's Naval Yard production during the Great War, but the held wisdom is that they're just waiting for it to collapse."

"Then why are we heading out there?" Kilroy questioned, racking bullets into her Sten gun. "That far out on the water, in full view of the harbor—there's no chance of getting to it unseen."

"What if we could fly?" Iosif asked, before he could stop himself.

The others looked at him. Snorky gave a little laugh. "C'mon, kid, if we's could fly, we'd just skip over half this shit."

"You might," Grey murmured. "I'd prefer not to set foot on any sort of flying vessel at all."

Kilroy gave a little smile. "Superstitious, Philip?"

"No. But I can observe trends. And I'd like for there to at least be a body to bury."

"The Shenandoah's not our final target," Hougan said. "It's just a useful place marker. Every Thursday, the Coastal Patrol sends a supply boat to our real target—" he pointed slightly off to the left of the balloon, "—Fort Sumter. And on its way, it always passes directly under the Shenandoah."

"If we can get on the boat, the captain should take us straight through the mine field and straight through the water gate," Grey observed.

"The boat comes through at around eight at night," Hougan said. "But we can't risk being seen setting up, so we'll need to be out there and hidden by first light."

"So we's gonna be out there from dawn to dusk." Snorky did not look happy.

"Longer," Hougan said. "We need to be in position before midnight, and that means we'll need to start setting up a good deal beforehand." He looked at Snorky. "You say you know a good man?"

"Good man? Nah." Snorky gave a cocksure grin. "But I know a *reliable* man, with a boat. Fisherman. Used ta help us smuggle stuff, back in the day. He'll do what we ask, for a price." He rubbed his fingers together meaningfully.

"Shouldn't be a problem." Grey waved his hand.

"Is good he is fisherman," Iosif observed, looking through the diagram in his hand. "Will help."

"Mm." Hougan eyed the device in the corner of the room. "You sure that'll work, Rusval?"

Iosif was still looking at the paper, so he did not notice that everyone had turned their eyes on him.

"Perhaps." He shrugged.

∽o∾

"Kid, your eyes are doing that glowing thing again."

"Sorry," Iosif said, practically on reflex.

"You may want to see an ophthalmologist, Mr. Rusval," Grey said, turning. "I was doing some reading, and I came across something called Coats' Disease. Cholesterol deposits, built up in the eyes, can sometimes shimmer when light reflects off them. If left untreated, the person could go blind."

"Possible." Iosif weaved his way around the long burlap sack sitting on the deck. Snorky missed it in the dark and stubbed his toe against it. The big man fell to the deck, cursing loudly.

"Shut it with all the yapping back there!" Captain Soates hissed from his perch. "We're just about underneath!"

The vast looming shape of the USS Shenandoah was obvious even to the others, and everyone fell silent as they approached. The balloon's great black shape blotted out the stars like a floating whale, and a giant mooring cable, about as thick around as a lamppost, drifted up from the water to disappear somewhere in its murky form. Dark shapes bulged out from its sides, and just the faintest suggestion of rusty metal catwalks could be seen. For a moment, Iosif thought he caught a wink of light onboard—one of the old searchlights, perhaps, reflecting the glow from the lighthouse. The very wind seemed to go quiet under its shadow.

Captain Soates cut the motor. They drifted for a few feet more. Kilroy checked the Morris Island Lighthouse against the angle of the Birstwiel Building, and nodded at Hougan. Hougan nodded at Iosif.

Together, Iosif and Captain Soates unpacked the metal fishing net they'd brought along. Iosif still wondered if this was strictly necessary—an ordinary fishing net would really serve their needs just as well, and be much less conspicuous. But no, he felt the small round rings fixed at equidistant points around the net, and he nodded. This was a sensible addition. Everyone took a side of the net and helped in getting it over the side.

"Buoy there," Captain Soates muttered, necessity finally breaking through the awe engendered by the floating machine above them. "Another there."

"Won't they see 'em?" Snorky muttered back.

"Weighted," Iosif clarified. "Float in the middle of the water. Not sink, not rise. Just hold up."

"Like a ship with ballast," the captain agreed. "Right. Now I'm going to just troll for a little ways. Drop the other buoys in when I say."

The air was filled with the churning of the boat's motor. "Now!" Captain Soates muttered. Snorky dropped his buoy in.

"Now!" The captain said again. Kilroy dropped in hers. "Now!" That was Grey. "Now!" Hougan at the end. The net was spread in a wide arc. The captain turned the wheel sharply, bringing them to the inside of the arc. Iosif continued to play out the second line, attached to the bottom of the net—this was a much thicker, heavier-duty cable.

"Right." Hougan came up alongside him and checked his watch. "Nearly midnight. We need to wrap this up, Iosif."

Iosif nodded and turned to the really big object under the tarpaulin. He ripped off the canvas and stood looking at it for a moment.

In principle, Iosif understood the idea of a bathysphere. In principle, he didn't see that there was much TO understand— it was a metal sphere with windows that helped you stay underwater. But this bathysphere had to be light, so the Coastal patrol ship wouldn't feel the weight; small, so that it wouldn't create much drag; and roomy, so that all four of them could fit inside. It also should probably have a fair amount of steering capability, so that they'd be able to make any small adjustments to avoid the mines on their way in (and on their way out, which was going to be the *really* challenging part).

Iosif really wasn't sure that the brassy, vaguely tear-drop shaped metal construct he'd cobbled together from steel plates and caulking glue would really do the job. But they didn't have the time to make sure.

"On the crane," he said.

Captain Soates' boat had a crane, used for hauling in the nets, nets that could be full to bursting of heavy, struggling fish. Captain Soates had modified it so that it could also lift nets full of moonshine or guns packed into watertight greaseskin containers. A bathysphere was a new challenge, but not an unsurmountable one. They lifted the metal oval, then swung it out over the water.

Iosif undid the bolts on the door, then opened it. Kilroy climbed in, undid the inner door, and disappeared. Grey went after her. Snorky gave Iosif a nervous look, and climbed in.

"Your fee." Hougan handed Captain Soates a wad of bills.

"Thought I only got half until after we finished the job." Soates said, thumbing through them.

"No guarantee we'll be back to pay you," Hougan said. "Drop us into the water once we're in, then go back to the shore and forget this whole thing ever happened."

"Not a problem." Captain Soates pocketed the bills. "I've probably forgotten more than you remember already."

Hougan climbed into the submersible. Iosif stepped over the slight expanse of water into the airlock and swung the door shut behind him. He felt the sub lurch downward and heard the splash before he even made it through the second door. Looking to the front of the bathysphere, he could see (between the tightly compacted bodies of his comrades) the dark water closing over the windows already.

"Damnit, I thought it was dark *before*." Snorky did not sound happy. "Ya got any lights on this thing?"

Kilroy snorted (At least Iosif assumed it was Kilroy. Between the growing dark and the sardine-packed closeness of the bathysphere, it was hard to tell.) "You jest, surely. Can you even imagine what a gas flame would do in here?"

"A moment," Grey muttered. Iosif saw him reach into his coat, but the others only realized what was going on when the tube in his hand lit up with a sickly green light.

"Lightstick," he explained to the others. "I have a few more, but we should use them carefully. I only used this one because, as I understand, Mr. Rusval ought to be at the front by the controls."

"That's right." Hougan's voice rang out, startlingly close to Iosif's ear. "Shift around, people. Let him through."

There was a great deal of pained maneuvering, full of bumped elbows, squashed fingers and awkward situations. The worst part, Iosif reflected later, wasn't the bashed elbows, or the part where he accidentally lurched forward and nearly faceplanted into Ms. Kilroy. The worst part was that throughout it all, every time they bumped against the sloping wall—nearly every time they moved, even—the entire submersible seemed to move with them, reminding them of the water pressing in.

At the end of it all, Iosif found himself sitting squashed against the front panel of windows. He had his knees drawn up against his chest, so as to allow space for Kilroy, who herself was arched at an uncomfortable angle against the slope of the sub, so that Grey, doubled over in the middle, could squeeze in far enough for Hougan and Snorky to be semi-tolerably squashed against the back.

Iosif actually felt pretty satisfied, looking at them all. He'd gotten the cubic space needed nearly exactly right.

"Why'd I ever agree to this nuthouse?" Snorky asked no one in particular.

"Because the alternative was life in a Federation prison," Hougan answered.

"At least there I'd get my own room." Snorky grumbled. "How long we gonna be here for?"

"Eight hours," Grey answered, shifting a little so he didn't have to be *quite* as doubled over.

Snorky sighed. "Great."

"Perhaps we play game?" Iosif suggested. "I spy…"

The lightstick went out, plunging the interior of the sub into pitch-black night.

"I hate you all."

Iosif did not answer. Under his left hand, he had just felt something that made him very worried.

He had felt water.

∽⚬∾

Time causes mass to settle. Iosif would not have phrased the concept this way, but he knew that if you pour a quantity of peanuts into a large bowl, they will start out randomly sized and spaced out, but if you leave them there long enough, the smaller ones will end up packed on the bottom.

So it was that after four hours in the bathysphere, the party had managed to find more comfortable ways of arranging themselves. Or at least, so Iosif assumed—even he could not see very much in this darkness. But he had managed to find a little extra room for his legs, and from the regular breathing to his right, he gathered that Grey had somehow managed to be comfortable enough to sleep. Snorky didn't seem to be quite that comfortable—or perhaps he was just less adaptable—but even he would have moments when his breath become slow and regular, before a sudden snort announced his return to wakefulness.

Whether Hougan was sleeping, Iosif did not know. He certainly knew, though, that Kilroy was not, he could hear her muttering to herself or shifting around every so often.

As for Iosif, it was quite impossible to sleep. He kept feeling the water under his palm, trying to decide if it had grown at all in the hours they had been submerged. His eyes kept fruitlessly tracking upwards, hoping to see the bracing of the sub. He ran the figures through his head, thinking about the different layers of plating that he'd installed, the sealant between each one, the rubber sheathing, the...

He would have liked to cast the whole thing in a single piece—that was how the best bathyspheres were made. But he knew nothing about casting, and this project would have meant nothing if they'd brought in someone from the outside. He'd done the best he could.

No, that was a lie. He'd divided his time. He'd been half-asleep through the whole process. All those late nights, down in the vault... If they all died down here because he couldn't put away a side-project—a hobby, really...

He wondered if he should say something. It wouldn't be easy to get out in a hurry, if the sub started to sink. It might already be filling with water. He might very well be on the driest spot; the others simply too asleep to notice the damp around them....

No. That was nonsense. They would wake up if they felt any water.

Still. The stress points on the hull—water would undoubtedly leak in between the joining points on the plates. Maybe the sealant hadn't hardened enough. The water could be degrading the sealant even now. In his mind's eye he saw the different possible leak points, calculated the rate of denigration of the sealant. It could be leaking all over, the sealant being destroyed everywhere, the whole bathysphere just seconds from suddenly collapsing around them...

"Are you claustrophobic?"

Iosif started. Ms. Kilroy's voice had come out of the darkness at him.

"Not... really," he said, with an effort.

"Well, it doesn't make much sense for you to be afraid of the dark," she said. "Although your eyes aren't doing that glowing thing anymore, so maybe this is the first time you've experienced real dark. Or are you afraid of the water?"

"No." Or yes, in a way, but not in the way she was thinking. "I... afraid of heights."

"Well... I don't know why that would be bothering you now, but you're breathing fast and shallow, so clearly you're afraid of *something* right now," Kilroy said, her voice even. "And you're sitting right next to the controls, and you're the only person who knows how this thing works, so *calm down*. Take some deep breaths."

Iosif did as she suggested. It didn't entirely help, but it certainly didn't hurt.

"Talk to me," Kilroy said, her voice still even. Cold. Clinical. "What do you like to talk about?"

Iosif gave this some thought. "I don't," he admitted.

Kilroy gave a sigh. "Talk to me about your home. Who's your father, what does he do?"

"No father." Iosif shook his head. "Die before me."

"...your mother tell you that?" Kilroy said. "Tell me about your mother."

"She nurse."

Silence. "... And?" Kilroy prompted him.

"Nurse... at hospital?" Iosif tried. He wasn't quite sure what Kilroy wanted him to say. "Not work there for some time. I work at watch shop before here."

"Very good of you. You're a very attentive son."

Iosif shrugged. "Work is something to do," he said. "Not as interesting as new job."

"That is certainly one way of describing it." Kilroy's voice was very dry right now. "Something of aesthete, aren't you? Doing the work for its own sake?"

Iosif frowned. He wasn't entirely sure what the lady meant. "Maybe?" he said.

Kilroy sighed. "Well," she said. "It's a sensible fixation, anyway. Better than all the other hormone-laced menfolk running around these days. Or all those silly girls dreaming after romance. Love of work is a more dependable joy than love of man—or woman."

Iosif winced a little. "I... is not... something I think about."

"*That* I sincerely doubt." Ms. Kilroy's tone was drier yet. "Never?"

"... sometimes, maybe," Iosif said. "But is better not to. No point."

"What, because of your face?" Kilroy snorted. "That sort of thing doesn't matter. Not for men, anyway. *Women* need to be fair skinned, beautiful, dainty. *Men* can have scars, warts, birthmarks, wrinkles, facial tumors—the more the better, really. It just makes them 'rugged.'"

Iosif frowned. The lady was very confusing sometimes. "Not for me," he said, sticking to what he knew. "Was one girl, once…"

"Did you tell her? Or talk to her"

Iosif stopped. "Not… much."

"Then you didn't love her. You had a crush," Kilroy said. "If you didn't actually ever talk to her, you didn't actually know her, you didn't *love* her. At best, you were in love with a delusional idealization of what your psychosis deemed her to be."

Iosif had again lost what the woman was saying. "I… suppose."

"And you can't honestly know if she would have liked you or not, because you never gave her the chance to reject or refuse you."

"When I went up to her she ran away," Iosif observed.

"Oh. Well, in that case, yes, that's a sign that she wasn't interested." There was the light ring of metal as Kilroy's head rested against the wall.

"Why you work here?" Iosif asked. It had nothing to do with their conversation, but so many people had been asking *him* for his thoughts on work, the question seemed fair.

There was a long silence. Then: "There weren't a lot of options." Something rustled in the dark noise, and when Kilroy spoke again her voice was muffled, as if she'd turned away. "You should try to get some sleep, Mr. Rusval. We have a big day ahead tomorrow."

Iosif doubted it, personally, but he stretched his legs out, leaned back, and rested his head against the metal. He felt Kilroy hadn't really answered the question.

Iosif supposed he must have drifted off at some point. However, he could not remember falling asleep—or more accurately, he supposed, waking up. He just remembered sitting and staring and shifting around to find a more comfortable position and wondering what it would take for him to fall asleep, for what seemed like hours.

Finally the silence got to be too much for him. "Ms. Kilroy, you awake?"

A voice at his other elbow made him jump and smash his head into the ceiling. "Ah, Mr. Rusval," Mr. Grey murmured. "Glad to hear you up. I don't think the others are..."

"Blast it Grey, how long have you been awake?" Hougan's voice floated from the back.

"Holy shit, boss, really?" Snorky sounded irritated. "I knew I heard something from ya a while back there. Hey, Kilroy, you up?"

"I am now," Kilroy muttered.

"How much longer we gotta sit in this thing?" Snorky asked.

"Let me check my watch." Kilroy's voice said. *Snap. Click.* "Ah yes. I had forgotten. I cannot see in this Stygian dark."

"Ya don't need to be a bitch about it." Snorky sounded put-out. "Any of you's others got any idea how long?"

"Long," said Hougan, and that seemed to be as precise as anyone was ready to go.

"I did bring some sandwiches, if anyone wants to try them," Grey's voice said. "Egg and cresswater. Ham if anyone is interested."

"Grey, I take back everything I ever said about ya!" Snorky's voice was full of excitement. "Pass me a couple, will ya?"

"I would like one as well, Phillip," Kilroy said.

"Just pass them all around the circle, why don't you?" Hougan still sounded a little irritated. "We could probably all use something to eat."

Somebody shoved a couple packages into Iosif's hands. He seized one at random and held the other out in the dark until a slender hand bumbled into his and grabbed the sandwiches. He bit down into his sandwich, and found he had one of the cresswater sandwiches.

The bathysphere was full of the sounds of chewing. "Seriously, Grey, you's a lifesaver," Snorky muttered, voice muffled. "Ya wouldn't have any scotch to wash this down, wouldja?"

"Unfortunately not."

"Hang on, I have a flask," Hougan said, with slightly more energy. There was a popping sound. "Just a few swallows, mind. There's not a lot."

"Ha! Mighta guessed, boss." Again the popping sound. "Damn, that's strong."

Pop. "And smooth," Kilroy agreed. Someone thrust a small metal flask into Iosif's hand. "What's the year, sir?"

"McAllister's 78." Hougan sounded satisfied.

Iosif felt a little self-conscious, but he undid the cap on the top and took a sip. He coughed.

"Rusval, did I hand that to *you*?" Kilroy said, suddenly sharp.

"Ha!" Snorky roared. "Ya gave the whiskey to the kid?"

"I sikteen," Iosif insisted.

"I thought he was Grey! I can't tell anything in this murk!"

Iosif didn't personally see what the problem was. He passed the small metal flask on to Grey.

"You all right, Rusval?" Grey sounded cautious. "Still good to pilot this thing?"

"I fine," Iosif insisted.

"Hmm." The popping sound repeated. "*Salud, hlaford.*"

"No problem."

"Do you know." Kilroy's voice had changed suddenly. "Something has just occurred to me. Is there a bathroom in this tub at all?"

There was an uncomfortable silence.

"Marvelous."

⚬◦⚬

"No."

"Aw come on! I'll give ya guys the first line, and then ya just repeat after me..."

"Capone, we are NOT singing "The Bar-Maid's Daughter.""

⚬◦⚬

"...is firm, out in Providence. Mostly make cargo lifts. Is very interested in safety prototype."

"What'd they give you for the patent?"

"Not sale. I get 20% of profits, and help with improvements."

"Bad call, kiddo. Always go for the money in hand."

"I agree for once with Mr. Capone. I'm sorry, Joseph, but I really don't think your business is likely to take off. There are plenty of cargo lifts companys out there already."

"Perhaps, Ms. Kilroy, but a safer model would give him a leg up. Mr. Rusval has fairly good odds, I should say. Though I am curious as to why he simply didn't release it to the Public Works department."

"Is boring. Also, lift still needs much work."

"Seriously, more work? Damnit, kid, don't you ever take time for fun?"

"But… is fun."

∽o∾

"A-Roving, A-Roving, since Roving's been my ru-u-in…"

∽o∾

"…I don't know *who* the invaders were, the story doesn't specify. Just that they were a powerful tribe from the southeast. I think the story actually just calls them unknown; as though even the Cherokee at the time didn't know. Anyway, not important. The point is, the Cherokee are losing badly and the city of Nikwasi looks about to be lost to these strange invaders. And then suddenly, a man appears next to the chief and tells him to withdraw from the field, that the Nunnehi will fight for them."

"Hang on, I thought ya said these Nunnehi guys were dwarves."

"Capone…"

"No, actually that's a good point. There's a lot of inconsistency in these old stories. Sometimes the *nunnehi* are fat-bellied dwarves with sharp canines, other times they're full grown humans of beauty and grace. You get the feeling that the storytellers were mixing up what creatures they were talking about."

"Hm. Not dissimilar from the 'faerie folk' in that regard."

"Yes, there are a lot of similarities like that. My ex-husband loved opera, and I occasionally wondered if there were any etymological connections between Wagner's 'nibelungs' and the Crow's 'nirumbee', which is essentially their word for the nunnehi."

"Eh. Sorry I asked. Can ya get back to the story?"

"Well, the Cherokee chief pulls his men back, and the ground rips open and an army of the nunnehi charge out."

"Dwarves or human-people nunn-e-whatever?"

"Capone, I thought you said you were sorry you asked."

"The story doesn't specify. I assume both. They attack, the enemy is slaughtered, Nikwasi is saved. The end."

"Why didn't they just take the whole city into the sky, like they did in that other story?"

"Or why not do it like the one about the Cherokee removal, where they took everyone underground?"

"*I don't know*, I didn't write the stories. Why do I ever tell you these things?"

∽૦∾

"Damnit, the first thing I'm going to do when I get out of here is smoke another goddamn cigar."

"I's gonna destroy a sandwich or twelve."

"I shall simply be glad to have the sun on my face again."

"I'm going to go to the bathroom."

Silence.

"Ya HAD to mention that, didn't ya."

"Okay, boss, your turn."

"All right. Let's see. Hm. What are the three main theories regarding Edison's death and the Menlo Park explos…?"

A sudden shudder shook the bathysphere. Iosif pitched forward and nearly planted his face into the floor. His left hand landed in a puddle. He could hear cries and curses from the other inhabitants of the sub.

"Well, I'll be!" Hougan, at least, seemed happy. "The magnets caught!"

"Will they notice?" Kilroy asked.

"Be able to tell soon enough." Hougan answered. "Grey, quickly, another one of those lightsticks."

The inside of the Bathysphere flared with sudden light, and the others cried out. Iosif himself winced. Still, the glow showed everyone in a tangled heap at the back of the sub, Grey holding out the glass tube.

Carefully, Iosif took the tube, glancing down in what he hoped was a discreet manner. The puddle his hand had landed in was small, but looking around, he could see it was far from the only one.

"We're still going up, Rusval," Hougan said, his voice tense. Iosif looked up, and their eyes met. Hougan gave a slow nod, and Iosif realized his boss had seen the leaks also. But he was going ahead anyway.

Getting a firmer grip on the glass tube, Iosif turned around toward the panel of windows. The controls themselves were simply a couple rods meant to angle the outside fins, but he'd also duct-taped a pressure meter and a compass next to the window, and these were what he was most interested in right now.

"Depth 31 feet… 27…" Iosif reported. "Direction 5 points South-Southwest." He did some rapid calculations. "Moving… 35 knots per hour. So stop at depth of… 7-10 feet."

"5 points South-Southwest is within the range of tolerance," Kilroy said. "They don't need to be making a straight shot, they might turn a little to make a path through the mines."

"The mines," Hougan said, his tone clipped, low. "Anything, Rusval?"

Iosif discarded the lightstick and leant toward the windows. Now that they were going up, there was more light from above filtering down—but it was orange-gold light from the sunset, already fading. And the water was murky with ships's rust and harbor silt.

"Not… much," he admitted.

"We's gonna die," Snorky muttered.

"Hang on." Iosif pulled a lever. The Bathysphere shuddered and immediately started to rise more quickly.

"What…"

"Ballast." Grey explained, as if it were obvious. "See anything now, Rusval?"

"Yes." He could see 10, maybe 20 feet in front of them now, enough to make out floating blobs with long trailing lines below them. They were more likely to attract a mine, now that they were higher up, but at least they wouldn't be bumping into the chains.

"Shit!" Snorky's voice. "The roof's leaking!"

Iosif couldn't turn to see if this was a new leak or an old one that Snorky had just noticed. They were entering the minefield.

"Shit. Shit shit shit shit shit… is there any caulking glue in this tub? Metal plating? Tape?"

"Wouldn't do much good if there was." Hougan's voice was level. "Stay calm."

"I'm calm. I'm being goddamned calm. Don't ya see me being calm right now?" Snorky swore again. "Shit."

They were among the mines. So far the boat had kept on a straight line. So long as it did that, they should be fine. Experimentally Iosif twisted the rods. He could make the submersible pitch up and to the right, or down and to the left, but nothing else. It was not ideal, but it was all he could manage.

"The floor's leakin' too," Snorky said. He did sound calm, now.

"We… we should be ready to bail out," Kilroy said. "If things go… badly."

"Right." Somehow Snorky's calm was more terrifying than his anger. "So lets work out who's goin' first. Boss, that's you…"

"No." Hougan interrupted. "Woman and children first. Kilroy, get in the airlock."

"Sir, I refuse to be—"

"Just to be ready. If I rap on the glass two times, you flood the chamber and exit. Rusval goes as soon as he can be spared from the controls. Capone, you're next. Then Grey, then me."

"Boss?"

"I'm getting to that island if it damn near kills me." Hougan growled. "Don't try to swim to the mainland. There's more than mines out here. Go for the boat. Your chances are better. Better to be in federal prison than in federal pieces."

"If you say so."

"Ms. Kilroy, what are you …"

"This coat isn't going to be any use in the water, is it? Or the Sten gun." There was the rustling of fabric. "Thank god I wore the pantaloons today."

Iosif could not spare very much time to think about what was going on behind him because the shadow of the boat above had just made a turn, a left turn, a very slight turn, but still a dangerous one that had brought a mine right into their path. Iosif turned the rudders, misjudged and sent them to the right, then re-adjusted and turned to the left. He hoped the others hadn't noticed.

"Didn't ya bring any scuba gear?"

"No room. Everything had to be streamlined."

The boat had turned again, now to the right. The sub was still going left, and was swinging out at the end of its lead like a trailer behind a train. Iosif turned again to match, but the momentum made the sub's movement sluggish.

"Well how fast is it leaking, do ya think?"

"It wasn't leaking a few minutes ago…"

"Well, it sure is now. This whole place could be about to go under."

Iosif was about to speak, but Grey spoke up first. "It's a slow rate," he said. "There was a spot of damp I was sitting on last night. For it to have leaked this much in 20 hours implies a rate of…"

Iosif's mind seized up. There had been two puddles? Then that meant that the rate during the night had been slower than he thought. But the water seemed to be spreading faster, now—he could feel it dampening his leggings. So something must have changed. But what? Perhaps the pressure...

A sudden shadow in the corner of his eye made him look around, and he nearly froze. The boat must have made a sharp right turn, because the sub was already listing pretty far in that direction, and there was one particular mine it was veering dangerously close toward.

Hougan had explained they couldn't be sure about the mines, but that they were likely to be magnetic and touch-activated. At this depth, it was more the chains than the mines themselves that were the problem—knocking one could set off a mine, which could prompt a depth charge from the ship.

Iosif twisted the left rudder down and the right rudder up. The submersible turned, agonizingly slowly, continuing to drift in a lazy arc, directly toward the chain with its explosive attachment. Closer, closer... it disappeared from Iosif's vision, but there was still the rest of the sub to clear...

There was a sharp exclamation and the sound of something hitting against the metal. Iosif nearly froze, but the next second he heard the air-lock door open and Kilroy speak. "Sorry. That was me. Something flashed right by the window."

"Rusval?" Hougan asked. His voice was calm and steady.

"Everything all right, sir." Iosif reported, shifting the rudders again to bring them directly behind the boat. The channel appeared clear for a ways.

"Water's getting deeper." Snorky noted.

Iosif had some concentration to spare, and he used it. "Sit down in the place you were last night," he said.

"What?"

"Were two puddles last night," Iosif said. "Leakage very slow then. But is going fast now. Only change—our position. Sit down where before."

"Kid, there's nearly an inch of water on the floor by…"

"Do what he says, damnit." Hougan snapped.

There was some splashing around behind him. Iosif didn't bother to look around. The channel seemed pretty clear. He could see mines looming in the darkness on the left and on the right, but nothing else.

"Damnit, my leggings are all wet."

"Quit complaining. It's working, isn't it?"

"Hard to tell. Wet is still wet."

The boat curved left. Iosif turned. It curved right. Iosif followed.

"We should have gotten through by now," Grey said. "What's going on, Rusval?"

Iosif looked at the compass and got his answer. "Going due west," he said.

"West?" That was Snorky.

"Must be going on a path around the island for a ways before they turn toward the dock." Hougan observed. "Smart. Very smart."

"Yeah, real damn geniuses, those guys."

"Sharp turn," Iosif confirmed, watching the boat up above curve to the right. He turned to the right and the sub responded, giving him a full view of what was beyond the curve.

"Er…" He blinked at it, unable to quite absorb what he was seeing. The water up ahead was shimmering; a flat sort of shimmer, like something in a painting. There was an odd design to it, too… Iosif put on his glasses. Yes, a sort of equilateral diamond pattern. Curiously regular, almost like…

"Net!" The words exploded from Iosif as the full implications burst upon him. "Is net… net ahead!"

"Net?" The other men said all together.

"Blast and blow," Hougan said, directly after. "Of course."

Grey used a word Iosif had never heard before. "Of course. Why wouldn't they have an anti-submersible system?"

"Time to go." There was a splashing of water as Hougan stood. "Everyone get ready, I'll signal Kilroy…"

"Wait!" Iosif barked. "I think… I try something."

Silence. He did not hear any rapping. He took that as permission and twisted the levers, letting the vessel dive. As it dove, he pulled another lever, and he felt the cable attaching them to the boat shoot lose. The sub shuddered with the momentum.

"Was that…?"

A squeak of metal. "We just lost the cable."

"Rusval…?"

"Is fine," Iosif answered tersely. They had enough inertia going; it should be enough to carry them past the net, if his guess were right.

He wasn't entirely sure how anti-submarine netting worked, but he'd studied nets in general a bit when building the device. And generally, nets did not go all the way to the ocean floor. It was too expensive, too difficult, and too uncertain—one could not be certain of how deep or how level the ground would be.

It was possible, of course, that the soldiers at the fort *did* know this and had a net reaching all the way to the bottom. But Iosif did not think so. He had observed, at the post office, that most people involved in the government were interested in working less, not more. Fort Sumter was a base at peace, miles away from any attack. It seemed unlikely the soldiers would have been perfectly zealous in their precautions.

They'd soon find out. But for now, going down just felt *right*.

"The water's going up," Snorky said.

"We're going down," Grey said. "Higher pressure..."

"Yeah, thanks, professor, I got that." Snorky snapped.

Iosif, who was half-lying down, could feel the water creeping up his chest. He chose to ignore it. He was counting. 1... 2... 3... He twisted the steering rods and felt the sub even out.

"Goddammit, Rusval! I can't see shit here! What the crap are ya..."

"That's not helping, Capone," Hougan said. "Rusval?"

"Past net now." Iosif sat up and turned around, aware they couldn't see him. "But bathyshpere is 30 feet down. No longer going down, but probably rocks..."

A grinding crash shook the entire sub as the floor flew out from under him, and he and the others smashed into the glass front of the bathysphere—the front, that was now crumpled, cracked, and leaking badly.

"Abandon ship!" Hougan shouted. The sub was already tilting, the floor becoming a wall. "Kilroy..."

They heard the steel door clang open.

"Kid!" Snorky roared. Iosif felt a hand grab into the back of his coat. "Get that door open!"

The big man heaved him, straight up into the darkness. For a moment, Iosif saw, perfectly, in his mind's eye, the shape of the sub he had built. His hands came together and clapped squarely on the handle of the door. Bracing himself against the wall, he ripped the air lock door off its hinges.

Water flooded into the room, filled it. Iosif felt the other men swim past him before he dared to let go of the air lock door. He swung himself through the doorway, climbed out through the air lock, and struggled into the outside water.

CHAPTER 9

0::218820::1284

Fresh shipment of Grubs required at Station 423. SXN-123 dispatched to Fort Sumter for resupply and re-distribution.

0::234842::2031

Iosif kicked. He flailed about with his arms. He realized, far too late, that he had no conception of what swimming involved.

Something big dove past him. He felt it rake up against his back. Then it came back from underneath—Snorky, stripped of his coat, in a white shirt and suspenders. He grabbed Iosif's hands (Iosif was too dumbfounded to struggle), and put them around his neck. Iosif understood immediately and clasped his hands together in a loop around the big man's neck. He felt the forceful *push* upwards as Snorky's arms and legs worked in powerful, sweeping motions.

They broke water, and Iosif's eyes burned against the sudden light. He felt them clamber up onto something solid, heard the others asking questions. Snorky's voice, strained tight, broke in on him. "Damnit, kid, leggo; you's choking me!"

Iosif let go and tumbled to the ground. Hougan and Kilroy were beside him instantly, as Grey supported Snorky.

"Did you not hear that stuff we were saying about coats and guns?" Hougan snapped, as he peeled Iosif's leather coat, soaked and heavy with water, off of him. "Shit, son, you're still wearing your blasted boots! How the sam hill did you get him up here?" he said, turning to Snorky.

Snorky was slumped against the concrete, coughing a little, but clearly fine. "Kid's barely 150 pounds soaking wet," he said, with a choked laugh. "Though ya wouldn't guess it from that death-grip of his."

Iosif looked up. "Thank you," he said. His teeth were beginning to chatter.

Snorky waved the compliment off. "Next time take some swimming lessons, will ya? And mebbe put some oxygen tanks on board."

"Yes." Iosif nodded, eyes flitting about. "Lower sealant needs work too, and a more controlled ballast system. Perhaps additional set of rudders. And a more sustained lighting system..."

"I dearly hope we're not planning on doing this *again* anytime soon," Grey said, sending a look at the others. "My best hat is down there somewhere, along with my old 37 revolver."

Hougan sighed. "Things are a bit more... complicated, now," he muttered.

Iosif looked around for the first time and took in their surroundings. They appeared to be on a concrete slab of some kind, underneath a raised walkway, which for the moment was deserted. There was a solid rock wall on their right, and some crates stacked high on their left. Iosif leaned a little to see, and saw three empty docks. Only the one on the far end was occupied, with the ship they'd come in on. Sailors were milling about on deck, but they seemed utterly disinterested in the rest of the facility.

"Well." Hougan shrugged. "Can't very well go back… or surrender. This is a Black Site, and I doubt they'd respect our Postal Enforcement badges."

"Now I feel better." Kilroy grimaced, standing and brushing herself off. Iosif couldn't help but notice that the lady's clothes were still very damp and clinging to her arms in a very arresting manner. "Perhaps we could take a ride back on the boat we came in on?" She jerked her head in the general direction of the patrol boat.

Hougan seemed to consider this. "Sounds like as good as good a plan as any." He shrugged. "We'll need guns, though. And disguises."

∽o∾

They took one guard at the end of the dock. Snorky grabbed him and dragged him behind the crates.

The second guard was at the foot of the stairs leading to the overlooking tower. He paid no especial attention to the new guard walking up, until that new guard brained him with a monkey wrench. Grey stepped over the body as the others began to strip him.

The third and fourth guards were chatting lightly up in the guard box at the top of the tower. They stopped and turned to look at Grey as he came in wearing the trooper's uniform. Their faces changed and they went for their guns. Grey was just too fast.

"Ya see anything in my size?" Snorky said, mounting the stairs after him.

"No…" Grey was looking out from the guard tower at the dock, absentmindedly wiping the blood off his knife. "But there is one *very* interesting thing I see…"

The others came beside him and looked out. Making his way down the dock toward a just-arriving motor yacht was a familiar egg-shaped silhouette in a dark black suit. Iosif recognized the small, spider-haired man with a suitcase at his elbow.

"Blackthorne," Hougan grunted. "How about that?"

"How are maritime operations any part of the Public Works department?" Kilroy asked.

"Public Works is authorized to commission Chamber agents for operational efficiency on select occasions," Grey said. "Though commissioning an entire Black Site is definitely beyond the purview of what the legislation is meant to cover."

"Have a feeling Blackthorne went beyond his purview a long time ago." Hougan grunted.

"But why come alone?" Kilroy persisted.

Iosif raised his shoulders in a small shrug. "His secretary is there."

"To keep a low profile, perhaps," Grey said. "And to ensure none of his underlings know of the details. Or perhaps the General here insisted on it—in order to preserve the base's own secrecy."

"Definitely unusual." Hougan rubbed his chin, as Blackthorne stepped onto the yacht, followed by the spider-haired Flistworth. "Man rarely goes anywhere without a whole army of staff members. Even if the base asked for it, he must *really* want something to come alone."

Snorky was interested in something very different. "There." He pointed. "That guy over by the crane. He looks about my size."

Grey cocked his head to look. "...he'll work, yes." He glanced around the tower. "I'll call him over here, shall I? There must be a speaking trumpet around here..."

"I'll wait for him downstairs." Kilroy turned to him. "Iosif, may I borrow your scarf?"

Iosif looked up at her. "...why you want scarf?" he asked.

"It's really better you don't know, dear." Kilroy smiled.

∞‧∞

"Every time we infiltrate a place, we always have to waste half-an-hour finding you a disguise," Kilroy said, as she stood over the big guard.

"Hey, it's not my fault all them feds are shrimpy little pipsqueaks," Snorky said, unbuttoning the man's pea jacket.

Grey sniffed.

"What... of me?" Iosif said, looking worriedly at the others. He didn't even think it was worth looking for one in his size.

"We'll have to do the prisoner routine." Grey glanced at Hougan.

"That didn't work well last time." Kilroy objected.

"Last time Capone didn't make for a very good prisoner."

"That guard was an asshole," Snorky said, frowning.

"We need to try," Hougan said, buckling the gun belt around his waist. He had been given the captain's uniform. It was slightly too big for him, but Grey explained that captain was the only role that made sense for a man of his age. "Capone, Kilroy, your job is securing our exit. The boat's a good idea, but keep it quiet—we don't know any of the passwords or signals, or how to get out through the minefield, so we'll need the captain at least, preferably the crew."

"Probably would be best if you just secured us a few seats, not a whole ship," Grey said.

"Yeah, yeah, we's adults, we got it." Snorky waved. He turned to Kilroy. "Hey, dame, wanna try putting those womanly wiles to work, huh?"

Kilroy held up the pistol she'd taken from the guard and just looked at him.

"Rusval, come on," Hougan said.

Iosif blinked up at him. "What?"

"You're our prisoner," Grey said, taking the handcuffs off his belt with a practiced twirl.

Fort Sumter, to Iosif's relief, seemed to be very clearly laid out. The hallways were all straight and simple, with clearly labeled doors at regular intervals. It was mostly concrete and rebar, and the doors were all steel. Guards walked around in drab blue uniforms, apparently unconcerned about the three of them.

Which was good, because Hougan and Grey were acting in what Iosif thought was a *very* suspicious manner. He supposed it must look convincing—Grey with his hand clapped on Iosif's shoulder, Hougan walking just behind, all of them marching, purposefully—but if anyone had stopped to mark their path, they would have quickly realized something was wrong. They doubled back on their steps, took false turns, went down blind alleys and constantly found themselves back where they had started. There was one point, when they walked a distance down the hallway, stopped at a door, opened in and marched inside, then turned right around and marched back out.

Iosif had never doubted his employer, but he was starting to wonder.

The mystery was unraveled after a few moments. "Any ideas?" Hougan grunted.

"I don't even know what we're looking for, sir," Grey muttered back. "Files? Labs? Secret maps? We only came here because Blackthorne was here, and that could have been on unrelated business."

"Our contacts said he visited this place 6 times in the last two months," Hougan said. "There's got to be something"

"We could check the lower levels," Grey suggested. "I saw some sailors going down there… this place must have a submarine dock. Or perhaps the barracks…"

"Attention!"

Both men turned around and immediately snapped to attention. "Sir!" "Sir!"

"At ease, captain. Corporal." A thick, but not heavy, man with a luxuriant mustache and an impressive uniform, nodded curtly. "Who's the prisoner?" Behind the officer, two guards in white gloves studied him.

"He was trying to break into the Fort, sir," Hougan said. "We weren't sure where to bring him."

"Ah, part of the new guard, are you?" The general seemed to be studying Iosif very carefully. "…no need to take this one to the brig, I think. We've got a place for infiltrators like him." The general turned to one of his men. "Sergeant Reynolds, you know where to take them?"

"Aye sir." One of the nondescript guards saluted.

The general turned back and nodded at them. "Good work, both of you. May I ask your names?"

"Corporal Phillip Grey, sir. Serial Number 9182883."

"Perry Hougan, sir. 2119124"

The general noted down the names in a small notebook. "Very good. Carry on." He passed by, with his guards.

Sergeant Reynolds, a slim man wearing a thin moustache and tinted spectacles, nodded to them. "This way."

Iosif had no idea what was going on. He wasn't sure Grey did, either—the hand on his shoulder was significantly lighter. They followed Reynolds through a litany of barred gates and armed checkpoints, ending in front of a massive vault door guarded by several machine guns and a small squad of men.

"Damnit." The burly lieutenant on duty in front growled. He too was wearing tinted glasses; Iosif wondered if they were standard for some reason. "This would happen now. We're still getting all the rest through processing. All my boys are helping with that. I don't have time for you two." He glowered at Hougan and Grey.

"The general said they were to be taken here," Sergeant Reynolds said. "Do you understand?"

"Right, right." The lieutenant waved. "But you can't go in there without someone from the PW present, and like I said, right now we're shorthanded." He shouldered his sten gun. "Right, I guess it'll have to be me. Lock the doors back there!"

Navy-suited guards swung shut the thick doors they had just come through, then locked them shut. The other guards hurried about into what were clearly pre-determined stations. Iosif tried not to look too interested in the whole process—particularly in a long side booth which seemed to be set actually lower than the floor in the hallway. He could almost see inside.

"All these damn protocols…" the lieutenant muttered, walking over to the vault door. He took a key from around his neck.

"Sir," one of the guards called from the side-booth. Iosif could now see, through the cracked door, a narrow trench and a control box. "The sub-trolley was on its way back, but with the outer doors closed—"

"Yes, yes." The lieutenant inserted his key in the vault and turned it. "There's no hurry. No one on it right now. This won't take a moment and then we can get it back in here." He spun the dials and the bolts retracted. "All this for one little…" he muttered, swinging the door open.

The room beyond was dark, but not so dark that they could not see how big it was. They stood on the lip of a vast, bowl, shaped depression, roughly the length of a football stadium (or so Iosif imagined; he'd never actually been to a stadium before.) Iosif's first thought was that it was a giant metal sieve of some sort, but then he realized that the metal latticework running around the bowl was formed of thousands of little cages, staring up at the tower in the center like little metal eggs.

It was a prison, Iosif realized with fascination. No—it was a zoo.

Then he heard the vault door slam shut behind them and heard the cocking of a Sten gun.

Iosif threw himself to the floor as the chatter of machine-gun fire filled the air. He rolled over, hands still cuffed behind his back, and was relieved to see Hougan and Grey already attacking Sergeant Reynolds and the big lieutenant.

Grey was a flurry of motion attacking the slim sergeant. He had clearly knocked the other man's pistol from his hand, but in all his darting strikes and kicks, Grey made no attempt to draw the gun at his waist. Nor did Reynolds make a dive for the pistol, lying on the ground some three feet away. Both men were fixed on each other, seemingly convinced that the slightest break in their attack would be fatal They danced back and forth, mere inches from each other, hands flashing in a rhythm of punches and chops.

Meanwhile, Director Hougan took a massive punch to the midsection, flying back a few feet with the force of the blow. He seemed to shake it off, like a boxer, and charged the big lieutenant again, even as the big man struggled to bring his Sten gun around. Hougan's hands contorted in an odd shape, and he gave the man several sharp, surgical jabs.

"Ha!" The lieutenant simply laughed, and grabbed the clearly-surprised Hougan in both hands. He threw the director, nearly over the lip of the bowl, then reached for his Sten gun.

Iosif, hands still cuffed, charged. He plowed into the man with as much speed as he could muster in fifteen yards—which is to say, not much. It staggered the lieutenant, knocking the Sten gun from his grip,but he simply turned—with astonishing speed for such a big man—and reached for Iosif.

Iosif dodged back, but misjudged the man's reach. Fingers dug into his throat as the big lieutenant hauled him forward and up. "What are you trying to do, you little maggot?" He sneered.

When he thought about it later, Iosif wasn't quite sure where the impulse had come from. He'd never seen any prizefights or moving pictures. But in the second where his face was hauled up next to the big lieutenant's, staring into the tinted sunglasses, it just seemed perfectly natural for him to slam his head into the man's face.

He hadn't quite expected it to be quite so painful. Stars danced in his vision and he barely heard the lieutenant's howl, barely felt it as he crashed back to the ground. His bones had all dissolved into water, and he could do little more than groan as a massive hand seized him by the hair and hauled him around.

Iosif looked straight up into a pair of *blazing* eyes, so bright they could have been twin jets of flame. The shattered sunglasses slipped off the lieutenant's nose as he roared at him with inhuman volume, displaying two overlarge, slightly sharpened canine teeth.

Hougan charged into the lieutenant, with twice the momentum of Iosif and much better targeting. His elbow caught the big lieutenant just under the ribs, and the man went down with a gasp. With his free hand he lashed out at Hougan, but the older man rolled away, leapt up, and dashed for Reynold's pistol, sitting unattended by the main door. The big lieutenant, strangling the handcuffed Iosif with one hand, reached again for his sidearm.

Iosif ripped the handcuffs in half and grabbed hold of the big lieutenant's arm. He felt something give under his fingers as the man howled in pain. The next second, three short cracks rang out, and the big man doubled over, blood seeping from several holes spaced neatly in his left pectoral.

Hougan turned around, presumably to shoot Reynolds, but it was unnecessary—the gunshots had caused the other man to freeze up just long enough for Grey to crush the man's windpipe with his forearm. Reynolds doubled over, choking, and Grey brought both his fists down on the back of the man's head. Reynolds crumpled over with barely a whimper.

Hougan holstered the pistol. "You all right?"

Iosif gave a nervous wave. He had just noticed that his fingers were covered in blood.

"Fine." Grey straightened his jacket. "You?"

Hougan let loose a groaning sigh. "I'm too old for this," he said.

"We both are," Grey said, stooping neatly to confiscate the Sten gun.

"What the hell even was that?" Hougan pinched the bridge of his nose. "Did they blow our cover?"

"It seems it would have been better to question us, in that case," Grey said. "No, I think they were quite honestly trying to kill two ordinary guards who found a prisoner they weren't supposed to."

"Thought the general seemed awfully interested in you, Rusval," Hougan said. He shook his head. "But why?"

Grey shrugged. "Dark secrets, it would seem."

"Those two were certainly Black Chamber. Probably everyone out there is too." Hougan grunted. He felt at his back and winced. "That lieutenant'd had some surgery done... or something."

"Indeed. The sergeant too... his eyes were glowing in a most unnatural way. It was most... peculiar." Grey was studying the room with a strange intensity "Perry... this place..."

Hougan turned, and seemed to absorb the massive bowl-shaped room for the first time.

"Oh," he said. "Oh hell."

"Perry?"

"Yes. Yes. Blast and blow, this is it, this is exactly the same. They could have picked it up and moved it straight here from Ellis Island." Hougan passed a hand over his face. "Or cloned it. Could they have more of them or did they rebuild..." His voice failed and he shook his head.

"Perry..." Grey said, in an odd voice. "You know I... I always believed you..."

"I know."

"But... seeing this..." Grey rubbed a hand over his mouth. "My word, it's exactly as you described it..."

"Doesn't matter, right now." Hougan seemed to have regained control of himself. "We need to hurry." He pointed at the long tower in the center. "They might have some records or something up there. There must be a way of getting to it."

Iosif found this all very confusing. Fortunately getting to the tower was a simpler puzzle. "Over this way." He'd already spotted an outcropping that looked designed to support a bridge of some sort.

"One moment." Grey stopped and pulled a card from the Sergeant Reynold's pocket, along with a set of keys. "This may prove useful."

Unfortunately, there was no control terminal, keyed or otherwise, by the outcropping. The support was clearly meant for a bridge—Iosif could even see the bridge, over on the watchtower—but there did not seem to be any way of signaling it to come over.

"It must ordinarily be password-controlled," Grey observed. "Only accessed at the discretion of guards already in the tower."

"Well they're not there NOW," Hougan snapped. "They must have a way of getting to it when no one's home."

"I think…" Grey cocked his head, quizzically, staring out over the chasm toward the tower. "But no… that is too transparently simple."

Hougan arched an eyebrow. "You see something, Phillip?"

Grey drew back a step. "We'll know in a minute, sir."

And with that, Grey dashed toward the edge of the pit and jumped.

Hougan and Iosif both started, but they had barely time to react before Grey landed—in midair. To Iosif's disbelieving eyes, he landed in a crouch on absolutely nothing at all, five feet out from the edge.

"Well, I'll be." Hougan breathed, as Grey drew back a few more steps, dashed, leapt, and again landed on nothing.

"What is it?" Iosif wanted to know.

Hougan pointed. "Little panes of glass, suspended on clear plastic filament. 'Silent Steps' we call them in Black Chamber. Used for training purposes. See them?"

"No…" Iosif shook his head. "My eyesight…"

"Odd for them to be used as a security measure, though." Hougan frowned. "Anybody with two eyes and a decent pair of legs could get across that obstacle course. I could probably do it, if I were ten years younger."

"No need to test that, sir," Grey called back, as he landed on the small ledge just on the edge of the tower. "I see the controls for the bridge. One moment…"

And a narrow tongue of metal, scarcely wide enough for two to walk abreast, extended out of the tower and landed neatly in front of Hougan and Iosif.

"Anything in here?" Hougan asked, as he and Iosif ran (Hougan ran. Iosif could only manage a plodding sort of jog) into the tower.

"Not of much worth, I'm afraid." Grey was rooting through the desk, completely ignoring the five Gatling guns strapped at the respective corners of the watchtower. "This doesn't seem to be meant for archiving, more as a guardpost or something. Oh, there is a safe, though. Rusval, if you would…"

Iosif happily jogged over to the safe. *Finally.*

"Other than that, not much." Grey shook his head. "There's a shipping manifest here."

"SXN-723" Hougan read off the paper. His eyes narrowed. "S… that's a submersible. They've loaded this cargo of theirs on a sub?"

"So it would seem." Grey toyed with his lip. "I did wonder why that dock was so empty. Unless they had a dedicated u-boat dock, of course… they were experimenting with underwater gateways at the Chicago pier."

A clanging noise at the front made them all glance around.

"That sounds like the guards at the gate, wondering where their lieutenant is." Grey glanced over.

"We can't fight off an entire army in this place," Hougan said, scooping up the papers.

"I think this may be designed for that exact purpose, actually." Grey studied the gatling guns at the corners of the tower with new interest.

"Even if we could kill everyone, we'd never make it out," Hougan said. "Rusval, what are you doing?"

Iosif had opened up the safe. "Is just metal plates here, sir," he said. The plates were large and thin, but otherwise unremarkable. He shook his head. "I… not understand, sir.

Hougan chewed his lip a moment. "Nobody locks up something unimportant. Bring them anyway."

"Yes sir." There was a leather satchel in the safe that seemed well-suited to the task. Iosif slid the discs into it and slung it over his shoulder.

"Across the bridge!" Grey shouted at them.

Hougan ran and Iosif jogged. Grey actually started to retract the bridge when they were three fourths across it. Hougan cleared the gap with ease, but Iosif, though the gap was small, landed on the very edge and nearly fell backwards with the weight of the disks in his pack.

"Damnit." Hougan grabbed him by the scruff of his neck and hauled him forward. "You can't…" A further clanging at the gate made him look over. "Never mind. Deal with it later!"

The vault door swung open. The guards outside rushed in, weapons at the ready. "Lieutenant Vanburen? Sergeant Reynolds?"

"Man down! Man down!"

One of the guards caught sight of Hougan and Iosif. "There they are!" he shouted, whipping his gun around to bear.

Hougan's pistol barked three times. The soldier collapsed, but already the other guards were turning around to face them, the muzzles of their rifles like gaping holes.

Then the gatling guns opened fire.

Grey's fire ripped into the guards' completely unprotected flank, cutting down three quarters of them before they even knew what was happening. Hougan finished off the few survivors as they ducked for cover.

"On!" Hougan roared, running for the door. "Quickly!"

A few stragglers were still trying to make it back through the vault door, presumably to close it. Hougan shot one, leapt over his body and clubbed the other on the head. "Hurry!" he shouted to Iosif.

Iosif waved. He was feeling a certain tightness in his chest. *Not now.* He thought. *Not now.*

Grey ran past him through the entrance. There was gunfire, shouts, a small explosion. Then silence. Iosif finally hobbled over the vault threshold to see Grey and Hougan amidst a few scattered corpses. He gulped. This was already worlds beyond the Coastal Defense Archives.

Both men were looking at the thick metal doors just beyond the guard post. "Those will stay locked until the vault closes, it seems," Grey said.

"Not forever," Hougan said. His hand was clutched to his side; red was spreading across his white shirt front. "Even if no one sounded the alarm, they're going to send a relief to this station soon. And our boat is going to be leaving in…" He checked his watch. "…ten minutes."

"We don't have a lot of options, Perry," Grey said.

"…wait…" Iosif managed to gasp out. "…one… option…" He gestured, almost desperately, at the side booth he had noticed before. "Sub… trolley."

The men looked at him, then at the booth, then back at him. "What do you mean, Rusval?"

Iosif stumbled to the booth and through the doorway. Hougan and Grey followed him. There, as he had guessed, was a control box, next to a narrow trench. Down in the trench, two narrow rails of metal could be seen.

Despite the tightness in his chest, Iosif grinned. "…sub… trolley," he said, grasping the control box terminal and fumbling with the cover. "Is… waycar. …is train."

Hougan still looked puzzled, but Grey's face cleared. "I should have guessed. Naturally they need a way to transport the prisoners to the subs quickly and discreetly, if their presence here is such a secret." He came to stand alongside Iosif. "This should run down to the docks."

"But they said the train is locked out until the doors open," Hougan said, finally grasping the idea. "How can we…"

"…o… o… over… ride." Iosif gasped, eyes scanning desperately over the control box. He was aware of another danger—the growing tightness in his chest.. "Sh… should… be…

Both men looked at him in alarm. "Take it easy, Rusval," Hougan said. "Deep breaths. Relax."

There was no time to relax. There was no time to take it easy. The waycar must be being kept out by a more mechanical safeguard; there was nothing in the control box. He saw, out of the corner of his blackening vision, bars locked over the trolley's tunnel exit. The hinges. There must be a catch on the hinges...

He let go of the box and stumbled toward them, but his joints were not answering. He fell to his hands and knees, gasping, desperately, for air. Hougan and Grey were both shouting, grabbing at him...

Not now... not now...

The last thing he saw was the metal bars over the trolley entrance.

CHAPTER 10

1::384902::4893

General Ramsford,

I am quite aware of the nature of this catastrophe. I am also fully aware of whose fault it is. Did you honestly not recognize the names they gave? Despite my frequent memos? You were confronted with Security Threats 1 and 2, one of them the least duplicitous infiltrator in the entire history of Black Chamber, and you sent them directly into the most secure section of the base?

You may count yourself fortunate that the grubs had been removed, and that currently the Dragon's Teeth project is at such a critical phase of implementation. It gives you an opportunity to redeem yourself. I shall count on your support when General Winters makes his decision. In the meantime, I have dispatched more Dragon operatives to assist you. Rely on their expertise, as clearly your own is so incredibly lacking. I will attend to this gross mishandling on your part.

0::000000::0000

Iosif woke up to the gentle rocking of the boat and a pounding in his head. There was, he realized gradually, a great thrumming noise as of engines, and he was lying on a thin blanket, which just barely kept out the chill of the metal beneath.

"Good, you're up," Hougan grunted, sitting a few feet away against the wall. "Now I don't need to work out how we're going to carry a comatose kid out of here."

Iosif sat up, feeling his head. "Sir?" The two of them were resting in a small metal room—no, container, Iosif realized, looking at the sloping, rusted walls. There was also a gentle rocking, which he recognized from the fishing boat.

"Decommissioned aerial bomb shell," Hougan said, noting his gaze. "Tried them in the war but they weren't much use. Dangest thing for the boat to be shipping. They must be taking them to the shipyards for scrap."

"So… we got to boat?" Iosif asked.

Hougan nodded. "Should make port in an hour." He winced and felt at his side. "Which should be fun, when we get to that part."

"How?" Iosif asked. Now that he was looking, he could see that Hougan's left side was bound up with thick bandages, marked with deep red blotches of blood. His right hand, also, was nearly entirely wound in bandages.

"Reynold's keys." Hougan shifted a little. "Grey had grabbed them, remember? You needed to insert them through a slot on the control box in order to activate the override. From there it was a straight shot to the docks."

"The others?" Iosif asked.

"Another shell, just next door." Hougan jerked his thumb to indicate. "These things can barely fit three at a time."

Iosif was about to ask about "three" when there was a rapping on the wall, and Grey slid in through the hatch in the side. "Kilroy is taking watch," he said. "So far no sign of anything wrong. There hasn't even been a signal from the island."

"Guard shift must not change for a while, then." Hougan said. "And it'll probably take them a while to get the doors open."

"They might not want to." Grey dropped to a crouch. "It seems even the other soldiers there aren't supposed to know about that room."

"Mm." Hougan grunted, then grinned. "Been searching for that place for years, and suddenly the enemy walks me right in. That's rich."

"What is… that place?" Iosif asked, feeling at his head. "Why… special? How you know it?"

Hougan and Grey exchanged glances. "I told you how I became Director of the Postal Department—why they think I'm insane," Hougan said, leaning forward.

Iosif nodded.

"The facility I mentioned? The one I mentioned in my report, that I had the pictures of that got lost in the mail?" Hougan said. "It looked just like that bowl place we found. Only the one I found was on Ellis Island, and it wasn't… completely… empty."

Grey glanced at Hougan, then began to speak. "Perry and I were part of the task force sent to liberate the island from the Zimmerman partisans in 1919," Grey said "It was completely Perry's idea, and the top brass were against it. But no one had really dealt with a situation quite like this before—hostages, terrorists and so forth, so they couldn't come to a decision. Finally Perry took me and a few other agents and we did the assault anyway."

"It went pretty well, all things considered," Hougan said. "We went through the place pretty systematically. We rescued the hostages, spiked the guns, sunk their boats… we were basically doing mop-up when I caught sight of Zimmerman and went running after him. It was crucial to get him; the man had been obsessed ever since he lost his job. If we didn't catch him, he'd be back with more men. So I chased him, and we went dodging through the hallway, until we somehow ended up in… that room."

Hougan shrugged suddenly. "Or a room that looked exactly like it. Bigger, perhaps, or deeper. I didn't study it extremely closely, Zimmerman and I were playing cat-and-mouse around it the whole time, and when I finally managed to plug him in the chest, he returned the favor by putting a slug in my right shoulder that sent me falling over back into the pit. I hit my head against something—" Hougan felt the back of his skull in memory, "— and everything went black."

"We could not find the director—or special agent, he was then—anywhere," Grey said. "Before we could do a thorough search of the island, the navy took possession of the island and we were ordered back to Washington. They ruled Agent Hougan either dead or taken prisoner."

"I woke up in a cell," Hougan said. "You saw the sort, there— more like cages than anything. Small, barely big enough for me; with only bars over the top; no privacy whatsoever. Normally, anyway. I wasn't a prisoner; I'd smashed through the bars and into the cell when I'd fallen into the bowl. I was pretty badly beaten up." Hougan frowned. "I would have died there, if I'd been alone."

"And then there… there just appeared this… small red man." Hougan shook his head. "I've tried, so many times, to think about how to describe him, but… He was the height of a small child, but he was wrinkly all over and had a great bushy beard that hung to his waist. He was wearing a rough sort of coveralls, but his skin was absolutely deep cherry red, like a man who drinks too much. But he was… skinny. So, so skinny. He looked like he hadn't eaten in a while."

"We've combed through the employee records multiple times." Grey looked at Iosif. "No such person was ever assigned to Ellis Island. Nor was there anyone like that among Zimmerman's partisans."

"I owe that man my life," Hougan said. "He tended to me, mended my bones, brought me food and drink. Never spoke a word the whole time. Then one day, when I was nearly recovered and he was getting me some food, he suddenly looked up, toward the lip of the bowl, and his eyes got very wide. He leaned in close to me, and whispered: 'Remember us.'"

There was a short silence. Iosif was seeing, in his mind, the small message he'd discovered so long ago, hidden in the screwdriver that started everything. *Help us.* "What… he mean?"

"I've been trying to figure that out ever since." Hougan slumped back against the wall. "All I can remember after that is dark shapes and a sharp pain on the back of my head."

"We found Perry wandering around downtown New York," Grey said. "He told us about the facility and the small man, but he couldn't tell us how he'd gotten to the city or what had happened."

"I knew how crazy it sounded." Hougan's mouth had a determined look about it. "So the same night they found me, I broke out of the hospital and went back to Ellis Island, with a camera. The place was still a mess, and security was all over the place. It took some doing, but I found the room again, and I took pictures. I had them developed and put them together in a packet along with my report. I sent both to my superior at Black Chamber." Hougan shrugged. "You know the rest."

"Apart from the addition that when we tried to find the room again, the week after, it had completely disappeared—replaced with a maze of offices," Grey said.

"Ah." Iosif's mind was still working on a different puzzle. "But… 'Remember us?'"

"It implies a larger body of people than the old man," Grey said. "Which would make sense, in a room of that size." A glance toward Hougan. "His focus on 'remember' and not 'save' or 'rescue' means he must've expected to die soon. Beyond that, the meaning is obscure."

Hougan gave a little wave. "The best theory we've come up with is that Public Works was doing experiments—is doing experiments—with genetics. At the time, Ellis Island had a pretty impressive genetics laboratory set up, supposedly for screening immigrants. And the war had just recently ended, so there were still a lot of war projects fighting for funding. That old man—" Hougan raised a finger, "—could lift me like a ragdoll, could easily navigate in the darkness, and was low enough to the ground to avoid gunfire. Someone like that—an army of someones like that—could've broken the lines at Verdennes a lot quicker."

"The idea is incredibly illegal, and almost fantastical." Grey shook his head. "Genetics... we barely understand it. It would take generations to breed a specific species of man. But... given what we saw today..."

"That lieutenant was not natural." Hougan glanced at Grey. "He has to have been part of Dragon's Teeth."

"Sergeant Reynolds as well." Grey nodded, staring at the wall in thought. "Both of them, inhumanly-strong, glowing eyes..." "My eyes..." Iosif had to know. "...they look like that?"

"No." Grey shook his head without looking at Iosif. "Your eyes... they're more reflective, like headlights. Their eyes were lit from within, like... burning coals."

"I cannot remember the old man having eyes like that. In any case, the program seems to have come a long way from a dying bearded old man," Hougan observed.

"Dragon's Teeth is genetics program?" Iosif was struggling to keep up. "For army?"

"Officially it's a cross-department military-enhancement program designed to increase the overall effectiveness of our armed forces." Grey nodded. "But reports of its implementation in Black Chamber have been... disturbing. Still there are talks of it being expanded into the armed forces also."

"So that's the conspiracy." Hougan rubbed his nose. "Tampering with the mail is conspiracy on its own, of course, but… I'll admit this is getting a lot more complicated than I initially thought. Things keep popping up. Hopefully, those discs can shed some light on it."

"We still have them?" Iosif asked.

Hougan nodded to the left. The bag was slumped out on the floor, with the metal plates stacked haphazardly across them. "Blast if I know what they are, but for all we went through, they'd better have some *incredible* information."

Actually they didn't get back to the APD until late the next day. The boat docked in Mclellanville, miles from Fort Sumter, but Hougan insisted they walk out of the city, holding that they'd gone through too much to get disks that they would be unable to hide. Iosif had never appreciated, before, how long it actually took to walk someplace. Once in the outskirts, they found a friendly farmer who was willing to use his tractor (it ran on some bizarre sort of oil-based fuel, which Iosif had never seen before but was given cruelly little time to examine) to drive them to the waycar station in North Santee, where they were able to take a waycar back to Pittsburgh.

The others quickly excused themselves to their rooms, but Iosif, who'd had perhaps more rest on the way back, went to lock the discs away in the vault (and take another quick peek under the tarpaulin to see if anyone had messed with his work) before heading to his workshop. There would be an enormous backlog of machining requests from around the plant, he knew, and he wanted to get started on them right away. Several steam lifts had broken down, the elevator in the administrative center was making funny noises, but top priority had to go to the heating problem in the engineering department.

The engineers were the only people ever allowed inside the Automated Sorting Engine, and only then to perform any necessary checks or maintenance. This meant that according to protocol, their requests had automatic priority. It also meant, unfortunately, that their wing was way at the back of the Postal Front Office building, where the vault door leading to the Sorting Engine was. It wasn't a huge walk, but it was more than Iosif had been hoping for.

Unlike most of the building, the Engineering department was clean and well lit, with cushioned carpet and cushioned chairs. The walls were tiled in their official certificates from the Carnegie Federal Engineering Institute. There were desks, but for the moment all the engineers seemed to be occupied at the far end, bending around a table. Iosif hurried over. "You have heating problem, sirs?"

One of the engineers, an older man with greying temples, swung round, flask in hand. "Ah, the little Machinist!" he barked. "About time! We've been freezing up here for days! Can't very well create the future if we're freezing, now can we? Well?"

"Yes sir." Iosif tried not to stare at the playing cards spread out on the table. "Where is problem?"

"In the calculating room," the older man said, turning around. He started to walk, and Iosif followed him. "Blasted things around here… always breaking. Put in a maintenance request, but our heating system is *apparently* done through a contractor. Fool decision if you ask me. Private contractors aren't worth horseapples. You hear about that accident in the hotel? That was a private contractor that installed that 'elevator' thing that crashed." He gave a snort. "That business is finished, mark my words."

Iosif blinked. He had seen a letter from his business partner, but hadn't had time to check it. His heart sank a little—he hadn't been in it for the money, but at the same time—money *was* awfully nice.

The room they came into was large, nearly twice the size of the entire office for the Postal Enforcement Division. This, though, featured large, metallic cabinets, decorated with numbers and letters, which paper was churning through at an alarming rate. Iosif followed the man through the rows of cabinets, trying not to stare around him too much.

"There," said the engineer, stopping. "That's my desk. And it's my desk because there's a heat vent right below it, so it's the only decent place to work in this freezing building. Except the *heat* isn't working, and *hasn't* been working for days now, so that's all gone to shit."

"I see." Iosif was trying not to look at the large metallic block next to the desk—roughly the size of an icebox. He could not possibly fathom why the engineers would store an icebox next to a typewriter, and why it would have a steam line running to it. It was puzzling, and wonderfully enticing as a result.

The engineer was not satisfied. He glared at Iosif. "Well? What do you intend to do about it?"

"Yes, of course." Iosif shook his head, returning to the task at hand. "I take look," he said, and got down under the desk to see the vent in question. A few minutes' work had the screws off, and after that diagnosis was easy. "There." Said Iosif, removing the dead rat from the pipe and stowing it in his toolbox. "Now should work."

"Is that all it was?" The engineer stared at the rat. "Damn, I could have done that. Thank you, young man."

"No problem." Iosif dusted his hands, again trying not to look at the metal box.

Apparently he was not quite successful. "Ah, interested in the Babbage engines, are you?" The engineer seemed gratified by his interest. "Marvelous things. Let me show you how they work."

Sitting down at his desk, the greying engineer gestured to him. "A typewriter, you observe. But notice that the paper—" He pointed at the sheet of paper, spread on a roll at the head of the desk, "—is in fact being fed from a different machine. Now:" He began to tap keys out on the machine.

Sq_rt(5729)

He pressed another button and before Iosif's eyes, the typewriter started to print its own numbers.

72.65672714897087

The engineer looked up at Iosif. "Impressive, eh? No need for abacus or even a slide rule. Absolutely brilliant. Then there's this." Again he typed on the keyboard.

Cos(56)

Again the typewriter spat out.

0.85322010772

The engineer looked at Iosif but seemed a little disappointed at his expression.

"Sorry…" Iosif blinked. "'Cos' is…"

The engineer sighed. "Oh of course. Machinist." He coughed. "'Cosine' is an expression of the alternate over the hypotenuse. Which means in this case, at this angle 56, the alternate over the hypotenuse is .85, which means if I know either the alternate OR the hypotenuse…" He trailed off. "Well. The point is, we used to have to look up these figures in enormous books. This little beauty actually stores them inside. And that's not all. Here." Again he bent over the typewriter.

Ref(file(R://Higgins/Doc/bignose.doc))

The typewriter again chattered into life, but it seemed to be doing something very different now. Instead of numbers, it was printing out lines and dots, forming a pattern…

Iosif's eyes suddenly got very wide.

"A trifle juvenile, I will admit, but the potential is fascinating." The engineer was clearly trying to suppress a smile. "One of the younger engineers made it. Oh, there was one remarkable one we had last year… One moment…"

Getting up from his desk, the engineer went over to the locker against the walls. Unlocking it with a simple key, he opened it on a row of shelves.

Shelves stacked with very familiar thin metal discs.

"Here." The engineer said, picking one up and turning around. "Johnson did this absolutely fascinating depiction of Charlie Chaplin with…"

Iosif was nowhere to be seen.

❦

The following night, Hougan and the others followed Iosif into the engineering wing.

"Babbage engines." Grey eyed the devices with interest. "The very pinnacle of American technology. Absolutely groundbreaking."

"Would you by chance know who invented them, Philip?" Kilroy sounded genuinely curious.

Snorky snorted. "It'd be Babbage, right?"

"…actually Babbage was the theorist who proposed the model that they're supposedly based on," Grey said. He paused for a few moments. "I… do you know, I don't think I've ever heard who actually realized the vision. Edith, you used to work with them, did you…?"

"No, never." Kilroy shook her head. "That's why I asked. It came up with the typists once and we realized none of us knew who had invented them."

Grey made a sputtering noise. "But that hardly seems possible. They're the wonder of the age, they've revolutionized industry…!"

"Really." Hougan picked up the top paper off a pile of printouts and turned it to show Grey. Iosif couldn't see all of it, just the head of a very pretty girl winking.

"Damn." Snorky sounded impressed.

"Of course." Kilroy sighed. "What are we here for, again?"

Iosif coughed. "This way."

Iosif hadn't actually seen how the discs were used, but it wasn't hard to work out. There was a slot at the front, with a small latch. He folded back the latch and slid the disc in, then folded the latch back into place. There was a series of rapid clicks from the device, then silence.

Iosif stood, but Kilroy was already at the typewriter. "If I may," she said, turning to look at him. "As Grey mentioned, I have worked with these before."

Iosif shrugged. The typing portion of it did not greatly interest him.

Kilroy began to type.

R://dir

    Supply12-2-54.doc

    Supply12-3-54.doc

    Supply12-4-54.doc

    Supply12-5-54.doc

    ...

"What's that series of dots at the end?"

"It means there are more documents further down. Probably of the same sort." Kilroy frowned. "This seems to be a record of supply accounts. Let me access one..."

open Supply12-2-54.doc

Instantly the paper began to churn through the typewriter, different numbers, columns, figures.

Grey picked it up. "It's a shipping manifest … parts, hardware, sheet metal, tools, food …" He frowned. "'Odd things to bring to a prison."

"There's an outgoing section too." Hougan said, his voice rising just a bit. "'Parts and technical equipment,' it says. And 'Grubs', again."

"The mutants, perhaps?" Grey said.

"Could be." Hougan agreed. "Not a lot to glean from these. Try one of the other ones."

Iosif ejected the disc and picked up another. He ran his fingers over the metal surface as he put it in … it had a curious feel to it. Something was strange about the texture. He picked up another to examine as the others continued to work on the computer.

"Occupancy list. What's that supposed to mean?"

"Try it."

The paper chattered through the typewriter, the typeset clacking noisily.

13-792834	102	07-30-27
04-024813	103	05-14-31
13-791494	104	07-30-27
09-184492	105	11-04-12
15-019349	106	09-22-19
09-831400	107	11-04-12

The paper continued to spew out paper. Hougan grabbed the end and looked through the list. "Not very helpful." He frowned.

"Thas a prison registry," Snorky said, looking over his shoulder. "These ones are prisoner SID's, these others here are for cells."

"Yes." Hougan nodded. "But no names. Nothing to actually work with."

"It could be somewhat useful," Grey said, reading a lower portion of the paper spool. "I see several distinct groups of SID's, here. They roughly correspond with some distinct groups of dates. They must have particular groups of these people that they move about at regular intervals. And of course, the amount of cells gives us an idea of the size and extent of the program."

"I think... let me see." Kilroy tapped a few keys on the typewriter:

13-792834

The engine made a succession of rapid clicking noises.

Retrieving...

Record:	*13-792834*
Cell:	*102*
Class:	*S*
Point of Origin:	*America*
Date of Acquisition:	*11-09-22*

Date of Transfer:	*07-30-27*
Date of Exit:	*09-21-33*
Notes:	*Fort Meade acquisition. Initially diagnosed with rickets by examining doctor Sven Farfield. Sub-par performance; several major incidents reported. To be kept in isolation if possible.*

"A data profile." Grey picked up the paper. "This is absolutely fascinating."

"Date of Exit—that'd be yesterday, hey? When they transferred all the... whatever was in there." Snorky waved.

"You can do this with all the records?" Hougan said.

"Presumably." Ms. Kilroy nodded. "Shall I try another?"

Hougan nodded.

09-184492

Retrieving...

Record:	*09-184492*
Cell:	*105*
Class:	*C*
Point of Origin:	*Germany*
Date of Acquisition:	*03-09-94*

Date of Transfer:	*11-04-12*
Date of Exit:	*09-21-33*
Notes:	*Ellis Island acquisition. Initial Examination completed by Dr. Timothy Rickenbacker; pronounced fully healthy. No issues noted with performance.*

"Timothy Rickenbacker…" Hougan frowned. "The name sounds familiar…"

"It does," Grey said. "Let me quickly check our files on Ellis Island to see if there's a connection there."

"Good work," Hougan said, as Grey ran off. "We'll have to print out a fuller accounting later. For now, let's see what's in the next one… Rusval? What's with you?"

Iosif had put on his glasses, and was holding the disk between himself and the lone gaslight they'd lit, squinting at the clear metal surface. He was pretty sure he'd worked it out. "Holes." He indicated. "Also groves." When held up to the gaslight, he could see fine rays of light shining through. That's what had made it feel so strange—it wasn't a smooth piece of metal, it was pockmarked with infinitesimally small holes. Thinner than pin-pricks, really, you probably couldn't see them even with the light if you weren't looking at the right angle… he looked up and realized everyone was staring at him.

"Sorry," he said, and inserted the disc. This time, though, there was not the usual series of dutiful clicks. Instead, the typewriter made an unhappy clacking noise.

Input password?

"What?"

Kilroy frowned. "Oh dear. I've seen this a few times. We need to type in a particular passcode to view the files."

"You're kidding." Hougan looked at her incredulously.

"These machines are quite remarkable, sir."

"A code... try Fort Sumter." Snorky suggested.

Kilroy seemed annoyed by this suggestion, but she typed it in.

>>*Fort Sumter*

Password incorrect

Input password?

"Dragons Teeth." Hougan suggested.

Password incorrect

"Reynolds," Snorky said.

Password incorrect

"What about—"

"Can you gentlemen please just admit none of you have any idea what the password is?" Kilroy snapped.

"Why, we got sometin' better to do?" Snorky said.

"This is a high-security closely guarded data disc," Kilroy said. "I highly doubt the password is going to be something blindingly obvious."

"Would the guard at the prison have known the password?" Hougan frowned.

"He would have had to," Kilroy said. "But we can't very well ask him now, can we?"

"Is there factory default?" Iosif said. The others looked at him. "Like on safe," he said. "Safe always come from factory with default setting. Perhaps Babbage engine is same?"

Kilroy sighed. "You do not *understand*. The Babbage engine isn't the safe. The disc is. And no, there's no default setting on these discs, they aren't encoded at a factory, they're encoded on these machines. The best we can hope for is that there's a universal password that all the guards are required to use."

"Hm." Hougan sighed. "Well. Put it away for now, then. Try the next disc."

"It's going to be more of the sa…"

"Sir." Grey came hurrying up. "I have something." He dropped the file on the desk. "Timothy Rickenbacker was one of the attendant doctors in the Genetics Lab on Ellis Island, prior to the Zimmerman incident. His name came up in our investigation."

"Well, that fits." Hougan opened the file and frowned at the daguerreotype of the man. "Unfortunately, it doesn't tell us anything we don't already know."

"Hang on, I know that guy." Snorky cocked his head.

Everyone looked at him. "What?"

"Well, I dunno any Tim Rickenwhatever, but that's Shifty Pete." Snorky picked up the paper. "Backstreet sawbones. Did sum rigging on the side. Hadda place in Detroit. He patched me up from a gunshot wound one time."

"Would you be able to find him again?"

Snorky shrugged. "If he's in the same area."

Hougan seemed to think for a moment. "All right," he said. "Get a good sleep tonight. In the morning, you, Kilroy, and Rusval leave to track him down."

"Already?" Snorky blinked. "Geez, boss, usually ya give us a little down time between…"

"We need to move fast," Hougan said. "Frankly I'm not sure I should give you tonight. I want you guys to find this man and see if he knows anything. Particularly about the password to the files."

Snorky looked puzzled. "Boss, I got ways of makin' people talk, and Kilroy's a psycho-whatever," he said. "But you's the expert interrogator, so why not you instead of…" He hesitated awkwardly.

"Why I go along?" Rusval asked.

"To keep you safe," Hougan said. "You realize we're running on borrowed time right now? Fort Sumter was the biggest job we've ever done. There are going to be reprisals for that." He stood up. "So while Grey and I handle that, you three are going to be on the run."

"Stay safe."

CHAPTER 11

2::324523::4201

Director Hougan,

Of course I remember you! You were instrumental in returning service to the island, and indirectly responsible for the final departure of the military garrison which had so impeded our own work. I thus consider myself indebted to you on multiple counts, and am very glad to have a chance to repay it in some way.

Much to my regret, however, it will have to be in some other way, as it seems there is little I can do for you here. I have consulted the records, and the name "Rusval" appears extremely infrequently, and then only in places that exclude the parameters you describe. It is an Eastern European name, perhaps originating from the Baltic States. Such immigrants were part of the "Germanic Invasion" of the 1870's, though that is, of course, a misnomer in this case. They were not an insignificant portion, but I cannot find anyone of the name "Rusval" of the proper age and background.

Alternatives exist, naturally. It is possible that your man immigrated to the Americas prior to the establishment of Ellis Island. However, the majority of Baltic immigrations took place after 1871. Therefore I think it is much more likely that your man was a stowaway. Cases of illegal immigrants are well-documented, the most famous being the Tiny Thirty. Of course larger immigrants would not have packed themselves in quite so tightly; there are plenty of instances of more normal-sized laborers found in cargo containers. Speculation abounds that Carnegie sponsored and funded many of these 'stowaways' in hopes of creating a workforce with no recourse to legal regulations or pay rates, which helped him break the labor disputes of 1880.

I'm rambling. I apologize. There is a third option, but I hesitate to mention it. I have, at times, noticed that our records, which were transferred to datadisc three years ago, have strange omissions. Some times even a name that appeared last year will vanish from the records. Personally I do not trust all these new-fashioned appliances; I do not find them as reliable as paper (but it must be admitted they are easier to search through.) Nonetheless I will have some of our men pore through the paper records for you, and see if our datadiscs are again lacking.

Thank you for giving me this chance to repay you! I only wish I could do more.

Jose Cortez

Director of Immigrant Affairs

1::214958::7764::328

"**T**his pisses me off."

"Surely in your past life you learned the value of a hasty getaway?" Kilroy asked.

"Well, sure." Snorky shrugged, carelessly sprawled over the opposite seat of the waycar. "I got no problem with no hasty getaways. I gotta problem with some otha guy takin' the heat for me."

"Loyalty. From you?"

Snorky snorted. "Just rubs me the wrong way."

Kilroy snorted in turn and looked out the window. "I'll confess I'm not particularly excited about having to meet with your business associates."

"Aw c'mon. They're no worse than me."

"Exactly."

"Look, Edith." Snorky spread his hands. "It's Detroit. Westinghouse's place collapsed, Carnegie bought out General Motors... bought out half ta town. And then the Feds shut him down. It's a big town with no jobs. Everybody's gotta eat. What's a guy supposed to do?"

"Make their own way. *Do* something with themselves." Ms. Kilroy had a sickeningly sweet tone to her words. "Or so that's what people have told *me*. I understand it's what America is all about."

Snorky looked at her. "Ya gonna be like this the whole trip?"

"Possibly." Kilroy sighed and pressed her fingers to the bridge of her nose. "I apologize. I didn't sleep well last night. This man, Shifty Pete... why do you call him that?" she asked. "Was he reliable? Is he likely to sell us out?"

"What's he gonna say? 'Hey, these characters are goin' after government secrets?' Everyone knows that already." Snorky spread his hands. "Anyway, no. Shifty Pete's more terrified of Feds than any man alive. His eyes, they do this twitch back-and-forth thing…" Snorky shrugged. "That's why we calls him Shifty Pete."

"You called him a 'rigger'…?"

"Sorta. Not really. Kind of a side job with him," Snorky said. "A rigger's kinda like a safe-cracker, ya know, 'cept they handle Federal Appliances, not safes. Sorta business I was in, ya don't worry so much about pryin' open the cover on a mail machine or whatever. But of course most of us boys didn't know nothin' about gears and switches. Riggers, those guys could open doors, shut off mail machines, break down waycars—the best could even hack waycars, from what I heard, make 'em go wherever they wanted to."

"Did any of them know anything about Babbage engines?" Kilroy asked.

"Not that I ever heard."

"Hmph." Kilroy looked away. "These people… if they were so talented, why not do that legally? Go to school, become engineers?"

Snorky snorted. "Ya ever tried applyin' to the Federal Engineering Institute, dame?"

"And you have?"

"I talk to guys," Snorky said. "Ain't no way of getting in unless you's some major egghead with a real swell top-dollar education. And unless you's in, you's not allowed to touch nothin'. So what's a rigger supposed to do, hey?"

Kilroy sighed and looked down. "You've been very quiet, Joseph. Everything all right?"

"Is fine." Iosif nodded. His fingers were splayed out against the control box. *Click. Whirrr. Tremor. ClickCLICK.*

In truth, he was thinking about his project down in the vault. With the professor's diagrams, he'd more or less worked out the aerodynamics (as they called it) of the alien's ship. There were a few parts of it that didn't make sense—which implied that the professor's model was probably inaccurate—but the principles were clear enough and he could see how the airship was launched and steered. Even the controls seemed fairly intuitive—when you got into the cockpit, there were two rings on either side of you, that you could fit your arms through to easily grasp the handles beyond. (Well, Iosif imagined it would have been easy for the alien. His arms were a little too short to make it comfortable.)

What he couldn't figure out was how to *power* it. There was no boiler, no air compression tank—not even fuel cells like the sort the farmer had used on its tractor. There were a lot of other things that he didn't understand, and he didn't want to actually start taking them apart.

"Is it anything to do with the Fort Sumter mission?" Ms. Kilroy asked. "From what I heard, you and the others got into some pretty brutal dealings, even by our standings."

"Grey said ya ripped your handcuffs clean off," Snorky said, sitting up a bit. "That normal for ya?"

Iosif shrugged. No one had ever remarked on him being particularly strong before. He'd helped out his mother and Mr. Whisterhorn, of course, but he'd always assumed that had more to do with their age than any particular strength on his part.

"Guess that explains the way ya had a death grip on my throat," Snorky said. "And the way ya ripped the sub door off its hinges."

"I wondered how you did that." Kilroy looked over. "Your sub had a rather enormous flaw, Joseph. There were no pipes to pump the airlock clear of water. I could fill it with water, easily enough but… the suction should have made opening the door nearly impossible."

Iosif nodded. "I fix in next model."

"That is not the…" Kilroy sighed.

"Ya got some freaky strength, kid," Snorky said. "Where'd you work before this again?"

"Watch shop," Iosif said.

∞◦∞

"Anything for the little lady?"

"Dry whiskey, straight," Kilroy said.

The man at the other end of the table whistled. "Quite a dame ya got there, Alphonse."

"Not mine, Maroni." Snorky raised his hand. "Really, not mine."

"Kindly do not suggest it again." Kilroy's hand had disappeared into her purse.

"Oh." The man raised an eyebrow. "I take it that kid's not yours either, then?"

"Again, no, and again, how the hell can ya even think that?" Snorky sounded incredulous now. "He even look anything like me?"

Maroni shrugged. "Hey, Mac, I try not ta judge. Maybe ya had a kid that went wandering in a leper colony or something. I dunno. Thought it was weird, never took ya for a family man."

Iosif really wondered about this man. He was dressed simply enough, in a suit with an open shirt collar, and lounged back against the deckchair, but there was a hidden menace to him. Apart from anything else, the fact that he called Snorky "Alphonse" seemed to imply that he was not a friend.

There was also the fact that Snorky himself, who had thrown himself with equal apparent carelessness on the other side of the booth, had drawn his pistol under the table. "Yeah, well, I ain't," he said.

"Glad to get that sorted." Maroni replied. His eyes, which had been lazy, hardened. "So if they ain't 'with' ya, than why *are* they with ya?"

"Workplace associates." Kilroy answered for Snorky. "We're private investigators."

"Like cops?"

Snorky's teeth flashed in a smile. "C'mon, Maroni. What's the only kind of private investigator in this town?"

Maroni chucked at that, but his eyes stayed hard. "Word was ya got caught on a big operation, Alphonse. How's it you's walking around free now and not in a jail somewhere?"

"I was," Snorky answered. "Ended up in a cell with my new boss. Broke us out, and now..." He shrugged. "...match made in heaven, I guess ya could say."

"Some might." Maroni was regarding them narrowly. He leant back. "Always said ya were into too shady of stuff, Alphonse. Told ya to stop with all that illegal stuff."

"Fine, ya don't believe me." Snorky gave a casual wave, his other hand still fixed on his pistol. "So as a perfectly law-abiding citizen who's never harmed a fly in his life, Maroni, do ya know where I can find the equally law-abiding Shifty Pete?"

That changed the hardness in Maroni's eyes. "Pete? Whaddaya want with that old fossil?"

"I gotta have a boil lanced." Snorky shrugged. "What difference does it make?"

"Well, it might." Maroni was still studying them, but with much less hostility now. "Pete's outta the game, Al. Disappeared about three years ago and no one's heard from him since."

"Yeah, that's what Fat Julio said." Snorky nodded. "Any idea as to why?"

Maroni raised an eyebrow. "Making the rounds, aintcha? Who knows why that crazy old coot would do anything?"

"Well, *you's* might," Snorky said. "I mean, why do ya think I went to you after Fat Julio? It ain't for ya sunny disposition, and it definitely ain't for the cannoli here." Snorky stabbed at the plate with his free hand. "Ya knew the 'old coot' better than almost anyone. So if he's disappeared, chances are ya'd know why, and ya'd know where."

Maroni grinned. "That ain't bad thinkin', Al. But why would I tell ya?"

"Civic duty as a law-abiding citizen? Bonds of mutual acquaintance? To get me outta here?" Snorky suggested.

"That last one would sound appealing to me." Kilroy murmured.

"Lossa ways to do them things." Maroni said. "I'm guessing ya've got a better offer."

Snorky grimaced and glanced sidelong at Iosif. "Fat Julio also said you's looking for a rigger." Kilroy looked at him sharply, but Snorky kept going. "A good one. Didn't say nothing as to why, though."

Maroni didn't say anything immediately. He gave Snorky a long look. "Mebbe," he said. "Ya know someone?"

✥

"Sorry, kid. It was the only thing I could think of."

Iosif shrugged. They were walking just behind Maroni now, down the alleys of the industrial district. There were no waycar rails down here, and everything was fairly quiet, but it was still hard not to feel unnerved by the four massive men walking a few paces behind them.

"You don't even know what he wants!" Kilroy hissed. "They could be doing a bank job or a gang war or…"

"Lady, I'm guessing whatever they's doing ain't gonna be anywhere *near* as dangerous and illegal as breaking into a Black Site military facility," Snorky said. "Damn, for all the cloak and dagger stuff we do…"

Kilroy growled. "I want it noted that this was all your idea."

"That a promise?" said Snorky, as they pushed through a green-stained door.

"All right," said Maroni, turning aside. "Let's see what ya man can do."

In the middle of the floor was a waycar terminal.

"Had a couple guys in to look at this." Maroni said. "It ain't like the old days, Al, it's hard to find any of the good riggers left." Reaching out, he tapped the terminal, lightly. "Used to be, any fool could figure out how to jury-rig these things so ya didn't have to feed 'em Morgan Dollars all the time. But after that upgrade they all went through in '21, ain't nobody can do nothin' with them anymore."

"Forgive me, but why don't you simply get a Federal Engineer to do it?" Kilroy asked. The men looked at her and she snorted. "I realize I'm new at this, but it can't be that hard to find a corrupt official."

"Boy, she is *really* not ya dame, is she?" Maroni said.

Snorky shrugged. "I told ya."

"And *I* told you not to suggest that again." Kilroy held up a finger.

"You's try bribing somebody on a five-figure salary in a cushy job sometime." Maroni said. "Ya know what kinda jail time treason lands ya?"

"I do, and I have. It's not that hard to bribe someone." Ms. Kilroy crossed her arms.

"I'm sayin' it's not cheap," Maroni said. "Ya tend to get a mixed bag. Some of them engineers specialize in waycars, some of them's specialize in mail machines, some of them's specialize in Babbage engines. 9 times out of 10, ya spend a buncha money bribing one, and it turns out they don't know nothin' about the one thing ya need 'em for." His gaze went to Iosif, and then to Snorky. "Now, ya say this rigger of yours is some sort of miracle worker, huh?"

Snorky shrugged and looked at Iosif. "Whaddaya say, Rusval?"

Iosif looked at the man, then stepped forward, pulling on his eyeglasses. The people who had come before him had already peeled the plating from the machine, leaving the workings naked to be studied.

His first thought was amazement at the intricately fine workings. His second was utter despair at making sense of them. The main block of the terminal was such a mass of wires, switches, levers, and catches, he did not have the first idea where to begin or end. He looked back at Snorky and Kilroy, and the men standing just behind them.

Then he looked back at the terminal and realized that the problem itself was actually childishly simple. The coin slot system was horribly complex, it was true—pins used to sense the size and denomination of the coins, switches to denote the needed value of money and the current placed value, etc., etc. But it was completely separate from the actual terminal system itself. The payment calculator basically was linked to the switchboard and ticket printer by a single catch, which kept the printer from engaging until payment had been made.

Iosif reached in and unscrewed the catch. Just to be sure, he typed in his home destination, and pressed the button.

The paper rattled through the machine. Tiny needles darted in and out through the hard baseboard, and the ticket spat out the front as a sharp blade cut it off at the designed point of entry. At the back of the terminal, a small hook wagged vainly as it tried to signal a rail line that wasn't there.

Iosif turned around and held up the ticket.

The others looked at him. "Ya done?" Maroni seemed incredulous. "How didja...? He pushed Iosif out of the way and typed in his own entry. Again the machine chattered, and again a ticket spat out.

He looked down at Iosif with a very strange expression.

"Was not hard." Iosif shrugged, feeling a little embarrassed. Quite frankly he didn't see what had been wrong with whoever this man had been brought in before.

Maroni looked to Snorky, who smirked, and then back to Iosif. "Kid, if ya ever need a job…"

"I think he's happy where he is," Kilroy said. "Now. Shifty Pete's address?"

∽o∾

The waycar slowed to a stop and the doors slid open. Iosif stepped out before the others and glanced up and down the street. They were on the south end of town, near the meat-packing district.

"Okay, Filterston Street." Snorky looked around the network of alleys. "That'd be … three down and two to the right, he said?"

"Four down and two to the right." Kilroy corrected him, already moving between the buildings. " 'the decrepit old warehouse' were his exact words."

"Why's it always warehouses?"

"Lots of room that can be easily adapted to any particular purpose?" Kilroy shrugged. "Who knows. Let's get moving."

The back streets were a maze, and not nearly so straightforward as Maroni's directions had made it appear. There were fences in the way, and drainage ditches, and at times great steam pipes that seemed to entirely close up the street.

Yet there was always something—some trick, some hidden alcove or unseen door that carried them past the obstacle. Once it took them a solid hour to find the pipe that was actually not fixed in place and could be swiveled out of the way.

"It would have been most helpful if your friend had mentioned this part." Kilroy grumbled, slipping through the crack.

"He's no friend of mine," Snorky said, forcing himself through after her. Then he stopped. "Aw, c'mon, ya gotta be kidding me!"

There was the warehouse they were looking for, right up against the shore of one of the many canals in the meatpacking district.

"We coulda taken a boat?"

"That non-friend of yours could've been *significantly* more helpful." Kilroy frowned.

Iosif, ducking in behind them, had another concern. "Where is lock?" he said. Then he amended that comment. "Where is door?"

The whole front of the warehouse was a collection of loose rubbish, plywood, and pipes piled over a collection of sheet metal and timber, such that it was impossible to tell what opened, and how.

"Mebbe we came around the back?" Snorky suggested.

Kilroy sighed, putting her hands on her hips. "There's not a back to this building. This pathway only reaches to here; there's no way on either of the other sides. There's a door somewhere here. We just need to find a way to unlock it."

Iosif cocked his head. The word jived something in his mind. Looking at it from another angle—if you looked at the warehouse as a box, and the front as the top...

Bending, Iosif pulled up on a piece of sheet metal. It slid up, allowing Iosif to fold the whole portion over. There were a few rods under that, locked in place, which he couldn't get to move, until he checked a panel further down, that he could push in and slide behind a block of wood, revealing some sort of clamp, which when you undid, allowed you to slide out the rods on the other side...

There were several other steps, and a few times Iosif had to go back and do things in a different order, but finally he clicked back a latch, and a large panel in the middle of the warehouse front swung open.

Kilroy watched him with a furrowed brow. "What... was..."

Five gunshots rang out in rapid succession, and all three of them immediately dove to the floor of the warehouse.

"Stay back!" called a quavering voice. "I'm armed!"

Snorky rolled his eye and pulled out his Tommy gun, aiming it well over where the voice was coming from.

Ratatatatatatat!

"...I have a defensible position!" the man called out again.

"Shifty Pete, its Snorky! Ya know, Alphonse?" Snorky called. "Fat Julio's friend? Mario sent us."

"Mario knows better than to send anyone here! And he never could stand you!"

Kilroy looked over. "Mario? Your non-friend Maroni? Sorry, why did you never mention your friend's full name was 'Mario Maroni?'"

"Because he hates that, and we needed a favor," Snorky muttered back.

Kilroy shook her head. "Dr. Timothy Rickenbacker!" she called. "We're from the government! We're here to help you!"

"You'll never take me alive!" The man's voice gained an edge of panic.

Kilroy winced. "We're the Automated Postal Department Enforcement Division!" she called again. "Conducting an internal audit into the Public Works Department! We think you may know something about the Dragon's Teeth program they're implementing, and we'd like to ask you some questions."

"So ask them!"

"I'm face down in a dirty concrete floor, that is *not* how I prefer to hold conversations, thank you!" Ms. Kilroy called back.

"I'm behind a barricade with my gun, and that *is* how *I* prefer to hold conversations!"

Snorky rolled his eyes and, taking off his hat, stuck it on a loose pipe. Slowly, he raised the hat up over the edge of the debris.

A gunshot went off, clipping the edge of the doorway and completely missing the hat. Snorky leapt up, dashed forward, and jumped over the barricade, wrestling the pistol away from the man behind it.

"There," he said, tossing away the revolver. "Now, ya ready ta talk?"

∞○∾

"The Zimmerman Incident was an excuse for me," Dr. Rickenbacker said, some time later. Iosif had found a coffee pot and was fixing some for everyone. "I'd been looking to get out of the program for some time. When Zimmerman's partisans took over and we cleared out, I used the confusion to run away here."

"What is this place, anyway?" Kilroy asked, glancing around. "It's … bizarre."

Iosif had to agree with that. A partially disassembled waycar from nearly ten years ago sat in the corner. Long grasping mechanical arms with strange attachments dangled from the ceiling, while above, gas lights flickered along dedicated lines. The walls were hung with various tools, pipes, and strange assortments of wires. Crowded against the back was a boiler, a workbench, several mechanized tools, a bunk, dusty and stained glass beakers, and what looked like on first glance some sort of metallurgy apparatus. Iosif even thought he caught the glimpse of a vault half-hidden at the back of the shop.

Snorky was poking around the chests and barrels. "Holy crap!" He pulled out a bolt-action gun—Iosif was not familiar with the sort. "Where'd ya find this dinosaur Petey boy? And the others?" He peered into the chest again and popped open another one. "Issat an axe?

"Most of it was here when I arrived." Rickenbacker said. "It's not my place, it … Nigrunir was going to live here."

Kilroy's brow furrowed. "Who?"

"So you don't know about that." Rickenbacker took a sip from the coffee. "Have to admit, that's something of a relief. I really did think you were from Black Chamber."

"You were involved in the Genetics Lab at Ellis Island," Kilroy said. "Screening the immigrants."

"Yes." Rickenbacker nodded. "In retrospect it sounds terrible, but at the time it was seen as a way of pacifying all the people worried about the 'Irish Invasion' or what-not. Of course, what we were really doing was far worse."

"Which was … ?"

Rickenbacker gulped down some more coffee. "You have to understand, I didn't realize what was going on," he said. "I inspected the people they told me to inspect, took samples, looked for diseases, prescribed medications, filed reports. I knew it was strange work, but… I thought I was just helping people."

"What struck you as strange?" Kilroy prompted.

"All my patients," Rickenbacker said. "They were all the same. Short men, with stubby legs and oversized heads. Sometimes short women. All very quiet. All giving one-word answers. Some with skin conditions, bone conditions, eyesight problems—one had scarlet fever, and I recommended he be put in quarantine where I could treat him. I never heard anything more about that one."

Iosif noticed Kilroy throw him an odd look. He wondered why.

Rickenbacker swallowed. "I thought… I don't know. I thought maybe they were just sending me those immigrants because of my work in achondroplasia. Or I thought that all Germans were short. I don't know what I thought… I didn't think enough, that was the problem. I didn't see."

"The experiments?"

Rickenbacker looked up. "They were doing experiments too?"

Kilroy exchanged a glance with Iosif. "We were hoping you could tell us."

"I didn't know anything. Not until Nigrunir." Rickenbacker swallowed again. "He was different than the others. He talked. About all his plans in coming to the New World, where he was going to stay, what he was going to do. And it wasn't until the end, when he asked when they were going to let him go, that I realized that there was something wrong going on."

Kilroy held up a hand. "Let him *go*?"

Rickenbacker nodded. "After that I started to ask around. The immigrants I was examining weren't coming from boats. They were coming from cargo containers in the hold. Stowaways, I thought. But then I wondered why they didn't send them back, or release them. I'd told Nigrunir he'd probably be released soon, and he promised to look me up. But he never showed."

Kilroy's brow was very furrowed indeed, but she said nothing.

"But I still didn't… *really* think anything could be wrong, until the… man came to visit." Rickenbacker shivered. "He asked… too many questions. Too many strange questions. Had I examined the subjects in question? What sort of strength did they have on average? Any notable trends across the data sets? Any differences between men and women? Did they ever mention family? Relatives in the States? Where they might be staying? Had I mentioned my patients to anyone? Did I love my country?" He shivered again. "That last question. Why ask that, unless they'd started to doubt me? Unless they knew my country was doing something significantly wrong?"

"What man?" Kilroy asked. "What was his name?"

"He… didn't give one." Rickenbacker said. He had a strange look on his face.

"What did he look like?"

"I… can't remember." Rickenbacker pressed his hands to his eyes. "That's the worst part. There's this… hole, in my memory. I can see him standing in front of me, I can hear his voice… but I can't remember either. He's just this… shadow. He's in the corner of my eye, and when I turn he vanishes. But I know he's in the room, because I can hear his questions."

"He wasn't a big man?" Kilroy asked. "Tall, dark hair, black suit?"

"No, he… he… I don't remember!" Rickenbacker said. He bit his knuckles. "It's this black horror, in my mind. You know we have these children's stories, about bogeymen. Elves, dwarves, fairies, dragons, genies. And we get older and we learn all about science, about how the world works. We mathematize the darkness and map out the caverns and explore the wilds. And we tell ourselves we know everything. But when I remember myself in the room, with that man… It's like I'm a child again, convinced there's something in my closet or under the bed or in the trees. All my knowledge from med school… it's just words, in that moment."

Slatey was leaning back. Her face was stiff and drawn. "You are speaking of legends, sir," she said. "Myth. Fairy tales."

"I know. I know." Rickenbacker's hands passed away from his eyes and rubbed back his drawn, hollow cheeks. "When I stop to consider it objectively, I know. But it's just… when I remember the event itself…" He shook his head. "There was no staying, after that. Nigrunir had mentioned the address where he was planning to meet his relatives. Once I had the chance—the Zimmerman Incident—I grabbed a rail and ran." He looked around. "And I've been here ever since."

Kilroy and Snorky exchanged glances. "We're looking into something called the Dragon's Teeth program," Kilroy said. "Did that ever come up?"

Rickenbacker considered a moment. "I never heard the name." He shook his head. "But they didn't tell me much. We had a lot of special programs going on… they were experimenting with in vitro fertilization, aviation, environmental monitoring… Some of the soldiers were in special training, I know, and some of them had special privileges in addition to that."

"They wore tinted eyeglasses?" Iosif asked.

Rickenbacker started and looked at him, surprised. "…yes, I think they did."

"Did you ever go to Fort Sumter? Or any other facilities as part of your job?"

Rickenbacker shook his head. "We had particular vessels going to there and other places, but they kept the different facilities tightly compartamentalized."

Ms. Kilroy gave a nod. "And… you left at the time of the Zimmerman incident, so you had no experience with Babbage engines."

"No… we never used them."

"Oh hey." Snorky spoke up suddenly. "Ya wouldn't happen ta know who actually invented Babbage engines, wouldja?"

Rickenbacker blinked at him. "…I guess I just assumed someone named Babbage?"

Snorky *tsk*'d quietly.

"One last thing, Dr. Rickenbacker." Ms. Kilroy said. She pulled a pocketwatch from her jacket. "With your permission, I would like to try something a bit more… unorthodox."

"Aw, Edith…" Snorky said.

"It is my belief it will do no harm, and it might possibly do some good." Ms. Kilroy insisted. "I think you may have been placed under hypnotic suggestion, so that you cannot remember the man's face."

Rickenbacker looked from her to the watch. "You want to try to undo it."

"I want to try to get under it." Kilroy held the watch in her palm. "Hypnosis has been used to great therapeutic effect by various psychologists, and at times accounts of alien abductions have been revealed under hypnosis."

Rickenbacker smiled. "Aliens," he said. "It used to be the elves who stole people. Now it's aliens."

"Will you try it, Dr. Rickenbacker?"

Rickenbacker shrugged. "Why not?" He stretched. "It can hardly worsen the memory."

Ms. Kilroy smiled. Taking hold of the watch chain, she slowly lifted it until the ticking watch dangled at the end, then gave it a little nudge to send it swinging back and forth.

"What I want you to do," she said, in a very mild voice, "is simply keep your eyes on the watch. Just keep your eyes on it. Do not worry about focusing on the watch, do not worry about its surroundings. Just simply watch it. Concentrate on my voice."

This was interesting in a bizarre sort of way, but Iosif had been meaning to look around a bit more in the warehouse, and this seemed as good a time as ever. He got up and began poking around. There was a mail sequencer in the corner—a very odd design, somewhat old-fashioned, but some sort of addition was hooked up to it.

"... You are listening to my voice, are you not? You are getting drowsy now. Your thoughts are beginning to drift away..."

There was a workbench in the corner. Snorky was leaning against it, watching the hypnosis with an irritated look on his face.

"Move please," Iosif said. Snorky looked at him with mild surprise, then got up and moved to the wall. Iosif began to look through the desks.

"Are you in the trance now, Mr. Rickenbacker? Good. You will remain in this trance until I tell you to awaken. Now. Go back to your time at Ellis Island. Are you there now? Good. You are in the room where you received visitors. There is a man there, asking questions. Do you see the man?"

Dr. Rickenbacker's voice became audible. "No, I... yes, I see him... he's standing in front of me, he... his shoes are pointed, made of leather. The floor under them is white tile."

"That's right. Very good. Now go up. What is on his legs?"

"He's wearing... pleated trousers... I think. His... it's a suit, he's wearing, a dark tie... a white shirt... cuff-links..."

"What about his face?"

"I... I don't know. I can't tell, I can't see... it's a... there's nothing there, it...!"

"Very good, very good. It's all right. Let's start again. You mentioned his tie. Focus on the tie. What cloth is it?"

"...polyester, I think. It's tied in an oxford knot."

"Good. What else?"

"It's... loose. His shirt's a bit too big for him, I think."

"Is it loose about his neck?"

"Maybe... I can't see his... it's blurring... maybe... I think."

There was a short silence. "Look at his neck, Dr. Rickenbacker. Look at his head. What do you see?"

"I don't see anything! It's... it's blurry, and... and dark, it's just a shadow, just a... oh!" The pitch of Dr. Rickenbacker's voice suddenly raised to a scream. "Oh! No! No, not... I see... Oh, I see..."

"The eyes!"

Click. Whirr, Tremor, Click. Jerk.

"I pushed too hard too fast." Kilroy frowned. "I should have stuck with what we had."

"What, wears a suit widda black tie?" Snorky scoffed. "That don't tell ya much, does it?"

"Well, 'the eyes' isn't terribly much more helpful," Ms. Kilroy said.

"Whaddaya expect? Hypnosis…" Snorky snorted and looked out the window.

"It's a useful way of lowering inhibitions and mental blocks," Ms. Kilroy said, passing her hands over her face. "Whether it has any inherent effect, the subject's belief in it often has a placebo effect, where they consider themselves less culpable for what they're saying, more able to confront painful memories without fear of the pain." She sighed. "It's… been useful before, but I'll admit it has mixed results."

"Well, Pete's not going to want to see ya for a while." Snorky grunted. "Or me. But that safehouse'a his might make a nice back-up if we need a place ta crash ever." He looked over at Iosif. "What'd ya get, kid? That's quite a satchel."

Iosif opened up the bag. "Found in desk," he said.

Inside were some twenty to fifty 'artifacts' of varying sizes and functions. The scrollwork on them was more evident, and many were grimed with age and rust, but the similarity was still obvious.

Snorky raised his eyebrows. "Well, that oughta cheer the director up."

"Very odd." Ms. Kilroy leaned forward. "They're not the sort of thing Dr. Rickenbacker would want."

"Maybe they came with the place." Snorky shrugged. "Like that other stuff."

Ms. Kilroy looked at him. "We've only found these in government facilities before this. Does that mean that warehouse is an old Black Chamber safehouse?"

Snorky frowned. "They'da found Pete ages ago, if that were the case."

Click. Tremor. Whirrr. Click. Jerk. They'd been picked up by an older model of waycar, where the control box was mounted near the ceiling. Iosif was looking up at it—the workings were so old you could hear the vibrations instead of having to feel them.

"What *did* he say about the warehouse?" Kilroy said. "I didn't think to ask."

Snorky rubbed his chin. "Not much, outside of that patient of his, Nigun-rear or whatever, owning it somehow. Not sure how he could have owned it, though, if he was on his way here still." *CLACK. ClickClickClickclickclickclickclick.*

Cocking his head at the ceiling, Iosif frowned. Something was wrong.

"Yes... Rickenbacker's 'patients.'" Kilroy frowned again. "That... is something we'll have to talk over with the director. If they were 'coming' to America..."

"Maybe these feds had a branch in Germany?" Snorky suggested. "They got a genetics program, don't they?"

"We're not friends with Germany."

"But this'd be before the war, hey?"

"Possibly. But why the questions about 'relatives,' in that—"

"Shh!" Iosif held up his hand suddenly.

... clickclickclickclickclickclickJERKclickclickclickJERKclickcl ick....

"What is it?" Miss Kilroy looked vaguely annoyed.

"Wrong." Iosif responded, listening closely. "Noises wrong."

The other two just looked at him. "I swear kid, I'd feel lucky to understand ya half the time you's talking." Snorky sighed.

"Wrong!" said Iosif, as the truth dawned on him. "Car has been called!"

Snorky blinked, a new expression hardening his face. "What?"

"Wait, he's right." Miss Kilroy glanced out the window, her face alert. "This is Jefferson Street, we shouldn't be going on Jefferson Street."

"Damnit." Snorky hissed, standing up. "And Jefferson so busy right now." Fishing a small crowbar from his jacket, he inserted it in the door. "Right," he said. "We get this open, and scatter. Meet back at the old man's place. Catch a tram if ya can."

"Better if we walk." Miss Kilroy argued. Her gun was already out of her purse.

"You honestly think that'll work for Short Stuff here?" grunted Snorky, already prying at the door. "Damn, they make these doors a lot tougher than ..."

"Wait." Iosif held up a hand. He was staring at the ceiling, thinking. Then he turned to Snorky. "I need to access ceiling panel," he said. "I stand on your shoulders, yes?"

Snorky just stared at him. "What the hell do ya need ..."

"Just go and put him on your damn shoulders!" snapped Miss Kilroy.

Grumbling, Snorky knelt in the narrow car and let Iosif clamber onto his shoulders. When he stood up, it brought Iosif face-to-face with the ceiling.

Iosif ran his fingers over the surface and smiled. Up close, it was easier to make out the scrollwork on the pattern of the metal, the interlocking four circles within the larger circle. And there, exactly as he thought, were the imperceptible bumps, the infinitesimal crack.

Out came the eyepiece. A moment's scan showed him the screws, a small adjustment revealed the star pattern on their tops. He fished in his coat and produced the screwdriver, clicked the star into position, and began to work at the tiny dots.

"What ya up to up there?" Snorky muttered, twisting to try and see.

"Hold still!" Iosif snapped.

The screws were not very deep, and were off in a second. Iosif placed his fingers to the crack and felt. There was no give if he pushed it forwards, backwards, or leftwards, but when he tried to move it right, ah, it slid naturally off into his hands. Before him lay the naked machinery, nestled in the bed of the ceiling.

It was beautiful. A neatly interlocking system of wires and catches so wonderfully complex and precise, for a moment Iosif felt truly lost in its glory. Absentmindedly, he let the access panel fall.

He felt his mount give a small jerk as it clattered to the ground. "Shit, kid, are ya takin' the tram apart? Are ya nuts?"

"Rusval, what are you doing?" Miss Kilroy hissed. "They're about to pull us over, if they find you taking apart a federal appliance..."

"Quiet." Iosif ordered, his mind elsewhere. All the switches had little wires attached to them leading back toward the box. Used for the ticket, certainly, but if this had been called...

Aha. There it was, a large clamp-like switch that settled over the others and made them click to its orders. *Its* wire came not from the box, but instead led outward, to the track and the police station calling it.

Snorky shifted under him again. "Oh shit."

"Iosif, the police station is up ahead and there are officers outside waiting." Miss Kilroy was using her calm voice. "If you have a plan, I would suggest you use it now. If you are merely entertaining your perverse curiosity in machines, then may I suggest you go to…"

"Box." Iosif commanded, holding out his hand. "BOX!" he shouted, frustrated by their dumbfounded expressions. Miss Kilroy, her face a study in fury, snatched up the toolbox from the seat and held it up, arms shaking.

Iosif hardly noticed. He rooted through the artifacts and picked out the pliers-like device he'd seen earlier. It would take too long to unscrew that clamp; the best method would be to cut off the order keeping it in place. Threading the tiny pliers through the intricate machinery, he found the offending wire and snipped.

The clamp swung easily away from the switches.

Iosif was starting to smile when a curse from Snorky brought him back to the fact that the car was still moving inexorably toward the station. "Ya little brat, if you's made me stand up and carry ya bony little ass just so's I can get twenty years in the can, I'll…"

"One moment more." Iosif insisted, diving back into the bag. Finding the tweezers, he selected a wire at random and pulled the switch back.

For one horrible instant, nothing happened. Then suddenly, forcibly, the car jerked to the left, away from the station and back into the main street. Snorky half-stumbled, nearly throwing Iosif from his high perch.

"Holy…!"

"Did …" there was a tone of disbelief in Miss Kilroy's voice. "…did *you* just do that?"

"Ya hijacked this thing?" Snorky's voice moved from disbelief to glee. "Oh, man… lookit them pigs! Lookit their faces! Oh, watch them run around; they's all messed up now."

There was a sharp crack, then another, accompanied by the sound of splintering glass.

"They're shooting at us." Miss Kilroy said dispassionately. The box disappeared and suddenly there was another, louder crack from the seat.

Snorky laughed. "Not a bad shot for a dame. How about ya hold up Shorty here, and I get to real work with my Tommy gun."

"Nonsense. There is no need for your violence; we're nearly out of gunshot already." There was a small whine as a bullet whizzed by the car.

"Sure, until they get those private cars of theirs out to run after us." Again Snorky laughed. "If ya ain't never seen a tram chase, lady, better buckle down and let the experts handle business. I… hey! What gives?"

"There. Now that I have the Tommy gun, I will deal with any pursuers. You, as the big strong man, are much more able to support Iosif than I."

"Ya gotta be kidding," Snorky said. "First tram chase since my mob days, and I'm stuck on stepladder duty?"

"But you make such a nice stepladder!" answered Miss Kilroy sweetly. She turned to the back window. "Iosif, turn right at the next street."

Iosif just nodded. He studied the workings. If *that* wire was left, then *this* one must be...

There was a grinding sound as the car's pole hit the side of the track, shaking the tram mercilessly. Finally the track split and the car moved off to the right lane and ground against ITS right side, completely bypassing the turn Miss Kilroy had asked him to make.

"What are you playing at, Rusval?" snapped the woman.

"I sorry. This system new, not certain..." Iosif let go of the wire and the car resumed its even keel down the track. "I do better next time," he promised.

"Very well. Turn right at the NEXT street, then. We'll just have to stick to the main roads for a while."

"Yes ma'am." Iosif studied the wires. So THOSE were for shifting lanes, and THOSE must be the ones for turning, but what was that ticking switch in the center for? It seemed to be on a timer of some kind.

"Oh, blast. Here they come. Get ready, you two."

"Yeah, I'm gonna get right on that," said Snorky. "Except I can't exactly duck or take cover or really do anything except stand here like some great slab of beef."

"Your skill set is hardly my concern, Mr. Capone."

Crack.   Crack.   Crack.   Whine.   Splinter.
RATATATATATATATATTTAT!

There was a muffled curse from Snorky. "Jeez, they're not that bad of shots, are they?"

Iosif saw the turn coming up. He pulled the wire. This time there was significantly less grinding before they sailed around the turn to lightly bounce against the side of the rail.

"Good!" shouted Ms. Kilroy against the gunfire. "Now continue on this until we get to Birch Avenue, and…"

Crack. The comforting support beneath Iosif vanished, and for a horrible second he was falling before his flailing fingers caught hold of a handy pipe in the ceiling. Glancing down, he spotted Snorky sprawled against the back of the car, fiercely clutching his leg.

"Damn!" he hissed. "That stings!"

"Forget the sting, get back up there!" Miss Kilroy shouted. "He can't damn well steer if he's hanging up there, now can he?"

"Well I can't damn well stand up there and support him with my leg like this, can I?"

"Oh for heaven's sake." A few quick steps, and Iosif felt new, slimmer shoulders under his feet. "Here," said Miss Kilroy, tossing the gun to Snorky. "See if you can manage to crawl around to that back window and protect us, you big strong man."

"Ah, now THIS reminds me of old times. Cops after us, my Tommy gun in my hand, a sassy dame in the car…"

"Do it, you great oaf!" Hands gripped Iosif's ankles, steadying him. "Joseph, we're practically a stationary target. They can line up their shots with perfect ease. Can you do anything about that?

RATATATATATAT!

Iosif studied the workings. "Maybe." He nodded.

The tweezers went up and plucked the "left lane change" wire. A short grind, and the car jerked to the left. Another wire, and it jerked back to the right. Then further to the right. And again. A quick jerk back to the left. The car weaved back and forth across the thoroughfare, grinds growing less and less as Iosif fell into the rhythm of the rails.

Snorky's delighted laughter could just be made out about the RATATATAT of his Tommy gun. "That's the stuff, kid! They're firing wild now!"

Twisting slightly, Miss Kilroy glanced back. "How is that car following us if we're not on a preset track?"

"Cop trams are special. They got a wheel to steer it, like Short Stuff is doing." Another burst from the submachine gun. "They got an engine in the car, too."

"Ah. I THOUGHT they were gaining on us."

"Oh yeah. No worries though, we've still got the advantage."

Iosif could practically hear Miss Kilroy's arched eyebrow. "Oh? And what is that, exactly?"

A *click* as a new magazine was loaded into the gun. "Firepower."

RATATATATATAT!

Miss Kilroy turned back to face the front. "Iosif, we're coming up on Birch Avenue. I want you to turn left and then duck down Seventh Street."

"Right." Iosif's tweezers darted back and forth amidst the wires. Right lane change, right lane change, left, right again, right…

Miss Kilroy was shouting. "I said LEFT, Iosif!"

"Hold on," said Iosif, hovering over the appropriate wires. Bullets came whizzing past, coming at an angle, less of an angle, now straight through the back window, one whizzed past his leg...

"The turn's right here, Iosif!"

"Right!" Iosif gripped the lane change wire and pulled it hard. *Click. Click. Click.* Their car swerved back across three lanes, coming to grind against the last just long enough for Iosif to pluck the "left turn" wire and send them hurtling round the corner.

The bullets vanished. Snorky gave one more burst with the Tommy gun and then let out a whoop. "There they go! Sailing right past! Ah, the numbskulls! Gonna take them a while to get turned around from that."

"Right." Miss Kilroy sounded relieved. "Good work there, though next time perhaps a bit of warning would be in order. Now, we could get out of here while we're out of sight, or else dart down a side street before they know where we are, or..."

"No." Iosif shook his head, thoughts flying.

"No?"

"I have idea." Or more appropriately, perhaps, a theory, about that odd ticking switch. It could be completely wrong, of course, but Iosif felt he had to at least try it out.

"Oh?" Miss Kilroy hesitated a moment. "Oh well, why not? This seems to be your show, go ahead and give it a shot." She shifted slightly. "You ARE heavy, by the way."

"Sorry." Main Street was coming up. Iosif flicked the switch and turned.

There was a short silence. "Iosif," said Miss Kilroy. "I realize you've done a lot today, but are you sure that was wise?"

"A lotttt of cops on Main Street," Snorky said. "Won't be five seconds before a patrolman spots us and sics a new car on our tail."

Iosif ignored the both of them, shifting lanes to bring them to the very center of Main Street. There was the Grand Column. He could hear the rushing air of cars hurtling past them. His eyes were fixed on the ticking switch. One, two, three… he pulled the switch.

Nothing happened. For a moment Iosif was confused, but then he nodded. Of course. The Grand Column would need to wait until there was an empty spot on the line for them to fit. In the meantime, the switch was ticking down again. One, two, three… He pulled it back again.

This time, as the train whizzed past, the car shifted left and latched onto its tail with a sharp *CLANG*. The whole tram jerked forward with renewed speed, throwing Miss Kilroy to the floor and leaving Iosif hanging for a few seconds before he carefully let go and dropped to the floor.

"There." He nodded to the two agents as they stared at him from the rear of the car. "No longer on local system. Ticket should carry us rest of the way." And feeling unaccountably tired, he collapsed onto the seat.

CHAPTER 12

4::124151::1596

ATTN: Federation Maintenance Department

MAINTENANCE REQUEST for WAYCAR RETRIEVAL SYSTEM.

PRIORITY: Orange

Federation application G-29310, the WAYCAR RETRIEVAL SYSTEM, is no longer working. When tasked with calling a designated car from the rail system, it managed to locate the car and bring it toward the station, then when it was on its final approach suddenly lost control. This resulted in the car and its passengers escaping our custody.

Please have some of your engineers down immediately to fix the control system, as this is a crucial part of our work and it must function properly.

FROM THE OFFICE OF:

Carnegieville Constable Commissar Derek Radcliff

4:000000::0000

"**F**ree access to the rails." Hougan considered and sucked on his cigar. "That could be huge."

"Could you modify some cars so that they could not be called?" Grey asked.

Iosif nodded absentmindedly. "Is possible," he said. His fingers ran over the rail ticket in his hand, feeling the tiny bumps on its surface. "With small lever, perhaps, to change between lanes. Modification illegal, of course."

"Easy enough to hide." Grey waved. "It's time you got a private waycar anyway, Director. And the rest of the team could use one also."

Hougan just grunted. "Well, not bad, not bad. Unrestricted travel arrangements and a hefty load of artifacts … very nice." He stubbed out his cigar. "We're all set for our next mission. As soon as we can find out where that's supposed to be."

"We could try seeing if any of the engineers knows about the password." Grey suggested. "Or if any of them have access to the facility."

"We tried that already."

"We could be more persuasive than hitherto."

"We're not torturing anyone, Grey," Hougan said. He looked at Iosif. "What're you doing, kid?"

"Is nothing." Iosif had his glasses on again. He held up the rail ticket between his eye and the light so he could make out the pinpricks in the thick paper. The dots seemed random, but they were clearly located on a grid.

"Perhaps we could try another tack," Kilroy suggested. "There are multiple targets that we couldn't approach because of rail restrictions. We could attend to those now. Or perhaps revisit an older target where we lost the intel…"

"The intel wouldn't be there anymore." Hougan tapped the ashes off his cigar.

"Other intel might be."

Iosif picked up a torn envelope on Hougan's desk. He ran his finger—again—over the higher portion with the raised bumps. He held it up to the light and saw a new pattern of pinpricks.

"No one would put useful intel in a compromised position," Hougan said. "Fresh targets, though—that's not a bad idea."

Kilroy nodded. "We never took a good hard look at where they were sending off all those supplies from the agricultural plant."

"There were some curious references to a facility at the Library of Congress I'd like to check," Grey said.

"That old geezer tol us about that plant where they took all the old stuff from the Carnegie Corp back in the day." Snorky rubbed his chin. "Mighta been nothing, but no reason not to look into it, if the fuzz can't stop us."

"Right, so we have ideas. Only question is how to prioritize," Hougan said. "We still don't even know what the Dragon's Teeth program is, but it's too far along…" He stopped. "Rusval? What is it?"

Iosif was walking toward the door, eyes fixed on the papers in his hands. "Idea."

"You… you can't come in here!"

"Really?" Hougan looked at the protesting engineer with vague bemusement. "I'm the Director of the Automated Postal Department. I'm really not allowed into certain sections of my own building?"

"You're not allowed within the Sorting engine." Grey pointed out.

"And you're not allowed in here!" the engineer said. "Viewing Federal Engineering techniques and patents requires Class A clearance in Public Works, which you do not have..."

"Patents, you say?" Grey moved aside some paper to expose the blackjack game.

The elder engineer blustered a little further, but he left.

The others turned to Iosif. "All right, Rusval," Hougan said. "What's your idea?"

Iosif had knelt by the computer they had been using before. He ran his fingers over the top. Again, the almost imperceptible bumps, the infinitesimal joint where the smooth metal joined. He produced his eyepiece and examined the tiny screws. They were marked with a hexagonal head.

Reaching to his tool belt, Iosif brought out the screwdriver. A quick adjustment, and he had the right heading. He unscrewed the casing and popped it off.

Grey winced. "Mr. Rusval..."

"As my ex-wife used to say, the shit's already out of the pot." Hougan held up a hand. "Seems a little late to worry about tampering with Federal Appliances now."

Iosif did not really absorb the words. The delicate web of wires in the way car had been beautiful, but this was a tapestry. The wires and switches were so fine as to nearly present a shimmering sheet of metal. He could barely make out the mini-motors that drove the little pins ticking over the disc's surface. Just by looking at it, Iosif knew that he had no possible chance of changing anything in this impossible fine, precise mechanism.

But that was all right. He'd only wanted a look to verify his idea.

He quickly reattached the casing. Then, with a quick press, he ejected the classified disc they had been trying to unlock. He ran his fingers over the metal surface, feeling again the small indents that marked the tiny holes. There. A narrow grove, all the way across the length of the disc, with a pinprick hole at either end. Iosif couldn't quite see them, but that would soon change.

Out came his eyepiece again. He also found a needle, and in another pocket, a jar of spirit gum that he used for sealing tires. As the others watched, he slowly, carefully, applied spirit gum to the groove, using the needle. The needle was really far too large—the whole process was a bit like trying to paint your signature with a roller brush. But Iosif kept his hands steady and his movements precise. His fellow workers fell silent, which he appreciated.

Finally, Iosif gave a nod of satisfaction, discarded the needle, sealed up the spirit gum container, and took out his jeweler's eyepiece.

"What was that all about?" Snorky asked.

"Maybe nothing." Iosif admitted. He was just guessing, really. But he felt pretty confident in his guess. "We try again."

He said, inserting the disc back into the slot. He looked at Kilroy expectantly.

Kilroy sighed, but walked up to the typewriter. Her eyebrow lifted in quiet surprise. "Well, no 'password' it's asking for so far..." She typed hesitantly.

R://dir

There was a whirring sound from the Babbage engine, and then the typewriter began to rap out its familiar rhythm.

log_09-10-33.doc

log_09-11-33.doc

log_09-12-33.doc

log_09-13-33.doc

"Well, I'll be..." Grey breathed.

"Try it, try it!" Snorky said, rubbing his palms together. Kilroy sent him an annoyed look. She typed again:

Open(log_09-13-33.doc)

The typewriter chattered into life. The other four turned to stare at Iosif. "Seriously, what did you do?" Snorky asked.

Iosif shrugged, but he couldn't help feeling a little smug. "Is holes, in disc." He pantomimed with one of the discarded discs. "Holes tell Engine what to do—with needle. Like music box. Is same principle they use on way cars." And, he felt sure, the mail system.

Kilroy was nodding, and Grey looked intrigued, but Snorky's expression was glazed. Hougan's attention had shifted back to the paper. "Men, I think we've hit the jackpot," he said.

The others turned to see.

LOG FOR: 09-13-33

    Orders completed: 249

    Orders received: 302

    Discipline Infractions: 27

    Deaths: 14

13-932984, 09-103945, and 10-304421 brought in for product evaluation. 13-932984 and 10-304421 product passed for review. 09-103945's product rejected. Appropriate incentives applied. 04-938453 condition diagnosed as bowel cramps, likely cause infection contracted during previous assignment (See attached report). 04-938453 terminated. Received instructions regarding 02-912034, on authorization: Cubbins. Severe incentives applied to 02-912034, transfer arranged to Los Angeles.

Inspection reveals possible damage on gas release valves. Maintenance requested. Plumbing facilities also in need of repair. Cells 239-286 approved for renovation. Inhabitants to be moved to Cells 347-391 during renovation. Request personnel to expedite renovation process.

Urgent request for grubs from Washington. Transfer date set for 09-21-33. Grub resource list attached. As emergency transfer will coincide with routine transfer, requesting additional personnel to expedite process. Disorientation protocols accelerated.

Grub level reaching critical scarcity. Distance toward gestation viability: 2 years. Renew request to Harrison for freshly harvested resources.

Log submitted by:

1ˢᵗ Officer Parsons.

Log reviewed by:

Agent Reynolds.

"Again with the grubs. Always with the grubs." Hougan chewed on his cigar.

"This does not sound like any sort of genetic engineering shit, boss," Snorky said. "I don't know what the hell it is, but..."

"That 'gestation viability' could fit." Kilroy glanced over. "But 'product evaluation...' do these 'grubs' secrete something?"

Grey's eyes were flitting back and forth. "Harrison... There is an undersecretary in the Public Works Department by that name. But why would he be involved? Or is it another Harrison?"

"Easy, people. Don't forget, this intel is nearly two weeks old." Hougan pointed out. "World's not going to end if we don't figure it out this second." But nonetheless there was a twist to his mouth. "Good work, Rusval."

"Welcome." Iosif nodded absentmindedly. He was studying the casing of the Babbage engine—the outside was smooth, but the interior was marked with the familiar scrolling pattern, and the four-circles in a circle. He really wasn't surprised anymore.

"We've got an edge, we need to press it," Hougan said. "With Rusval cracking into Federal Appliances, we're past the point of no return already. And I'm tired of…" He stopped as the door to the engineering office burst open.

"Sir," said the senior engineer from before. "There's someone here to see you."

"Who?" said Hougan, apparently unaware of Snorky moving to block the engineer's view of the Babbage engine.

"A senator, sir."

❧❧❧

"Perry." The senator's former good nature had evaporated. He was flanked, as before, by bodyguards and secretaries, but this time there were also a few extra men in suits and hats who seemed to be neither. "Perry, this is not good."

"You'll have to be more specific," Hougan said, pushing straight past the massive senator on his way to his desk. "I'm aware of a great many things in the world that are not good."

"This Fort Sumter business, Perry!" the senator snapped. "I've received reports that you were seen there! Are they true?"

"It's true that I was there," Hougan said. "As to whether the reports themselves are accurate, I'd need to see them to judge."

"Damnit, Perry...!"

A tall, spare man next to the senator spoke up. "How did you gain access to the facility? We have very strict security safeguards in place. This represents a major security breach."

"Then I accept your thanks for testing the security measures," Hougan said, routing through his desk. He pulled out a thick file and selected a particular sheaf of papers. "Here is my report regarding our infiltration of the base. You will find it is correct in every detail."

Iosif heard a small curse behind him and looked back to see Kilroy biting her knuckle. Grey and Snorky both looked very grim.

Neither man touched the file. "Damnit, Perry, people are *dead!*"

Perry nodded. "How many do they say are dead?"

"At least five!"

"Really? Interesting. I would have said ten or twelve at least," Hougan said. "Mostly by the hand of my second, Philip Grey, though I myself shot a number of men, including a Lieutenant VanBuren. Is his name familiar to you?"

The two men exchanged glances.

"It is to me," Hougan said, pulling out a couple other files. "Lieutenant VanBuren was court-martialed four years ago for firing upon—in fact, murdering--civilians. Sergeant Reynolds, who my second killed, was indicted two years ago for his role in the Osterman bombing, and is currently supposed to be serving time in Alcatraz. What he was doing at Fort Sumter, I can't pretend to know. Nor do I quite understand why he tried to shoot me in the back of the head."

"By the Military Secrets Act of 1900, any unauthorized person found within a Black Site facility may be shot on sight without..."

"Which is an interesting point, considering that neither Sergeant Reynolds nor Lieutenant VanBuren were authorized to be anywhere but in prison," Hougan said. "Nor, for that matter, were the other nine people we shot." He spread out more files on his desk. "My Mr. Grey has a remarkable memory; he never forgets a face, even one that he has glimpsed in the heat of battle before it is mangled beyond recognition. It seems a remarkable amount of these men have no military records at all, and appear on no government registry lists." He looked up at the two men. "You are, of course, free to check these against your own reports."

Senator Blackthorne and the lank man exchanged glances.

"The five which, perhaps, you were told we killed are these five right here." Hougan spread out some sheets. "I am sorry, but not surprised, to hear they are dead; we took great care not to kill them. Mr. Capone gave this one a slight concussion, Mr. Grey incapacitated these three with a series of very clever attacks he learned in Black Chamber, and Ms. Kilroy smothered this one with a scarf until he passed out." Hougan leaned back. "You are free to dispute those facts, but facts they are and facts they shall remain, and I shall defend my staff against any allegations that they have committed murder."

The lank man reached out and picked up the profiles. "Eleven men, you say."

"You admit that you have killed Federal Employees." Senator Blackthorne said.

"I admit that I have shot persons on Federal ground, but there are certainly no records of them being employees. In which case, the evidence would suggest I shot infiltrators that had no more right to be there than I did." Hougan folded his hands on his desk and looked up at the two men. "Less, in fact."

The lank man's eyes flickered down to him. "And why should we believe your account that you had nothing to do with the murder of these five other men?"

Hougan did not blink. "I do not make a habit of lying, Secretary Yardley, as I would hope my earlier admissions would make clear. I anticipate that you will be conducting a full investigation into the nature of these men's deaths. I welcome it, and you are free to take my report as evidence in that investigation." He nodded toward the sheaf of paper. "But if you wish to detain any of my staff for questioning, I will refer you to the Postal Enforcement Statute, which permits the Postal office to retain individuals under investigation."

Secretary Yardley did not blink either. "I would remind you that that statute holds the Postal Director responsible for their availability for questioning."

"Understood." Hougan nodded. "Is there anything further?"

"No." Secretary Yardley handed the file off to Flistworth, who stuffed it into a suitcase. "Senator Blackthorne, if I might have a word…"

Snorky exhaled loudly as the other men filed out. He turned as the door slammed shut. "Jeepers Creepers, boss. Would it kill you to act like a spy?"

"Why would I, if there's no need to?" Hougan said, knocking the ash off his cigar.

"It would have been counterproductive in this case anyway," Grey said, though he did not look happy. "General Ramsford would have been able to testify to having seen the director at the fort, and likely myself as well."

"And Iosif, unless he was overlooked," Ms. Kilroy said.

"Which tends to happen," Hougan said. "He would not have mentioned Rusval in any case; it would have drawn attention to the sort of person he thought Rusval was. Which is why I concluded it was extremely unlikely anyone near that jailing facility was listed on the records." He gave a long pull on his cigar and let the smoke drift out. "And why I expect this investigation will go nowhere. Like my original inquiry."

"What would you have done if the men had been listed on the records?" Kilroy asked.

Hougan glanced sideways at her. "Admit to that. Claim self-defense, though it would have been shakier ground claiming that they were trying to execute two fellow soldiers and not two unlawful trespassers." He shrugged. "The chances were pretty good, though."

"You are *way* too lucky for your own good." Snorky shook his head.

"I don't think you quite get it, Capone." Hougan looked at the big man. "We're investigating a government conspiracy engaged in extremely illegal and undemocratic behavior. Of course they're going to be breaking rules left and right. This works *because* we're fighting against immoral men." He rubbed his forehead. "And because someone way back when granted the Post Office with jurisdiction approaching Black Chamber's."

"It is very peculiar." Grey frowned. "I was aware the modernization process was difficult and that a lot of red tape had to be cut out of the way, but I had no idea…"

"It bears looking into," Hougan said. "Can't imagine I'm the first to use these powers so broadly. Maybe some corners had to be cut in taking down Carnegie, but I wonder what else got chopped away."

"So what's next?" Kilroy said.

Hougan looked up. "They're extremely unlikely to question you, and they need to give us 24 hours notice anyway. Unless and until we receive a summons to that effect, we pursue the different targets we were talking about, using Mr. Rusval's new rail-jacking method."

Iosif rubbed his head awkwardly. He felt slightly uncomfortable with all the approving looks he was getting.

"But I think I've decided our first priority," Hougan said. A grim smile was spreading over his features. "I've had enough of being treated like some juvenile delinquent. It's time I started directing more than the Enforcement Division. I'm the Central Postal Director, damnit, and I'm tired of being locked out of my own building." His gaze moved to the back wall, and they saw him looking through it, beyond, to the engineering wing, and the gleaming vault door at the back. "Grey, get that engineering fellow back in here. I think it's time I saw what this 'Sorting Engine' is like."

CHAPTER 13

0::305494::4950

Report thus far inconclusive. Investigation into Iosif Rusval thus far reveals typical upbringing and lower-than-average education. No known connections with Black Chamber or crime syndicates. Applied multiple times for higher-level schooling but was never admitted.

0::581033::4710

"I don't actually know… *how* to open it, sir." said the engineer, licking his lips.

Hougan's gaze was level. "You don't know how to get inside the *one* thing you're responsible for here."

"We're responsible for many things!" The elderly engineer insisted. "We perform analytics, we provide technical drawings, we brainstorm and develop new devices for the American government, we fine-tune and maintain the sorting engine…"

Kilroy's eyes narrowed. "You *just* admitted that you don't know how to get into the sorting engine."

"I haven't seen a single analysis from you people cross my desk during my entire tenure here," Hougan said.

Iosif turned and looked at his boss. "Federal Engineering Academy not produce innovations for over seven years."

Snorky looked at the engineer. "What do ya guys do, exactly?"

"Technical drawings!" the senior engineer insisted.

A much younger engineer behind him spoke up. "There's not a lot *to* do, to be honest. They don't really give us a lot of clear objectives, and they don't provide much feedback, either. They basically just... leave us alone." He shrugged as they looked at him. "It's a really cushy job."

"The academy only hires and trains the top 0.5% of students." Grey looked incredulous.

"Well, yeah," the younger engineer agreed. "I mean, you need to have the best grades and such... need tutors and all sorts of other coaches to pass the exams. But once you're in..." He gestured. "We can't look at patent diagrams. We can't request information on other government projects, or sometimes even our own. Technically we're allowed to access federal appliance machinery, but only if we submit the proper paperwork several weeks in advance, and then it needs to go through several different review boards. So there's no access, no information, no materials... I mean, you can put in requests and submit ideas, but usually they just get passed on to some higher bureaucrat and get tied up in paperwork, or worse yet, hit a brick wall and just disappear." The engineer shrugged helplessly. "So what's the point, basically?"

Hougan let out a deep sigh. Grey grinned. "'I stand upon the air and contemplate the sun,'" he muttered.

The older engineer was nearly sputtering with rage. "Albert has *no* idea what he's talking about. He's too darn young, with absolutely no respect for the..."

"Get out of here." Hougan waved both engineers out. After they left, he stood staring at the massive, circular door leading to the Sorting Engine for a long moment, chewing on his cigar.

"Rusval?"

Iosif started. "Sir?"

"You've been breaking into the downstairs vault nights, correct?"

"I... sir... it..." Iosif looked over at Kilroy in terror.

Kilroy rolled her eyes. "I can tell when things have been moved, Rusval. Especially that tarpaulin and the iron lung."

"Sir..." Iosif said, turning back to Hougan. "... is just private project sir, I..."

"Got a feel for opening it?"

Iosif halted, taken aback by what seemed like, to him, an abrupt subject change. "I... suppose, sir."

Hougan took the cigar out of his mouth and stabbed it at the massive door. "That look pretty similar to you?"

Iosif looked at it. He cocked his head and squinted. "Possibly, sir."

"Give it a go, why don't you?"

Iosif chewed his lip and stepped forward. It did seem, standing up close, that this was of the same approximate brand as the vault they kept the alien and the artifacts in. However, that was a little like saying that SecurStrong had made the bike lock as well as the Administraion safe. The "Lost and Found" vault was, for all its complexity, still an arrangement with straightforward wheels and dials. This was not. It indeed had several formidable and complex-looking dials, but a quick turn revealed them as fakes—there were no gates, no catches, no momentum like a dial should have.

Quite simply, Iosif did not have the first idea how to even go about unlocking it.

"Difficult," he said, turning back to his boss. "Difficult."

"Impossible?" Hougan arched an eyebrow.

Iosif shrugged.

"Good enough." Hougan grunted. "Take as much time as you need—I'll order the engineer boys to leave you alone—but get it open."

"Hey, hang on, I thought Rusval was going to be working on getting us free access to the rails," Snorky said.

"He is." Hougan lit a cigar. "He's just going to do that *and* the safe-cracking bit at the same time."

"Don't… you think that seems little bit… excessive, sir?" Kilroy looked concerned.

"Oh!" Iosif suddenly remembered and turned around. "I have parts request for new bathysphere—upgraded model."

Grey blinked at him. "Mr. Rusval, we have no need of a bathysphere anymore."

"Yes, yes." Iosif nodded. "But I still make better one. Yes?"

"See?" Hougan puffed on his cigar. "Rusval's fine. Oh, but no, Rusval, can't let you make a new bathysphere. Having one sitting around would just look suspicious."

Iosif felt a bit disappointed, but he nodded.

"Focus on the transit cars. Work on this after you've got that sorted out. If you need something to keep you busy…" Hougan shrugged, "…well, you've still got that project in the basement.

The rest of you." He turned to the team. "Let's prioritize some of those ideas we were talking about."

Iosif did not mind being left to himself—in some ways he preferred it. It gave him time to think. Which was good, because even though he'd been staring at the vault for a solid hour, he couldn't begin to form the faintest notion of how to open it.

The dials were all fake. It didn't matter what order he tried them in, none of them had the weight that a real dial would have. He'd studied the door, too, to see if it was a puzzle door variant, but again, nothing showed itself.

Things like this frustrated him. Things like the alien's ship, still in the vault. He was pretty sure he'd found the power source—it looked like it ran on voltaic energies—but he couldn't figure out how to turn it on. It wasn't a real surprise, he supposed—in some ways he should be happy he'd gotten as far as he had. He couldn't even identify what sort of metal it was made out of.

The metal...

Iosif stepped up to the door again, and this time, instead of touching his fingers to the dials, ran his fingers over the metallic surface of the doors themselves. It was a very odd substance, he could not help feeling—it looked hard and unyielding, it even felt fairly substantial, and yet there was just the slightest... flexing? As though the pressure could...

Pressure. That was the trick here.

He passed his fingers over the door several times. The door was very large, but fortunately, all the significant spots were located low to the floor. He felt at least three spots where the pressure was particularly pronounced. He varied the pressure at each spot, pushing in, releasing a little… Feeling back and forth. Yes… there was just a slightest catch, right… there! Decidedly so.

After a few minutes of trial and error, he believed he had the pressure approximately right on all three spots. But still the door remained locked. He pressed them in different orders, and even simultaneously, using his head.

Then, something occurred to him and he nearly groaned with the implications. Hoping he was wrong, he applied the right amount of pressure… and then turned his hand.

He felt something *rotate* underneath his palm.

This wasn't going to be easy….

"…and then we just came back! No trouble at all." Snorky smiled. "I tell you man, those private cars you whipped up are a wonder. Could have used them back on the Denver job. I ever tell you about the Denver job?"

"You did." Actually Iosif had no memory of the Denver job, but he was having trouble focusing on the dials, and he was hoping Snorky would leave. It seemed rude to ask, but perhaps, if there was no reaction to his stories…

"Denver was a gold mine." Snorky did not seem to have heard him. "Like, a literal gold mine. They had the gold locked up tighter than a duck's asshole—didn't think to cover the payroll nearly as well, though. Course, job went bad and someone got shot, so when the cops called our waycar, we knew it was break or bust.

Smashed out the doors and went running. Ended up having to grab a tractor for most of the way back—you remember how we got back from Fort Sumter?"

"Yes." Iosif had studied the vehicle while they were riding it. The farmer had started the fuel-cell engine with a key, he remembered. An anti-theft device, apparently, that one needed to spark the initial process.

A key... something about that seemed interesting to him. He looked at the doors. No, nothing with that. No place to insert a key there.

"Could've used a rigger on that job." Snorky mused. "I saw one hack a car once, like what you did. Did I ever tell you about that one?"

"No." The ship! Of course, that was what he was thinking of. The alien's ship probably would have a 'key' of some kind—it must have, or else the Federal Engineers would have already figured out the power source. Or not, given their apparent levels of ability. But no, the government must have good ones— scientists—hidden away somewhere.

"Well, that job... we were working with this guy named the Tickler. Big guy, great bald head. This guy... this guy was *so* good, he didn't even need to come himself, he just sent his apprentice, this little old man with huge spectacles and a big black beard. So we needed to get into the docks..."

"These give you an idea of the different points on the wheel— the gates, you say?" Grey was studying the bits of sticking plaster Iosif had attached to the vault's engraved surface.

"Yes." Iosif had actually asked Grey to come down, he'd been hitting a road block, and hoped the spy could suggest something. "No dial on outside, but dial on inside…"

"But you can only find one number per wheel."

"Yes," Iosif said.

"But there must be more."

"Yes."

Grey was silent for a moment, staring at the door. "Do you know, the Black Chamber used to just be a codebreaking organization," he said, almost absentmindedly. "There wasn't a war going on; they actually founded it after the war ended. All about intercepting diplomatic messages and breaking their codes. Very unusual to have a peacetime intelligent force."

"Yes?" Iosif waited.

"That was why I was on board; I'd done some code-breaking in the war. The director was a straight up MI-8 field agent they brought on once we started to become a bit more… hands-on. Herb—that is to say, Secretary Yardley, you saw him here the other day—he was our old boss."

"Yes?"

"The Secretary of State at the time, Henry Stimson, he never liked our work, particularly the way we worked with the telegraph companies—you might not remember them, they're mostly now used for emergency signals. 'Gentlemen do not read each other's mail' he used to say."

"Yes?" Iosif coughed.

"But he still used us," Grey said. "Sometimes I wonder if he was trying to tell us something."

"Yes?" Iosif said, politely.

"Yes." Grey heaved a sigh. "Sorry. We visited the old HQ in New York today. I suppose I'm just troubled at running up against old friends. And of seeing what's happened to the Chamber since I left." He leaned forward. "In our codebreaking work, we sometimes encountered layered code, where you needed to break a second code before moving on to the next step of the first one. Perhaps the additional 'gates' cannot be found until you have the right combination of the first three."

"Is worth trying," Iosif agreed, moving back to the door. "Much thanks."

∽○∾

"So you've got it pretty well narrowed down?" Kilroy stood, arms crossed, eyes running up and down the doors

"I think so," Iosif said. "No false gates. Still many combinations to try."

"No kidding." The young engineer from earlier, whose name seemed to be Albert, had come over to watch. Iosif wasn't sure why, he'd never shown any interest before.

Iosif looked at the long list of possible combinations he'd tacked up next to the door. He'd crossed out about roughly a third so far. "Getting there." He turned his attention back to the door—the circles were marked out, along with little black and red bits of tape to denote the different gates.

"How do you turn the dials, under the metal?" Ms. Kilroy asked. "You can have no traction on them, and the outer casing doesn't move at all—how does the dial behind move?"

Iosif frowned. He had honestly not considered that. "Perhaps magnets?" he suggested. "If owner wears rings, works as key for dials to catch?"

Kilroy looked at him. "Iosif, you don't wear rings."

"Ah." Iosif had to admit that was a hole in his explanation.

"Perhaps electrostatics?" Albert suggested. "They're doing some fascinating work with electrostatics in Los Angeles. You can use your own body to interact with…"

"Would be strong enough to move dial?" Iosif asked.

"I don't actually know," Albert said. "They haven't gotten into practical applications yet."

"Heat, perhaps," Kilroy said. "Some sort of compound that is sensitive to heat, and reacts to it when your hand touches the metal."

"Is possible," Iosif said.

"That's an excellent idea, lady," Albert said, holding up a finger. "A grand idea."

"I'm sure it is," Kilroy said, in a somewhat dry voice. "Iosif, I came down here to ask you… I noticed Sleeping Beauty had been moved." She looked at him squarely. "Does this have anything to do with your… project?"

Iosif winced. "Some," he admitted. "Is idea… not yet confirmed." He thought he'd found the key, he just didn't know how to test it.

"Mmm." Kilroy's gaze was very level. "Mr. Rusval, I do hope you have not been doing anything unbecoming."

Iosif blinked at her, unsure of her meaning. "Work has all been very careful," he said. "No risks. I use very precise tools."

Kilroy studied him for a moment more. "Well, it doesn't seem to have been opened, so there's that at least," she muttered, looking away. "Have you done any more work with the artifacts?"

"Some." He'd nearly filled out the tool belt they'd found—he had a whole array of hammers, screwdrivers, pliers, and assorted devices at his command. Digging around, he pulled one out. "This," he said. "Is drill… augur. Maximizes force. Very precise."

"Are… all the artifacts you've found tools?" Kilroy looked at it with a contemplative expression.

"Nearly." Some of the ones from the Rickenbacker's workshop had turned out to have less utilitarian functions—the one they'd found on the desk was a child's toy, some sort of little clockwork man.

"Curious." Kilroy turned it over. "Odd that… soldiers would carry around ordinary hand tools." She was clearly conscious of Albert eavesdropping on their conversation. "And such beautifully carved ones at that."

"Is it?" Iosif considered and decided that yes, it was odd. Most of the artifacts were more intricately engraved than his mother's ashwood prayer necklace. For genetically engineered super-soldiers to spend the time crafting such things… he had not considered it at all.

"Do you know, I think there's some variations in the design," Kilroy said. "These ones from Rickenbacker have a faintly Celtic look to them—all knots and interlocking designs. And I've sometimes thought that the ones we found in the vault—some of those were here when we moved in, you know—look vaguely Germanic. But this… is this from Grand Central Station?"

"Mm." Iosif nodded. Hougan had dropped it off after the team had gotten back from the infiltration of the rail center, along with the blueprints to the Grand Column Engine they'd discovered.

Kilroy turned and looked at it again, then shook her head. "It's odd," she said at last. "But I could swear… it almost looks Cherokee."

Iosif raised an eyebrow.

"Sorry…" Albert said. "What are you two talking about?"

Kilroy turned to leave. "Nothing for you to worry about."

∽o∾

"How's it coming, Rusval?" Hougan knocked the ash out of his cigar.

"Is good, sir, I think is almost…"

The door handle caught, he felt the bolts slide out, and the door swung open.

Hougan's mouth gave a twist. "Good work."

∽o∾

Hougan waited until Grey and Kilroy were back from the Environmental Monitoring Archives before proceeding, and ordered both to reload and refit before anything further was done. Iosif was again given a revolver, despite his own protestations. By that point, the engineers had all gone home for the afternoon, so there was no one to see the five of them as they stepped through the doors.

The first two feet were pure metal—the solid steel of the vault shielding. Then, for about five hundred feet further, there was a tunnel of solid rebarred concrete. The ground underneath their feet was dusty, and the curving walls were full of cobwebs, showing that the spiders, at least, had had no trouble in breaking

251

in. The tunnel was quiet, and the entire team was utterly silent as their footsteps echoed against the concrete.

Eventually, they became aware of a low rumble, which rose to a rattle, growing and growing as they passed along the corridor, till the very floor seemed to be vibrating. Then there was another door—solid, but not secure, a thick metal gate clearly meant to guard against accident, more than intruders. Snorky shoved it open with an easy elbow, and the thunderous rattle burst in on them like a wave, clear, cacophonous, and ear-shatteringly vast.

The big man stepped through the now-open doorway, and suddenly froze.

Grey pushed him aside, and froze also.

Hougan stepped beside him, and his cigar fell to the floor

Kilroy wormed her way around all three men, and then stepped back, hands rising to her mouth.

Iosif tried to go around, but the quartet made a solid wall across the doorway, and no amount of gentle nudging seemed to budge them. Finally, in a frustrated surge of embarrassment, he got down on his hands and knees and crawled between Snorky's legs.

Halfway through, he looked up, and froze.

It took him a few moments to even make sense of what he was seeing. Across what seemed like miles of open air between them and the back wall, innumerable rattling chains and tracks ran back and forth, crisscrossing, fusing, splitting, and losing themselves in a vast metallic spiderweb. Up, down, sideways, diagonally, and vertically raced tracks, each stacked full of the light beige envelopes firmly bolted to them.

It looked like a hopeless tangle. And yet it wasn't, Iosif saw. Already the dizzying tapestry was collecting itself into a discernable pattern. Struggling through the last bit of Snorky's legs, (first noting, and picking up, Hougan's cigar on the floor) Iosif stood to his feet (handing back the cigar to his boss) to study the pattern better.

Each track, or at least the ones that he could see, when coming from the outside, hit first a small (comparatively; Iosif guessed it must be a little shorter than Snorky) box-like device. From there, they split up into several different directions. Some raced toward adjacent boxes, but most continued onward toward nine boxes—no, Iosif corrected himself, looking again, 26, in all, stacked like a elephantine dice—much larger than the previous ones, at the center. These took in small tracks from all directions, and sent them out again back toward the smaller cubes on the outskirts, which collected tracks from several directions and united them in a single track that raced out again.

Kilroy was shouting something, pulling at Grey's shoulder. He looked where she was pointing, nodded, shouted back, then pulled on Perry's sleeve and pointed. Iosif turned and looked. A few feet further on, a small enclosure about the size of Hougan's office was raised on stilts. A winding staircase led the way to the glass-paned room. Iosif followed the others up the stairs and shut the door behind him, mercifully shutting out the bulk of the thunderous din.

The others were up against the windows, craning their necks around to look at the workings. "It's a maze." Grey shook his head. "An absolute labyrinth…"

"How would ya ever make a place like this?" Snorky took off his hat and passed a hand through his thick black hair.

"They made the pyramids," Grey said, still looking around.

"Yeah, with a lotta slaves and a hunnerd years a hard labor."

Grey frowned and turned to glare at Snorky. "The Egyptians did *not* use…"

"How does it keep working?" Kilroy said. "The intricacies… I mean, surely something must break down! Look at how fast they're moving. How is it possible?"

Iosif didn't say anything, but he had just noticed a maintenance tunnel set into the floor down below, just to the left of the room's stilts. And if he squinted, he could see several others in the automation machine itself.

"I'll be jiggered." Hougan shook his head. "If I'd known what was pounding away in the back of my own building… my word. I've never seen anything like it…"

Iosif snapped his fingers suddenly. "Way cars."

Hougan looked at him. "What?"

"Way cars," Iosif said again. His finger trailed along the tracks to the cubes. "Stations." They moved on to the thicker tracks. "Columns." Then to the enormous cubes. "Grand Terminal. Is way car system." And, he felt sure, a model of the Babbage engine. This was what it must be like, to stand inside one.

"How does it keep track of all of them?" Grey said.

"Whatta it matter?" Snorky said, apparently shaking himself free of the wonder. "Hey boss, what're we doing here, anyway?"

"Right," Hougan said, looking around. "Well, as I've said before, it's a bit much to hope my original report is still in the system, but I'm interested in how they might have gotten it *out*."

"Looks pretty damn impossible to me," Snorky muttered.

"A lot of people have said that, but I doubt any of them saw this place." Hougan was studying the room around them. The space under the glass panes on three sides of the room was covered by various switches, knobs, dials, and gauges, reminding Iosif vaguely of daguerrotypes he'd seen of battleships when he was younger. Hougan pointed at a console in the exact center, dominated by a keyboard. "How about we start tinkering with that thing?"

"And by 'we', you of course mean Mr. Rusval," Grey said.

"Unless YOU want to start hitting buttons and levers at random," Hougan said, as they gathered around the instrument panel. "I don't think any of the rest of us has any idea what we're doing."

"Um...." Iosif hated to contradict his boss, but he'd grown better at it. "Actually... Kilroy better for this."

"Yes, I was about to say..." Ms. Kilroy, who had crouched over to study the keyboard, nodded. "This setup seems remarkably similar to a Babbage engine. I think I might be able to provide some insight."

The other men looked at her. "I stand corrected," Hougan said. "Ms. Kilroy, if you would care to take a look?"

Kilroy pulled up a chair next to Iosif, who stepped away from the console. There were two icebox-sized boxes on the left of the typewriter, which he'd guessed contained the actual Babbage engine, especially since there were four or five discs already slotted into openings. But Iosif's eyes were already being drawn back to the wonderful tapestry of the Sorting Machine itself, outside the windows.

"No password or anything..." Kilroy observed. "They probably figured whoever got past that enormous door was authorized enough already. The only thing that seems really very interesting is this file—'Flagged Accounts.'" Kilroy pointed at the entry on the page. "Let me see..." She typed a few keys and immediately the computer began to print out a series of figures.

1::001283::0192

1::120018::1894

1::913773::4785

1::782166::9144

2:: 324523::4201

2::439921::9381

2::819033::1778

2::784023::2213

2::245119::3423

2::324523::4201

2::324523::4234

3::582011::1834

...

"Wait," Hougan said, reaching out a hand. "Can you pause it?"

"Apparently not," Kilroy said.

Hougan seized the paper spiraling out of the machine and ripped it off just at the point where the "2" numbers started to transform into "3" numbers. "This number, right here," he said. "This is the number for the postal service main office."

"Holy shit." Snorky looked over his shoulder. "They've got the sequence for my flat on there."

"And mine." Grey agreed, looking over Hougan's other shoulder. "And… Perry, isn't that the number for your ex-wife's parents?"

"…yes," Perry said, after a moment. "Kilroy, what does this 'flagged accounts' thing do?"

"I can't do anything further with the system until the output's finished." Kilroy answered. "Until then, I'm in the dark as much as you."

"Redirect," Iosif said. His eyes were wandering back and forth across the crisscrossing tracks again. "Letters from sequences. Redirected elsewhere. Letters opened. Then sent elsewhere." He shrugged. "Or not."

"That's extremely… bureaucratic." Hougan snorted.

"These '1' sequences…" Snorky said, stabbing a finger at the list. "…that's for DC, ain't it?" Hougan nodded, eyes still flicking over the numbers. "And those Null Sequences are for Black Chamber accounts."

"Spying on the spymasters." Grey looked over at the console, which had gone silent. "Ms. Kilroy, now that it's finished printing… you said you could figure out the details of this 'flagging' system?"

"Ah, yes." Ms. Kilroy's fingers clattered over the keys. "Operation list… yes. 'redirect all messages to 0::000000::0000.'

From that point I imagine that could be put back into the system or... not. It also looks like... there are flagged... locations? Where every message from a particular region gets sent?"

"Possibly cross-referenced with the way-car system," Grey suggested. "We know they monitor what cars we get into... it would be easy to monitor the various mail machines in the area also."

"At least this explains how they've been monitoring us." Hougan scanned through the list. "Any chance of tracing where 0::000000::0000 actually is?"

"Not that I can see," Kilroy said.

"Oh c'mon," Snorky rolled his eyes. "We all know it's Blackthorne."

"Maybe not." Hougan set the list down and pointed at a particular entry. "That's his private number right there."

There was a silence. "Well shit," said Snorky.

Hougan took out a cigar and lit it. For a few moments he puffed smoke contemplatively. Then he raised his head. "Kilroy," he said, can you have them send messages from a particular account here?"

Kilroy raised her eyebrows, but turned back to the keyboard. "It looks like it... 0 sequences are automatically excluded from the system, though, at least from this terminal. Let us see... options... set up database... review station... what sequence did you have in mind, sir?"

Hougan stared at the floor. "Grey, what's the sequence for Harrison?"

Grey blinked, once. "1::729491::4892. But he's in Human Resources, none of our work indicated... "

"Done," Kilroy said. "Oh. It says, 'retrieving record.' It must have found something already." She turned. "I'm afraid I must have set it to send them to this terminal, rather than the one at the front, sir."

Hougan shrugged.

A letter rattled out of the mail machine next to Iosif. With a strange feeling of foreboding, Iosif took it and slowly, handed it to Director Hougan.

CHAPTER 14

1::729491::4892

Re: Dragon's Teeth Project

Director Harrison,

Scouts from Fort Smith indicate signs of a fresh nest of grubs near the Crooked Creek headwaters. Size and strength of grubs calculated low, given lack of indications. Requesting intel and resources to collect grubs.

8::428101::8210

"Are ya sure ya know where we're going?" Snorky asked, from the rear of the group.

"Not in the least," Hougan said, consulting a map. "None of this corresponds to the terrain pictured in the official Pryor Mountain park guide. This canyon shouldn't exist." He shifted the cigar from one side of his mouth to the other.. "Means we're in the right general area."

"Unless you's just lost." Snorky shrugged

"Crooked Creek was formed when the boy Burnt Face tore up great boulders from the ground to show the great strength he had gained among the Nirumbee." Kilroy shaded her eyes to look across the landscape. "He piled them in tall columns to show the skill and magic he had gained also." She pointed at the tall thin stone pillars near the water.

"Looks like all ya stupid trivia was useful for once," Snorky said.

"It's not *mine*. The Pryor Mountains are Crow country. Or were, at any rate, until President Harding decided they didn't need them anymore." Kilroy crossed her arms and glared out across the landscape. "And I'd like to stress, sir, that this is extremely slip-shod, what you're asking me to do, applying folk legends to locations. The tale of Burnt Face is a prepubescent male fantasy about the ascendence of the outcast, it's not meant to indicate geographic locations with any level of precision. The stories themselves aren't consistent and vary wildly from one teller to another."

"Mm." Hougan nodded. "Too bad we couldn't get a map from those Indians."

Kilroy closed her eyes. "This is sacred land to them, sir. *They* don't set foot on it if they can help it; of course they're not going to help *us* walk all over their holy grounds."

"Well, no wonder Harding snapped it up, then." Snorky said. Kilroy glared at him and he waved an apology. "Look, all this nature is killing me, ya know? We goes too far out here, we's gonna meet some gap-toothed hillbilly who thinks we look mighty tasty."

"More likely more scouts from Fort Smith, looking for 'grubs,' whatever those are." Grey carefully climbed down a heap of stones.

"Grubs, right." Snorky scratched his head. "What's the idea with those, now?"

"Before the letter, the theory was that they were super-soldiers in training," Hougan said, knocking his cigar against a handy rock. "But if they need to 'catch' them ..."

"Perhaps some escaped?" Grey suggested.

"Or perhaps this is some sort of training ground where the ordinary soldiers need to hunt the grubs," Hougan said. "Or maybe we've been going at this the wrong way and the super-soldiers aren't genetically modified, but surgically modified, made out of kidnapped test subjects. Crow Indians, for example."

"I keep telling you, they don't live here." Kilroy insisted, though she looked a little green. "No one lives here."

Snorky cast an uneasy glance over his shoulder at the mountains towering above. "And ... anyone wonder *why* that is?"

A grin curved Kilroy's lips. "Oh dear. Does the primordial fear of the overarching wilderness and a sudden awareness of your comparative feebleness unsettle you, Alphonse? Or are you superstitious?"

"Hey, sweetheart, I am *not* superstitious, just a bit creeped out is all." Snorky glared at her. "What, do you folks have stories about baby-snatching shapeshifters out here?"

"*Everyone* has those stories, Alphonse," Grey said.

Kilroy's grin turned absolutely feral. "They say the skinwalkers, the yee-naaldooshi, can take the form of trusted comrades and even of the very trees and stones themselves."

Snorky winced and looked around. "Edi ..."

"Can you two stop?" Grey snapped. "We're right in the path of a military operation, here. We don't exactly have a lot of time."

"We have some," Hougan said. "That military operation is waiting on Harrison's go-ahead, after all, and he never received the request." Hougan answered. "But they'll probably send another request before too long, or Harrison will ask, so yes, time is important. Rusval, you feel ready to go yet?"

Iosif, who did not intend to faint again, was taking deep gulps from his inhaler. He nodded desperately. This felt so deeply uncomfortable. The others were wasting valuable time waiting for him to muster enough stamina to climb over rocks. "Perhaps… you… go…" He managed to choke out.

"Splitting up would be a bad idea even if it weren't likely that Dragon's Teeth confederates are in this area," Grey said.

"We needed to stop for lunch anyway." Hougan shifted his cigar around. "It's not a major problem."

Iosif told himself not to be upset that they were making excuses. Being upset would just make things worse. He focused on his lungs instead. Breathe. Breathe. Deep. Regular.

"I think… I think I good now. Sir," he said, at length.

"Good." Hougan glanced over. "Got a pretty good idea of where to go from here, Kilroy?"

"Yes sir," Kilroy said, stepping from the slope of gravel to the more solid rock. "And sir, may I say I appreciate how little occasion you give me to wear heels?"

"Gratitude noted, Kilroy," Hougan said, as they started to climb over the rocks again.

"Whassa problem with wearing heels?" Snorky asked. "They give dames a certain… air."

"If by 'air' you mean causes them to thrust out their bust and buttocks, then yes, I would agree." Kilroy cast a disdainful look back at him. "If by 'air' you mean leg and back problems, then again I agree. I suppose I just disagree in how beneficial that particular 'air' is." She climbed over a log. "Especially in an occupation where running or climbing is so often involved."

"You coulda gone into a different field of work."

"Not if my ex-husband had anything to say about it. Besides, you miss the point. I *like* not having to wear high heels."

"Do you two ever stop talking?" Hougan looked back at them. "It's like you've never even gone hiking before."

"Why would I ever go hiking?" Snorky said.

"I have been on hikes," Kilroy said. "Long ago. I just… don't enjoy thinking about them."

Hougan's face changed subtly. "Bad memories?"

"Very good ones. That is why I dislike thinking about them."

Iosif was confused (as, he was gratified to notice, were Grey and Snorky), but Hougan nodded. There didn't seem to be much to say after that, and they hiked in silence for a half hour or so. When Hougan called them to a halt Iosif felt certain they must be stopping for supper. But instead, the director was frowning at a tall stone.

"Any of you feel something fishy about this rock?" he asked.

Iosif looked at the others, but all of them looked equally puzzled. "You do, sir?" Grey asked.

"I do." Hougan nodded. He tapped his cigar against the standing stone, knocking loose the ash. "Not sure what it is. It just looks… conspicuous."

And tilting his head, Iosif saw what his boss meant. The stone was positioned just oddly enough to be unnatural. It shouldn't be—it was simply the largest rock in a random pile—and yet it was sticking out just a little *too* far, it looked just a little *too* clear of debris.

"Hold on." Grey squinted. "The surface has an odd texture…" He walked forward and stared intently at the surface. "Rusval, you don't happen to have that jeweler's eyepiece, do you?"

Iosif had started bringing the toolbelt, complete with all the assorted artifacts, everywhere with him. He dug into the left side pocket and tossed the jeweler's eyepiece to Grey. It was a bad throw, but Grey still caught it effortlessly.

He stuck it to his eye and peered intently. "Yes," he said, after a moment. "There's a pattern of sorts here, etched faintly into the stone."

"Like a code?" Hougan stepped up.

"A code would be more regular and follow a logically consistent internal structure," Grey said. "This looks more… artistic."

Hougan hmmed thoughtfully. "Native American relic, maybe?"

"For crying out loud, how many times do I need to tell you?" Kilroy pushed her way forward. "Sacred land. They don't come here." She grabbed the eyepiece and after a moment grunted. "… it does look Crow-ish," she said, grudgingly. "Perhaps an offering of some sort."

"Offering ta what, exactly?" Snorky said.

"Odd sort of offering in any case," Grey said, taking up the eyepiece. "It's fairly recent if you ask me—the carvings are small and thin, but the edges are hard, there's no erosion. And I can't make out any iconography—it all seems to be gathered around a single point, which…" He looked. "Hm. Seems to indicate a direction. Down that gully." He pointed.

The party hesitated. Everyone looked to Hougan, who seemed to be considering.

"Clearly it doesn't have anything to do with Fort Smith," Grey said. "Or any hidden facilities Black Chamber might have. It might have nothing to do with us at all."

"We don't even know what we're supposed to be looking for," Kilroy said. "There's no telling what the 'signs' were that the Fort Smith team found in the Pryor Mountains. But we're looking into the strange and unnatural, and this would definitely qualify. I say we look at this as a lead."

"An' I say we look at this mess as a mystery of the dark unknown which man was not meant to probe," Snorky said.

Everyone looked at him. "Those dime store novels are really not helpful for you, Mr. Capone," Grey said.

"They seem to have done wonders for his vocabulary, at any rate," Kilroy said.

Hougan kneaded his forehead. "Rusval, any thoughts?"

Iosif started. "Not… really," he said. "I… I tired. And hungry."

Hougan gave a grunting sort of laugh. "All right. Let's stop for a short break and decide after supper. Grey, break out the sandwiches."

As the others sat and argued, Iosif used his eyepiece to look over the stone himself. It did little more than confirm his suspicions—the pattern was the same sort of scrollwork he'd seen on the artifacts. The 'single point' the scrollwork was all gathered around was the familiar four-circles-in-a-circle sign.

No one was very surprised, though Snorky was visibly dismayed, when Hougan decided to follow the path. The path wound along the narrow gulch and came out on an mountainside which stumped them, until Grey pointed out another conspicuous stone—not identical to the first, but again drawing attention to itself in a slightly uncanny way. And like the first, it was marked with a scrolling design indicating a new direction.

After that, the only real difficulty was finding the rocks. Each one, when found, would point the direction to the next leg of the journey. Grey theorized, as they were climbing, that there were many of these rocks, spread out like a web across the country, pointing like roadsigns to the main path. It wasn't an exactly straight line, and once they climbed along a snaking ridge for half an hour before finding the next stone. But as they got better at determining which stones were missing, it got easier. Iosif had a private theory that part of what made the stones so indefinably conspicuous was the near-invisible carvings on the surface, making them subtly different to the naked eye.

Hougan was a little less happy. "If I'd known this was going to be so complicated..." He grumbled, eyeing the sun sinking low in the west.

"No pain, no gain, sir," Grey said. "When I was a child they told us that the Fair Folk hid their treasure at the center of an impenetrable maze guarded with spirits and charms."

"Damnit, is it always the fairy tales with ya people?" Snorky said. "We's adults here! Huh? We gotta job, right? All this talk about garden gnomes and mazes and what not... whadda we, in the dark ages still or something? Ain't this the 20th century, hey?"

Kilroy turned to look at Snorky, with just a tiny smirk. "They say the tariaksuq, the shadow men, can only be glimpsed in the corner of your eye, and if you try to look at them, they disappear."

Snorky winced and looked around. "Damnit..."

Hougan smiled but he did not laugh. "Everyone still believes the stories, Alphonse," he said, climbing over a tree. "Maybe just in unguarded moments, just when a floorboard squeaks or when you can't see what's in the corner. Maybe sometimes in moments when things fit together just a little *too* well for a coincidence. But everyone still believes the old stories, even if we give them new names. They can say demons are just in our heads, but that's the same as admitting they're real."

The rest of the team stopped and stared, but Hougan continued on, apparently unaware of the stir his words had caused. After a few moments, Grey turned to them, shrugged, and followed after.

"The phrase 'inner demons' is a holdover from literary metaphors, not from psychoanalytic studies," Kilroy muttered, as they resumed walking.

"Even I know when to let things go, lady," Snorky wiped the sweat from his forehead

Finally they seemed to come to an impasse. There was no stone visible from this point, nothing but solid rock walls on three sides. They were in a sort of box canyon, and they could not see any way to go over or under the surrounding rock.

"Maybe we missed something back there?" Kilroy suggested.

"Maybe the whole thing was just some kinda prank," Snorky said. "We wasted enough time on this."

The others ignored him. Hougan pulled out a cigar and lit it, puffing contemplatively. "Rusval, you're up," he said, extinguishing the match.

Iosif blinked. "Me?"

"You're the idea man," Hougan said, turning to look at him. "And right now I'm out."

Iosif wasn't sure how to take that—it was an uncomfortable level of responsibility. He cast a quick glance around at the three box canyon walls. Nothing struck him. He looked up at the reddening sky. No inspiration dawned. He walked straight to the rock wall directly in their path and examined it.

Enlightenment.

Digging out his jeweler's eyepiece, he grinned in triumph. "*Wall* is rock." He informed the others, tapping the mountainside. He saw their uncomprehending looks and tried again. "Is design… is destination. Rock back…" He waved vaguely in the direction they had come from, "…was pointing here." Proffering the eyepiece, he nodded again at the wall. The silvery scrollwork could be barely made out on the rock's undulating granite surface.

"What direction does it say to go?" Grey asked. "The only way we CAN go is back."

Iosif frowned. That was true. Also, this scrollwork did not seem to be exactly aimed in any one direction over another. It wound around and over and through with no particular bias toward any direction, seemingly almost random.

But no, the design was too deliberate to be purely random. There was a pattern...

He brushed some rocks off a ledge. That gave him enough room to pull on the outcrop of rock just above.

It swung 125 degrees.

Iosif felt a surge of triumph. "Puzzle box," he said, by way of explanation. He pushed another rock back into a small crevice. That gave him the clearance to slide another rock from one side of the cliff to the other. He pulled down a small shrub (which turned out to be made of metal). A particularly large bolder, it turned out, was on a swivel and could be turned to line the crevices up properly, so that a stick jutting out of the top could be pulled all the way to the bottom. Iosif found a jutting portion of the rock that was on a hinge, and he folded it back.

And then he pushed.

It wasn't *merely* a forceful push; it was a push in a very specific spot, with a specific amount of pressure. But though Iosif had carefully judged how much force to push against the stone with, he still was not quite prepared for the rock face to suddenly give way and fold inward. With a startled yelp, he tumbled forward and nearly landed face-first on a smooth tile floor.

A wild collection of jabbering noises made him look up.

His first thought was that they were children, and then he realized that their beards made that impossible, and that their large eyes were in fact merely goggles, expanding what must be normal-sized eyes to a much larger ratio. The dying light glinted off the metallic armor they were coated with, and also off the long-barreled items they were pointing at him—some sort of blunderbusses, Iosif presumed, though the steam line running to their backpacks indicated that they fired their projectiles through some sort of explosive steam pressure—not ideal, but it could probably punch four or five holes in a man in rapid succession before....

Iosif's mind caught up to the fact that these blunderbusses could probably punch four or five holes in *him* in rapid succession, and were all pointed at him for that exact purpose.

He also registered, now, the presence of Hougan and Snorky standing on either side of his still-prone body, with Grey and Kilroy just behind them. All had their guns out, and all were tense.

"Take it easy, everyone." Hougan slowly shifted his cigar from one side of his mouth to the other. "Iosif, you all right?"

"Y-yes." Iosif managed. He'd caught himself just before hitting the ground, but quite honestly his mind wasn't on that at all. Nor was it, despite everything, really interested in the potential death still staring him in the face. It was still studying the instruments of that potential death.

"Keep it calm, everybody," Hougan said, raising his free hand (keeping his pistol leveled.)

The little men made no answer.

"*Guten tag, meinen herren?*" Hougan said. "No? Thought I caught some German there."

Still silence.

"Perhaps Old Saxon, sir." Grey licked his lips. "Mine's a bit rusty, but... *wir ne ofslagen, wir...*"

Still silence.

"Thissa waste of time." Snorky seemed much more confident, now that he was faced with flesh-and-blood targets. "Boss, them weapons of theirs can't fire more than a coupla rounds a minute..."

The little men suddenly broke out in an excited jabber, pointing at Snorky.

Iosif, who was more in the dark of the cave, noticed something. "Sir?" he said, carefully. "There are... much more. Back there. With guns." The light from the entrance reflected off the little men's goggles like gimlets. They were lined up, three deep, blunderbusses over each other's heads, shoulders. And further back he caught glimpses of others, half-hidden behind large rock slabs.

"That so?" Hougan chewed on his cigar a bit more. "About how many would you say?"

"Twenty... thirty?" Iosif shrugged, as well as he could while nearly lying on the ground.

"Perhaps we should hold off on the gunfire until we know more about the situation," Grey said.

"We's got position," Snorky said. "No way they could make us if they rushed. I says..."

"Don't shoot!" A new voice rang out—in English, but with a strange accent—from farther back in the cave. "Don't shoot!"

Another short man—big-nosed and long-bearded like the others—came jogging up into the light. He carried no gun, and was in a simple flannel shirt with canvas trousers and a newsman's hat.

"Don't shoot!" he said, walking forward, palms up. "We come in peace!"

The others stared at him.

"No." He lowered his hands and seemed to think. "Not right that is. Brought we in peace? We in peace are come? We..." He coughed. "We... want not shoot you," he said, carefully. His voice was thick and gruff, but still decipherable. "Do... YOU... come in peace?"

There was a beat of silence. "Yes." said Hougan.

The strange man relaxed incrementally. "Proving of this have you?" he asked.

"Hm..." Hougan glanced at the others. "Not that comes to mind," he said. "This wasn't exactly part of the plan." He thought for a moment. "Let me turn this question around. Do you think your companions will shoot us if we lower our weapons?"

The little man seemed a little taken aback. "No."

There was a short silence.

"All right then." Hougan holstered his gun.

"You can't be serious, boss man," Snorky protested.

"Sir..."

"Do as the Director says." Grey's machine pistol vanished into his coat.

Kilroy reluctantly followed suit, but Snorky refused to lower his gun. "Youse all are nuts," he insisted, glancing back at the others. He fixed his gaze on the little man. "Just 'cause the boss man thinks he got some sorta lie detector bullshit ability..."

THUNK.

The rock in Grey's hand collided with Snorky's skull, and the big man's eyes lolled back. Hougan yanked the Tommy gun out of his hands as the man crumpled softly to the ground.

"There." Hougan turned to the little man and his armored companions, facing the row of blunderbusses. "Satisfied? Mount a guard over him if you like."

Another short silence. The little men were all glancing at each other in bewilderment, even the English-speaking one seemed a little taken aback.

"Is content." The speaker said something to the others in their queer little jabbering language. There seemed to be some back and forth—a discussion—before the lead guard was apparently satisfied and lowered their weapons. Most of them, anyway.

"Excuse us if trust not repaid in kind," the speaker said. "Not… accustomed are we to strangers. Or yes, but…" He shook his head. "Come within. Much there is to talk."

∾⊙∾

"I am merchant," the speaker told them, much later, as the company was marched through a collection of tunnels. "I ore sell, devices, trinkets to the above-world. Needful, but risky. Every year less. I am of few who speak the common tongue of overlanders. Gate-guards me signaled when your bondsman they heard."

"Hm," Hougan said. "And you are?"

"I am Otr," the little man said. "We are the *nirumbee*."

The party froze. Otr noticed and turned. "Is something matter?"

"The *nirumbee*." Hougan's gaze was level. "Those… folk from Kilroy's stories."

"I… I called them the *nunnehii*," Kilroy whispered, staring at the little man. "That's what they were in the stories my father told me. *Nirumbee* is the Crow word. They're called the... the Yunwi Tsundi among the Cherokee, the Ishigaq among the Inuit...."

"Many clans there are here." Otr said. "I myself am *dvergr*. Home of Germania. Dwarves, other name, or gnomes called sometimes."

Iosif stared back at the man with wide eyes. His mind went back to his mother's stories—small men in tunnels under the mountains, making magical kingdoms of glittering gold and jewels, stealing children from their cradles...

"Those little people from Kilroy's stories," Hougan said. "That's you? Picked up a townhouse and carried it into the sky? Opened up a mountain and hid Iroquois villagers inside?"

Otr looked uncomfortable. He shrugged. "I not of the knowing... I am *dvergr*. Newcomer. Came in ship's cargo container, years ago. Know not of stories. But..." He hesitated. "...possibly exaggerated."

"Do you have leprechauns here, too?" Grey said. Iosif glanced up at him, but could not tell whether the man was being sarcastic.

"A few of the Tuatha de Danaan there are here." Otr studied them carefully. "So... Human you are not?"

Hougan seemed to rouse himself at this. "Course we're *human*, kid."

Iosif felt a momentary impulse to point out that the 'kid' had a beard reaching to his ankles.

"Then American are you not?" Otr asked.

"No, we're all Americans." Grey shook his head.

"Then how..." Otr shook his head and turned away. "Come come. Much to discuss there is."

They continued down the dark corridor. Iosif, who was directly behind Kilroy, could hear her muttering under her breath. He felt like he should say something, but it was difficult … there were so many interesting things around them. The blunderbusses, for one—he'd gotten a better look at them, and he realized that in place of a bayonet, they had an axe-head. They also seemed to fire shells, which—he could see the cartridges on their belt—looked to be loaded with mini-projectiles. Like a shotgun, he surmised.

At length they stepped through a door. "Talk we here," Otr said.

Gas flames lit up at various points along the wall, and the others suddenly saw a large, wide room. It was roughly circular, with a large, vaulted ceiling, and a deep pool in the middle, filled to the brim with not-quite-glistening water. There was a raised dais at the back, but it was piled so high with crates and bags that it was impossible to see what might have been once back there. They could just barely see the blunderbuss packs stacked everywhere and the axes, the bedrolls, and the thousands of glaring eyes looking back from the darkness. Pewter pipes from the octopus-like boiler next to the dias had been bolted over the intricate carvings on the wall.

The chamber, though not small, was also not quite full. The little people clustered all together (though they maintained a safe distance from the intruders) but their numbers were far from filling the room. It had the look of a curiously badly-attended party, where not quite as many people had shown up as the organizers had planned. Iosif could see, looking at them, what Otr had meant—there were clearly several different sorts of dwarves huddled together there. They looked curiously… afraid.

"Look," Mr. Grey whispered. He was pointing at a large symbol, etched into the opposite wall. "That symbol's on the vault in the APD centre, isn't it?"

"Is in many places." Iosif nodded. The four-circles-in-a-circle, of course. But it was different. More detailed. He could finally make out the pictures. The lowest circle showed a little bearded man, in a pillared underground chamber, jewels streaming through his fingers. The leftmost middle circle showed a man with dark braided hair, standing in a field of stylized corn. The circle to the man's right was utterly dark, save for a pair of glowing eyes. The topmost circle…

Iosif frowned. It looked again like a man, this time with pale hair. But there was something off about the neck, and the hands were…

Iosif's eyes went round. The hands. The hands.

"Ones that came before, you look like," Otr said, turning to look at them closely. "But, acting different are you. Surrender, finally, to accept of us?"

The others looked at him. "What?"

"Terms, of any, we will accept." Otr raised his hands. "Must end, the parties of raiding. People of us… too many gone now. Too many taken. Greenhouses and great pumps stand empty with no hands to work them. Cannot run longer. Tribute of any conditions we will trade, so long as you return our people to us."

Hougan took the cigar out of his mouth. "What," he said carefully, "are you talking about?"

Otr looked from one to the other. "America is not your tribe?"

"Well… yes," Hougan said "Post Office. We're… we're doing a… a mail investigation…" his voice trailed off as he looked around the room. "Blast and blow…" he exhaled, loudly.

"You said, 'raiding parties,'" Grey said. "What do you mean by that?"

"The raids… the soldiers," Otr said. "They break stones, invade tunnels, take women, men, children, and give nothing. Kill chiefs, warriors, many others. In many places, for long time, this happens."

Grey's brow furrowed. "America wouldn't declare war on a fairy-tale country. Who are these men? Why are they doing this?"

"We know nothing." Otr's eyes glimmered in the light of the gas jets. "Reasons we have none, people we have few, and surrender only to give. But you will not trade."

"Grubs," Hougan muttered.

"Sir, it doesn't make sense." Grey looked over at Hougan. "Why would the army—why would Black Chamber—commission a war to kidnap and imprison garden gnomes and dwarves?"

"Why indeed." Kilroy sounded bitter.

Hougan looked at the end of his cigar. "Y'ever read that one children's story, Philip," he said, almost absently. "About the clockmaker in the village?"

Grey looked absolutely blindsided. "I don't…"

"There's this old, miserly man," Hougan said. "Makes the best clocks in town. Wonderful clocks. Beautiful clocks. Never lose time, with little automatic figures that come out and play tunes ever half-hour. And no one can figure out how he does it, because they never see the man working."

Slowly, Grey nodded. "The young man..."

"There's a young man comes to visit the old clockmaker. Wants to be his apprentice. Old man throws him out." Hougan dropped his cigar on the ground and crushed it with his shoe. "But the young man comes back. And while snooping around the store, he finds this door locked with seven locks. He undoes all the locks, and opens the door, and there's this strange little man sitting in this room the size of a closet, chained to the wall. Making clocks."

"Everyone loves free labor." Kilroy's mouth had a grim set.

"But Public Works doesn't make clocks," Grey said. "They don't make anything. They just run the APD and the Waycar system. Carnegie made..." He froze and his eyes went wide.

"How'd Carnegie do that, anyway?" Hougan said. "Man was a businessman, not an engineer. Didn't even invent the Bessemer method, just brought it to America. But he develops this amazing public transit system and this practically magical mail delivery network. And implements it across the city in *one night*."

"What was it they said in the indictment trial against Carnegie?" Kilroy said. "The men who testified against him? 'He treated his workers like slaves.' Never realized they didn't say 'men.'"

Grey slowly nodded. "But why would Public Works keep it going? For maintenance workers? A massive, inter-governmental conspiracy, all for a slave force to keep the engines running?"

"Is not just maintenance." Iosif spoke up. He felt like he was starting to understand. "Is innovation." The others didn't seem to understand, so he tried to clarify. "Federal patents," he said. "Federal Applications. But no Federal *Inventors*. Or not enough."

"The Babbage Engines…" Kilroy muttered.

"Someone must have noticed this before," Grey said. "Carnegie came to power in the 1880's; you couldn't have hidden it for so long! You couldn't have kept so many people from talking!"

"Maybe someone did," Kilroy said. "Maybe they talked to the wrong official. Or that official talked to the wrong official. Maybe they just submitted a report that never arrived and everyone wrote them off as insane because it got lost in the mail."

Hougan gave a small, grim smile. He looked around at the room and the frightened dwarves clustering inside. "In that case," he said, folding his arms, "they really shouldn't have put that somebody in charge of the mail service."

CHAPTER 15

1::729491::4892

Harrison,

I'm aware the lapse in communication was not your fault, and I thank you for bringing it to my attention so readily. We'll have to correct that. In the meantime, I would order the Fort Smith garrison to proceed with hunting out the grubs they found. Don't worry about the mail, I will sort that out myself.

0::000000::0000

"How wide a message are we talking about here?"

"Over the whole system," Hougan said. "Pittsburgh, Washington, Chicago, Los Angeles, Denver... we send it out to everyone. A full summation of everything we've found."

"Youse turning us into newsmen, boss?" Snorky looked very irritated, and he was nursing a bump on the back of his head.

"Not to worry, Alphonse," Hougan grunted, as the waycar pulled up to the post-office terminal. "Pretty sure the moment it gets sent out, Black Chamber will be on us like flies on a picnic, as my ex-wife used to say."

"Your ex-wife had very strange sayings." Kilroy frowned, stepping out of the car.

"Yes. Yes she did." Hougan gave a little smile as everyone exited.

Iosif followed them up the steps, thinking through the logistics. "Post works by sequences," he said, as they passed through the doors. "Need to send message city by city. And mail machine not news press. Will take time."

"Right." Hougan nodded, as they passed through the lobby at the front. "So we'll need to hold them. Locking ourselves in the Sorting Engine should give us some time, but we have to guess they'll know the combination."

"A standoff." Snorky started to grin. "Heh. Haven't had one of them jobs since Zoltan Bank." He hefted his Tommy gun.

"Birds and trees make you nervous, but guns make you excited," Kilroy said. They passed through the door at the back marked "Employees Only" and weaved their way through the abandoned offices. "Are we really doing this?"

"Gone too far to turn back now," Hougan said.

"We could send out the message to all of Washington and count on it to spread," she suggested, following the others through the door to the Engineering Wing.

"Politicians would just bury it. Or people might not believe them." Grey shook his head, pacing up the line of empty desks, filing cabinets on one side, Babbage engines on the other. He halted halfway. "I have trouble believing it myself."

"People might not believe *us*. Assuming we live long enough to even send out the message." Kilroy crossed her arms.

Hougan shrugged. "Doesn't change what we need to do."

Kilroy was studying him narrowly. "Sir… this is, actually, illegal. I sincerely doubt there's anything in the postal jurisdiction that makes this permissible."

"Giving away secrets of postal development? Yes, that's against nearly the very first statute," Hougan said. "If we live through this, I will resign. Happy?"

Kilroy grinned, slowly. "Just wondering, sir."

"Glad you're happy, then." Hougan took his revolver out of his overcoat. "Rusval, I can't have you staying—you're just a kid."

"I sixteen," Iosif said, but it was mostly an absentminded reply. He was staring at the door—something about it seemed wrong.

"Sixteen's still too young to die," Hougan said. "And you're no use in a fight. Unlock the door, then get out of here."

It *clicked* in Iosif's brain. He turned to face Hougan, eyes wide.

"Door already unlocked," he said.

The fact had just time to register on Hougan's face. "Cover!" he shouted, dodging behind a desk, as he vault door swung open to reveal a line of black-suited soldiers, machine guns at the ready.

Bullets sliced through the engineering offices, kicking up splinters from the desks, punching holes in the tile. Iosif, who had been knocked back against the wall by the swinging vault door, blinked stupidly at the battleground before his eyes.

"Kid!" Snorky shouted, from behind the drafting desk in the corner. "Get the door!"

Enlightenment hit immediately—the massive vault door loomed just above him. Iosif jumped up and took hold of it, heaving with all his might. He heard shouts and yells as the door swung around over the opening, and tiny vibrations thudded against the metal, but the door was just too thick, and the vault door slammed shut, trapping the gunners behind it. Iosif gave the hidden dials a quick spin, unsure if that would actually do anything.

"Black Chamber," Grey said, coming out.

"That puts the plan on ice," Snorky said. He was holding his leg and wincing. "Think those guys anywhere else around here?"

Grey and Hougan heard them before the others. They whirled around just as the stream of men came pouring through the side doors, their weapons blazing. The first three or four black-suited soldiers fell to the ground, but five or six managed to get into a position behind the Babbage engines.

"Pull back!" Hougan said, ejecting the spent shells from his revolver. His other hand was grabbing a ring of bullets—Iosif had never seen that before, it was really fascinating how the ring kept the bullets in a sequence that could easily be loaded into the…

"Iosif!" He heard Kilroy shout. He looked up to see her up against the pillar. "Grab Al!"

Snorky was half-lying behind a crumpled desk, propped up on one shoulder, firing away with his Tommy gun. The submachinegun was spraying indiscriminately across the lobby, out of control in Snorky's single hand. The big man made no move to join the others dodging toward the door—his left leg was lying completely flat on the floor, blood leaking across his upper thigh.

Iosif ducked behind the filing cabinets and half-ran at a crouch to him. Snorky didn't even turn to look at him. "Okay kid!" he shouted. "Just hold to the line of desks until ya get to that pillar there, then wait for me to give them a *real* burst so ya can..."

Iosif picked up the man under the shoulder blades and dragged him along the line of desks.

"Holy *shit!*" Snorky struggled for just a moment before quickly adjusting, bringing his other hand around to actually aim his gun. Iosif paused at the pillar, waited for Snorky to give a burst from his machine gun, and then he was trotting across the floor as fast as his short legs could carry him.

The others were already gone. Gunshots were echoing through the empty offices. "Shit, kid." Snorky gasped. There was a rattle—he was probably reloading his gun. "I keep forgettin' how freaky strong ya can get..."

A huge rumble shook the building, throwing Iosif to the ground and sending Snorky tumbling several feet away. Plaster rained down from the ceiling. *Explosives?* Iosif thought disbelievingly. Had they planted them while they were out? Could even Black Chamber bomb a building in the middle of Pittsburgh?

He was picking himself up to go grab Snorky when a series of bullets popped close to his head. He ducked and rolled over behind a toppled filing cabinet, fumbling for his pistol. Sticking it over the edge of the filing cabinet, he fired wildly in the general direction of the shots. Several more bullets punched holes through the filing cabinet, and he nearly fell over trying to avoid them. His last two bullets went into the ceiling.

Snorky was on his back, a mere two feet away, shooting and shouting—but he might as well have been a mile. Iosif knew he would never make it.

He tried. He made a mad dash out from behind the cabinet, but just as he did, another explosion shook the building, and Iosif tripped, pitching forward, tripping completely over Snorky's leg, and going flailing through the door just beyond. He slammed into the opposite wall and for a moment saw stars. He was just getting up when he felt two hot knives of pain searing into his shoulder. Crying out, Iosif recoiled on instinct. He caught the flash of black through the doors on his right, and stumbled as quickly as his short legs would carry him. Gunfire was everywhere.

He half-fell into the warehouse area, saw the workers lined up against the wall, and immediately fell back. He no more than glanced at his workshop before he saw the Black Chamber agents and heard the sounds of crashing.

He managed to batter in the door to the offices, only to have a burst of machine-gun fire whistle over his head. "Damn," Kilroy breathed, lowering her Sten gun. "Don't you know better than to go smashing into places? We're in a war zone here!"

Hougan was crouched by the window, a double-barreled shotgun in his hands. "Damnit, Rusval, Grey just left to look for you. Where's Snorky?"

"Back … Engineering Department …" Iosif panted, shutting the door again. He pushed a desk against it, called it a barricade, and sat back against it.

"Shit." Hougan swore. Something outside the window caught his eye; he half stood and fired. Cries echoed up from the street as he ducked down again and half-crawled, hugging the wall, to a new window. "I knew they'd be desperate, but I didn't expect them to be so *fast*."

"Sir, we need to go," Kilroy said.

"Right." Hougan gave a quick nod. "Best to split up and meet again at the safehouse in Dallas…"

A shadow fell over the windows. Hougan looked up at something outside. Kilroy glanced over too. None of them were watching as the door blew open.

Iosif, whose back was to the barricade, went flying forward. His arms went up to shield his head, and he smashed straight into the bank of desks, right into a bookcase beyond. The entire contents of the bookcase crashed all around and over him. Dazed and confused, he watched with a curious detachment as black-uniformed men swarmed in through the door, hiding behind huge metallic shields. They bore only batons, he noted. No guns.

Hougan fired, and an array of sparks danced off the shields, but the men did not even slow. Hougan went down under the lashing of batons. Kilroy backed up, her sten gun rattling with desperate energy. Iosif saw her eyes tracking back and forth and wondered what she was looking for. Suddenly she seemed to gather herself and leapt through the paned glass window, firing at whoever was down below.

He heard a groan, and looked at a bloodied Hougan, getting dragged to his feet, hands cuffed behind him. Four soldiers held him on either side. Other Black Chamber agents had drawn strange-looking weapons, and were firing through the windows after Kilroy. Still others were charging on into the director's office, or beginning to check under the desks.

Awareness came flooding back, and Iosif suddenly realized his deadly peril. A thin layer of tumbled-down books and paper were all that shielded him from Hougan's fate. He could feel something warm running down his left arm, but did not dare to move… hardly dared to breathe.

And then Secretary Flistworth walked into the room.

It took Iosif a moment to place the small, thin little man, with the spidery black hair and the oversized eyeglasses. Then he remembered the job interview, the work inspection, and it came flooding back. Senator Blackthorne's underling. Mailing secretary. Responsible for all inter-departmental communication.

Flistworth studied the scene of the office. "Have we found any, ah, records?" he said, ignoring Hougan and the others for the moment.

"Not yet, sir." A man with a white sword etched on his helmet said in answer.

"The woman?"

"Went through the window, sir."

"Hm." Flistworth looked over at the shattered window. "And the boy?"

I sixteen. Iosif managed to bite his tongue.

"Still looking, sir. They said he was in this sector."

"Hm." Flistworth's eyes swept the room, and Iosif closed his eyes out of sheer fright, horribly afraid that somehow, their eyes would meet and he would be discovered. "Clean up that, ah, mess." He heard, and opening his eyes, he was relieved to see Flistworth gesturing vaguely, the commander standing stock-still as he listened to the orders. "Make sure you search everything and take every scrap of paper you can find. This place is too valuable to, ah, *completely* burn down but we may as well do the next best thing."

Hougan groaned.

Flistworth looked over at the man and smiled. "Are you, ah, still with us, Central Postal Director?" he said, walking over. "It's all right. See me. Recognize me. Remember me."

Hougan looked up. His eyes seemed to focus. "You…" He said. "I… know you. From somewhere."

"Yes, you do." Flistworth smiled. "We've, ah, seen each other many times. And we'll be seeing a lot more of each other now." He looked over at his men. "Take him to the airship."

"Yes sir."

"Oh ah. That reminds me. Higgins. Morris." Flistworth snapped his fingers, and two of the uniformed soldiers came forward. "This is your first field mission, isn't it?"

"Yes sir." Both men saluted.

"Captain Davis," Flistworth turned his head slightly. "These men acquitted themselves well?"

"Quite satisfactorily." Captain Davis answered.

"Very good." Flistworth faced them. "Gentlemen, if I recall your profiles correctly, that means you have fulfilled the last requirement for entry into the Dragon's Teeth program. There is… just one more detail to attend to." He held up a finger. "Minor technicality, really. The program requires a final test of, ah, resolve."

One of the soldiers drew his pistol and shot the other one in the head.

Iosif gave a little gasp, which fortunately was covered by the roar of the gunshot. The stricken soldier made a little flailing motion as he crumpled into a heap at the mailing secretary's feet.

"Hm." Flistworth looked at the body. "Interesting. What made you so, ah, sure that that was the test?"

"Bosworth, sir." The soldier answered, holstering his pistol. "Didn't say outright, but dropped enough hints."

"Really." Flistworth glanced over, and Iosif caught—not really a glint, but an actual *flame* in his eyes behind the lenses. *His glasses… they must have some sort of filter.* "I see. Well. All that remains is the final augmentation procedure."

He held out his hand. The soldier gripped it … and screamed.

Flistworth's hand melted into a fleshy goo, winding around the man's hand and arm, racing up his shoulder with deafening speed—Iosif noticed, with fascinated horror, the corresponding mass vanishing from Flistworth's other arm—and flattening itself in a doughy, flesh covered mass over the soldier's screaming mouth. A hook-like proboscis grew out of the tentacle and poised, for a moment, before the man's wide eyeball.

And then the proboscis was plunging deep into the eyeball and Iosif was erupting out of the books because he just couldn't take it anymore he couldn't and he was running for the stairwell and bullets were whining around him and something hit him on the leg but that was okay because he was on the stairwell and falling, falling down the stairs and there was the vault, the forgotten vault, which somehow had been left unguarded, and Iosif was swinging it open and tugging it shut behind him as shouts filled the stairs.

He sat there for a moment, gasping, until the rattle of gears reminded him of the danger. Someone might very well know the combination to the lock.

It was all right, though. He knew exactly what to do. It was all going to be all right.

Quickly he stumbled—something was clearly wrong with his leg, but he couldn't worry about that now—over to the iron lung, where the alien girl still lay in her deep sleep. He grabbed hold of the handle on the side and hauled the cylinder over to the tarpaulin.

The vault shook with a thunderous *boom*. Someone was trying heavy ordnance. But someone else had done a damn good job on that vault.

Iosif tore the cover off the ship—only it was not the alien's ship, not as it had been. Rough metal and canvas had been bolted onto sections of the ship, along with some controls that looked like they may have once belonged to a motorboat.

This was the risky part. Iosif undid the locks on the side of the iron lung and opened it up.

Iosif knew next to nothing about medical science. Questioning Grey, he'd learned that iron lungs were used to help with people who had difficulty breathing—particularly people with polio. Kilroy had told him that the girl had arrived in the machine and it'd made sense to keep her in it.

But if this girl had been kidnapped by the same people who were now hammering on the door, her welfare was probably the last thing they had in mind.

Iosif reached into the lung and picked the girl up—one hand under her shoulder blades, one hand under her legs. She was astonishingly light. The hospital gown draped around her form, and her pale hair hung down nearly to the floor (not terribly far, given Iosif's height)

But Iosif was not interested in that. He was watching her chest. It rose and fell with a regular rhythm. He had been right.

The rattle had stopped, it was now more purposeful, a rapid, smoothing grinding. Someone knew what they were doing. Someone had opened this door before.

Quickly Iosif opened up the chassis to the ship. He put the girl into the front seat of the cockpit and fastened the straps around her. Her head lolled around as he grabbed her arms by their silver bracelets and fitted them, one at a time (the hands *oh the hands,* but he had no time for that puzzle now), into the dual rings that extended from levers on either side of the aircraft.

The controls lit up. The engines fired blue. He had been right about that, also.

The vault made a *click*.

Iosif jumped into the back seat and swung the windshield shut, just as the door to the vault swung open. He had just barely the presence of mind to strap himself into the seat before he was punching the throttle, sending them smashing through the room beyond, crashing through the splintering wooden stairwell, up through the tall skylight at the top. A vast ballooning shape blotted out the sky above. Iosif swung the controls wildly and he was pitching left, just sailing past the zeppelin. The ship continued to pitch left and he spiraled upward in a wide circle, giving him space to appreciate the view.

The vast, hulking form of the USS *Shenandoah* hung over the smoking ruins of the Automated Postal Department. The Administrative Center was dark, but the Automation Centre was still churning out steam. He could make out the blockades at the waycar stations, the frozen train line, and the barricades erected everywhere. He could see the lines of waycars in the city beyond, bustling about on their way through the city, and just barely, the thin threads of mail-tracks, spreading out like a vast metallic spider web, carrying the mail throughout the city and country.

And then his aerocraft pitched into the cloud and the sight of Pittsburgh was lost to him.

CHAPTER 16

2PITTSBURGH HERALD

MOB HIT ON POSTAL DEPARTMENT LEAVES THE MAIL SERVICE BATTERED BUT STILL RUNNING.

Honest citizens of all sorts were shocked when remnants of the Moreni family gang opened fire yesterday on the National Headquarters of the Automated Postal Department, situated downtown. Despite gunfire, melee combat, and firebombing, the core of the government agency remains operational, and no interference in mailing operations is expected.

Motives for the attack remains unclear, but most sources point to a recent armored delivery made to the mailing center warehouse, which the gangsters were perhaps intending to steal. Police spokesman Captain Davis confirmed that the delivery had not been stolen, but said it had been removed from the premises as evidence.

According to witnesses, the mob rolled up in private waycars. They attempted to gain entry to the building, and when denied by the security guard, opened fire. They managed to penetrate the front offices, the warehouse, and even made it into the engineering division before being repulsed by a joint attack from Postal Enforcement employees and Law Enforcement officials arriving on the scene.

Among the casualties was Director Percival Hougan, who was shipped off to Pittsburgh Intensive Care shortly after the attack had been repulsed. "Director Hougan is a man of uncommon strength and resolve." Interim Director Higgins said, in response to inquiries. "I have every confidence in his eventual recovery, and wish him the best of luck."

ID Higgins went on to assure our readers that the mail would continue to run on time. "The attackers did not quite penetrate to the Automated Centre—if indeed they would have any interest in doing so. The machinery was undamaged. Though we may have suffered an incalculable loss today, we will not let that stop us from carrying on the job the people of America have entrusted to us. The mail will continue to run on time."

Such a high-profile attack has already garnered attention on Capitol Hill. Senator Vandermuelen (R, PA) called the attack "an act of unmitigated gall and an affront to our modern way of life," while Secretary Yardley said that "our thoughts and prayers are with the fine men and women of the Postal Department in this difficult time." Secretary Yardley also stated that a committee is being *formed to look into the attack. Senator Blackthorne of the Public Works Department also expressed his concern, stating that the "the usage… of private waycars in the attack underscores the rogue element that they represent in public transit."*

Donations for the reparation of the Postal Headquarters, as well as gifts for the families of those killed in the attack, may be directed to 1:392113:8411. Anyone with information regarding the attack is also encouraged to contact the authorities by any means possible.

2::428440::5204

For a moment Iosif nearly panicked. In the cloud, he could not tell what direction was up, or down, or sideways. The control panels in front of the alien flashed strange symbols. The compass he had installed on the dashboard was *no* help whatsoever; it spun wildly and gave no indication as to the height or orientation. What was it that professor had said? A gyroscope! Why had he not thought to include a gyroscope? Of all the ridiculous omissions…

And then the plane broke through the cloud layer and the window before him was sheer bright blue.

Iosif winced against the light, stifling a gasp. He had never seen such a crystal clear blue, nor such a pure, gleaming white as the clouds from above. Towering mountains, cliffs, and impossibly poised monuments towered around his tiny plane on every side. He shied away from them, unable to decide if this was paranoia or awe on his part.

Iosif actually felt surprised he wasn't panicking more. He had not, as he now realized, ever really intended to take the alien ship up at all (*that* was probably why he'd neglected the gyroscope), but when he had toyed with the idea he had felt nearly stupefied with terror at the mere thought of being up *that* high, soaring that far above in the open air, with no supports, in a device that had never been correctly made, that had never been *tested*…

But the adrenaline had carried him past the critical point of launch, and now what he felt was mostly a sort of curiosity. It was practically academic at this point, he decided, how high he was. His mind literally could not grasp the idea of how far below the ground must be. It was just a colored mat below him, no more terrifying than the sea

He turned the ship left and noted how the handling was sluggish, he banked right and noticed how it overcorrected and nearly sent him into a tailspin. He tried to determine whether the craft was indeed tilting slightly, and if that was because of a misaligned rudder or if some of the canvas on the wings had ripped off somewhere. He'd never really had the chance to get a feel for how these parts worked together.

He was surprised with how well the steering mechanism was working, to be honest. He'd just jury-rigged it over what he'd guessed the alien's "key" to be—the two rings at the ends of long levers. His own levers were basically bolted onto these; he moved them and, marionette-like, the other levers followed his motions.

The alien, still slumped over, also followed his motions, which Iosif found a little creepy. There'd been no way around it. He'd been pretty certain that the armband embedded into her wrist was supposed to match up with the rings, and theorized it had some way of activating the ship's engine (which still confused him, but he'd decided to take a shortcut) but it had been entirely guesswork. It'd been a risk, but he hadn't had much of a choice.

It felt a little like kidnapping. Was it kidnapping? The Black Chamber agents would probably have just locked her up somewhere new. They had probably kidnapped her to begin with. He shivered a little with the thought. A whole life, simply being juggled from one agency to another…

That might be Hougan's life now. Or the others. Assuming they hadn't simply been shot, or wouldn't be, before too long. Iosif thought about the others—the warehouse workers, the seniors in the administrative centre… What had happened to them? And then a new thought struck him: What about his mother?

He could not really say how long it took him to think through all this. Time seemed meaningless up here, amidst the huge, lazy clouds. He must be traveling at an incredible rate (he hadn't thought to add a speedometer, either), but against the mountainous white clouds, he seemed to be going along almost lazily. They looked so delightfully fluffy—so soft and yet solid. Like you could jump down onto one and go an amazing journey up and down and over its great bulbous sides. Iosif caught himself wondering if the great window at the front could unlatch; if he could get out… he wrenched his eyes away from the skyline and focused on the console.

He supposed he should be less worried about getting captured on the ground, and more worried about whether he would ever get back there. He had surely passed the Marceloni barrier—maybe, he hadn't included an altimeter either—by this point; if he didn't disappear it would be another first. At any rate it seemed nothing to do with the clouds themselves. In a sudden surge of boldness he decided to bank the plane through another cloud just to make sure.

He realized his mistake the moment the grey vapors closed around the craft, and for a minute he DID bank the plane, in an attempt to get back out. Again, he quickly realized the mistake, and straightened out—perhaps, he couldn't be sure—but the damage was done. He could see nothing but grey mist. His hands strayed to the controls and then he stopped. The best thing to do would be to just leave them alone.

Anxious moments ticked by, moments as tense and nervous as the outside flight had been lazy and carefree. The plane did not seem to be dissolving, at any rate, so the 'acid cloud' theory could be considered disproved.

Finally the vapor thinned and faded away from the front of the cockpit, and Iosif gasped.

Again he saw the blue sky, again the high, towering white mountains of vapor—but now imposed against them was a vast blue-green shape, like an enormous, upside down flower lily. Its enormous, bottle-blue petals overspread a tiered collection of twinkling shapes. It was bigger than the Automated Postal Department, bigger than the Maritime Authority, possibly bigger than a small town. And with a solid point of reference against the sky, suddenly Iosif realized how fast he was in fact going, very fast, straight toward the enormous structure.

He tried to bank away, but the floating structure grew and grew in his vision. Left and right he yanked the levers; the ship refused to answer. Terrifyingly quickly, the glittering shapes were resolving themselves into great blue-glass gourds, suspended in what looked like green discs. Tiny objects—or they looked tiny from this distance, at any rate—detatched from the sides and seemed to head toward him with definite purpose.

"*Vaas mana?*"

Iosif yelped and nearly fell backwards. A small, blue man had seemingly jumped into the air just above the alien's wrist.

"*Vaas mana, Aeorol imgitata.*" The figure repeated. Iosif now realized it was an alien, not a man, and also that the man seemed to be slightly transparent. He peered at the girl in the chair, seemingly unable to see Iosif.

Suddenly the man recoiled. "*Lumohiris!*" he said, and winked out of existence. Iosif watched in confusion as the shapes headed toward him suddenly wheeled and banked around. This was the chance. Now or never. He grabbed the levers and pulled with all his might.

The levers snapped away in his hands.

Iosif stared helplessly as the disc came nearer. He was going to crash. He was going to crash, and going to die, miles up here under the blue sky and he would never get the chance to make a better version of this aircraft where that sort of stupid mistake wouldn't happen. The speed was nearly blinding, now, he was coming up fast... well, not so fast... no... no wait.

Iosif frowned as he looked out the window. What was happening? The aircraft seemed to be... it definitely *was* slowing down, and that was against everything he understood about aerocrafts and how they were supposed to work. And really just velocity in general. And now the engines were shutting down, which also wasn't supposed to happen.

Iosif's thoughts on how planes weren't supposed to behave this way were interrupted by what was happening outside the window. He could see the discs up close, now, and see people— no, aliens, he corrected himself, noting the strange profile— walking around the blue-bottle gourds, which towered above them. Looking straight ahead, he saw something on the very edge of the disc, right in his plane's line of flight—it looked like some sort of harness, or a hook, very close to the ship's own shape…

The plane slid neatly into the harness and latched onto the front. Without Iosif even touching the window, the front cockpit slid open. He let out a small yelp and glanced back at the alien girl, but she remained comatose in the seat behind him.

Looking out, he saw something else. About ten or twelve figures in long pale blue cloaks were slowly converging on the craft. Little could be seen under the shadows of their hoods save for their glowing eyes, but there was a deadliness to their movements that left little doubt as to who they were.

Iosif had one chance, and he knew it. Raising his hands, he stepped out of the aircraft. "I unarmed!" he shouted. "I in peace! I Iosif Rusval! I… I sixteen…"

One of the hooded figures stopped and seemed to point. Something, small, round, and glowing shot past him, and then, before he could react, looped back around to hover in front of him.

Iosif had just enough time to wonder how it was doing that before it fired a pair of wires into him, and he had a whole new problem to worry about.

∽∘∾

Some time later, Iosif lay in a holding cell, trying to remember what exactly that had felt like and how the pain had been so completely different from other sorts of pains he'd felt before. Because it really had been. Not simply in degree, but also in kind—it was unlike heat, or force, or cuts, or any other sort of pain that he could remember.

It was tricky to remember because the whole event was rather hazy in his mind. He couldn't even remember how he'd ended up in this room.

A bizarre experience, Iosif decided.

A bizarre cell, for that matter. The walls felt like glass, that bottle-blue color that was everywhere, but they were completely opaque, and the texture felt very different too—harder, somehow. The only opening was in the ceiling, and there was some sort of film over it that flickered every so often. Iosif wondered if it could replicate the pain from before, but decided he wasn't curious enough to test it. And anyway it was out of his reach, and the ladder had been retracted.

Even as he looked up at the opening, he heard some steps above him, and one of the blue hooded figures appeared on the edge, alongside a tall figure in a flowing robe. They held some sort of conference—or so Iosif assumed, he could hear nothing—and then the hooded man adjusted something on his bracelet.

The film over the door disappeared. Iosif stared at the hooded man, trying to figure out how he could do that without some sort of telephone wave, but before he could give it much thought, the robed man had leapt down into the cell, with an inarticulate cry. Iosif had no time to react before the tall alien wrapped him in an embrace, jabbering wildly.

Iosif was very confused.

Iosif was still confused. They had taken him out of the cell, then out of the larger... building, he supposed he should call the enormous glassy pods looming on every side. He had walked with the emotional alien in the robes for a distance, past more impossibilities than he could keep track of, to another glass gourd bigger than the last. He'd been brought in, met another emotional alien—a woman, he was pretty sure—and was currently sitting on some sort of hammock that was slung from the ceiling, sipping a strange purple drink that left an aftertaste in his mouth. The aliens had not stopped talking since he arrived, but he understood them no better when he arrived. So he just stuck to nodding and smiling pleasantly. It usually worked pretty well.

At length another alien—this one wearing a less flowy garment, it had a sort of uniform feel to it—entered the room and spoke. The two aliens jumped up and gestured to him to follow them.

They went into another room, and standing there was a man Iosif recognized from his obituary in the newspaper: Orville Wright.

Iosif blinked. "Er..," he said.

"You must be the pilot." Wright said. He gave a dry smile. "Don't worry. Things will make sense soon enough."

Iosif blinked. "Er...," he said.

"I suppose I should introduce myself, though you seem as if you might recognize me already. Orville Wright, bicycle mechanic and aspiring aviator." He executed a half-bow. "And you, obviously, are the rescuer of this couple's delinquent daughter."

Iosif blinked. "Er...."

Wright smiled again. "The girl—whose ship you took back up here." He indicated the aliens, who were gazing with rapt attention at their conversation. "Her parents lost her a number of years ago. Salali. Sweet girl." He grinned, slightly less drily. "I knew her as well, actually, she was always bothering me about the 'Under-lands.' Bit too curious for her own good. Suppose that's how she crashed." He shrugged. "Anyway, they are very grateful to you for returning her."

Iosif blinked. "Er..."

Wright's face took on a little more of a concerned expression. "Are you all right?"

"Er... ...yes," Iosif said. "Thank you. I fine. I sixteen. I Iosif Rusval. I..." he paused and gathered his thoughts. "Girl is ... fine also?" he asked.

Wright relayed his question to the parents. "They say she's with the doctors and she's expected to make a full recovery," he said. "She's been in a sort of coma—they're not used to the air pressure down at our level. You've probably noticed how thin the air is up here."

"Ah." Iosif nodded. He had, but the comment reminded him of something. "I… have breathing problem," he said. "How…?"

"Asthma?" Wright seemed to think it over. "They might have something. I think the Osaka family made some rebreathers for Underlanders with lung problems."

"Osaka?" Iosif tilted his head.

"I'm not the only aviator being kept up here." Wright gave another dry smile. "Not even the first. Just the closest. Tell you what, how about we go for a walk and take a look at your airship."

∞o∞

"They call themselves the Tywlyth Teg." Wright told him, as they walked. "Elves, you'd probably know them as."

"Nu-nne-hi, maybe?"

Wright glanced at him, impressed. "Well, you're a surprising one. Yes, that's one of their names—technically more the name of an alliance, I understand. A coalition they were a part of. With humans, presumably—not sure who else there could be. The word means 'people of all places,' but they don't use it much anymore."

"Alliance… why?" Iosif asked.

Wright shrugged. "Not sure. Probably for a war or something. Alliances usually are."

"Ah."

"You've got a good eye for airships, kid." Wright told him, turning back to the aircrafts, stacked in their curving hanger like peas in a pod. "I mean, mostly what you've got there is a retrofitted Tegn flier, but in a way that's more impressive—you've already grasped the basics of their tech and how to use it."

Iosif nodded. "Interesting how they fix," he said, squinting at the aliens (*Tegs*, he reminded himself) who were rapidly taking apart his work and adding in more of their components.

"Yes." Wright said. "If you can follow it you're further along than I am—I'm still floored just by how they use manage to employ electricity on such a massive scale—for nearly everything. They have some way of getting it from the sun—" he waved his hand vaguely. "Has to do with those giant roof panels at the top."

Electricity. That explained why none of this made sense, but at the same time it just added yet another thing that didn't make sense.

"They have ground stations they land at from time to time." Wright said. "To get supplies and such. Always out in the middle of nowhere, though, where no one can see them."

"Why hide?"

Wright frowned, still looking out at the sky. "I don't know," he said. "It just seems to be a general assumption. I wouldn't say they're afraid of humans, and I wouldn't say they scorn them either. They'd hardly let us walk around free up here, if that were the case."

"But… you prisoner," Iosif said. "Yes?"

Wright exhaled loudly. "Essentially. You're not allowed to take out any airships, a *martilon* keeps track of all your movements, etc." He shrugged. "It's not so bad. They give you a house, *and* a living stipend. It's comfortable here—certainly beautiful." Again he looked around at the city. "They have wonders here we never dreamed of in Ohio. We could have been millionaires and never lived this well." There was a short silence. "It's not so bad."

Before Iosif could make any sort of reply, the bracelet Wright had on his wrist chirped. He glanced at it.

"C'mon." He gave a hand to Iosif. "They say Salali's woken up. I suspect she'll want to meet you."

Salali's eyes were blue, Iosif discovered. He'd never seen her with her eyes open before, but when he arrived with Wright and saw her glancing about the hospital room like a lost little girl (she even was gripping her parents' hands rather tightly), his first thought was how startlingly blue her eyes were.

Those eyes grew even wider when they landed on him, and immediately she launched into a flood of speech, directed at her parents. Iosif could only assume it was about him, based on the amount of pointing.

Whatever she learned, she eventually turned around and spoke to him in slow, halting words. They sounded vaguely like English, but there were so many stops and starts and stammers, Iosif really wasn't sure. She was a lot redder than she'd been before, too, he noticed.

Wright turned to him. "She's thanking you, and she says she'd like to know your name."

Iosif looked at Wright quizzically. "Iosif Rusval," he said.

Wright elbowed him. "Say it to *her*."

This whole thing seemed very unnecessary and uncomfortable, Iosif felt. Turning to the girl, he gave a little half-bow, as Wright had done, and said "I Iosif Rusval." A pause. "I sixteen."

The girl repeated the words, slowly, haltingly. "Ai—Ee—oh—sehf—Rross—vull." A pause. "Ai—secks—tene."

Wright chuckled, and the girl looked at him with startled eyes. Wright said a few words, and the girl covered her mouth with her unnaturally long hands. She mumbled a few words quickly.

"She says she's very happy to meet you, and that her name is Salali te Laynetha." Wright shrugged. "But you knew that already. She says she hopes you will come see her again, when she is better able to receive visitors, and tell her all about the outside world." Wright paused and cocked an eye at the taller male, who was speaking very rapidly to Salali, and chuckled. "Her father is telling her that she is far too interested in the Underworld for her own good." He waved Iosif toward the door. "We should go, this is likely to drag on for a while."

Indeed it seemed so, as Salali cut her father off in mid-sentence with a fiery question. The mother spread her hands to silence both of them, but the argument was already taking off and nothing could stop it now.

"They'll patch it up eventually." Wright said, guiding Iosif toward the exit. "You'll have plenty of time to visit later."

It soon became apparent that 'time' was all Iosif had. As Orville had said, he was given a small place near to the center of the construct, and a stipend of food, which seemed mainly to consist of vegetables and assorted birds. He was allowed to wander the city, but not to approach the edge of the disc without an escort. And it was made very clear that he would never be returning to the world below.

His pleas to the Governor's Council were unavailing. "Iosif, the Council has been holding aviators here for hundreds of years." Wright told him, after yet another fruitless meeting with the ruling body. "They're not going to suddenly stop doing it now."

"But … is problem with nirumbee! America!" Iosif protested.

Wright shrugged. "They've passed that on to the other cities—they might even convene a Parliament to discuss the matter. But until then, nothing can be done. Technically the Isolation Decree isn't even theirs to change—it was a decision made by the Collective for the good of all the cities."

"But… is not… were not nirumbee part of alliance… of nu-ne-hi?"

Wright shrugged. "Possibly? I'm surprised enough to learn they exist, no one here has ever mentioned them before."

Iosif sighed. He missed Grey. Grey would have known how to handle the Council. He missed Kilroy too—her biting wit would have been a pleasure to witness when aimed against the Council. Or Snorky, who could have least made some amusing comments. Or Hougan—Hougan would have cut through all this red tape by now and made some real progress on the matter. Iosif couldn't help but feel he was standing still, stuck on a beautiful, but unrelated, event in his life. He was incapable of thinking of this strange world as his home for the rest of his life. He wanted to get back to his real home, his world, his friends. But he wasn't sure how to do it.

Wright told him to find a hobby, and he tried. He had Salali (who had recovered quickly) explain their technology to him. He went around the city and visited the different parts—there was an older section near the core that was really fascinating, you could see how the technology had evolved from when the cities had lifted off years ago. Wright had hosted a little party where some of the other Underworld aviators from other cities came over to hear Iosif's halting account of the world below— he even met Wilbur, Orville's brother. They all agreed it was very horrible, but, well, after all, there was nothing further they could do.

Iosif understood that. He was beginning to understand it all too well.

Somehow, staying in the city helped him regain his fear of heights. He became terrified of going too close to the edge, even if it hadn't been against the rules. He stopped going to the older, less reliable, core segment, or even to any of the other levels. He found that even when he walked around the disc, he was feeling the structural weaknesses underfoot and thinking all about the ways they could fail.

"She says she's been worried about you, Iosif." Wright said. He stood with Salali in the anteroom of Iosif's gourd (he'd learned they were called *vil-rayneth* but honestly he had a hard time as seeing them as anything other than gourds). "You haven't been outside in days."

"No?" Iosif thought about this. "Days... so hard to tell, here."

Salali sighed when Wright relayed this. "She says you need to get out more. It can't be healthy to stay inside all the time."

Iosif shrugged. "Maybe."

"Look, I'm a little worried about you myself." Wright said. "Everyone has trouble adjusting—things were a little rough for me too—but this... what have you been even doing in here, all this time?"

Iosif's eyes refused to look at the sketches spread on all the desks and tables, technical drawings, diagrams, data visualizations—of aerocrafts, gliders, and parachutes. "Nothing really." He shrugged.

Salali sighed again. "She asks if you would at least come with her today. She promised you to take you to someplace special for your birthday."

"Did she?" Iosif considered. He didn't remember that. Then something else occurred to him. "Is my birthday?"

Now Wright sighed. "You really should get out, kid."

"I sixteen," Iosif said, absentmindedly. "Seventeen." He corrected. He probably should go out today, it'd been a while... "Maybe later," he said, turning back toward his desk. "Not... today, I..."

Salali crossed the room. Her elongated fingers gripped him by the arms. "Eee...ooo... sehf..." Her eyes sought his. "Pl... EESE... coohm... whit... mehee." She seemed to gather her thoughts. "Ooouuu... WHIL... like."

∽∘∾

"Central column?" Iosif halted when he saw what they were going for. "Where we go?"

"She hasn't told me." Wright said. "Come on." And stepping into the thin air of the central column, he rose in the air, floating upwards.

Iosif really hated this part. It was half the reason why he had stopped going between levels. He understood just enough of the principles behind the levitation fields to be terrified of them failing. He looked at the opposite wall and tried to imagine that he was just walking forward, just stepping forward, that there was a completely solid floor where his foot was about to step…

The floor dropped out from under him, and Iosif nearly threw up as he ascended into the air. He kept his eyes fixed on Wright's shoes—looking down was bad, but looking up was almost worse, somehow. Just to imagine being up as high as the top of the column was dizzying.

Yet as they went up, and up, and up, and floor after floor passed them by, Iosif's dread grew and grew as he realized they were, in fact, going up that high.

Finally, Wright's shoes made a motion, and Iosif pushed his arms back, signaling the lift to take him toward the side. He floated through the exit port with a gulp of relief, entering just a little above the floor and dropping to meet it. For a minute he stood, panting, hands on knees.

A gentle exclamation made him look up. Salali was standing at the head to a set of stairs. *Stairs?* Iosif wondered. *Here?* Mostly those tended to be found in the older sections of the city. Salali looked at him quizzically, then beckoned again. "Ou wihl like," she said again.

Iosif doubted it. He was regretting the whole thing already. His heart was racing, his limbs felt like lead sticks. He felt the city moving beneath his feet and felt all the thin air beneath that. For a moment he seriously considered turning around—but

JD Kloosterman

that would mean facing the levitation field again. Groaning, he followed her up the stairs, and Wright followed him.

The staircase was narrow and claustrophobic, curling around in a wide spiral. "I believe we're right up against the field generator here." Wright explained, gesturing to the inside wall. Occasionally a glow would pulse through the wall (all the walls here seemed to be translucent). "The real reason for it is to support the solar roof—and lift the city itself, of course. The column is just a happy side effect."

"Ah." Iosif was trying not to think of the possibility of the staircase crumbling underneath them.

An exclamation from Salali made him look up the stair, and to his astonishment he saw not the underside of the ever-present solar panels, but only the clear sky above them. Salali ran up the last few steps, and then stood to the side of the staircase, smiling and beckoning them out.

He and Wright emerged onto a small grassy knoll amidst the clouds. An impossibly clear sky stretched above a perfectly lush, green garden, dotted with small white flowers. Clouds towered above and around them, and the sun gleamed down above them both.

"My word…" Wright whispered.

Salali spoke, hands clasped shyly behind her. "Haaa… peee bURth… daey, Eee-oo-sehf."

Iosif said nothing, standing perfectly still, staring all around him. This place… it was impossible. Magical. He felt again the timeless serenity from the aerocraft.

"Ooh" Wright said, stepping close to the edge. "So that's where we are. They really ought to have up a railing."

313

Salali launched into a babble of explanatory jargon. Iosif took one step toward the edge, and realized what Wright was talking about.

The edge of one of the vast petals that made up the solar roof crept into view. The platform they were on was just high enough above the sloping glass that it was possible to completely lose sight of them if one was standing in the exact center. Iosif wondered if that was by design.

He certainly wished he hadn't seen the panels.

"Oh, that's interesting." Wright *hmmed* thoughtfully. "Is that why we're not feeling the wind up here either?"

Salali made an affirmative noise. Glancing at Iosif, she said something that sounded more interrogative.

"She's asking if you like it." Wright clarified it.

"Is… very pretty." Iosif managed. Despite himself, he took a few steps closer to the edge. He had wondered what the solar scales looked like from above. How they actually worked was as elusive as ever—all the electricity stuff was a lot to wrap your head around—but they were still fascinating puzzles. The glimpse he'd caught when he'd flown in had been far too short, and he hadn't even realized what he was seeing. Now he could make out the rain-water sluices, the maintenance crabs walking over the glittering tiles, and the air vents.

He felt someone behind him and turned his head. Salali was standing a little ways back and to the left, looking at him questioningly.

"Is… very nice," Iosif said again. He looked around, but Wright, for whatever reason, had decided to vacate himself to the clear other side of the platform.

Salali said nothing. She just kept staring at him.

Her gaze made him nervous, somehow. He turned back toward the terrifying vista. How far did the petals stretch? A half mile? Surely not. 2000 meters, perhaps. Again, it was hard to tell with the slope. Iosif wondered why this platform had ever been built. They must be… twenty feet, perhaps, above the petals. More than enough height for someone to dash their brains out on the solar scales (or smash through them and get shards embedded in them before dashing their brains out on the floor below).

Iosif shivered. "I… not good with heights," he said to Salali, fully aware she understood nothing of what he was saying "Not know why. When up high like this... I think… well, mostly I think of how other things might break, smash… all that might go wrong… but… also…" he swallowed, staring at the sloping blue glass. "Also… I wonder. How it feel… What it would be like…" He stepped forward, to the very edge, staring down. "… to jump. Or just… step." His feet were on the very verge. "I… I want to, almost. Just to see what it would be like." He looked over at Salali's uncomprehending eyes. "I am curious, you see. And I feel curiosity, what would it be, to fall, through the air, just …" He lifted his foot, ever so slightly.

There was a silent moment. Iosif felt how simple it would be. Simple as moving his foot a few inches forward. That wasn't such a big deal, really. Just taking a step. What would that be like?

He stepped back a little, and shuddered, looking up to the clouds. "Is so." He turned around fully to look at Salali, who was still watching him, and he gave a tight smile. "We go now?"

But to his surprise, Salali grinned back, a wide smile, with a twinkle in her eyes. And then, before he realized what she was doing, she darted forward and pushed him off the edge of the platform.

∽∘∾

Iosif couldn't even hear his screams for the first five seconds or so of falling. The air sang over his eardrums, and the blood thundered in his head. The tower flashed past him, surreally slow.

He heard a whoop from above and looked up to see Salali jumping after him, Wright's arm making an unsuccessful grab at her cloak. She had her arms tucked closer to her sides, blue cloak and flaxen hair streaming out behind her in the speed of her fall. Iosif had a bizarrely precise impression of her face, laughing gleefully as they fell.

And then he realized that he really should not have time to notice all of this, and that some force was starting to pull him out, away from the tower, translating the speed of his fall into a different velocity.

Iosif tumbled over in the air, and saw with feverish gaze the solar scales not rushing up to meet him, but rushing *past*, like rippling water, as he flew mere feet from their glittering surface.

A slender hand with elongated fingers grasped his, and there was Salali, laughing beside him, also flying over the sloped surface of the petals. Her mouth was moving, she was saying words, but Iosif could not hear them over the roaring wind.

They shot along, darting past the maintenance droids, crisscrossing over raining sluices. Salali shouted something at him and angled her body, sweeping off to the right. Iosif tried to copy her movements and also coasted—more of a yaw than a sweep, but he followed her. She looked at him with wide, happy eyes and laughed. And he laughed back.

He did not even have a chance to see the edge of the petals coming up.

He and Salali shot over the edge, into thin air. Before Iosif even had time to register the yawning expanse below them, the levitation field was pulling them back in, slingshotting them along the underside of the solar petals.

But Salali was done playing. Her face suddenly serious, she grabbed Iosif with one hand, and with the other, pressed a button on her belt. They plunged discward, landing at high velocity in an unused catwalk high on the city.

Right next to a flyer.

Salali pulled Iosif to his feet. She pushed him toward the flyer. "Youuu ... goh," she said.

Iosif's startled mind was still taking in the fact that there, in front of him, was a flier—a glider, he decided, absorbing the notable lack of engines. The wings had an odd curve to them, and there was a cockpit where someone small could sit, and he was next to a glider on the upper levels on a deserted catwalk.

Where the *martilons* couldn't stop him.

He turned at Salali with wide eyes, seeing the girl for what he felt was the first time.

"You goh," she said, more distinctly. "N-ow."

Yet Iosif lingered.

"N-ow!" She stamped her foot in frustration.

They were short on time, he knew, it was only a matter of time before the *martilons* found out where they were, but suddenly, he had so much he wanted to ask this girl.

She saw the question in his eyes. "Salali kno-ghs wuat… eht ehs…" she said, carefully. "…t-ooh bee cay-gede ahnd wahnt… toh fly."

Iosif felt he ought to do something. Thank her; give her a hug… something.

But then there was a shout, and he saw two workers on the lower levels pointing up at them.

Salali hissed under her breath and twisted something on her bracelet. There was a series of bright flashes, and the workers flailed about, blinded. Salali practically pushed Iosif into the glider. "You goh!" She slammed the canopy behind him and kicked over something on the side.

There was an explosion, further down the catwalk, and suddenly the world was tilting. The glider slid at an incline off the catwalk, clearing the edge of the disc by inches, and then it was out in the air.

Iosif had managed to spend enough time around Tegn aircraft by this point to have a pretty good understanding of how the controls were supposed to work. He had not gotten a much better understanding of how flying was supposed to work, though. Wright had told him about updrafts and rising air columns and air pressure—but it had been mostly theory, and a little outside Iosif's usual field.

But after all, he was not flying so much as falling, and as the glider coasted downward, he spared a look back up to the Tegn city, already fast vanishing behind him. He couldn't even see the Martilon fliers launching—they would not venture far from the central construct, he knew.

"Goodbye," he said.

CHAPTER 17

4::931077::9103

Sally,

I've looked everywhere for the hog and his piglet. Nothing yet, but I'm almost positive they were never sent to the butcher's shop. But they're not in any of the usual pens—though apparently we have a lot more of those than I thought. I'll keep at it—things aren't too hot here yet.

How's the horse?

Gary

9::231844::1005

9::231844::1005

The horse is well, though his constant braying gets on my nerves. Hopefully he'll be out in the yoke again before too long.

Cheers,

Sally

4::931077::9103

Iosif didn't like the hat. It was big and floppy and kept getting in the way of his eyes. He didn't like the tinted eyeglasses either. But he didn't like being a fugitive, and he suspected he would like being a captive even less, and this was the basic sort of costume the Dick Tracy villains wore when they were hiding from the law, so it was all he had to go on.

He didn't much care for San Francisco. It was too bright, too hot, too salty. Apparently Wright had been correct when he said the cities wandered around. He'd crashed in some sort of vineyard, walked two hours to an adjoining farm, and stolen the farmer's tractor. He did feel bad about that, but if the farmer'd known who he was, he doubted Black Chamber would have been very merciful with him. So it was really for the best.

Hacking a railcar would be easy, but he had to get inside one first, and he had no money to call one. Most of his belongings he'd left with the Teg. He had the toolbelt, of course—even in the elven city, he'd worn it everywhere—but he was loath to sell any of its components. They might be traced to him.

So he paced the blinding pavement of San Francisco, wracking his brain furiously. Get a job? Too slow. Rob a store? Too illegal. Sell his coat? Who would buy it here? He had to get to Dallas, some way, any way; nearly the only thing he could remember from the attack was that the others had been going to a safehouse in Dallas. But he couldn't walk there, and it was starting to look like…

"Rusval! Iosif Rusval!"

Iosif froze. Should he run? Should he act natural and keep walking? But he'd already frozen, so that was…

"Don't be like that!" A meaty hand grabbed him by the shoulder and he was whirled around to face a potbellied man with a pencil mustache, in a yellow striped suit and a sunhat. "I'd know you anywhere!"

Iosif stared. He, most assuredly, did not know this man.

"Vern!" The man said, gesturing to himself. "Vern Bankston! Don't you know your own business partner? With the elevators, eh? You sent me the blueprints!"

"Ah." Iosif slowly nodded. "Yes... yes, of course, Bankston's Silos, yes." It seemed a lifetime ago, the modified elevator he'd created, the entrepreneur he'd reached out to... yes, that had been a Bankston. "Forgive me, I... have never seen you before... not in person."

"What?" The man seemed injured by the admission. "Well sure, I know we only *made* the agreement over the mail system, but... Never seen my billboards? My pamphlets? My lovable mascot Billy Bankston the Barley Loaf?" He waved away the question before Iosif could protest. "Oh, never mind, never mind. But I know you, Mr. Rusval!"

"Ah?" Iosif could only think to say.

"Yep!" The man draped an arm over his shoulders and began to pull him along the street. "C'mon, we'll find a watering hole and I can tell you all about it!"

∞

"It was some government men." Bankston said, some time later, pouring out a glass of some fizzy drink. "Dunno what department, but they came in asking if you'd contacted me. And I said, shucks, I been trying to contact you. And they said, you sure? And I said, whadda I look like, some idjit who don't know his own business? And they said, okay, but if he shows up you let us know. Showed me your picture and everything." Bankston gulped down his drink in record time.

"Ah." Iosif sniffed the drink cautiously. It had a faintly malty touch to it. "Yes... those men... they are after me..."

Bankston held up a finger. "Not a word, Joseph my man, not a word! Can I call you Joseph, by the way? Not a word about those men. Here in 'Cisco we know how a man often has side businesses, knowwhatImsaying? I don't judge. Not me. I'm a practical man. I looked, you know, and I saw that business in Pittsburgh, and looked it up. You were in that postal building that burned down, weren't ya? But why'd they come asking questions, if they thought you were dead? Now I don't know if you're covering your tracks or if they're trying to kill ya, but hey, s'all good, y'know?"

"...good," Iosif said.

"But I *was* tryin' to get in touch with ya!" The man said, his eyes widening as he leaned in closer. "That elevator thing... its sellin' like hotcakes! We're making more of them than silos now! That whole accident—man, we couldna asked for better publicity! Any other lift woulda absolutely plummeted, knowwhatImsayin'? Killed everyone on board. But your little gadget? Boom!" He clapped his hands together. "Everyone survives. Just the ticket. People get to see the safety functions inna really dramatic way."

"Oh!" Iosif nodded. "So... is good, then?"

"Good? My man, it is the latest thing! Everyone's wantin' a Bankston elevator in their building! No more stairs! People don't feel terrified a tha lift no more!" Bankston sat back in his chair.

"Seriously, my man, you have made. My. Day. I cannot tell you how grateful I am for our partnership. Words cannot express it."

"Good." Iosif couldn't help but feel this was very much *not* what he was interested in at the moment.

Bankston seemed to notice his disinterest. "Hey man, you okay? Is it the thing with the feds? Listen, if there's *anything* I can do to help out..."

Iosif's head came up. He suddenly saw the potential in this. "I try to get to Dallas..." he said.

∽o∾

The seat beneath him was plush leather, and the clear glass windows gave a beautiful view of the Rocky Mountains as they roared past. Iosif felt a little annoyed with the little cabinet under the seat with all the bottles—it kept popping out and banging against his legs.

It was Bankston's own private waycar, but he'd insisted he was meaning to get a new one anyway. Iosif felt that the permission to hack the control box had been implied in that statement. The bills in Iosif's pocket were not Bankston's, he had been very specific that they were actually Iosif's cut of the profits, which he had not yet received. Iosif took them out and flipped through them, feeling rather pleased with the look.

The gun in Iosif's other pocket, that had been bought by Bankston's man Hemenford. Its presence did not reassure Iosif greatly—he was still not a good shot. But it was something.

The bottom of the waycar was littered with news bulletins. Iosif had been paging through them for a while. It seemed everyone had accepted the "mafia attack" story, though the committee investigating the matter said the case was still ongoing. It was a relief to learn that none of the 'administrative employees' had been killed—apparently Black Chamber felt that no one would listen to a community of insane and infirm agents. There was no mention of the warehouse workers, though. Iosif wondered about that.

There was no mention of Hougan's condition or any of the others. He supposed they wouldn't be likely to announce shooting Grey or Kilroy, but they might announce their *deaths*. They were probably still alive, then, probably still out and on the run. He rubbed his nose. Probably.

"The safehouse in Dallas," he remembered Hougan saying. Unfortunately he had absolutely *no* memory of what house in Dallas that might be, and the city map indicated that Dallas had a *lot* of houses.

Not for the first time, he reconsidered. He had plenty of money in his pocket, now. He could easily turn this car around at the next junction—head to Detroit instead. Pick up Mother, go to Canada. Buy a house. Fix watches.

He shook his head. No. He had to know. He had to find out what had happened to the others. Help them, if he could. Anyway, they were probably watching his house. Going there would just get his mother arrested. He might never be able to see his mother again. That was a thought. He and the others, they might spend the rest of their lives on the run, living double lives, unable to ever see again the people they loved.

Iosif again shook his head. These long rides really made your mind wander.

Dallas was, if possible, brighter and hotter than San Francisco had been, though at least it was not quite as humid. Iosif had originally thought of going to the Post Office, but realized halfway there that it was too obvious. Then he'd thought of getting in with Snorky's underworld contacts, before realizing that he had no idea who those underworld contacts would be. Then he considered talking to Grey's friends, only Grey didn't really have friends. He even briefly toyed with the idea of seeing if Kilroy's ex-husband lived in the area, but he knew virtually nothing about the man and it seemed a doomed enterprise.

Still. It seemed like the place to go would be a bar. So he went to a bar.

"We don't serve minors here, kid," said the woman behind the counter, polishing a glass.

"I seventeen," Iosif said.

The lady spared him a glance. "Then come back in four years."

"Perhaps I have glass of milk?" Iosif suggested hopefully, laying a five-dollar coin on the counter.

The lady looked at the coin, looked at him, and sighed. "Sure, why not," she said, turning around. "Lemmee see what we have in the icebox. It's only the middle of the day, why wouldn't you want milk?"

Iosif frowned as she disappeared. He had the vague sensation that she was unhappy with the arrangement, but he wasn't sure why. It was true that it was an unusual time of day—nearly all the seats in the bar were empty.

Truth be told, Iosif was hoping for a miracle. Some stray conversation, some random stranger—some pure happenstance event that would tell him where the safehouse was. It was a bit much to hope for, maybe, but happenstance had served him well so far—it had sent Bankston to him, for one.

But so far nothing was happening. And it did not look like he had chosen the best place for a miracle. Accepting the glass of milk with a nod, he walked back to the booth, settled down with a sigh, and decided to think.

All right. A safehouse. What would a safehouse look like? Low profile, presumably. Secure, isolated, but with ready access to a getaway route. Boat? But no, Dallas did not have much of a waterfront to speak of, only a reservoir. Close to the Grand Column? But that would ruin the low profile.

He frowned. This was going nowhere. Approach it from another angle, perhaps. *If* they had planned to go there, they must have felt confident it had not been compromised. But they had known about the letters and the rail tracks. So it must not have been a place they'd been to before, not a place they'd ever written about, nor a place directly connected to any of them.

So he knew what the safe house *wasn't*, and he had a few ideas about what it *was*. That still left a lot to figure.

Another thought. If they'd never been in the area, how could they feel confident they would all know the address? Unless it wasn't a particular address; but just a location everyone would be familiar with. But then it wouldn't keep a low profile. Unless it was a *famous* location that *no one* would think to look in…

Iosif groaned and rubbed his forehead. This was pointless. He was a machinist, not an investigator. If Black Chamber's agents couldn't sort it out, how was he supposed to?

Because he was a member of Hougan's team. He should know how they thought. Except apparently he wasn't, because he didn't.

Suddenly he had a thought. There *was* a source of quick getaway routes in Dallas, aside from the waterways. They even tended to be located in rural areas, where the rails didn't reach. The only problem was that there were a lot of them. How to narrow it down?

"Yeah, this here ranch used to be a Pony Express Station," the foreman said as he led Iosif around the farm. "Still technically part of the post office, I s'pose, but buried so deep in the funding everyone's forgotten about us. Ain't no problem for me. They use it mostly—or at least they usedta—as a retirement home fer old service horses. We've still got a few from the Great War that they sent here—ole warhorses, ya know. I mostly jest come out here to give 'em feed and a good rubdown. They've earned their rest, I reckon."

"Ah." Iosif had not really asked for the tour, but the old cowboy had insisted. "What is house there?" He pointed.

The cowboy looked. "Ah, now that there's the old riding post where the stablehands usedta stay. Bunks and such. Bit of a museum now, though a'course no one visits it much, so I keep it locked up. Bit of an eyesore, but historical building, y'know, so not much you can do. Now, ya oughta see the water tower…"

It was half an hour before Iosif could slip away from the talkative wrangler and run over to the historical barracks house. He halted outside the door. Should he call out? Knock? Was there a secret knock? Should he just pick the lock? But no, the last time he had barged into a room he'd nearly gotten shot. He gave a few experimental raps on the door.

No response. That wasn't much of a surprise. Maybe it was a secret knock, maybe he was the first one here.

Maybe he was the only one left.

Iosif pushed the thought away and knelt next to the door. His lockpicks were stored in the belt. He took them out, and a few minutes work popped open the lock.

He swung the door open, and found himself staring into the barrel of a Tommy gun.

He had just time to absorb that he did not know the grim-faced man on the other end before a sharp pain exploded at the back of his head and everything went black.

∽o∾

Iosif woke up in a narrow coffin of metal. His arms and legs were shackled, and he could barely move for the tightness of the container. He could only stare out the small glass window directly before him, at the bruised and bloody form of Percival Hougan, Central Postal Director.

"Rusval." Hougan nodded, as best as he could with his hands chained behind his back. "Terrible to see you again."

CHAPTER 18

1::931815::2416

Hello dear Director of Missing Persons

This is Nancy Rusval again. I'm sorry for constantly bothering you, but I'm afraid I still have not received any word regarding my son, despite your assurance. Agent Smith was very considerate, but I haven't heard a peep from him since our first meeting together, and he hasn't responded to any of my letters.

If you could simply get in touch with him and ask him to touch base with me, it would be great to have some sort of word. Iosif was a Machinist in the Automated Postal Department—I believe he worked directly with the Director. I don't know if he was working at all that day, but he used to mail me every week, and it's been months since I last heard from him. His ID number was 592-4113.

If you could tell me what Agent Smith has discovered, or have him contact me, I would be ever so grateful.

Sincerely,
Mrs. Rusval.

4:115123:983

"**Y**ou too, sir," Iosif said. The reply was automatic; it was only after he said it that he realized that the director hadn't in fact said it was *good* to see him.

Fortunately the statement, as it held, was perfectly accurate. Hougan sported one eye nearly complete swelled shut and a purplish-grey bruise on his jaw. There was caked blood under his nose. The old man was on his knees, and quite clearly chained to the floor.

Iosif could see more now, but he almost wished he couldn't. He could see long rows of coffins like his own—dull metal tubes with fins on the top--stretching away into the dark, hanging on chains like slabs of meat in a packing house. Bombs, he realized. Bombs hollowed out with small windows cut in. They swayed gently back and forth with a sensation that made Iosif feel a little ill, particularly as it made him conscious of his own rocking.

"Mr. Hougan tried to, ah, escape recently." Flistworth loomed out of the darkness between the bombshells just opposite Iosif. "I, ah, apologize for his appearance, but in my defense… the men he ran into on his way out look much worse."

"Good to know I've still got it." Hougan gave a little smile.

Iosif swallowed nervously, looking at the thin man.

"Oh, you may relax, Mr. Rusval." Flistworth smiled, just slightly more widely than was natural. "I shall not, ah, keep you long. Ar-range-ments have already been made." Stopping between the two of them, he looked from one to the other and steepled his fingers—Iosif thought the fingers actually grew as he did so. "I merely wanted to, ah, show you to your… former employer, so that he, ah, understands the situation."

"You're going to try and break me by threatening him." Hougan gave a level stare.

"That would be a, ah, waste." There was something odd about the way Flistworth's eyes rolled behind the thick glasses. "Mr. Rusval is far more useful to us in another capacity. Besides, such a plan would depend on your... hope that we would eventu-al-ly release your, ah, subordinate, and you are far too... practical a man for such things."

"Hm." Hougan nodded and glanced up at Iosif. "Sorry, Rusval. I told you this was dangerous, but I thought we could avoid it."

"I suppose you may have, ah, loved ones." Flistworth glanced over at Iosif. "The few you have must be e-spec-i-ally dear to you." He shrugged. "But their... disappearance might raise an, ah, inquiry, which would be troublesome at this juncture."

Hougan frowned at him. "You attacked a major government headquarters in broad daylight using a zeppelin."

"Which no one of any, ah, consequence was stationed at." Flistworth raised a finger. "The entire... purpose of the Postal Department is to be, ah, ignored. Before you, of course. Ver-y few people will miss your merry band of outcasts." Again the too-wide smile. "No, Mr. Hougan, I have brought your subordinate here in order to, ah, crush your hopes. To persuade you that your stubbornness is... meaningless."

"What... you even want?" Iosif asked. He was pretty sure the only things of value the conspiracy had held were in the vault, which Flistworth himself had opened.

"What he knew, who he told, and where they are." Flistworth shot him an annoyed glance, as if irritated with the interruption. "Things that I, ah, im-a-gine you know very... little about."

Iosif was pretty sure that there had been no accumulation of evidence, and he was also relatively sure that Hougan had told no one outside the group of his plans. But a look from Hougan convinced him to keep his mouth shut. Anyway, Flistworth had a point—that was the sort of information that he could hardly be privy to, as a Machinist.

Flistworth was still looking at him. "Your eyes are most… fas-cin-at-ing, Mr. Rusval," he said, stepping forward. "I, ah, noticed them when we first met. As you, ah, noticed me, which was itself very, ah, noticeable. Not many people do."

"I know what you are." Hougan struggled to sit up straighter. "You're…" he seemed to search for the word a moment. "…Edith told us about your kind. Shadow-man."

"*Tariaksuq.*" Flistworsth smiled. "That is the, ah, local name. Yes. A name, for that thing they say you only see moving in the corner of your eye. The thing that disappears when you try to look at it." Flistworth smirked. "It can be very useful, in government service, to only be seen when you, ah, *want* to be seen."

Iosif remembered. No one seeing Flistworth when he reminded the senator about Iosif. The others talking about how the senator was at Fort Sumter 'alone.' Rickenbacker's strange questioner.

"The, ah, original inhabitants also called us skin-walkers, *yee-naaldiooshi,*" Flistworth said, walking a little ways away, "even if they didn't know we were the, ah, same. Like *wendigo. Jinni. Changeling.* How can you know what a, ah, shapeshifter truly looks like?" He smiled, and this time it reached nearly to his ears. His hand stretched longer than it ought to and caressed the side of one of the bombs, hanging from the ceiling. "What a shadow *is*?"

He looked back at them. "They, ah, forgot about us." His face actually flickered, the flesh rippling in a disquieting manner. "They wanted to. This, ah, modern world... they tried to banish the dark... explain away the shadows. They pushed the unknown to the stars and, ah, told each other the earth was *safe.*" Again the flesh rippled. "They thought they killed us all, and so they tried to forget us."

Iosif remembered an old daguerreotype, hanging in the abandoned room on the upper level of the apartments. "You... with Carnegie," he said. The others looked at him. "In picture. Of businessmen."

"Been at this a while, haven't you?" Hougan said.

"It *has* taken a while, yes, thank you for noticing." Flistworth turned to look at the director. "A long, and slow, job, but it is quite, ah, rewarding to see it coming together at last." His eyes glowed, even through the filtered lenses.

"Why gnomes?" Hougan said. "What do you have against them?"

Flistworth considered. "Why do I need to, ah, have a reason? They were useful and they were at hand. They were also in the co-a-li-tion that destroyed my people; the Nunnehi, the Tuatha de Danaan. They were at the Last Push of Nikwasi. But so were many others." He shrugged. "They were simply, ah, convenient." A grin spread across his face, a small one, almost natural. "Though a part of me is, ah, *amused* that the resurrection of my race has come about through one of our greatest enemies enslaving one of their own allies."

"Ressurection?" Hougan asked.

"The eyeball…" Iosif said. "…man you stabbed in eyeball… Dragon's tooth?"

"So you *did* see that." Flistworth's eyes glowed momentarily. "The Dragon's Tooth Program is simple, ah, reproduction at its core. I have used it to create suitable, ah, hosts for my people." His hand grew long, slender, stretching in various segmented sections to loom up and tap the glass in front of Iosif's face with its bone-like probiscus. "I cannot implant simply, ah, anyone, you understand. It has taken me many years to create a world safe for my children, years more for me to devise a successful process to ensure their health and, ah, loyalty, and several additional years for our numbers to swell from one to a hundred." The long finger shrank back into his hand. "I *have* been working on this a long time, but it is finally coming to fruition."

"It won't last," Hougan said. "Your conspiracy is too large. Sooner or later, someone will slip up—someone will notice. My team won't be the last."

"Your, ah, team was not the first," Flistworth said, turning fully to face the director. "People *have* slipped up, and people *have* noticed. But again, so many of them have decided they did not *want* to notice. You don't somehow believe that the Carnegie Empire fell and no one, ah, noticed the army of slaves he'd, ah, accumulated? The government did not, ah, care about Carnegie's abuses so much as the fact that they did not control them. They did not want to, ah, explain to voters why suddenly their mail, their rails *cost* so much more." He grinned, a small one this time. "It was as unavoidable as it was predictable. Like clockwork. And people did not ask how it was accomplished because they did not care. *You* did not ask. Very few people actually want to know how the world, ah, ticks."

"Uh-huh." Hougan grunted. "And despite that, you work so hard to keep it secret because … ?"

Flistworth rolled his glowing eyes. "Being the sole survivor of one's species gives one a taste for, ah, subtlety. It is easier to control the process when no one knows how the workings, ah, work." He waved a hand. "Doubtless, if the … camps were made public there would be, ah, troublemakers."

"Doubtless." Hougan's voice was very dry. "I seem to recall we fought a war over such things."

"Yes, yes," Flistworth said. "After over a century of the practice, but yes. The moral outrage would make conflict eventually unavoidable. Just as it was with you." Flistworth shook his head, staring at Hougan. "You could not abide a falsehood in the records. Your… honesty made acceptance of the lie un-ac-cept-a-ble. When it comes down to it, Mr. Hougan, you were not particularly bright or brutal, you were simply stubborn. I should have seen that, ah, armed conflict with you was in-ev-i-ta-ble, but then…" he shrugged. "…I didn't calculate on your bullheaded investigation actually, ah, getting anywhere. It shouldn't have. It wouldn't have. If you hadn't bumped into *him*." And at this he turned to glare at Iosif.

Iosif felt strangely happy to be included in the conversation, then guilty about feeling happy.

"You gave him a puzzle he couldn't crack." Flistworth turned to face Iosif fully, eyes glowing. "As, ah, intolerable to him as a lie you couldn't believe was to you. You dragged Mr. Rusval out of his shop to a path that could only end here." Flistworth gestured around at the dark room. "Predictable. Or it should have been." He grimaced. "I should have foreseen the outcome, if I'd realized sooner your machinist was half-gnome."

Iosif blinked. He himself was not very surprised—he'd started to guess it among the elves—but he was astonished Flistworth knew. And equally astonished at how little surprised Hougan seemed to be.

Flistworth noticed this also. "So you knew?" he said, turning.

"Not exactly," Hougan said. "But it was pretty obvious there were some links after your man in Fort Sumter mistook him for one of the 'prisoners.' Plus there was the strength … and the eyes."

"Yes." Flistworth's glowing eyes looked up at Iosif's shining ones. "Also the ugliness and the need to shave every day."

Hougan looked at Iosif. "While Grey dug up the employee records, I visited your mother. She said your father showed up on her doorstep some twenty years ago, bleeding from four or five bullets. Said he was a small, bearded man who never told her much about his past, and that he disappeared to help some friend." He shook his head. "I should have told you. I thought, at the time, your father might have been a super-soldier experiment that escaped. Didn't know how to tell that to a man."

Iosif wasn't sure how to react to that. It seemed one should have some sort of reaction to revelations about one's ancestry, but he was more astonished that Hougan had hidden something from him. Almost as though Hougan had lied.

"Un-fort-u-nate, you two meeting each other." Flistworth gave a tight, almost pouty, frown. "For all involved. Otherwise you might never have died for such a, ah, point-less cause."

"Even if you were right," Hougan said, looking at the shapeshifter, "I'd do it again."

Flistworth simply nodded. "Of, ah, course you would, Mr. Hougan. As would Mr. Rusval. As would I, even if I believed I was wrong. This whole conversation is a simple, ah, formality."

His arm shot out suddenly and yanked on a lever just beside Iosif's coffin. Iosif felt the chain above him come loose, and then his bomb was screaming downward through the air. He had barely time to register the lights of Fort Sumter in the bay before he hit the water.

∞∞

It was a sub that picked him up, gliding up through the water within seconds of his arrival. Silent men took the bomb and loaded it below decks, without so much as looking at him. He was brought out again, much later, onto the loading dock of one of the beetle-like Water Environmental Monitoring Stations. Dark-suited men emerged from the steam and took his coffin, under the station, down a long shaft.

A crane's long pincher took hold of the coffin. As it swung him around, Iosif caught a flashing, frenzied view of a ring of open-ended concrete cells, suspended in air around a single column. One in particular grew closer and closer as the crane stretched out toward it. Words rang out above Iosif's head, garbled through the glass, and before him, shining eyes appeared in the dark of the cell. Small, warted men with long beards came out of the gloom, craning their heads around to look at him.

Iosif heard a *click* above him, and the front of the coffin suddenly opened up, sending him sprawling into thin air. He caught sight, far below, of churning dark water…

And then pale arms grabbed hold of his and pulled him into the cell, even as the crane pulled up and away with some last garbled words of warning.

"Just one?" He heard one of the bearded men mutter. "That's odd."

"Disciplinary case, maybe," said another, a white-bearded man with a horribly scarred face. "Big fella, isn't he?" He gave Iosif a quick slap on the shoulder, clearly meant more to rouse him than to cheer him. "Hey? You. What's your name?"

"I Iosif," Iosif said. "I six—" he corrected himself. "I *seven*teen."

"Hm." The gnome seemed unimpressed. "Greetings and Peace to you, Iosif." He turned away. "For however long you survive."

CHAPTER 19

4:115123:983

Mrs. Rusval,

Thank you for your continued patience with us. As it happened, there have been no signs of your son. We did manage to find his office in the administrative centre, though that was, as you have doubtless heard, badly damaged by the fighting. We were only really able to recover an old prayer necklace, which is enclosed with this missive. We do not consider this positive proof of your son's fate one way or another, and will continue to work tirelessly to answer your concerns.

Thank you!

Missing Persons Department

1::931815::2416

T he water woke Iosif. It came gushing out of the grate in the back wall, spraying over the racked beds of the gnomes and over Iosif's little bedroll, spread out on the floor. It was cold, wet, and salty, the sort of irritant impossible to sleep through and ignore, especially if you knew that would only bring more.

"Enough nap time, maggots!" The trumpet at the end of the crane blared, as the gnomes stumbled out of bed. "You've got a rail car to work on. Look sharp!"

The rail car in question was dangling at the end of the crane, a few inches from the open end of the concrete cell. It was pretty easy to see what the problem was—the entire frame was riddled with bullet holes.

"Another one of these," the gnome with the scarred face grumbled. "Iosif, drag it in here with those long arms of yours."

Taking care not to look down, Iosif reached out and grabbed the rail car, hauling it in obediently. He wasn't entirely sure whether Gripgut, the scarred gnome, was officially some sort of leader of the cubicle or whether the others followed his orders out of shared respect, but he knew enough that when Gripgut asked you to grab a rail car, you grabbed it.

Other arms reached out as he pulled it within reach, and soon all seven of the gnomes were maneuvering the rail car into a resting point. "Easy, half-breed," one of the other gnomes, Hogslip grumbled. "Clumsy ox."

"Enough of that," Gripgut snapped. "Get these panels off already. I want an inventory."

Hammers, wrenches, and screwdrivers came out. The little men went to work on the damaged vehicle, tossing the punctured metal aside as they worked it free. Iosif scrambled to pick up the scraps and pile them as neatly as possible.

"Gonna need a new sequencer."

"Transfer switch is all busted."

"Doors are pretty well shattered."

"And the paneling itself is all shot to pieces, obviously," Gripgut muttered, noting down all the observations on a sheet. "Right then." He glanced over at Iosif's pile. "I think we can fabricate most of the parts here, but we're going to need some large pieces for the paneling, and I'll have to send off for the new sequencer. Wheezer and his boys should be able to get one done by tomorrow." He ripped the paper off and stuck in on a hook on the outside of the cell, flipping up a red sign as he did so.

The air filled with whirrs and little *tang* sounds as the gnomes swarmed over the metal vehicle. Steam drills and power saws ground away at the metal with ear-splitting whines. Rapid commands were barked. "Saw! Tooling hammer! 5/8 socket! Gas torch! Screwdriver!"

Iosif grabbed one from the toolbox and dropped it into Gripgut's hand. Gripgut's thumb manipulated the control on the handle without even looking at it; the desired bit extended; and the gnome started unfastening the casing to the old sequencer. "Careful with the pressure tank!" he called suddenly, glancing over. "That's still intact. We'll want that to…"

BOOM!

The cell shook. Iosif and the others looked over to see steam erupting from one of the cells on the other side of the ring. Even as they watched, several figures fell, screaming, from the scalding clouds, plunging into the blackness below.

"Accident?" Hogslip asked.

But Gripgut shook his head, a grim expression twisting the scars on his face.

There was a great whirring noise, and the steam was sucked back into the cell, before it could drift higher. The interior of the cell looked blackened, almost scorched. Iosif thought he could see someone still moving around, but he wasn't sure.

"Why…?" he asked.

Gripgut shrugged. "Maybe they were up to something. Or looked like they were up to something. Maybe they exceeded the catalogued weight for their cell. Maybe the guards were bored, or they bumped a switch. Maybe a valve somewhere failed." He turned away. "Back to work, everyone."

The others did so. But now that the idea had been brought to their attention, the gnome's minds started to work on it.

"I heard in Charleston one cell tried a bathysphere," one gnome said, busily cutting out a section of pipe. "Refilled steam tanks with oxygen and sent it over the edge deliberately. Plan was to dive beyond the sea wall and come out on the other side."

"Did it work?" Hogslip asked, glancing over.

"No. Not sure why. Leading theory is that they have a grate down there."

"Make sense. Couldn't risk bodies popping up outside."

"I heard in Boston someone used a catapult to try to make it to the tower. Didn't even make it half-way."

"When I was in Chicago some idiots tried to use a bridge for that." Another gnome put in. "Used suspension wires anchored to the back wall as supports."

Hogslip scoffed. "Seriously? You think they'd be able to tell the stresses would be too great on the metal."

"You'd think. The other guys said it was a couple newcomers, some *nirumbee* they'd just brought in from the mountains. Desperate."

"That's why they split them up." A dark-haired gnome warned, wagging his finger. "Those nimrods are crazy when they're together."

"They split us all up, Vinoka," Gripgut said. "You know that. People are always being redistributed. They don't want to give us the chance to form teams."

Vinoka grunted. "Caught them off guard, at any rate. The guards know *our* tech inside and out. All these safeguards… I'll bet there's some of *our* folk working with them, actually helping them to predict ways we might try to escape." He glared out at the tower in the center. "A bridge was at least a novel idea."

"I wonder what happened in Seattle," Hogslip said.

"Must've been close, whatever they did."

"That's why I'm wondering about it."

"Wonder about it too much, and they'll dump this whole station into the water," Gripgut cut in again. "Whatever they did in Seattle, all it gained them was a lot of little floating bodies. You want that for everyone here?"

There was some grumbling and muttering. "No sir." "Course not sir." "You're right of course, sir."

Gripgut's dark eyes darted from one of them to the other. "Look over my shoulder," he said. Five gleaming eyes flickered up and then down. "How much you want to bet there's a guard behind that window in the tower? What're the odds he's looking at us?"

"About 1 in 12," Hogslip said.

"1 in 15, I'd say." another said. "After whatever happened with Block 49 over there."

"1 in 3," Vinoka said flatly. "They know *he's* here." He nodded at Gripgut. "And *him*." He jerked his head at Iosif.

Iosif felt a curious pang at being noticed—more, at being considered significant; though he was not sure the comment was complimentary. He liked these men ... admired them, even, but even after a good month among them, he still felt like something of an outsider.

"What, the half-breed?" another gnome snorted.

"If you'd talked to him, you'd know the 'half-breed' broke into the old Fort Sumter station," Gripgut said. "And broke out. Like Vinoka said, the watchers in the tower know all our tricks; they don't know him as well. If they're not stupid, they're keeping an eye out."

"Plus, it means there are seven of us here." Vinoka's movements were smooth and precise as he worked; his voice low and quick. "We're a particular risk. You can bet they're watching us through spyglasses right now."

"And covering us with those machine guns of theirs," Gripgut said. His scars were white against his red skin. "So for the sake of all of us, *shut up* and *keep working*."

The gnomes fell silent and went back to work. Iosif was a little disappointed.

He'd wanted to hear more ideas about escaping.

A crane came by about an hour after and dropped off the parts. Iosif supplied the gnomes with them, but there was not much more to be done until the sequencer arrived. So the crane took the half-finished waycar out of their cell and stored it away someplace else. They were given a police barricade to work on instead. Then it was a central heating boiler. Then a whole array of small orders for each gnome to work on individually. Even Iosif got a turn, working on a power sweeper for—he assumed—another machinist's shop

Gripgut was working on some sort of plated shield—not unlike the ones Iosif had seen in the Post Office raid. "Hang on, I need this bolted in." He reached and pulled a cord hanging in the middle of the cell ceiling.

A telescoping column unfolded from the ceiling. The apparatus at the end of it sported a bolt-gun, a power-drill, a circular saw, a focused gas-light, and an elaborate magnifying lens.

Iosif watched as Gripgut used the boltgun to finish the plating on his shield. It wasn't the first time he'd seen his old invention being used, naturally, but it was still not a particularly pleasant reminder. It brought back happier memories, which right now he could do without.

Gripgut finished and looked up at him. "What is it, half-breed?" he asked, bushy eyebrows lowering.

Iosif ducked his head, then nodded at the apparatus. "Device… it seems could be better managed," he said. "Combine boltgun and power-drill into single head… Attach chain hook for hoisting purposes…"

"Hm." Gripgut cast an appraising eye over the apparatus. "Could be." He gave it a little push and sent it sliding back up into the darkness. "Might want to talk to management about that." He gave a little nod toward the tower. "They love new ideas. Could net you an extra ration or so."

"Best to troubleshoot first," Vinoka cut in. "Bolt-gun combined with the drill might not work so well. A drill requires a hardy central shaft that spins; a bolt gun needs a hollow center that stays in one place."

"A power drill needs to be able to channel the force up the center," another gnome agreed. "Pressing down on something with a hollow center might just send the drill bit shooting up into the bolt-gun-barrel."

"Design is different," Iosif assured them. "Is two shafts that can switch…"

"Later. Talk about it later." Gripgut cast a wary eye back toward the tower. "But worth pursuing, Iosif."

The rations were dropped off toward the end of the day, and Iosif sketched out his idea with pieces of hardtack.

"Could work," Hogslip admitted grudgingly.

"Mm." Another shook his head. "The power source would be insufficient. The steam drive couldn't handle it."

"He's got a plan for that, though." Vinoka eyed Iosif. "Don't you?"

Iosif beamed. He'd never found anyone so interested in his work before. "New power source," he told them. "Copper wire around iron core, set spinning by steam, produce electricity. Then…"

"Hold it." Gripgut leaned forward. "Electricity?"

Vinoka raised his eyebrows. "You've been among the *svartelfein*?"

"The Tywylth Teg?" another gnome said.

"And you saw their technology?"

"And understand it?"

"*Quiet!*" Gripgut's voice was scarcely above a hiss, but the intensity made the gnomes immediately fall silent. "We're nearly out of time for dinner," he said, glancing again at the tower. "I don't want to hear another word about this. And half-breed—best to keep that design to yourself, for the time being."

∽◦∾

The sequencer arrived later, just before the lights faded to a dull red and a loud klaxon blared out. The gnomes started packing up their tools and tidying up the workshop.

"Looks like they're taking some of the boys out on a trip," Vinoka said, casting his eyes up at another cell slightly across the ring. "Block 45… that'll be Rupert's gang."

"I don't envy him," Gripgut said, already swinging up into his bunk. "Rupert, with his arthritis? The tunnels are in a terrible state in this city. Mold everywhere."

"It *is* a problem," Hogslip agreed. "Baton Rogue hasn't been redone in a while, perhaps. Plus there's the climate."

"Mm." Vinoka said, stowing his tools and walking back to the bunks lined against the grated back wall. Again he cast a glance toward the tower in the middle with its dark windows. The searchlights on its base were still, but as Iosif knew from experience, they would snap on and scan over the cells at a moment's notice. The red lights were still bright enough for the guards to keep an eye on them.

Iosif, for his part, was spreading out his rubber mat on the floor. It did not especially bother him, sleeping on the floor, he was simply too big for the beds against the wall. The only time when it was inconvenient was when one of the others felt the call of nature in the middle of the night.

He lay back against the mat, feeling the unyielding concrete cold against his back, and pulled the wool blanket up to his chin. At the moment everything felt like hard edges, but he knew that, bone-weary as he was, it would not take him long to fall asleep.

But tonight, that would not be an option.

"Okay, Half-Breed." Gripgut said, in a barely audible murmur, as he stared fixedly at the grate against the back wall. "Tell us everything you know about the Tylwyth. Especially about their flying machines."

CHAPTER 20

1:145241::2947

Senator Blackthorne,

The data your man sent over on the Dragon's Teeth project is very impressive. I was especially interested in your figures from the trial runs and optimization phase in Black Chamber. The increased records are most promising, and the mission success figures speak for themselves.

However, I am concerned by the casualty rate of the program. No amount of improved strength and resilience can make up for a 73% loss rate. Even if one soldier could have the strength of four, he could not fill the same four places on the battlefield, nor be in four separate places at once. Implementing the program in the US Army at large would leave our forces decimated and our nation vulnerable to attack. I must also repeat my inquiry as to the natures of the 73% dropout rate, and what has rendered them all uniformly unfit for service.

Unless and until I can be confident that implementing this new training regimen will improve the army's overall strength, I cannot adopt it, even on a volunteer basis. Of course, if you could persuade your development specialists to work with my own, perhaps we might be able to develop something with a greater survival rate. I urge you to raise the subject with them again.

General Winters

1::885201::4810

"A lot of boys ask about the face," Gripgut said.

Iosif paused between blows to look at the man. Gripgut was tightly holding the pinchers that gripped the red-hot iron Iosif was shaping.

"It's just, you haven't," Gripgut said. "Not much of a talker, are you?"

Iosif shrugged. "Never good," he said, and went back to beating. The hammer had a very small head, but it needed to be swung with great force. Exact precision was required here.

"Yeah." Gripgut nodded. "Noticed the accent. Weird, that. Even the most recent boys from the old country have lost theirs by this point. And none of the kids have accents."

"Kids?" Iosif looked up.

A flash of pain crossed Gripgut's face. "They… keep them elsewhere. The women too. Different stations. Sometimes they put us together, but usually you only get to see them as part of the incentives program." A snarl twisted the scars on his face. "Like animals…" He looked away.

Iosif felt he should say something. But as he'd just observed, he had no idea what to say, so he resumed pounding the glowing metal.

"Anyway," Gripgut said, turning back. "We've had some kids here, and none of them have accents. One of the doctors one time—they have doctors check up on us, run experiments—he had this theory he was talking about, 'genetic memory.' Like elephants, you know? Elephants, their children remember watering holes that their parents went to before they were born. This scientist thought gnomes might have something similar, with machinery and so on."

"Oh yes?"

"Just a thought." Gripgut shrugged. "Maybe you got your accent from your daddy, whoever he was. Or you're just wrong in the head. Who knows."

"Ah." Iosif certainly didn't, and couldn't say he cared to know. He needed to focus on this job right now, and Gripgut wasn't much help.

"The athsma, though... that hasn't bothered you here, has it?"

That did bring Iosif up short. "...no." He admitted.

"Mm." Gripgut gave a smile. "Thought not. It's got to do with the air. It's too dry on the surface, I think. Or too thin. Not sure which."

Iosif picked up the red-hot metal with the tongs and peered at it carefully. The point was sharp, but it also needed to be hard... iron folded over several times. And the wide part needed to be wide enough to block the pipe, but thick enough to withstand the pressure...

"Well?" Gripgut looked at him.

Iosif gave a firm nod. "Is good," he said, plunging it into the seawater.

"Good." Gripgut glanced around. "Vinoka, the panels in place yet?"

"Nearly there." Vinoka was fastening the sheet metal from yesterday onto hinges on the ceiling. He craned his neck around. "I'm not sure the blankets will quite seal the joints between the panels, though."

"It doesn't have to hold for long." Gripgut said.

"The launch strip's nearly ready too, boss." Said another gnome. He was positioned in front of the rail car with the sequencer, but in reality was fixing the bed rails—newly scored with guide tracks—to the cell floor.

"You've got the orientation right?"

The gnome threw a seemingly casual glance over his shoulder at the tower. "Accounting for some drift, yes."

"Good." Gripgut looked back at the back wall. All but the front façade of the bunk beds had been removed, but the grate, with its gaping pipes, was still behind that. "Good."

"Is good," Iosif said, taking the sharpened iron pole out of the water. He stashed it behind the bunkbed façade.

A klaxon blared as a crane lowered in front of the cell, a net hanging from its hook, heavy with baggage. Two of the other gnomes grabbed the net with hooks and pulled it in. "Leather covers for the seats," one said, looking up with a smirk. "We'll get them cut up to your measurements and then bring them in."

Iosif nodded, and he and Gripgut walked to the waycar, shiny new panels covering its sides. It could just barely be seen, but the panels were not bolted in place as they had been yesterday, but were hanging on hinges from the frame.

"It was an escape attempt," Gripgut said. Iosif looked at him, and Gripgut pointed to his own face. "The scars," he said. "From the steam, you understand." A light grew in his eyes. "I've been wanting to try this again."

"Okay, so once more, you're sure this will work."

Iosif shrugged as he tightened a gasket. The interior of the way car was closer now to a basket. Both the old and the new sequencer lay in pieces, and instead, at the front was a complicated series of levers and pulleys.

Gripgut winced. "But you saw the blueprints to this place."

The I-X93 facility. Iosif nodded.

"And you were among the Tylwyth Teg for a while."

Again, Iosif nodded.

"And you've built one of these before."

Iosif stopped and considered this last question. "Not... exactly."

Gripgut looked at him for a second, then looked around at the surrounding framework. The gutted skeleton of metal, its outside panels just barely hiding the folded fingers of aluminum and leather waiting to spring out.

"Well, it seems a sound principle." He shrugged. "Too late to do anything now. I'll tell the others to get ready. You'd better get in position."

Iosif gave the gasket one last turn and swung a panel out of the way to exit to the workshop.

"No weapons." Gripgut was telling the others in a low tone. "If we make it, we'll have all we need, and if we don't, it won't matter. Keep the weight load down."

"Should we strip?" Vinoka asked.

Gripgut considered this. "I don't think that'll make much difference one way or the other," he said finally.

"Every little bit helps," Vinoka said.

"Steam..." Iosif gestured toward the back wall. "Could get in. Clothes good for protection."

The gnomes looked at the wall. "Fair enough," Vinoka agreed.

"All right." Gripgut looked to Iosif. "Whenever you're ready."

The gnomes gathered around the waycar, hammers and screwdrivers in their hands. Their hands moved in busy, quick movements, disguising the fact that they were doing nothing whatever. Iosif moved to the back, toward the sharp spear he'd left by the bed frame.

A crane suddenly lowered down in front of the cell front. "Block 43, you have yet to complete job 29." The speaking tube blared. "Return job 29 to processing and prepare to receive incentives."

Iosif froze. Then kept walking. The plan wouldn't work if that crane was in the way the whole time, but it also wouldn't work if the guards in the tower (almost definitely watching now), thought he was acting suspiciously. He couldn't go to the beds, though, they might notice the beds were gone. The wall, walk toward the wall.

Gripgut had stood up. "The bolts on the sequencer are rusted," he said. "We're having trouble getting them loose. One actually cracked in half."

Iosif had reached the wall. Now what? He bent to pick up something at its base. A screwdriver. He started to walk back to the waycar, clicking it thoughtfully as he did so.

The speaking tube was silent. "Return job 49 to processing," it said again.

"We can't." Gripgut said, giving an annoyed growl to his voice. "The damaged bolt critically destabilized the waycar. If we move it now, it'll fall apart. We need a vise to keep the differential skeleton together before it can be put back on the crane."

What? Iosif couldn't quite keep the disbelief off his face. Several of the other gnomes also looked incredulous; even downright terrified. The guards might not be engineers, or even machinists, but surely even *they* could tell that none of those things were real. They couldn't possibly fall for… …

"…very well," the speaking tube said. "Vise being acquired. Prepare to return job 49 to processing."

The crane lifted out of the way. Gripgut swung around. "The pipes, Iosif, *now*!" he hissed. "They'll be back any second!"

Iosif darted back across the room, fumbling desperately for the lance. He ran up against the grate and scanned the mass of pipes just beyond. *What happens if this… valve gets blocked?* Rearing back with the lance, he drove it straight into the relevant valve and twisted.

There was no time to tell if it'd been successful. Iosif ran back across the cell, shouting, "Now!" Secrecy meant nothing—indeed, it might speed things up if the guards thought they were up to something.

Vinoka pulled on the cord hanging from the ceiling. The bedframes closed over the back half of the cell in a giant funnel, a bottleneck with the waycar as the cork. The other gnomes flipped up the panels and spread out the webbed wings of aluminum and leather, hooking braces into place even as they themselves clambered into the skeleton-like frame. And Iosif dove for the controls as he heard the rumbling behind.

… if we assume the pipes and valves to be for some sort of steam drive system, generally there would be some sort of emergency vent. But here, if this valve were blocked, it would instead build up in this pressure tank and explode outward.

Violently.

For one horrible second, nothing happened.

And then there was a great BOOM that shook the whole waycar and the steam was rushing outward, practically bursting the funnel but more importantly punching the waycar out over the track shooting out into the air the thin air and there was the tower coming up and the wide window where the guards oh too HIGH…!

The top of the waycar-come-aerocraft slammed into the upper lip of the wide window, swinging the lower half full into the glass and smashing into the room just beyond.

Iosif never saw the guards—whether there had never been any or whether they were crushed under the plane, he never knew. By the time he came crawling out of the wreckage, Gripgut and Vinoka had ripped the machine guns off their mounts and turned them on the black-suited guards charging down the spiral stairs in the center.

"Come on!" Gripgut roared, running for the stairs, Maxim machine gun blazing.

Iosif just barely absorbed they were in a circular room, with machine guns at each point of the compass. The other gnomes had ripped off the other ones already; Iosif had to instead grab a solid girder of metal that'd been ripped free in the crash. Then he charged up the stairs after the others.

There was quite a jumble of noises, and Iosif couldn't be sure, but he didn't think they were all coming from inside the tower. The gunfire, certainly, was all inside—there was the rat-tat-tat chatter of Gripgut's machine gun, and the slower staccato of the Sten guns of the resisting guards. There were screams, also, and howls, and curses. But Iosif also caught the sound of far-off crashes and yells.

He had to pick his way up the last few steps of the stairs— several guards had slumped over the steps, and the floor was slick with their blood. He came out into an upper room—logistics of some sort, he decided, based on all the tables and charts and…

A bullet bounced off the wall next to his ear and Iosif decided to stop thinking about it. He dove for the ground and crawled to where Gripgut and the others had knocked over a few tables. It was not so much shelter as cover, as bullets were shredding through the wood already, but Gripgut and the others were not looking to stop. They pushed the upended table forward with their shoulders, firing their machine guns around the corners at the guardsmen and assorted workers cowering behind a makeshift barrier of filing cabinets, right against the back windows.

Iosif caught a glimpse out the windows. The cranes, he saw, these were where the operators of the cranes must sit, there were the long arms of the cranes, and what were those things running along up toward…

The windows behind the guards shattered, and more angry gnomes poured into the room, leaping on the humans from behind.

Something cracked overhead. Iosif looked up just in time to see a supply cabinet, falling over. It slammed into him, full force; he went down; his head knocked against the floor, and he knew no more.

CHAPTER 21

4::234253::4354

Mr. Whisterhorn, this is former apprentice. You remember me, yes? I cannot give name. Reasons complicated. Could you perhaps contact mother? I cannot write her directly—again, reasons complicated. I have some friends I would like her to meet. If she could come to this address [2::985182::5660], it would be most helpful. Tell her to use the station over on Rutherford Ave.

Many thanks. Also thanks for watch, it was very useful.

4::023894::8538

Mrs. Rusval stumbled into the waycar carriage and collapsed onto the seat, mopping her brow. "Wooh..." She said, fanning herself. "Oh my. I haven't walked that much in some time." The car underneath her rumbled as it moved off into traffic. "I don't know why William had to be so mysterious about the whole thing... If Iosif visited him..."

THUD.

Mrs. Rusval's eyes flew open to see a small, red man with a horribly scarred face and a long iron-grey beard beneath it clinging to the side of the car. He smiled in what was evidently meant to be a reassuring manner, and said something she could not catch through the glass.

Mouth gaping, gulping at thin air, Mrs. Rusval could not think of anything to say.

The small man fished some sort of prybar from his jacket and wedged the doors open with it. Mrs. Rusval stumbled back as he dropped into the compartment.

"Greetings and peace." He smiled at her. "You must be Iosif's mother." He clambered up the interior of the car with disquieting ease and began to take apart the control box at the top. "Half a moment. This won't take long."

∽०∾

"The dvergr?" Mrs. Rusval said, some hours later, as the car rumbled through Chicago. She passed a thermos cup of tea to the little man, now propped up on the seat opposite her. "Well, I never."

"I will say, you're taking this better than I expected," the little man, Gripgut, as he'd introduced himself, answered. He sipped the tea.

"Oh, I always held on to the old ways," Mrs. Rusval assured him. "Iosif was always raised to leave a little food out for the household gnomes. For good homekeeping, you know. I do hope he's treated you respectfully. He's a good boy, but he can be very thoughtless, some times, in dealing with other people."

The man Gripgut had a very strange expression on his face. "…that's not quite what… well, never mind." He stretched. "Anyway. He thought you might be in danger, so he arranged… all this. Knew you'd have to pass the bridge if you took that station to that destination; told me to stand on lookout and get ready."

"And you made this?" Mrs. Rusval glanced around the car.

"Not this… precise one, but things like it, yes." Gripgut nodded, sipping the tea. "Easy enough to change up the sequencer."

"Marvelous!" Mrs. Rusval shook her head in admiration. "Simply marvelous! And where are we going now?"

"Some warehouse in Chicago," Gripgut said. "The others were headed there when I broke off. Iosif seemed to think we could hide out there for a while—some doctor or other who he said would be happy to help us."

⚬⚬⚬

"Oh my word," Dr. Rickenbacker said. He stared at Iosif and the alleyway full of little bearded men. "My… my word."

"We were hoping we might stay," Iosif said. Vinoka snorted for some reason.

"Yes, yes of course you can." Dr. Rickenbacker nodded, a little too quickly. "Of course, of course you must, but it's just that…" he looked back over his shoulder. "…it's… ah…"

Something was wrong. Iosif looked over his shoulder and caught, just inside the doorway, the sight of a massive man in a trenchcoat…

"Short stuff!" Snorky said, coming out of the warehouse, Tommy gun slipping back under his trenchcoat. He eyed the army of gnomes. "You's been busy, hey?"

Iosif couldn't even nod. He was staring at the slim figure just beyond the big man.

Salali waved to him. "Hey-low, Yo-sef."

∞◦∞

"Sh-shee was the first one here, actually," Rickenbacker said. He and the others were all seated around the table. All around them, the gnomes—with the exception of Vinoka and Gripgut (who had arrived in the meantime)—were busily examining the warehouse's many goods. "She said she went to the nirumbee in the mountains, after her folks threw her out. They sent her here because this place is a ... waypoint?" He looked at Salali, who only looked confused.

"A trade depot," Vinoka said, still glancing around. "I hear we used them to trade with the humans—and the elves, when possible. That door—" he pointed to the hatch set in the floor "—probably leads far outside the city."

Iosif did not answer. He was still staring across the table at Salali. His mother put a mug of coffee right by his hand, and he didn't even notice.

Salali smiled back. "Gode to see yo, Yo-sef."

"She's been remarkably quick at learning the language," Rickenbacker said.

"After they blew the Dallas safehouse, it was evident that the Black Chamber knew all of our hideouts," Ms. Kilroy commented, walking up to the table and sitting down. "This was the only place we could think of." She glanced over at Salali. "I will admit to feeling very… startled on recognizing our 'alien' talking with the good doctor here. But her information has been *most* helpful in making sense of things."

Snorky punched Iosif in the arm, bringing the other to with a start. "Didn't expect ya to come calling, neither. You's a barrel of surprises, kid."

"Indeed." Grey was standing just over Dr. Rickenbacker, leaning against a crate, coffee mug in his hand, eyes roaming over the gnomes working all around them. "Most astonishing."

Iosif shrugged, a trifle uncomfortable with all the attention. He felt he'd been essentially pushed into most of his accomplishments; there just hadn't been many other options available at the time.

His mother beamed at him. "More coffee, anyone?" she asked, holding up the pot.

"Please." Mr. Grey smiled. He turned to Iosif as she refilled his mug. "I suppose it would be too much to ask if you knew where Director Hougan is being held."

"Shenandoah," Iosif said, almost without thinking.

The others blinked at him. "My word." said Ms. Kilroy.

"They questioned me there," Iosif said. "Is Flistworth's base, I think."

"It would make sense." Grey nodded, staring off into space. "Their use of it for the assault is particularly telling. The mooring cable is probably a communications line."

"That raises other problems." Ms. Kilroy was frowning and had crossed her arms. "How are we to attack it?"

Everyone looked at her and she snorted. "This is an issue of some urgency, gentlemen. You realize Flistworth will take action once he realizes one of our conspirators has led a massive prison break?"

Snorky shrugged. "Not like he can find us."

"Not the point." Kilroy waved her hand. "He knows we want to reveal this conspiracy, and now we have proof. He doesn't *have* time to seek us out; he needs to act to make us irrelevant."

There was a silence.

"Damn," Snorky said.

"He has control of Black Chamber… he could orchestrate a coup and set Blackthorne as a figurehead." Grey straightened from his leaning poise. His fingers tapped against the palm of his hand.

"Why bother?" Vinoka shrugged. "He has an army and loyal military encampments all over the Pryor Mountains—he could retreat there and set up his own slave kingdom."

"Or he might decide to take us all down with him." Gripgut's teeth were clenched. "Bury the evidence. There are still prison islands in every major city. If he gave the order…"

"He might not care," Iosif suggested. "He said…"

"The point," Ms. Kilroy said, cutting through their talk, "is that we cannot know for certain until we have attacked the *USS Shenandoah*, and we must do it *soon*."

"But they'd see us coming. That far out in the water?"

"Pa-leese ex-coos." Salali interjected. She had been following things with a furrowed brow. "This Shae-nan-doe-aah… it is an airship, yes?"

The others looked at her. "Yes…" Snorky said.

Iosif smacked his forehead with sudden realization. "Ach."

Grey looked at him. "Oh... yes, that... could work."

"Your airship..." Gripgut looked at him with interest, "... would it work?"

"Is it safe?" Kilroy asked.

"I... I don't know." Iosif admitted. "I never really... *make* airship... not from scratch... not that size. Not that many. I... know not if... I can" He looked at Salali. "But... she might."

CHAPTER 22

0::000000

Dragon's Teeth:

PURGE.

0::000000::0000

In the end, of course, the project was a joint operation, involving Salali, Iosif, and various gnomes who had insights to offer (particularly on the subject of landing gear).

Supply was the major problem. They could only have two aircraft, as Iosif and Salali were the only ones with anything approaching flight experience. That meant they would have to be big—bigger than they could make with what they had on hand. Snorky was given a list, and he disappeared off to his underworld contacts. He returned with mysterious crates carried by dour-faced men.

Kilroy and Grey both vanished to do some intel-gathering. Mrs. Rusval, it had been decided, was too obvious a target for her to return to the house, so she stayed in the workshop, distributing food to the gnomes and chatting with them about their families.

"No move from the Shenandoah," Kilroy reported, early the next morning. "In the same harbor it's always been in."

"Why would it move?" Grey shook his head. "A Black Chamber takeover would be far more subtle than a giant blimp."

"Zeppelin," Iosif said, absentmindedly, tightening a lever in the front cockpit.

"And he could give the kill order from it as easily as from Washington," Gripgut said, poking his head from the guts of the engine. "Hundreds of my people could be dead by now."

"If they are, then we would not have been able to save them in time and we certainly can't save them now," Kilroy said. "At the very least, it seems we can exclude setting up a Pryor Mountain slave-kingdom from his list of plans." She looked over at Grey. "Is there any reason to think the coup has not happened already?"

Grey shrugged. "It would need to be VERY smooth for it not to have made any ripples at all. And at least one major official would need to die for Blackthorne to take his place."

"Oh!" Iosif knew he had forgotten to mention something. "Flistworth is a skin-walker."

The others looked at him. "Well, ain't that nice." Snorky grunted. "Gnomes, Elves, and now goddamn... what's a skin-walker, again?"

Kilroy's hand had flown to her mouth. "If he's able to take any form... it could be all over already..."

"That... seems unlikely," Grey said suddenly. "If he can imitate anyone, why Flistworth? Why not Blackthorne?"

They looked at him. "Because no one notices Flistworth," Kilroy said.

"Which would be incredibly useful, to a spy," Grey said. "But not to a changeling. Being noticeable means little if you can simply shift to another form."

"He … is Flistworth for long time," Iosif said, thinking. "In Carnegie Corporation, he was Flistworth."

"Maybe he likes the face?" Snorky shrugged

"Maybe the legends aren't comprehensive," Kilroy said. "Maybe he can't change to whatever he wants. He's got to be pretty old by this point—perhaps its only young ones that can do that."

"Oh." Iosif remembered something else. "He has young ones. That was Dragon's Teeth program."

"You's just full of unpleasant surprises today, ain't ya?" Snorky tilted his head.

"Sorry, I need to ask." Gripgut said, climbing out of the aircraft. "Does any of this actually change our plans?"

The others looked at each other. "I suppose it does not." Grey sighed. "Is everything ready?"

"As ready as it can be." Gripgut slammed the maintenance hatch shut. "For the record, I'd still feel better if we were sending a party to the Pryor Mountains."

"We don't …" Grey started.

But Gripgut held up his hands. "I know. We can't spare the time or the men. And it's not a likely target and there's not much the nirumbee could do even if they knew. I'm just saying I'd feel better."

"Then I suppose we are all in readiness," Grey said. "Mr. Rusval?"

Iosif nodded.

"Then it's time to get going," Grey said. "Half of us in one, half in the other. Let's move."

"Iosif." Mrs. Rusval came shambling up, as the others clambered into the vehicles. "Take this." She pressed the prayer necklace into his hand. "It was all they recovered from your old office."

Iosif, irritated at the delay, tucked the little necklace into his coat. But he knew he should feel more affected by it, so he gave his mother a kiss.

∾o∾

"Are you sure you know how to do this?" Kilroy asked, from somewhere behind him.

Iosif shrugged.

"Very comforting."

Iosif didn't know what she wanted from him. He'd really only done this twice before—the first time he'd had a computer helping him (apparently) and the second time he'd crashed. The Tylwyth had done their best to keep him from learning much about flying while keeping him imprisoned in the city. He honestly didn't have much to work with

The plane was shaking horribly. That was to be expected, he supposed, though neither of the earlier models had done that. Also, perhaps, to be expected, was the way clouds left water all over the windshield and made it hard to see (he'd meant to put wipers on this model. That'd have to go on the next one).

He did like the new compass, and the gyroscope, and the altimeter. At least he had some idea where he was going.

"Th-this rate…" said Grey, whose teeth had not stopped chattering since the start of the flight. "If th-th-this m-meter is ac-c-curate, th-this r-rate is in-incredible. We should nearly be at the harbor now."

Iosif nodded and tilted the lever (Gripgut had insisted he call it a "tiller", like in a boat) downward, sending the aircraft into a slight dive, straight toward a particularly fluffy cloud.

"Oh shit, not again." That was Snorky.

They hit the cloud, and immediately lost all visibility. Iosif could see no further than the nose of the aircraft, watching as clouds shredded over its metal skin. The shaking grew even more extreme, and somewhere in the back there was the wet sound of someone throwing up. Iosif kept one eye fixed on the gyro compass, watching as the angle dipped steeper and steeper… he pulled back a bit on the lever and it evened out again.

The plane broke through to the underside of the cloud, and there, stretched out before them, was Charleston and its muddy bay. The *USS Shenandoah* hung over it like a black pall, mooring lines trailing down to the water.

"Okay." Iosif bit his lip. "Now… this is tricky part."

"Oh swell," Snorky said. "I was worryin' that was over already."

Landing had never been Iosif's strong suit, and here the only place to land was the unshielded rubber top of the dirigible. The skis they had underneath the plane were designed for this specific circumstance, and Salali had said she *thought* it would work. Still. It didn't *look* like a lot of space to land with.

Iosif shrugged and banked the plane in a wide arc.

Salali's plane came down in front of him and he let her take the landing first. Carefully he noted her steps—flaps out, engine reversed, angle the plane so the back skids touched first, letting the front skids crash down afterward. Deploy the parachute. The aerocraft wobbled a little back and forth on the dirigible, but it mostly held on course and coasted to a stop just shy of the nose.

Okay. So the concept was sound. Iosif held his breath. He pulled the tab that opened the flaps all the way. The plane lurched and shook, and there was a crashing noise from the back. "Oh… hold on!" he shouted.

"Thanks kiddo!" Snorky shouted back.

Iosif didn't answer. He had cut the motor, now he restarted it in reverse. The motor coughed a few times before turning over and sending the rotor twirling in the opposite direction. The dirigible was coming up very fast—Iosif noted with dismay that they would not be coming *quite* straight on, but it was too late to do anything about that. He tilted the plane down, then at the last minute angled upward.

The back skids touched the dirigible.

The lever came alive in his hands, struggling furiously. It wanted to go left, right, up, down. His chair was rocking up and down—the whole plane was. Cries, thuds, and curses echoed from the back. Under his feet, the metal flexed and groaned. The dirigible shot under the plane at a disturbing rate… but the plane was slowing, slowing…

…it was headed for the edge, Iosif realized.

He reacted slowly—he'd come to do everything slowly, in the aerocraft, as sharp turns were impossible—and pulled gradually back on the tiller. A few seconds reflection made him realize that had he jerked the wheel back, it would have overcorrected, possibly throwing the whole plane over, certainly sending it shooting off the other side. Instead, it remained upright as it drifted closer and closer to the edge—but at a shallower angle than before.

"We're going to fall, we're going to fall!" Someone screamed behind him—the direction of the plane was becoming obvious.

Iosif didn't answer. There wasn't much he could do, but... they were slowing. He could make out the forms of the other gnomes and Salali out of the corner of his eye. He thought... he thought they might just make it... it was stopping now, surely stopping... The grey edge of the balloon shrank beneath the nose, then vanished completely... they were hardly moving, now... he could feel the nose begin to dip...

The plane jerked suddenly to a stop, and Iosif nearly slammed face first into the controls, making him realize how fast they had in reality still been going. The plane had stopped, but how...?

"Hurry!" Gripgut's voice shouted. "Get out of there!"

The door slid open. There was shouting, clamor, Grey and Gripgut barking conflicting orders over the chaos. The sound of tearing metal. Iosif could feel the plane tremble on the edge of the precipice, like a giant lever. He could feel the point of tension—something was anchoring them, in the back. But it was giving... the horizon dipped, he saw the ocean...

"Kid, MOVE!"

That was Kilroy. Iosif turned from the cockpit, as if in a dream, just in time to see Snorky reaching for him. Iosif wriggled out of the harness just as the giant man grabbed his arm and tore him from the seat. The aerocraft rushed past him in a blur, the door flashed by, and suddenly he was out on the surface of the dirigible, Snorky tumbling after him.

"Let go!" He heard Gripgut roar, and Iosif turned just in time to see twenty or so gnomes rip their picks free from the plane's metal. The plane slipped a few inches further, tipping more; than its tail flipped up, and disappeared, with a great crash of metal.

"So much for stealth," Gripgut said. He looked around, and Iosif looked with him

There were approximately a hundred gnomes gathered on top of the zeppelin. Most were armed with hammers, picks, or axes. A little over ten of them had automatic weaponry.

These gnomes had spent the last hundred years in slavery to the men below them in the dirigible.

Gripgut hoisted his Maxim repeater. "Let's go, boys!"

With roars of rage they swarmed over the side and charged the catwalks.

∽o∾

Plans, as Grey had pointed out, were mostly intellectual exercises that immediately disintegrated under the weight of combat. However, he also argued that they gave useful purpose and direction to said combat, so he and Gripgut had worked out a three-pronged strategy.

The primary assault team—Gripgut and the gnomes—were to storm the base and take out the main points of resistance—the guard posts, the barracks, and the gun turrets.

The secondary assault team—Grey, Snorky, Kilroy, Wheezer, and a number of others, were hunting Flistworth. Assuming they found him in the zeppelin's command post, they could use that to pinpoint and attack other points of interest.

The tertiary assault team, which was a grand name for a party of approximately six gnomes and one elf, was to rescue Hougan and seize control of the ship's engines. Iosif and Salali's presence on the team had been objected to—Grey had argued they ought to stay by the planes. But Vinoka pointed out that it would take more men than they could spare to guard the planes, and neither Iosif nor Salali thought the planes would be capable of a second flight anyway. So they were to keep behind the other five gnomes on the assault team, and provide what help they could.

Iosif really wished he'd been a prisoner for longer here. "I asleep most of the time," he explained, as they rushed over the catwalks. "Did not see most of ship… they put me in metal… bomb."

"The prisoner pods, yeah." Vinoka nodded. "A couple nirumbee mentioned them."

Iosif felt a bit more confident now. "Was dropped out of the bottom, through doors. Many other… pods around me."

"Main bomb bay." Vinoka nodded. "Makes sense. Large place, isolated enough to store prisoners. And if you think they're about to be rescued…" He gestured with his hand. "You just let them drop into the water.

Iosif winced at the thought. It made too much sense. "Must hurry. Where?"

Vinoka waved his hand and led the small party down a side corridor. Iosif trotted after them. With all the work on the plane, he'd been too busy to study Grey's blueprints and diagrams—however altered those probably were by this point. He was blind in the dark here, and could only make rational guesses.

There was probably a release valve—a switch that opened the bomb bay doors. It probably was running somewhere among the pipes overhead. But it was impossible to know where among the pipes, or what it might look like, and hitting the wrong one could just as easily blow the doors open. Iosif cursed his lack of time to study diagrams, he cursed his lack of knowledge on valves and switches, and he cursed his general stupidity.

"Here!"

Vinoka, who apparently *had* had time to study the diagrams, was peering up at a particular tangle of pipes just above the catwalk. He pointed. "That 3 mm one—all rusty with glue piled up on the left. Jam it."

Iosif could *just* reach the valve in question with his hammer. He swung.

CLANG!

"That'll work." Vinoka nodded. "This way. Quickly!"

The door to the former bomb bay was long and garage-like. The guards barely had time to react before the gnomes were on them. In close quarters like these, the little men with their melee weapons were devastating. Iosif barely got off two shots with his pistol before all four of the guards (and one of the gnomes) lay dead. Vinoka heaved up the door with an easy hand, and then they were in the prison.

The long lines of bombs/prisoner pods were just as Iosif remembered them; dull iron cylinders dangling by chains from the ceiling. By the light of day, Iosif could see the fins and the bulbous flotation devices on the sides. There was something on top, too, just below the chains—some sort of parachute pack. He couldn't remember one opening on his, but then everything had gone awfully fast.

"What the devil is going on out there?" He heard a shout.

Iosif let out a glad cry. "There!" he shouted, breaking into a run. There was Hougan, jammed uncomfortably tightly inside one of the larger 'bombs'. The small glass window just barely showed his irascible expression.

The irascible expression lifted an eyebrow as Hougan saw Iosif. "Mr. Rusval," he nodded, his voice slightly muffled by the glass. "Good to see you again."

Salali came along Iosif and Hougan's other eyebrow lifted. "Miss," he said. "I believe we've met, in a way. You look well."

Vinoka, and the others came jogging up.

Hougan said nothing at first. Then: "Gentlemen, good to meet you." He looked back to Iosif. "I see there've been some interesting developments."

"Sir," nodded Iosif, unable to stop smiling. "Is much to say... have you out soon," he said, peering at the lock. One of the other gnomes stepped around to the side to examine the hinges on the door. Vinoka snorted and heaved back his hammer.

Salali stepped in between them and inserted the key in the lock.

The others stared at her as she clicked the lock open. "Ees wrong?" she said, noticing their gazes. "Salali sees kee-yes on dead man's belt, Salali tha-ought..."

"No…" Iosif assured her. "Is fine, is…"

The coffin sprang open and Hougan practically fell out. Iosif just barely caught him in time.

Up close, Hougan looked a mess. His face was a mass of bruises, and he had three teeth missing. He'd noticeably lost a lot of weight, and the lines around his face seemed deeper, harder. But his eyes had lost none of their brightness, and his face none of its set.

A loud clatter from above awakened them all to the reality of the situation. "We move on… seize the engines," Iosif said, holding out a hand to the Director. "You able to walk, yes?"

"Get me a gun and I'll be fine," Hougan said. He took a step, almost fell, and grabbed Iosif's shoulder, hard.

"This is no good." Vinoka frowned. "He'll slow us down. We need to get to the engine room fast."

"They'll tank it quickly," Hougan agreed.

Vinoka cast a look around. "Guardhouse at the back should be defensible. Long aisles, clear firing lane. Iosif, you know how to use a gun, right? Hole up in there and you should be fine."

"But…" Iosif started to protest, but the others were already running for the door.

"Gah-nzzz…" Salali tilted her head, looking after them.

"We can't stay here," Hougan said, pushing himself upright. Iosif felt the hand on his shoulder trembling with exertion. "The others… where are they looking for Flistworth?"

"Command deck." Iosif answered.

"He's not there." Hougan shook his head. "It's too public. He'll be in his office—where he receives all the intercepted mail. It's low on the ship…"

"The underbelly…." Iosif saw once again the dark looming silhouette of the ship against the sky, the night they went out on Charleston harbor. He saw again the long mooring cable leading up to it, the lit window at its top that winked out. *He was there… then.*

"They'll… lose him," Hougan said. He pushed himself forward a step and nearly fell over again. "We… need to… go."

Iosif and Salali exchanged nervous glances.

Progress was slow.

"We need to *hurry!*" Hougan insisted, for the twentieth time, as Salali and Iosif struggled under his weight. "He can communicate with everyone from up there! Our only chance is that he hasn't yet realized how serious things are yet! You need to drop me…"

"You… are… reason… we… came." Iosif gasped. His asthma was once again choosing the worst time to flare up. His arms were strong enough, but his lungs refused to cooperate.

A guard poked his head around the corner. Hougan swore, pushed off from Iosif and Salali, and fired with the Tommy gun in his hands. The guard went down in a hail of bullets, but the recoil sent Hougan crashing into the wall. Something cracked. "*Damn*it!" he said, dropping the gun and grabbing his leg.

"Hoe-gahn?" Salali questioned, running over to him.

Hougan felt his leg, winced, and looked up at Iosif.

In his mind, Iosif could see the calculations lining up. He didn't like them; but they had a horrible inescapable quality to them.

Hougan let go of his leg (wincing) and picked up the Tommy gun. "That hallway," he said, pointing. "Turn left at the end, follow it all the way, take the door on the right. Should be a few guards. Door combination is 35-82-16." A breath. "The idiots took me down there once, so I could watch him sift through the letters."

Iosif looked at Salali, almost in desperation. She seemed to be thinking along the same lines, for she paled and shook her head. "Salali not ken guns. Not ken mail system. Not ken Flistworth."

All good points. There was nothing for it. Trading his revolver for the Tommy gun, Iosif, with a small moan of terror, stumbled down the hallway, gasping for air.

The first guard he ran into just as he was turning the corner. The guard seemed absolutely astonished to see him, and equally surprised by the bullets that went ripping through his torso, neck, chin, and lower face. Iosif was mostly surprised by the violence of the recoil—he barely managed to get it under control before it could go spraying up at the ceiling. His mind was too keyed-up to be very shocked by the fact of the death itself; he simply stepped over the guard's body, grabbing his keys as he did so.

There were mercifully few guards in this corner of the base, it seemed. The second had his back turned to Iosif. The third came out of one of the side doors, presumably to see what all the gunfire and screaming was about. That one was a bit... messy, and actually ended with Iosif dodging around the man (as best he could). He'd managed to make it to the door Hougan had mentioned, and was fast approaching the anteroom before Flistworth's office.

There were nearly five guards there. Worse, they had clearly all heard the gunshots, and their automatic weapons were out and trained on the hallway. Iosif caught sight of them in a fortunately-positioned pane of glass and flattened back against the hallway.

Should he charge in there, guns blazing? Snorky probably could manage it. Grey almost certainly could. Maybe all he needed was to take the bull by the horns, do something really dramatic for a change...

Iosif's eyes caught sight of the words "maintenance hatch" just under his feet. His eyes traveled over to the keys in his hand.

The key slid into the lock quietly. The lock made a click as it opened, and Iosif heard someone say something in the next room. He threw the hatch open with a loud clang and swung himself out.

It was only when both legs were already out the door that it quite registered that there wasn't actually a catwalk there, only a ladder that ran along the underside of the zeppelin itself.

He still had a grip on the edge of the hatch. He tried to haul himself out—and found he could not. The asthma was still clutching at his chest. Gunfire was filling the hallway above; guards were sure to follow.

It was too terrible to think about. His hands moved. They gripped the first rung. Then the second. A third. They started to work up a rhythm. He was going along at an impressive rate when his fingers missed a rung and he slipped off the ladder, falling into space.

He probably screamed. He certainly flailed, tried to grab the already-out-of-reach railing. He twisted in mid-air, flipped over, and just managed to register a thick dark line between him and the water when something barreled into his midsection, hard, and he reflexively grabbed it.

The skin ripped off his palms as he hugged it—hard—and he felt friction eat away at the leather of his jacket. But he slowed, and eventually he stopped, dangling from a great metal hose about twenty feet below the hulking monster. The mooring line, he realized distantly. It must be nearly a foot in diameter. Even at this distance, he could faintly hear the gunshots, and in some cases explosions, echoing from the airship.

He could also see the windowed chamber situated just where the mooring line met the airship.

Adrenaline seemed to have cleared his lungs, for the moment. Slowly, he inched himself up the cable—gripping first with his legs, then with his arms. His hands felt raw, and the wind whipped cruelly at his face, but inch by torturous inch, he crawled up the mooring line.

It took a long time. Too long, he felt certain. Perhaps Washington had already fallen. Perhaps the gnome prisons were already flooded.

No. Iosif shook his head. He refused to believe his friends could fall so easily. More likely the fight was probably over. He no longer heard gunshots or explosions. The others had probably finished retaking the zeppelin, Iosif told himself as he finally reached the underside of the chamber. Flistworth was probably long gone, he considered, as he found the maintenance hatch just to the left of the "mooring cable" assembly. Probably, Iosif reasoned, as he climbed the little ladder that dropped out of the hatch, probably, given how quiet it was, he'd come up to see all his friends in the room, standing there waiting for him.

Instead, he saw Flistworth crushing a man's skull in one hand. One massive, dark, clawed hand.

Flistworth turned and saw him. "Ah, Mr. Rusval," he said, as if blood were not squeezing through the mottled fingers on his left arm. "Forgive me. I was legit-i-mate-ly not expecting you. I'll, ah, be with you in a moment."

Iosif's hands flew to his belt—but of course there was nothing there. His Tommy gun was out in the hallway, on the other side of five fully armed guards.

Flistworth's great hand unclenched, and the corpse fell to the ground. A thin, frail corpse—it looked like a secretary, perhaps. "Now." Flistworth said, shaking the bits of brain from his massive hand, even as it shrunk back to an unassuming hand in a suit. "You *must*... tell me how you, ah, got in here."

Flistworth's other hand surged outward and caught up Iosif in a wave of flesh, slamming him against the front windows. Iosif heard the glass crack, a little.

"It's nothing short of a-ma-zing." Flistworth said, walking forward, his distended arm shortening as the skin-walker's body caught up with it. "This is easily the most, ah, secure room on the Shenandoah. Which, I hardly need add, is the most secure facility Black Chamber, ah, possesses. I... assume you also had something to do with that? And the jailbreak?"

He shook his head as he finally came within spitting distance of Iosif. "Re-mark-a-ble, Mr. Rusval. Truly, ah, remarkable."

Iosif clawed at the hand, but it was like trying to bend granite. His lungs were starting to burn, in a way that had nothing to do with asthma.

"I'd like to, ah, make a skin-walker of you myself." Flistworth said. One long finger extended in a fleshy spike, bobbing playfully before Iosif's eyeball. "You would certainly be, ah, useful. Still." The spike suddenly and violently retracted. "Your loy-al-ty would be difficult to, ah, ensure."

Iosif's hands went to his tool belt. Virtually nothing left. A screwdriver. He stabbed it upwards into the hand. No effect. A hammer. He flailed against the arm with it. The skin-walkers did not even blink. He found a length of wire and tried to wrap it around the arm. Flistworth sighed contemptuously and snatched it away from him.

"I'd, ah, a-pol-o-gize, but that would be … dishonest of me." Flistworth said, cocking his head at an unnatural angle. The glasses slipped off, completely, showing the flaming eyes set in the pale skin. "In … truth I'm quite glad to have the chance of ah, kill-ing you before I leave."

Iosif's vision was turning black. His hands patted away at his pockets. His left pocket had some things in it. He started throwing them at the arm. A napkin, an Allen wrench, a little bit of pocket lint…

"Fare-well, Mr… RUSval." Flistworth's teeth shone in a pointed smile.

Something was tangled up in his hand but he tried to throw it at the arm anyway.

"HSSSSSSCHHEEEECCH!"

Flistworth's bland face suddenly distorted into something misshapen and cruel; great hollow flaming eyes and lips shrinking back from fleshy teeth. The claw around Iosif's throat vanished with a burning smell, and Iosif nearly collapsed to the floor. He just managed to catch himself on the desk and looked up. Flashing legs, claws, teeth, flaming eyes rushed toward him in a sensuous rush. Iosif fell back with the horror of it and threw up his hands to protect himself.

"HRRRSSSCCH!" There was a scrabbling noise, and a crash. Glass smashed outward. Iosif looked up just in time to see a long, distended leg vanishing out the window. Running to look out, he saw something like a great spiky spider climbing over the underside of the zeppelin with blistering speed.

Uncomprehending, Iosif looked at the thing he had tangled in his hand—a necklace. The prayer necklace mother had given him. What was special about that?

A roar outside the window made him look up again, just in time to see the second plane come into sight. It was flying at a very shallow angle—almost falling, really--and even as Iosif watched, it pitched into the sea.

Iosif started to grin before he realized that it probably wouldn't make much difference to a shapeshifter. It still felt good, though.

The chattering of machinery caught his attention and he looked down. The metal track of the mail machine brought a letter up to its peak and stopped, expectantly.

Another chattering noise, this time from the typewriter. White-House_81 read the printout. Apparently Flistworth had a Turing engine set up to tell him where messages were coming from. Below, it typed out Options?, which Iosif could only guess at.

Gingerly, Iosif reached forward and took the letter. He slit it open with his fingernail, and read the contents.

> 0::018390::0001
>
> *Removal successful. Hoover and Curtis eliminated. Agent on site awaiting further instructions.*
>
> 0::000000::0000

Bile surged in Iosif's throat as he realized he was holding news of the President's death. Probably from an agent in the White House.

Another letter popped up in the reader before he could quite parse all of that thought. Again he ripped it open.

> 0::244511::4955
>
> *Receiving conflicting reports from mainland. Please update with instructions for Grubs*
>
> 0::000000::0000

Iosif didn't understand at first, until he glanced down at the Turing Engine. Fort Sumter64, read the printout. Options?

With a strange feeling of unreality, Iosif sat down at the mail machine and typed:

> 0::000000::0000
>
> *Report status.*
>
> 0::244511::4955

The reply came back almost immediately

Status at Fort unchanged. Suspicious behavior observed on Mobile Platform Shenandoah. Possible attack in progress. Orders with executive callsign received from unrecognized address: "Shenandoah compromised. Terminate grubs and open fire on airship." Requesting confirmation.

Iosif panicked. The countermanding order could only be coming from Flistworth. He could understand a soldier being hesitant about firing on a friendly ship, but the soldier would soon get beyond those qualms. Iosif needed to work quickly. But what was the executive call sign?

The word *Options?* glared at him from the Turing Engine. He pressed a key.

Options:

[1]. Return to Sender

[2]. Remove from Database

[3]. Add to Permanent Database

[4]. Add an Entry to Temporary Database

[5]. Remove an Entry from Database

Iosif's eyes lit up.

4

Please enter the sequence to add to Temporary Watch Database.

0::244511::4955

0::244511::4955 accepted. Review station?

0::000000::0000

0::000000::0000 accepted. All incoming and outgoing mail from 0::244511::4955 will now first be directed to 0::000000::0000 for review.

Options?

Before he could select anything further, the mail machine made a rattling noise. Iosif grinned triumphantly as an intercepted letter appeared..

0::293041::1894

Call sign: Nirumbee. Repeat: All grubs are to be exterminated immediately. Open fire on Mobile Platform USS Shenandoah. Any forces from the mainland without proper authorization are to be fired on immediately. Await further instructions from this station.

0::244511::4955

All right. Iosif bit his lip and typed out his own letter into the machine.

0::0000000::0000

Call sign: Nirumbee. Disregard orders from mainland. USS Shenandoah is not to be fired on under any circumstances. Grubs are not to be harmed.

0::244511::4955

He waited with baited breath. A moment later, a new letter popped up.

Acknowledged. Orders?

Iosif sat back and let out a breath. The two words stared him in the face.

Acknowledged. Orders?

He thought for a moment longer, and then he began to type.

CHAPTER 23

1::380244::4901

Director Hougan,

Allow me, on behalf of Congress, to express the heartiest congratulations on your recovery. I am relieved to hear that rumors of your demise were so greatly exaggerated, almost as distressed as I am to learn that accounts of your confinement were significantly underrated.

In light of your instrumental actions in restoring order to Washington in the wake of the attempted coup, I am offering you the position of acting Supervisor of the Black Chamber Investigative Committee. Your duties as yet are broadly defined, but they involve looking into the extent of the Blackthorne Conspiracy and determining how best to reconstruct the department. There may also be some cross-over with immigration affairs as you discuss how best to situate the new citizens we have welcomed to our shores.

We look forward to receiving you shortly at Washington, and await eagerly the many ideas I am sure you must have as to how to proceed.

President Yardley

1::394001::4258

Hougan tossed the letter across the desk. "Well, suppose it was inevitable," he said, taking a drag on his cigar. His face was covered in bruises and bandages, but it had lost none of its ill-humor. The old man got up and walked in heavy, solid steps to the window. "Bureaucrats…"

"Hot damn." Snorky chuckled, looking through the paper. "'Broadly defined,' I like the sound of that. Guess you're going to be top dog for a while, boss."

"Top scapegoat." Grey took the paper and gave it a passing glance before handing it over to Kilroy. "Yardley's passing this off because he knows the whole job's one prolonged political suicide. A major investigation, a costly public works program being dismantled, AND an immigration crisis? No one's happy here, and no one's going to *be* happy. The best Yardley can do is throw the mess onto someone who he can blame for the whole problem once it predictably makes voters mad."

"Or perhaps he might appreciate having someone he knows can't be bought by all the different forces jockeying for power right now in Washington," Kilroy said. "Poking through every politician's secrets, rebuilding a department from scratch…"

"Mm." Grey shrugged. "In any case. They wouldn't be the first to underestimate the Director."

"No need to talk about me like I'm not here," Hougan growled, still staring out the window.

"Sorry, sir. You are planning on going?"

"Of course." Hougan's shoulders slumped. "Call of duty and all that. Can't say I trust anyone else to handle the job, given circumstances." He turned back to the office. "Flistworth's still out there, somewhere, and at least seventy of his Dragon's Teeth Operatives."

"We know how to stop them, now," Grey said.

Kilroy glanced over at the other inhabitant of the room. "The legends do say you can kill a skinwalker with an arrow coated in white ash." There was a twist to her mouth. "Or a necklace, hm?"

Iosif turned the prayer necklace over in his hands, nervously, the wood inlay with its silver engravings flashing. "Was simple chance," he protested.

"The Battle of Hastings was decided when an arrow fell by chance into the eye of King Harold," Grey said. "Such chances are rarely random."

⚬∾⚬

Iosif met with Salali the next day. "Sorry I late," he said. "Director... he have me meet with nirumbee, help with talks ..."

"Is all right, Yo-sehf." Salali placed a long hand on his arm.

Iosif sighed. "I no good with talks."

Salali's cheeks dimpled. "Salali neither. But Salali goes to speak to Tylwyth Council. Maybe council listens."

Iosif snorted. He'd talked to the council. He did not have high hopes there.

He glanced around. "You like building?"

"Is nice." Salali glanced around, clearly unsure what she was seeing. "Please excuse… what you call this?"

"Factory." Iosif articulated the word as clearly as he could.

"Fak-toe-ree." Salali sounded the word out.

"We make new lifts," Iosif said. "Apparatus's too. Perhaps more—gnomes coming to work here. They have patents for Federal Appliances they made, Public Works is being…" He struggled to articulate the complexities of Washington politics. "Is smaller," he said finally. "This." He gestured. "Is for making things," he said. "Is making things gnomes invented. To sell" And then, moved by an odd impulse: "I am owner."

"Truth you say?" Salali beamed, throwing her arms around him. "Salali congratulates!"

To be honest, Iosif felt a little nervous about it. There was still a lot of risk involved. And there were going to be a lot of complications—employing all the homeless gnomes, helping to privatize the mail system and the waycar transit lines (Hougan was convinced no one should be able to repeat what Flistworth had done), working on the new flying machines… it was all so very new, with so many challenges and worries. So many things could go wrong. There could be any number of accidents.

But as he stood there in his new factory, with Salali's arms around him, Iosif felt that accidents were nothing to be afraid of.

AUTHOR BIO

JD Kloosterman teaches English in Michigan, writing and drawing in his spare time. A devotee of JRR Tolkien and Terry Pratchett, JD loves vibrant and imaginative worlds that delve into what was as well as what might have been. He is currently working on *The Teutonic Doctrine,* the next installment in his YA urban fantasy series The Solomon Code.

Also by JD Kloosterman

The Nephilim Protocol

Chad Dickson has never liked being himself, and that was before he ripped off his friend's jaw and punched a hole in a brick wall. Now, he finds himself in Camp Solanas—a prison camp on a tiny frozen island designed for "Nephilim," half-angel hybrids with a nasty history with humans. Campers are disappearing, and Chad needs to find a way out. But at the edge of the world, can even an angel escape?

The Hospitaller Oath

A crippled arms heiress, and a legendary blade (or at least a hilt). Chad wasn't expecting to crash—literally—into either, but now he's sworn to protect both. In the wrong hands, the Skofnung Sword could upset the balance of power in Europe. Pursued by deadly Nephilim commandos across Norway and Ukraine, Chad and his new friends must race desperately to find the last piece of the sword before either the Russians or the Templars find it. But someone among them is a traitor.

www.ingramcontent.com/pod-product-compliance
Lightning Source LLC
Chambersburg PA
CBHW020930020726
47495CB00002B/429